SHATTERED BONE

SHATTERED BONE

Chris Stewart

M. Evans and Company, Inc.
New York

M. Evans and Company, Inc.
216 East 49th Street
New York, New York 10017

Library of Congress Cataloging-in-Publication Data

Stewart, Chris, 1960–
  Shattered bone / Chris Stewart.
     p. cm.
  ISBN 0-87131-831-8
  I. Title.
  PS3569.T4593S48   1997
  813'.54—DC21   97-20580

Book design and typeformatting by Bernard Schleifer

Manufactured in the United States of America
10 9 8 7 6 5 4 3 2 1

Disclaimer
In accordance with the Joint Ethics Regulation, Chapter 2, para. 2–207, the views presented in *Shattered Bone* are those of the author and do not represent the views of the Department of Defense, its Components, or the United States Air Force.

To my wife,
the best friend I have ever had,
and my children,
who remind me every day
that life is good.

SHATTERED BONE: the code word used to signify the theft, hijacking, or unauthorized flight of a B-1B bomber loaded with nuclear weapons. Such activity would be considered a class "A" security violation. The incident aircraft will be destroyed using any and all means available. Its destruction is the highest priority.

Follow notification procedures appendix three.
Follow command and control procedures
appendix ONE HELP JULES.
Implement Emergency War Tasking Operations Plan
"SPLINT."

Air Force code manual 13–12

We are deceiving ourselves if we believe that we have a clear understanding of the developing political landscape in Russia. The hard truth is, the economic situation has become nearly intolerable for the large majority of its citizens . . . who have lost all faith in reforms. To a large degree, Moscow has lost control of its army, and the former republics are crawling with strife. Despite our support, none of us can guarantee who we will be dealing with, nor even what type of government we will face, next week, next month, or next year.

Internal State Department Memo

PROLOGUE

MOSCOW, RUSSIA

THE SUN WAS JUST SETTING AS THE PRESIDENTIAL MOTORCADE TURNED onto the Minskoje Road, its waning haze barely burning through Moscow's sulfur-rich air. Gennadii Sakarovek, the President of Russia, was on his way to the British Embassy for another meaningless conference on trade where he would spend the next three hours begging for money from men who were less than his equal, while smiling at their jokes and enduring their wives. In exchange for the cash, he would make promises of further reform. It would be a long night. He was in a bad mood.

Two cars behind Sakarovek in the motorcade, the Prime Minister of Russia, Vladimir Fedotov, sat in the back seat of his limousine alone, separated from his driver and bodyguard by a thick panel of reinforced, bulletproof glass. Gazing out the window, he watched the sun set over the city.

A soft chime sounded from Fedotov's breast pocket. Reaching under his overcoat, he pulled out a tiny cell phone, flipped it open and placed it to his ear. After listening only a moment, he grunted and glanced at his watch.

"I thought you took care of his car," he said sharply.

A slight pause and then, "Yes. Okay. But keep this in mind. If he lives, if he makes it across the border, you know what I will do."

Without waiting for a reply, Fedotov flipped the phone closed. Shoving it back into his pocket, he took out a cigarette and lit up with a scowl, the orange glow illuminating his face in the darkness.

The motorcade rounded a corner. Fedotov glanced ahead. They were approaching the threshold of the Borodinski Bridge. Built immediately after the revolution, the bridge spanned the Moscow River at its narrowest point, a massive structure of stone, sweat, and steel. With multi-pillared towers rising along the river's steep bank, it stood as an impressive monument of human labor. Narrowing to only four lanes, the Minskoje Road ran 30 feet over the Moscow River's icy waters as it crossed the Borodinski Bridge.

Fedotov smashed the cigarette out, then flipped a switch positioned alongside his armrest. Instantly the window separating him from his driver and bodyguard went black, the result of a tiny electrical charge that passed through the ionized glass. Reaching into his briefcase, he pulled out a small flashlight which was wrapped securely to a strong magnet by strands of black tape. Turning the flashlight on, he screwed a small red lens cover over the bulb, then rolled down his rear window and attached the flashlight to the roof of the car.

After rolling up his window, the Prime Minister pulled on a pair of thick safety glasses, then lay down on the floor of the limo. Under his crisp white shirt, a bulletproof vest was cinched tightly across his chest, making it uncomfortable for him to breathe. He hated this part of the plan. He felt like a coward as he hid on the floor. But it was important that he survive, while at the same time giving a credible appearance of having been endangered himself.

He glanced at his watch once again, then felt the limousine slow as the caravan approached the Borodinski Bridge.

Fedotov sensed his bodyguard shift his weight in the front seat. Both the driver and his bodyguard were long time members of his staff, and Fedotov had come to consider them allies and friends. He knew that they would give their lives to protect him, and so he considered it fitting that these friends would be allowed to give their lives for his cause.

The limousine bumped as it crossed the steel threshold of the bridge. Fedotov covered his face with his arms.

Inside the president's limousine, Gennadii Sakarovek was enjoying a drink. His Foreign Advisor sat quietly beside him, scribbling notes on a small pad of paper.

SOUTHERN RUSSIA

The Russian crashed through the night, the whites of his eyes shining in the darkness as he frantically pushed through the trees. Dressed in a dark suit, leather shoes, and silk tie, he looked ridiculously out of place in the mud and slush of the forest. Being fifty pounds overweight, it wasn't long before he was gasping for breath. Tiny beads of sweat matted his thin hair against his forehead and stung his eyes, but he made no effort to wipe them away.

Half a mile behind him, his stalled car sat on the side of the road, its hood raised, the oil pan dripping, black smoke wafting from the still scorching engine. Everything he had left, every possession he had not already abandoned, was left sitting in the two trunks that filled the back seat.

Fighting for breath, the Russian pushed on through the forest, cutting across a loop in the road toward the rendezvous site. He made no pretense of stealth. Those games were now over. Now it was only time to run.

Coming to a narrow patch of open wood he sprinted as fast as he dared, running recklessly through the darkness. Reaching the thick brush on the other side, he slowed and held himself back, picking his way across the rocky terrain, fighting to stay in control.

Though he knew he was followed, he never looked back.

The light rain had stopped and the night air was heavy with cold mist. Overhead, the clouds began to break, allowing the half moon to cast occasional shadows. Huge drops of moisture dripped from leaf to leaf and branch to branch as they made their way to the soggy forest floor. Dripping birch leaves slapped at the Russian's face and shoulders while the thick, wet underbrush pulled at his feet. He was soaked and chilled to the bone. He glanced at his watch only once, its luminescent face glowing green in the night. 21:17. He doubled his pace. There wasn't much time.

With the document in his possession, his fate was now sealed.

Two hundred meters through the forest, and slightly to the west of the fleeing Russian, was "the Horse," the man whose responsibility it was to get him out of the country. Like his charge, the Horse was of Slavic descent. He was hairy and squat, with stubbly black hair, huge biceps and thick thighs.

This was a dirty job, and incredibly dangerous, and he was one of the few men willing to do it. To penetrate an enemy border. To go in alone and without any contingency for assistance. To go in without any cover. It was something any agent was loath to do. Perhaps once in a generation did an operation warrant taking such a risk.

And tonight was one of those times.

The Horse wore a dark cotton jumpsuit and black leather boots. Every exposed piece of flesh was smeared with gray cammy, including his eyelids, lips, and even his teeth, allowing him to blend nearly perfectly into the night. He crouched under the thick brush that lined the side of the rutted, gravel road. A tiny radio transmitter was strapped to his waist. With its pea-sized speaker stuffed tightly in his ear and the tiny microphone clipped to his collar, the man could communicate without using his hands.

The Horse glanced at his watch. 21:26. Three minutes to go.

"Trojans up," he whispered to the darkness. His ear piece crackled just slightly as his transmitter scrambled and broadcast his voice over the VHF frequency.

Twelve miles to his south, level with the tops of the trees, a tiny helicopter sped through the night, controlled by a single pilot. Despite years of training and a thousand hours of combat flying, the pilot was tight as piano wire.

Pulling his chopper over the top of a ridge, he banked slightly to the right and pushed the noisy machine down a small valley. He navigated only by feel, never referring to a chart. Indeed, he didn't even have one. He had rehearsed the mission so many times, he could have navigated the route in his sleep.

The pilot reached down and keyed his mike. "Say status?"

"No contact."

The pilot swore violently under his breath. "Say position?"

"Charlie."

"Say time?"

"Three minutes."

The pilot swore once again, cursing in fear.

The Horse didn't respond. Settling deeper under the brush, he scanned the road once again.

The Russian pushed himself to his feet and brushed the mud from his eyes. Far, far in the distance a dull "whoop" rolled through the forest, barely perceptible to the human ear. The Russian turned and ran without notice. The darkness began to break, deep shadows giving way to dim light. Without warning, he burst through the trees and onto the road, his shoes crunching across the wet gravel.

Lifting his face, he searched the night sky for the north star to show him the way, but the tree line blocked his view. In a panic, he ran to his left, then suddenly stopped and turned back to his right. Frozen in the middle of the road, he listened.

He could hear him out in the trees. The man had followed him through the deep forest. The soft rustle of dead winter leaves. The snap of a twig. Soggy branches being pushed out of the way.

Turning quickly, the Russian took a deep breath and gathered himself for the run.

MOSCOW, RUSSIA

Two hundred feet across the Borodinski bridge stood the Klanublsky Towers. Resting atop a small outcropping of granite and sand, they lined both sides of the bridge, standing as twin sentinels over the eastern side of the river. Four arched capstones rose more than 100 feet into the air, providing a perfect view of the road down below. High atop the northern tower, two unidentified men lay in a prone position, their blackened faces barely visible over the high granite wall. As the motorcade approached the bridge, they each dropped ANVIS Night-Vision goggles down in front of their eyes. With the goggles in place, the two men could easily make out the individual features of the men who sat in each of the cars, their faces ghostlike and surreal in the faint, green light of the goggles. As they counted the cars in the caravan, both men noted the small red light shining brightly from the roof of Fedotov's car.

The first man picked up a rifle-like object. It was small and light as an umbrella. The man looked through the telescopic lens and focused on the first car in the motorcade, then flipped a switch and pulled the trigger. An invisible beam of laser hit the car squarely on the wind-screen, scattering billions of protons of energy in all directions. Meanwhile, the second man picked up a much larger weapon. He quickly loaded two huge shells, just as the motorcade was crossing the threshold of the bridge. Traffic had been stopped for the oncoming dignitaries and the sedans in the motorcade were now the only cars in sight.

"Ready?" the second man mumbled, his breath emitting just a hint of moist vapor into the cold air.

His companion took a deep breath and held it, then nodded his head in reply.

The first rocket was fired. Sensors inside the small warhead immediately picked up the scattering pool of energy that was washing around the window of the first sedan. It honed in like a missile, traveling the distance to the car in less than a second, then impacted the windscreen with a crash. The shell didn't detonate until it had passed through the glass and into the interior of the car, where it exploded with a fury, blasting seat fibers, glass, and jagged pieces of hot metal in all directions. Mingled among the exploding debris were charred pieces of clothing and broken fragments of bone, the remains of the four men who had once occupied the now-burning car.

The car rocked up on its front tires as it exploded. The second car in the motorcade crashed into the wreckage, creating a sufficient roadblock to stop the remaining cars from going any further across the bridge.

Within seconds another shell was on its way. This one honed in on the third car in the procession. Before the driver of the Presidential sedan had any time to react, it was over. The President of Russia was now dead.

A huge fireball rolled across the bridge, splitting the night air with a roar. Shadows burned and flickered across the empty road as the fireball rose in the air. The driver of the Prime Minister's sedan slammed on the brakes. He knew instantly what had happened, and realized that the only thing he could do to save his life was to get his car off the bridge. He shoved the heavy sedan into reverse before it had come to a stop, the transmission grinding and jerking from the strain. As he started to back up, he tried to look through his rearview mirror. But he couldn't see a thing. The interior glass panel that separated him from the back seat was nothing but a flat sheet of black glass. Turning to his sideview mirror, he accelerated backward, weaving like a madman through the maze of limousines that now lay strewn across the bridge.

It would only take a few seconds to get off the bridge. Then he would steer the car off the embankment and onto the safety of the low ground by the Moscow River. A few seconds was all he needed to save the Prime Minister, as well as himself.

The second assassin was reloading his weapon. Reaching beside him, he pulled a red-tipped shell from a black leather pouch and shoved it down the muzzle of his weapon. The shell was very short and not as round. Inside its hard steel casing was a mixture of gunpowder and sawdust, giving it only a fraction of the explosive power of the shell that had been fired at Sakarovek. Leveling the missile launcher against the side of the granite balcony, he pulled the trigger once again. His companion had already focused his laser on the faint red light on the roof of the fleeing limousine. The shell honed in on its target. Another explosion rocked the air, noticeably less forceful than the first. The blast blew out all of the windows and buckled the roof of the car. The two men in the front seat of the Prime Minister's sedan were instantly killed.

Broken glass and burning powder exploded into the rear compartment, tearing at Fedotov's neck and arms and scorching his hair into tiny, white curls. His suit was tattered and his face was smeared with blood. However, the front seat and thick privacy glass had absorbed most of the shock, and for the most part, Vladimir Fedotov had been protected as he lay on the floor.

After the shell exploded, his car continued to roll backward before it crashed against a high cement guardrail that lined the side of the bridge. As the limousine crunched to a stop, Fedotov rolled out the back door and crawled over to the side of the bridge. From where he crouched, it was only a twenty-foot fall to the water. He looked around quickly, then let himself over the side rail, just as the fourth and final shell hit another sedan. The explosion rocked the bridge and shattered the air, sending a burning tire to bounce over the guardrail and drop into the cold river down below.

Then it became very quiet. Only the crackle of the burning cars filled the air. Off in the distance, sirens began to wail in the night.

No one saw the two assassins scramble down the side tower and speed off in the small rubber raft that had been secured to the footings of the bridge.

A few minutes later, the new president of Russia, Vladimir Fedotov, emerged from the icy waters of the Moscow River and fell into the waiting arms of one of the few surviving security agents. He was shivering with cold and shock, his shirt torn into tatters around him.

Thirty feet below the surface of the Moscow River, jammed between two moss covered rocks, lay a discarded bulletproof vest.

SOUTHERN RUSSIA

Without warning, the Horse slipped from the shadows and grabbed the Russian by the shoulders with astonishing force. Lifting him by his jacket and shirt, he pulled him off the road and dragged him back into the forest.

The Horse dropped silently to the wet ground, pushing the Russian beneath him. He covered the target with his body, positioning himself between the man and the road. He knew the Russian would be followed. He knew their lives were in great danger.

The Horse held his gloved hand over the Russian's mouth. The Russian didn't move. His eyes were closed. Even through his gloves, the Horse could feel the man's pulse pounding in his neck. The Russian held perfectly still.

The Horse watched the forest for at least 60 seconds before leaning forward and speaking into his mike. "Trojans in," he said in the tiniest voice, his breath hot against the Russian's face.

The agent turned to the Russian and planted his mouth next to his ear. "Do you have it?" he whispered.

"He's going to kill me!" the Russian sobbed. "Please, he's gone crazy. He's already . . . my wife . . . two of my children . . . please." The Horse covered the Russian's mouth and pressed down once again. "Mr. Secretary, I will protect you. A helicopter is on its way. It is only minutes out. But I have to know! Do you have the document!?"

"He will kill me," the man sobbed. "He will kill us all. A million people are going to die! The Duma is gone. I saw the soldiers myself. They were everywhere. The constitutional court. The parliament. Everything. All of it gone."

"Quiet! Yes, we know!" the Horse hissed. "We know. I will help you. Now, Mr. Secretary, I will ask you for the last time. Do you have the document? Is it in your possession?"

The Secretary shuddered and nodded his head. Freeing his arm, he reached into the crotch of his pants and pulled out a single piece of paper.

Handing the paper to the agent, the Secretary lay back in exhaustion and dropped his head to the ground. He stared blankly into the darkness, eyes unfocused, his lips tightly drawn.

"He's already killed Komisarenko," he whispered, more to himself than the Horse. "Komisarenko was my friend. And General Azov. Both of them dead." He paused to swallow, forcing the bile down his throat. "Now you've got to get me out. Please, I've done my part!"

The sound of approaching rotors beat through the air, steadily growing. The Ukrainian grabbed the paper and held it up to his face, looking for the signature at the bottom of the page. The dull *whoop* of the blades cut ever closer. In seconds, the helicopter would be overhead. After studying the paper, the Ukrainian broke into a quick smile.

Then without hesitation, he lifted his gun and shot the Russian square in the head.

The small chopper appeared over the trees, already stabilized in a twenty-foot hover. A harness and rope dropped from the left side of the chopper. The Horse broke from the bush in a run. Grabbing the harness, he slipped it over his shoulders and cinched it around his chest even as the helicopter climbed into the air.

KIEV, UKRAINE

Yevgeni Oskol Golubev, the Ukrainian Prime Minister, sat back in his chair and pushed his fingers through his thick, bristled hair. Andrei Liski, the Director of Ukrainian Border Security, dropped the analysis on the desk and stared the Prime Minister straight in the eye. A bony man with limp shoulders, thin neck, and delicate fingers, it was hard to imagine the cold and cunning heart that beat in his chest.

Leaning toward the hapless Golubev, Liski lowered his voice and got right to the point.

"Mr. Prime Minister, it is just as I said. He has already made great preparations. Last night's document only proves what I have already told you. Now, clearly we have to do something. If we sit on this information and pretend the threat doesn't exist, then, when the time comes and we are caught unprepared, we both will then deserve to die."

BOOK ONE

The central question is no longer how to avoid a nuclear exchange, but rather, how to predict one. It is our opinion that a deliberate nuclear detonation is now unavoidable and is likely to occur within the next 10–15 years.

CIA Report to the President

ONE

OSAN AIR FORCE BASE, SOUTH KOREA

OSAN AIR FORCE BASE IS SITUATED APPROXIMATELY FORTY-FIVE kilometers south of Seoul, Korea. It sits low in the Son Mihn Valley, surrounded by gentle hills, cypress trees, and musky, slow-water creeks. A steady stream of C-141 and C-5 cargo aircraft make their way across the Pacific to Osan in an effort to keep the enormous military machine on the Korean peninsula adequately supplied. Twice a day, huge KC-10 transports bring in a fresh supply of reluctant troops. However, common as these transports and cargo planes are, most of the flying activity is generated by Osan's resident fighter wing—the Fighting Fifty-First Aces of the south. Their motto—"Death from Above."

The 51st Fighter Wing is a front-line wing, consisting of three squadrons of F-16s. Because of the tense political climate in which they operate, air operations continue twenty-four hours a day, and the whine of jet engines constantly fills the air.

The flight line is a nest of activity, vibration, and noise, with maintenance troops and technical specialists scrambling among the jets and aircraft equipment. Fuel and fire trucks lumber carefully among the fighters while bomb and missile trolleys are carefully positioned under the F-16's wings to load them with weapons for upcoming sorties.

After spending six hours to prepare an F-16 for take off, the crew chiefs breathe a weary sigh of relief when their jets finally begin to taxi, rolling from their parking spots in groups of two and four. However, their respite will be brief, perhaps as short as an hour, for that's all the time it takes for the little fighters to burn their 7,000 pounds of jet fuel and fire off all their missiles. Upon their return to Osan, the pilots over-fly the runway at 1,000 feet before breaking into a hard turn to line themselves up for final landing.

Then the whole process will begin once again. Within minutes after touchdown, even before the jet engines are shut down, the aircraft are surrounded by their maintenance crews and fuel trucks, all rushing to prepare the aircraft for another sortie.

Scattered among the parking ramps are aircraft suffering through various stages of repair, surrounded by tool boxes, cooling hoses, fire extinguishers, maintenance stands, and teams of hustling mechanics. The technicians hunker around the broken aircraft, sweating in the early morning sun as they study their maintenance handbooks that lay spread across the baking cement.

This was Senior Airman Stacy Derby's world. This is where she belonged. Working on the fighters was all she had ever wanted to do, and once she was given the opportunity, she considered herself very lucky. As a crew chief on the Fighting Falcon, she loved her work on the flight line. She loved it all; the smell of burning jet fuel, the overhead floodlights that illuminated the ramp at night, the pressure of pushing to have her jet ready for takeoff, then watching with satisfaction as it taxied on out to the runway, the ground vibrating under her feet. She found so much satisfaction in what she did. So why was she taking such an enormous risk? Was she really willing to give it all away?

Greed is an evil thing, she thought, as she made her way across the ramp toward her aircraft. Sometimes people do stupid things for money.

But maybe things wouldn't have to change. In fact, if she were careful, everything would turn out just fine. She would hear the terrible news when she reported to work in the morning. Then she would mourn with the others. Tears of pity and grief would stain her cheeks, but that was as far as it would go. There would never be any suspicion. No evidence. Nothing to trace back to her. If she were careful and did exactly as she had been told, none of the tragedy would affect her directly.

Airman Derby walked up to her aircraft and gently patted its nose. This one was her baby. Aircraft number 87-341 had not flown the night before because of a faulty generator and Airman Derby had spent the morning troubleshooting, trying to find the source of the problem. Around ten o'clock, she had discovered a fault in one of the relays. Once she knew what the problem was, she could have fixed it within an hour. But she didn't. Instead she tinkered and puttered around, always trying to look busy. She had to delay until the evening flying schedule was posted at twelve o'clock. She had to check on something before she completed the job and called her aircraft back in the green and ready to fly.

Just before noon, she left her toolbox by the aircraft and walked into the hangar that housed Maintenance Control. There she found the newly posted evening schedule, written in bright red marker on a large sheet of Plexiglas mounted on the hallway wall. Derby quickly scanned the schedule, looking for her aircraft. She found it on the eighth line down. Aircraft number 87-341 was scheduled for a 23:38 local takeoff. It would be loaded with four Mark 82 bombs and two sidewinder missiles. Its pilot was Capt Richard Ammon.

That was what she needed to know. After checking the schedule, Airman Derby stopped by her locker to get her lunch. She also picked up a small package containing a box of cigarettes. Derby had only recently begun to smoke, a nasty habit for which she seemed to take unending guff from her supervisor, but though still a rookie, she had learned early to keep her cigarettes inside a tin box to protect them from being crushed as she crawled around the aircraft. Stuffing the tin of cigarettes into her front pocket, she closed her locker door and began to walk back to her jet.

Forty-five minutes later, she finished the work on the faulty generator. She then began to replace the aluminum panels that covered the aircraft's electrical systems. When that was complete, she took an inventory of all her tools. If anything was missing, she would have to ground the aircraft until the missing tool could be found. More than one accident had been caused by a missing pair of pliers or a screwdriver that had been left behind, only to get jammed in an aircraft's flight controls.

When Derby had accounted for all of her tools, she walked around the entire jet, opening access panels and doors to ensure that everything was in order.

The last thing Airman Derby did was climb on top of the aircraft and open the slip door that covered the air refueling receptacle. But before she climbed onto her jet, she glanced up and down the flight line to make certain that her supervisor was not around. Then, with a quick jump she climbed onto the fighter's wing and stepped over to the fuselage to where she could reach the small door that covered the air refueling port. Before pushing the door open with her left hand, she glanced around once again.

Working quickly, she pulled the tin of cigarettes out of her pocket and peeled back the wrapper with her teeth, exposing a strong adhesive which she used to attach the tin box to the inside of the slip door. Then, very slowly, she removed the last cigarette from the tin box. This activated a tiny switch which armed two ounces of plastique explosives. The explosives would remain armed until the slip door was opened during flight for air refueling. Once the door slid open, micro-sensors inside the box would sense the change in air pressure and send a fire signal to the explosives.

And while two ounces of plastique explosives were hardly enough to down an F-16, she had been assured that, given the close proximity of the explosives to the aircraft's fuel system, it would more than do the job.

Airman Derby looked around once more before allowing the door to spring closed, then climbing from the aircraft, she gathered up her tools and headed back to Maintenance Control. As she walked across the flight line, she found herself deep in thought once again. Knowing she would soon be very rich she found herself wondering. What was it going to be like to have so much cash? How could she possibly spend so much money?

TWO

OSAN AIR FORCE BASE, SOUTH KOREA

CAPT RICHARD AMMON DIDN'T REPORT TO WORK UNTIL LATE AFTER-
noon. He slept in until nearly ten, then spent the morning browsing
through the tiny shops that lined the narrow streets of Song Tan
City. For lunch he ate at the closest McDonald's, where he paid the
equivalent of eight dollars for a Big Mac and chocolate shake. Silently
he nibbled on the burger and sipped at the frozen chocolate, forcing
himself to eat, knowing that if he didn't, by tonight he would be very
hungry. But still, the burger made his stomach roll and turn. Lifting
the bun, he stared at the soggy meat and marveled once again at the
Koreans' ability to make even one hundred percent beef taste like fish.

Before he left the restaurant, Ammon walked back to the counter
and ordered another Big Mac and fries. He packed three tiny bags of
ketchup and a couple napkins into the paper sack, then turned and
walked out onto the busy street. The dank vapor of sewer and mildew
filled his lungs. But he didn't notice. After seven months in Korea, he
no longer noticed the smells.

Half a block down the street, he found Kim La Sung. The old man
sat at his usual location, his back propped against a crumbling brick
wall, his bare legs and dirty feet stretched out into the sidewalk. The

man stared straight ahead, holding a small cardboard box filled with hand-carved wooden toys.

"How ya doing ol' man?" Ammon asked as he approached the wretched street vendor. His Korean was barely understandable.

The man's face brightened at the sound of Ammon's voice, but he didn't turn his blind eyes away from the street.

"Hey there, you ugly American," he replied through tea-stained teeth. "Bring me anything to read?" The old man chuckled. It was the standard greeting between them, a personal joke that stemmed from the first time they had met.

"Not today, Kim," Ammon said. "I'm in a bit of a hurry. I'm flying tonight, so I don't have much time."

"Okay, Captain Richard. But next time come and stay awhile."

"I will, old man," Richard Ammon replied as he placed the bag of food next to his friend. The blind Korean immediately smelled the grease-soaked fries. He reached down and located the bag with his right hand and gently tore it open.

"I hope you didn't forget the ketchup," the old man said.

"It's in there," Ammon reassured him.

Ammon turned to leave, then stopped and pulled out his wallet. Without even counting the money, he took all of the bills that were tucked inside and dropped them into Kim's cardboard box. Kim immediately sensed the presence of the cash. Without so much as a nod, he reached out with unseeing hands, extracted the folded bills, and stuffed them into his shirt.

"Next time, bring me more ketchup," he demanded as Ammon turned and began to make his way back down the street.

Ammon walked to the base, flashing his identification card to the guards that manned the sidewalk gate. Then he went back to his quarters to sleep. Normally when he flew at night, he didn't take an afternoon nap. But tonight he wasn't scheduled to take off until 11:38, which meant he wouldn't land until after 3:00 A.M. By the time he finished debriefing and had completed the required paperwork, he wouldn't be back to his room until nearly sunrise. He figured a little afternoon siesta would help him get through the long night.

It was somewhat unusual for him to fly such a long sortie.

Normally he would fly about an hour, maybe two hours if he did air refueling. But tonight he would climb up behind a tanker to get gas not only once, but twice. Both times he would meet up with his tanker just off the western coast of Korea and refuel as they flew out over the

Yellow Sea. After topping off his tanks for the second time, he would turn back toward home, knowing he had enough fuel for several practice instrument approaches before he would have to land.

Inside his Q room, Ammon stripped to his underwear and settled himself onto his bed and tried to sleep. But although he felt very tired, sleep did not come. After laying on his bed for an hour, Ammon gave up and turned on the television to a rerun of "The Beverly Hillbillies." "The Hillbillies" were a favorite of the Korean people. It reinforced their concept that all Americans were somewhat dim, but rich nonetheless. It was laughable to watch the voice-overs that mismatched the actors' lips. Although Ammon couldn't speak Korean well enough to follow the story, the familiar sight of Granny and Ellie May brought him some comfort when he was so far from home.

At four o'clock Ammon picked up the phone. He dialed the international code for the United States, then a California area code and number. It took several seconds for the call to go through. When it did, the phone on the other end of the line only rang three times before an answering machine clicked on. Ammon listened to the message, then waited for the beep.

"Jesse, I've got bad news," Ammon said quickly. "I've been trying to call you since yesterday, but you haven't been home. My father is sick. I think he'll be okay though. Reggie is with him now. Don't worry. I'll call you when I can. You have my word."

He immediately hung up and looked at his watch. It only took twenty seconds to make the call. Less than the required thirty seconds it would have taken to trace the number he had been connected to out in California. Good. That was extremely important. After checking his watch, he reached down and dialed again. This time he talked a little bit longer, but he didn't really care. It was to a number that couldn't be traced.

Fifteen minutes later, Ammon was stepping out of the shower to shave. He studied his face in the mirror, looking for any signs of the stress or anxiety he was feeling. Nothing showed. In his reflection he saw only the same trusting smile and even features that had served him so well in the past.

Richard Ammon was not tall, only a fraction of an inch above six feet. But at twenty-nine, he was still solid, his shoulders and back sculpted into graceful lines by frequent workouts at the gym. He had tan skin and blond hair, which he wore in the same tight cut as most of the other pilots in his squadron. His teeth were white and straight.

His jaw was square and taut. His face was friendly, for he frequently laughed, which helped to soften the intensity of his hard black eyes.

Ammon quickly shaved and then sat down on the edge of his bed to dress. Opening his nightstand drawer, he took out a long elastic sports bandage and wrapped it tightly around his left knee. He put on a clean flight suit and pulled on his boots, then grabbed the flight bag which he kept by the bedroom door. The last thing he did was stuff a plastic Ziploc baggie into his pocket. He then walked out of the room without turning out the light.

He drove to the fighter wing complex where he parked his battered Isuzu in front of the wing intelligence building. He punched the keys to the cipher lock on the side entry and greeted the Sergeant who let him in. As one of the squadron tactics officers, he had an office inside the building. He quickly made his way down the wide corridor of the empty building to his door, where he paused for a moment before pushing it open. He shared the room with two other officers, and was relieved to find himself alone as he slipped into the darkened office.

He glanced around. Government-issue metal desks faced each other in the center of the room and three large file cabinets lined one wall. The only decorations were the standard framed pictures of various military aircraft and a two-foot model of an F-16 hanging from the ceiling. Because the occupants of the wing intelligence building always dealt with classified documents, the structure had been specifically designed with security in mind. None of the rooms had any windows, and all the doors were sealed and soundproof. Every room had a built-in safe or vault to store classified material. On the rare occasion that a visitor was allowed into the building, a bright red light flashed in every room and corridor as a warning for the occupants to protect their secrets. With sealed doors and no windows, the air in Ammon's office was always stale and cold.

Reaching into his flight bag, Ammon pulled out a pair of rubber gloves and quickly put them on as he walked to the three desks in the center of the room. Passing by his own, he sat down at his friend's, Major Billings. He unlocked the Major's desk with a stolen key, pulled out the center drawer, and, with a practiced hand, began to feel underneath for the sheet of microfilm. His fingers quickly explored the underside of the drawer, running along the corners in an effort to find the thin piece of film. He felt his heart quicken and his head began to pound as his hands groped along the underside of the drawer. Then he found it. The slippery film was stuffed way up in the right hand corner, exactly where it had been left the day before.

With a careful tug he pulled the film away from the tape and quickly placed it inside the baggie he had pulled from his pocket. After he sealed the plastic bag, he checked it to ensure it was airtight, then pulled up the leg of his flight suit and stuffed the bag under the wrapping around his knee.

Walking from the building, Capt Ammon stifled the urge to run as he made his way to his car. He glanced over his shoulder. No one was there. Nothing was amiss. And yet one thought continued to turn in his mind. If he were discovered with the microfilm in his possession, he would almost certainly die in a South Korean interrogation cell. The South Koreans, while trustworthy allies, were very intolerant of those charged with treason.

Tucked inside the baggie was a microfilm that contained the codes and frequencies that were used to guide the GBU-15 optically guided bomb. This precision weapon was one of the most powerful and useful American Air Force bombs. And since the Americans had invested billions of dollars in the weapon, they had to rely heavily on its performance, particularly during the first and most critical opening days of a war.

But the GBU-15 was a very vulnerable weapon. If the enemy ever discovered the radio frequencies that were used to guide the weapon to its target, the bomb could be easily jammed. And once it was jammed it went from an extremely smart and accurate weapon to a very expensive stupid bomb.

It was hard to estimate the difference that having these frequencies could mean to the North Koreans. It was information that could provide them with a decisive advantage. And it was worth a huge amount of money.

Except for one thing. The codes which Ammon carried were more than three years old. Since then, the GBU-15 had undergone a major upgrade in avionics. Part of the upgrade included a change in software. As a result, the codes that Ammon carried out of the wing intelligence building were completely useless. They were of no value to anyone. And Ammon knew it.

Just over four hours later, Capt Ammon found himself circling over the western coast of Korea. It was a beautiful night; clear with a full moon and not a cloud in sight. That was very unusual for August.

When the weather briefer forecast clear skies for the air refueling track, Ammon had not believed him. During the day, thunderstorms would usually develop over the mountains of central Korea. They then would move eastward and blow out to the Yellow Sea, reaching the ocean by nightfall.

But here he was, level at 23,000 feet, with nothing but twinkling stars and the bright yellow moon.

Seventeen minutes earlier, Ammon had taken off from Osan and climbed immediately to 23,000 feet. He was a little early for his air refueling and had spent the last five minutes in a lazy orbit while he waited for his tanker. Sealed inside the cockpit, the earth passed silently below him, interrupted only by the sound of his breathing and an occasional radio transmission from Air Traffic Control.

To pass the time he tried to identify as many constellations as he could, but his gaze was continually drawn to the water below. He noticed the sparkle of the moon as it reflected on the sea. Following the coastline, he could see the lights of Seoul sprawled along the Han river. Further to the north, P'yongyang, the capital of North Korea, caused a dim glow on the distant horizon.

As he circled, the KC-135 tanker that was scheduled to refuel his fighter was enroute to his position. It would be there in a little less than five minutes. Ammon had already talked to the tanker pilots on the preassigned radio frequency. He reported that he was orbiting over the start point of the air refueling track at flight level 230. Once the tanker was within thirty miles of Ammon's position, it would descend from its cruise altitude of 29,000 feet to 24,000 feet. As they met over the start point, they would both begin to fly eastbound along their designated refueling track.

In the tanker's tail lay the "boomer," an enlisted crewmember whose job it was to maneuver the air refueling boom into the fighter's refueling port. He lay on his stomach on a padded board that looked very similar to a weight bench. From this vantage point he could look out a large bubble window and watch the thirsty aircraft maneuver behind the tanker as they moved into position for gas.

The boom extended twenty feet below the belly of the tanker and had small winglets and hydraulic actuators that allowed the boomer to move it into position and connect with another aircraft's refueling port. Once a "contact" was established, fuel could be transferred at a rate of 3,000 pounds per minute.

When Capt Ammon had the lights of the tanker in sight, he would begin a gradual climb to tuck himself under the tanker's tail. Once in position, he would open his refueling door to allow the tanker's boom to hook into his F-16's fuel port.

On a dark night it could be fairly difficult to maneuver into position for refueling. The tanker's lights would blend in with the starry background, making it nearly impossible to see the outline of the aircraft or refueling boom in the darkness.

But as Capt Ammon looked around him at the bright moon and clear sky, he realized that it would be easy to refuel tonight.

"No problem," he muttered to himself through his oxygen mask as the tanker flew into view. At three miles, Capt Ammon could clearly see the outline of the tanker as it positioned itself ahead of him. He completed his air refueling checklist, checked his own airspeed and altitude and added a little power to begin his climb up to the tanker. Thirty seconds later, he was in position twenty feet behind and slightly below the tanker's extended boom. This was considered the "precontact" position and it required a final radio check prior to moving any closer.

"Kingdom two-two, Devil six-seven is established precontact," Ammon transmitted over the radio.

Inside the tanker's belly, the boomer had watched as Ammon had maneuvered his aircraft into position. Now he could clearly see the outline of the pilot sitting inside the cockpit, illuminated by the moon and the lights of his instrument panel. The boomer keyed the radio switch in his left hand and replied.

"Roger, Devil. You're cleared in. Are you going to want all five thousand pounds? That's a lot of gas for such a little plane."

The tanker was scheduled to offload 5,000 pounds of fuel. But like most tankers, they were feeling a little stingy. Their thirty-year-old engines were very inefficient and burned enormous amounts of fuel, so they figured it never hurt to try to keep a little extra gas. They especially hated to give away fuel to unappreciative customers. Their attitude was, if Ammon didn't really need the gas, then maybe they would just keep it for themselves. Unfortunately for them, tonight Ammon needed it all.

"That's affirm, Kingdom two-two, I'll need all five thousand pounds." Ammon replied.

"Okay Devil, we copy," the boomer said. Then after a short pause he commented, "Beautiful night, isn't it?"

"It really is. Kind of makes you sad to think of landing and losing this view."

"Roger that, Devil. Well anyway, if you're really going to steal our gas, then come on in to Mama."

Before closing the final distance between the two aircraft, Ammon scanned his instruments to complete a final safety check. He would not be able to look inside the cockpit once he hooked up to the boom, and he wanted to know everything was normal before the refueling began. He also reached up with his right hand to brighten his exterior lights. That would make it easier for the boomer to see his refueling port against the backdrop of his gray painted aircraft. Finally, he nudged the throttle forward ever so slightly and moved in on the tanker.

Now there was only one thing left to do. He had to open his refueling door so that the boom could make a contact. But before he opened the door he lifted up his left hand and gave the boomer the customary wave. He saw the boomer return his wave, then give him a thumbs up signal.

Not until then did Ammon reach down to his side console to find the switch that would open the refueling door. He felt for the switch and found it without looking, keeping his eyes on the tanker above him. He hesitated for just a second, then moved the switch to the open position.

The boomer could only stare in bewilderment when the aircraft exploded before him. The dazzling flash filled the night sky with a white-hot ball of fire and burning metal. For several seconds, he was completely blinded by the searing explosion, leaving him confused and disoriented, his mouth hanging open in silent horror. He was only eighteen years old, and his young mind took a moment to comprehend the fact that he was in the process of watching a man die.

When the boomer could finally speak, he forgot to key his microphone switch, and no one heard him screaming. "What! No! Climb! Climb! Get away from the fireball!"

Capt Ammon's F-16 was now a dazzling ball of flying fire. However, the pilots in the tanker had no idea what was going on. They didn't see the flash of the explosion or feel any of the shock wave it produced. Their only indication that something was wrong was a slight bump and lift in the tail. The boomer was the only one to witness the fighter as it descended and rolled inverted, its left wing and fuselage completely engulfed in flames. As the fighter's engine flamed out, it quit producing thrust. With its airspeed decreasing rapidly, the aircraft began a near vertical fall. Spinning wildly, it descended to the ocean more than four miles below.

Capt Ammon was knocked nearly senseless by the explosion; his head smashed against the Plexiglas canopy with enough force to fracture his helmet and mask. Inside the belly of the aircraft, splintered fuel and oil lines fed the already billowing fire. Precious electrical wires that allowed the pilot to control the aircraft were burned almost immediately. Within seconds of the explosion, Ammon was little more than a passenger in a scorching, smoke-filled cockpit. A soft female voice in his headset announced the obvious.

"Warning! Warning! Fire! Fire!"

It took the onboard computer less than two seconds to analyze the deteriorating situation and reach a conclusion. Based on the increasing rate of descent, the presence of the fire, and the lack of thrust, the computer considered the aircraft to be in a situation from which it could not recover. After reaching its conclusion, the computer offered this advice.

"Eject! Eject!" the computer-generated voice called through Ammon's headset, this time an octave higher and with a significant degree of urgency.

But Capt Ammon wasn't ready to bail out yet. Although he knew that the burning aircraft would probably not recover, pride and training forced him to try.

He pushed the fire-suppression button, then threw the control stick left and right. No response. The aircraft tucked into an even tighter spin, the G forces pushing him against the sides of the canopy. By now enough smoke had filled the cockpit that he could barely see the instrument panel. The acidic air filtered through his splintered oxygen mask and burned his lungs. "Warning! Fire! Eject! Warning! Fire! Eject!" The voice repeated itself every three seconds, making it even more difficult for Ammon to think.

Peering through the smoke, Ammon searched for the airspeed indicator. Eighty knots! That wasn't even flying airspeed. He would need at least 200 knots before he could break the spin. And to accelerate, he would need more power.

He jammed the throttle forward into the full afterburner range. But nothing happened. No gentle push of acceleration. No vibration or muffled roar. It wasn't until then that he noticed the silence. The familiar drone of the engine was no longer there.

Only twenty seconds had passed since the plastique explosives had been detonated, but in that time Ammon's aircraft had lost more than 10,000 feet. At the rate it was accelerating downward, it would take only fifteen seconds more before it hit the water. His engine was gone, he had no control, his jet was on fire.

It was time to get out.

As he reached for the ejection handle between his knees, Ammon pushed his back straight up against the seat. After tucking in his legs and elbows, he yanked on the yellow-striped handle with all of his might.

In less than a second, explosive bolts fired his canopy clear of the aircraft. Two rocket motors then ignited under his seat, propelling him upward with enough force to shoot the seat two hundred feet into the air. As he began to accelerate up the ejection rails, the first thing Ammon encountered was the incredible wind. It pulled the breath from his lungs and sent his arms flailing like a tattered rag doll at the side of his head. The skin on his face was stretched against his teeth and cheekbones. His left boot was ripped from his foot. The overall effect was like being fired from a cannon into the vortex of a powerful tornado. Ammon had talked to pilots who had survived an ejection before, but nothing prepared him for the sheer force his body now encountered. Although he remained conscious during the entire ejection sequence, disorientation and shock made him only dimly aware of what was happening around him.

Fortunately, the seat and parachute deployment was completely automatic. Seven seconds after pulling the ejection handle, Ammon found himself hanging in his parachute harness as he drifted down toward the sea.

For several seconds he hung in a stupor. Time seemed to have stopped and his mind seemed far, far away, floating in some kind of haze. But as he descended, the initial shock began to wear off and the cool breeze helped to clear his head. Quickly, he looked around him in an effort to regain his bearings. Out of the corner of his eye he saw a trace of flame and followed it as it spiraled downward. He could clearly see the splash and spray in the moonlight as his F-16 impacted the water. For several seconds Ammon stared at the spot, watching the foamy water, illuminated by the moon as it gradually spread and then slowly disappeared. For just a moment he imagined what it would have been like to have been inside the cockpit of his F-16 when it was shattered by the force of the impact. He pictured sections of the cockpit exploding around him and the wave of the incoming sea as the aircraft broke into a thousand pieces and began slowly sinking to the ocean floor.

Looking down at the black-gray slate of wrinkled sea, the water seemed so cold. So dark. A horrible place to die. He shook his head and tried to clear the image from his mind as he stared at the glistening ocean below.

Finally, the flapping of his parachute demanded his attention, reminding him that there were certain things he needed to do in order to survive. He couldn't just hang there in his parachute. He needed to prepare for his water landing or he would drown before he could get inside his life raft.

What had they taught him in ejection seat training? There was a little song that would remind him what to do. As he tried to concentrate, the jingle he had learned several years before slowly came back to mind.

> "Canopy, visor, mask,
> seat kit, LPUs.
> That's what you need to save your life.
> So do them or you lose."

He worked quickly to prepare for his water landing.

Canopy. He looked overhead to make sure his parachute was fully deployed and that none of the nylon canopy lines had wrapped themselves around the top of the parachute.

Visor. He needed to remove the visor that protected his eyes so that it wouldn't shatter if he fell during landing. Too late, he thought, as he reached up to disconnect the visor. It was already broken and gone.

Mask. He reached up and pulled off his oxygen mask so that he wouldn't suffocate from sucking water through the airhose and into his mask. After disconnecting the mask, he let it drop to the empty darkness below.

Seat kit. His survival raft was now hanging in a small pouch under his parachute. By pulling the D-ring by his left hip he activated a cylinder of oxygen that would immediately inflate the raft. He listened with relief as the raft hissed and crackled, spreading out below him.

LPUs. Life preserver units. These were the inflatable life preservers attached under each of his arms. Sensors would inflate them automatically when they were submerged in salt water. At least they were supposed to. Ammon felt for the inflation tube under his chin that would allow him to manually inflate the life preservers if necessary.

Looking around now, he tried to judge how high he was above the water. The moon still reflected on the open sea, but everything looked exactly as it had a few minutes earlier when he had stared down from his jet as he circled at 23,000 feet. He felt from the warm temperature and humid air that he was quite low, and guessed that he had only a few thousand feet to go.

Suddenly he was engulfed in the cold and salty water of the Yellow Sea. He had completely misjudged his altitude and the air was knocked out of him when his body slapped the water. The complete blackness and brutal chill made him nearly panic. As he kicked his way to the surface, he felt his arms being forced above his head as his LPUs inflated. Spitting and coughing, he found himself on the surface of the water gasping and sputtering for air. But what was this slimy sheet above him? It took a moment for him to realize that he had surfaced under the canopy of his parachute. Taking a deep breath, he ducked under the water and swam out from under the chute, being careful not to get himself tangled in its many canopy lines. Once he was clear, he released the parachute from his harness. The chute would soon become water-logged and sink and he didn't want to be strapped to it when it did.

Looking around, he saw his life raft bobbing in the four-foot waves. It was securely tied to his harness by a twelve-foot lanyard, and it didn't take much time to pull the raft to him and hoist himself inside. As he fell into the tiny raft, he lay back and rested his head against its side. He could feel his heart still racing in his chest. Suddenly he felt exhausted. For several minutes he lay motionless, his feet dangling in the water as he listened to the waves lap against the side of his raft. Staring into the darkness, a heavy weight seemed to spread through his body. He felt very tired and very alone.

The salt water began to sting Ammon's lips, and he was very thirsty. Reaching into his leg pocket, he took out a small water bottle and took a long drink. As he put the container back into his pocket, he felt the wrapping around his knee and hoped the microfilm was not getting wet.

Finally, he sat up and looked around him. Nothing but water and the open sky. Occasionally he could hear the sound of an aircraft in the distance, but it seemed to come and go with the wind, and he never could get a good fix on its location. That would be the tanker, he thought. They are already looking for me. He was opening his survival kit to take out a signal flare when he suddenly figured it out.

He wasn't supposed to signal the tanker. They were supposed to think he was dead.

Ammon shook his head in disgust and rage as he realized that his ejection had been a setup—a carefully thought-out plan to convince the United States government that Capt Richard Ammon no longer existed.

They would never know the truth. Richard Ammon was not dead, he had simply been called back home.

When he had been told that he would be brought in, he had expected instructions to land in North Korea. Or maybe a simple early morning kidnaping on his way home from work. He had imagined any number of ways they could have brought him in, but not this.

What idiot had come up with this plan? Didn't they know that people died in airplanes that exploded at twenty thousand feet? Didn't they know that ejecting from an aircraft could break your back? And now what was he to do? Bobbing around in the Yellow Sea, he felt completely helpless. Did they have a plan to recover him before the Americans did?

Even now, the tanker would have reported the accident and Ammon's last known location to the rescue forces that were stationed at Osan. Even now, an emergency locator beacon in his life raft was broadcasting his location to every aircraft flying within a hundred miles. The rescue forces would easily find him. It wouldn't even take until morning.

But his friends would find him first. Surely they would. They would have it all worked out. He had to trust them. At least for now.

Ten thousand feet above him, the crew of the KC-135 tanker was busy. It had taken some time before the boomer had calmed down enough to tell the pilots what had happened to the F-16. For a second they didn't believe him. But the obvious panic in his voice soon convinced everyone that he wasn't playing around. They listened in stunned silence as the boomer described the explosion and fireball. Then they acted together in a flurry of activity.

The pilot immediately banked the tanker into a steep descending turn. The boomer began searching the night sky for a parachute. He watched the burning F-16 spiral into the darkness. As the fireball descended, the boomer followed it as long as he could, but eventually he lost sight of the trailing flame. He never did see Capt Richard Ammon eject or the splash of the F-16 impacting the sea.

While the pilot flew the aircraft, the copilot radioed for help. "Mayday! Mayday! Mayday!" he cried, talking much too fast to be understood. "This is Air Force tanker call sign Kingdom four-six. No disregard. Disregard." The copilot took a deep breath and started again.

"This is Kingdom two-two. We've got a downed aircraft. I say again, we have a downed aircraft. We need an immediate rescue response."

The air traffic controller's voice came back, much more calmly than the copilot's hurried call. "Aircraft calling Mayday, say again your call sign and state your position."

"This is U.S. Air Force tanker Kingdom two-two. We are on the two-five-six radial, seven-three DME off of the Hung tacan. I say again, we've got a confirmed downing of an Osan F-16. Unable to confirm any ejection. Will you initiate a rescue response? We will orbit the area to assist in the coordination."

"Roger Kingdom two-two, standby. Korean Air flight three-fifty-six, turn right heading one-three-zero. Climb and maintain twenty-thousand feet. Air Japan flight, turn right heading three-six-zero. Proceed direct to Seoul when able."

The controller was already starting to vector other aircraft away from the crash site. Not only would this make rescue efforts easier, but it was not unheard of for an aircraft to unknowingly hit a descending parachute. He had also motioned for his supervisor, who immediately called the command post at Osan Base Operations. On the north end of Osan's runway sat a small alert facility with an HH-60 rescue helicopter waiting outside. The rescue helicopter was airborne within minutes.

Meanwhile the tanker continued to orbit overhead. They had now descended to 2,000 feet and were searching the darkness for any signs of a survivor. They listened on the radios for the sound of Ammon's emergency beacon and watched the sky for any flares. If the F-16 pilot had survived, he would surely try to signal them. If he was down there, they would find him.

So they continued to orbit. But the hours slipped quietly by, and eventually the sun began to break over the horizon. Finally, they were forced to return to Osan, for they were running low on fuel. For five hours they had loitered over the crash site, trying to find a survivor. For five hours they searched the dark sea and listened on the radios, but found only darkness and silence.

THREE

LOS ANGELES, CALIFORNIA

ABOUT THE TIME AMMON FOUND HIMSELF FLOATING AROUND IN HIS LIFE raft, half a world away, the sun was just coming up and a light mist floated off the Santa Monica Bay. Jesse Morrel had spent the last forty-five minutes walking along the boulevards and watching the sunlight filter through the huge oak trees that lined her neighborhood streets. Although she had started her daily walk in the deep shadows of early dawn, by the time she returned home, the morning sun was shining through her kitchen window.

Jesse was dressed in a bright blue jogging suit and white hightop sneakers. Her hair was tied back with a simple white ribbon. Around her wrist was a small silver chain attached to a two-ounce can of mace. Smart women didn't walk in the early hours without some form of protection.

She was tall and slender, with olive skin, high cheek bones, and dark eyes. She had the sharp features of her Italian father, though somewhat softened by her mother's Norwegian side. Shiny, brunette hair dangled from the thin white ribbon and bounced around her shoulders. A set of perfect white teeth flashed between her lips. Her eyes were clear and bright and generally sparkled, though they could become moody and narrow when she was angry or sad.

Jesse kicked off her shoes and poured herself a glass of orange juice before she noticed the blinking light on her answering machine. She punched the play button and walked to the kitchen window as she waited for the tape to start playing. As the message started playing, she smiled. It was so nice to hear his voice.

Then she heard what the voice had to say. She hardly breathed as she listened to the entire message. She continued to stare out the window as the tape stopped playing, clicked, and rewound itself to accept another call. Without thinking, she poured the orange juice into the sink and walked slowly to the answering machine again. With trembling hands she pressed the play button and turned up the volume.

She listened to the message again, rewound it and listened once more. She could have listened to the tape a thousand times, but the message wouldn't have changed.

After listening to the tape for the third time, she turned the machine off. She left the kitchen and walked through the apartment's small living room. As she passed by the front door, she slid the dead bolt closed, then hurried down the hall into the bedroom.

Opening the closet, she rifled through the clothes until she found what she was looking for, shoved in the back of the closet under an old umbrella and yellow raincoat. It was an old flannel shirt. She hadn't worn it in years.

She took out the shirt and fingered its worn flannel as she walked over and sat on the bed. It was a man's shirt and much too big for her, but it was the most valued piece of clothing she owned. She fumbled with the shirt until she found the left breast pocket, which was buttoned closed and hard to get open. Finally she undid the button and pulled out a folded piece of paper.

She carefully unfolded the paper and looked at it for the first time in over a year. It had a line drawn down the middle, with words written on both sides in tiny but legible writing. She studied the paper closely, reading it one line at a time. It contained twenty lines of code words and phrases, along with their deciphered meaning. Quickly, she scanned down the paper, not finding what she was looking for until she got near the bottom of the page. She sucked in her breath just slightly as she began to understand what Ammon was trying to tell her.

My father is sick = they are bringing me in
Reggie = I don't know what they want
I'll call you = wait for me—follow the plan

After reading the paper, she folded it up again and put it back into the shirt pocket. Picking up the phone, she dialed a number and spoke in a pleasant voice. But she only talked for a minute. After hanging up the phone, she stuffed the flannel shirt into the one travel bag that she would take. Within minutes Jesse had packed and showered. On the way to her car she stopped at the manager's office and asked him to check her mail. There's been a sickness in the family, she explained. She would be gone for a few days. Maybe even longer.

In the attic above Jesse's bed was a small black electronic box about the size of a large pack of gum. It was attached to a crossbeam by four small screws and lay immediately on top of the ceiling drywall. It had been placed there by a man named Valori Antonov. For three weeks it had lain dormant.

Nine hours before Jesse came home from her morning walk, a tiny red light on the side of the box shone for the first time. Silently, a microphone the size of a pin was forced through the ceiling and into the room below. Only one eighth of an inch of metal was exposed on the bedroom ceiling, but that was enough to pick up even the quietest whisper, no matter where it was spoken in the apartment. The box had already picked up and broadcast in a digital format the message that Jesse received on her answering machine. While Jesse was busy packing, three voice recognition analysts were trying to determine who had made the call.

FOUR

YELLOW SEA

RICHARD AMMON WAS IN HIS LIFE RAFT LESS THAN AN HOUR BEFORE HE heard the sound of an approaching boat. He peered into the darkness, but could see nothing but the faint outline of the horizon against the star-covered sky. The approaching sound was deep and throaty and seemed to come from all around him so that he couldn't determine in which direction to look. He thought for a moment about shooting off one of his flares but immediately decided against it. He knew the tanker was still somewhere overhead and he couldn't take a chance.

Out of the darkness emerged the shadow of a black speedboat. It appeared to be about thirty feet long, but its low profile made it difficult to see. It was heading directly for him, and for a moment he thought it would run him over. Just before reaching him it turned sharply and cut its engines. The wave and splash from its wake sent Ammon's small raft reeling and once again, he found himself in the water. As he sputtered to the surface, a rope was thrown over his head and a voice yelled to him in Russian.

"Ti ponimayesh yeshcho rodnoi yazik, tovarishch? Do you still understand your native tongue, my comrade?"

After a long pause Ammon responded in English. "Who are you? Can you help me? I need your help."

He didn't recognize the voice, and the man had not given the proper code.

For a second the only sound Ammon heard was a gentle laugh. Then the voice responded, this time in English. "It's a cold night for such happenings."

"Yes, especially for this time of year." Ammon called back. As he pulled himself alongside the boat, a massive pair of hands reached down and pulled him from the water. Shivering and exhausted, Ammon found himself staring into a bearded face he had never seen before.

"Who are you?" Ammon asked, once again in English.

"I am Amril. But no time to talk now. Your American helicopter friends are only a few minutes away. They want so much to be heroes, so we must go. I will answer all of your questions soon. Very soon."

Ammon didn't move. His eyes narrowed in the darkness. "Who arranged for this little accident?" he finally said dryly. "I could have been killed! You fools are lucky you're not pulling a waterlogged corpse from the sea." Ammon paused, then, slipping into Russian, he continued, "It was a stupid idea," he said flatly.

"No, no, it was not," Amril shot back. "It was a stroke of near genius, little man, so be quiet and do as I say."

The distant sound of the circling tanker pulled Amril's eyes toward the sky. Turning away from Ammon, he yelled as he ran to the front of the ship. "Quickly! Pull in your raft and take off your flight suit. Do it now! We don't have much time!"

Ammon hesitated just a moment. The night wind began to stir, cutting through his wet clothes and leaving him chilled to the bone. Overhead, the sound of the circling aircraft drifted across the open ocean. Four-foot waves slapped at the bow of the boat as it bobbed in the water. A high overcast was beginning to form, stealing the light from the moon. Ammon shivered once again, his jaw stammering from the cold, then moved to do as he was told.

Bending over the railing, he reached over the side of the boat and pulled on the lanyard that was attached to his life raft. The raft was light and easy to pull from the water. He hauled it aboard and dropped it on the narrow deck of the boat. He then turned and, leaning against the brass railing for support and balance, he slipped off his parachute harness and wet flight suit, letting them drop to the deck beside the raft.

Meanwhile, Amril was pulling a black canvas bag from under the forward bow. Reaching into the bag, he pulled out a small bundle of canvas and rubber. It was a rubber raft identical to the one Ammon had just pulled from the sea. He gave a quick tug on its activation cord and with a hiss and crackle, it began to inflate. But only on one side. The air chamber on the left side of the raft had a broken valve and would not hold any air. Later, when the investigation of the missing F-16 was complete, the accident investigation board would determine that the faulty valve on Ammon's raft was at least partially responsible for his death.

With a jerk, Amril took Ammon's raft and read the serial numbers that were painted under the lower rim. Working quickly, he took out stencils and a can of yellow spray paint and painted his raft with the identical numbers. He knew that the Air Force would easily confirm that this was the life raft from Ammon's jet, once the serial numbers had been traced. Then turning to Ammon, he said, "I need some blood. Lay down and lift up your arm."

Ammon was startled by the request. After a short pause he asked, "Is it your feeding time already?"

His weak attempt at humor went unnoticed, and he felt silly standing there in his wet underwear, shivering. He noticed Amril staring at the wrapping around his leg, but Amril didn't mention his apparent injury.

"Quickly, lie down," Amril said again. "I need blood from an arterial vein. And don't worry about the pain, I am very good at this." Ammon didn't miss the sarcasm in his voice.

Ammon did as he was told as Amril approached him with an enormous needle. As he stepped to Ammon's side, Amril jerked his arm above his head and held it while he smoothly inserted the needle into the axillary artery that ran under his arm and directly to his heart. It took only a moment to fill the syringe with blood. He then walked over to the partially inflated raft and squirted the blood all over, smearing it with his hands. After tossing the raft overboard, Amril turned to face his shivering passenger. "Now, we must get underway."

Amril led the way forward to the small cabin and started the boat. Gunning the throttles he turned northeast. After throwing Ammon a huge towel and cotton bathrobe, he motioned to a vinyl chair. Ammon sat down, and Amril closed the hatch door behind them, cutting the sound of the engines to a muffled roar. Amril had turned off all of the boat's navigation lights, making the speeding watercraft impossible to see in the darkness.

After a moment of silence, Ammon asked, "Why did you have to stick me?"

Amril glanced at his passenger for a second before he replied. "For several reasons," he said. "First, your death will have to be positively confirmed. By giving them a blood sample, they will have the DNA evidence to do that. But more importantly, by drawing from one of your arterial veins, we will help them identify a probable cause of death.

"You see, blood from a major vein, such as the axillary artery, is easily identified by the amount of oxygen it contains. When they analyze the samples taken from your raft they will conclude that you have suffered a major wound, probably a compound fracture of the arm or leg. It would be expected that you would lose a large amount of blood. Loss of consciousness would shortly follow, and since your raft was only partially inflated, the Americans will then theorize that you must have passed out and slipped peacefully into the cold, dark sea."

Amril paused for a moment, then chuckled as he continued.

"I can see the accident report now:

"On 18 August, Richard Ammon, Captain, U.S. Air Force, was on a routine training mission over the Yellow Sea. For yet undetermined reasons, his F-16 exploded just prior to air refueling. The aircraft crashed at sea and was destroyed upon impact. Capt Ammon's body has not been recovered, and we suspect he was a midnight snack for a herd of migrating turtles. The investigation continues."

Amril continued to chuckle as he poured two steaming cups of coffee into capped mugs with his free hand and passed one over to Ammon. Amril sipped at the bitter brew in silence, then finally concluded. "It is a simple deception, but it will work."

Ammon said nothing. By now the overcast had thickened and had completely obscured the once bright moon. They traveled in complete darkness. He felt dizzy and had to hold the brass side rail to steady himself in his chair. He began to realize how tired he was. Instead of the coffee, what he really needed was some rest and some time to think.

He stared into the darkness. As the boat sped on, bouncing from wave to wave, Ammon's head began to slowly bob in rhythm. He listened to the drone of the engines. It was a pleasant sound, somehow comforting. It reminded him of when he was a small boy. Ammon could still picture himself as a child, huddled in the back seat, surrounded by thin wool blankets as his father drove the back streets of the Kasakstov and Preshingtovalon districts. His father, more adept at drinking than holding down jobs, had finally found a job he could live with delivering newspapers between boroughs in eastern Kiev. The money wasn't great, but it was enough to buy vodka and food. And since his mother had passed away several years before, his father had insisted that he accompany him on his rounds, rather than be left back in their tiny apartment alone.

As a young boy, Carl Vadym Kostenko was identified as having the potential to complete one of the Kollektive Sicherheit's most rigorous tracks. He was separated from his family at age nine, and for the next nine years was indoctrinated with the theories of Marx and Lenin. He learned perfect English (with a slight southern accent) and American history and culture. Like American boys his age, he grew up to the music of Tom Petty, U2, and the Boss. He hated country and western. He loved the Dallas Cowboys.

But Carl Kostenko's education didn't end there. He also learned how to manipulate friends, communicate secretly with his handler, and operate miniature photographic and communication equipment. He learned how to evaluate others for tendencies of sympathy to his cause. He learned to exploit and deceive and lie. Finally, he was taught how to kill. Efficiently. Quietly. Without a trace. Without leaving a mess. It was a skill he anticipated he would never use, but if it ever became necessary, so be it. It was simply something he would do.

At the age of eighteen, Carl Kostenko found himself planted in the United States, complete with papers, a solid background, and a new identity as Richard Ammon. He entered UCLA, and graduated in three years with a B.S. in mechanical engineering. He received a reserve commission in the United States Air Force. A year later, he completed pilot training and had been flying the F-16 ever since.

During his first years at college, he had literally no contact with his handler. He didn't even know if he had one. Many times he was left to wonder if he might be on his own. It wasn't until he was ready to graduate that he was contacted. He was told that they had decided that he should accept his commission in the Air Force. This was very good news for Ammon, for although he would have done whatever was expected of him, he very much wanted to fly.

But like everything about the Kollektive Sicherheit, there were strings attached. No rewards were ever free. Richard Ammon was told that if he didn't do well enough in pilot training to get a combat aircraft upon graduation, then the agreement to allow him into the Air Force would be terminated. In addition, his superiors would be extremely disappointed in his performance and would have to question his ability to successfully complete future assignments. His whole situation would then be re-evaluated.

Few student pilots entered undergraduate pilot training with as much hidden baggage or secret motivation as did Richard Ammon.

But once he started to fly, Ammon began to relax. He discovered that he was a natural pilot. Flying just seemed to come easily to him.

He remembered clearly the day he knew he would make it. It was on his second sortie in advanced aerobatics in the T-38. The instructor pilot, who occupied the rear seat, was in a sour mood and nearly impossible to please. While completing a simple loop, he had suddenly grabbed the controls from Richard Ammon and snapped back hard on the stick.

"I said, pull more Gs!" he screamed, while pulling the little fighter around in a sharp bank. "You've got to G up this aircraft to get it around. Now do it again, and this time keep it coming. When I say pull, I mean pull! Don't nanny around with the stick!"

Ammon shook his head with disgust, both at his own mistake and at his instructor for being such a jerk. Taking the stick in his right hand, he set up for another loop. Pushing the T-38's nose toward the earth, he shoved both throttles into afterburner and accelerated quickly to 500 knots, then with a sudden snap, jammed the stick back into his lap. The Talon's nose arched gracefully skyward as the G meter pegged at seven Gs. Grunting against the strain, he kept the pull in through the top of the loop, then accelerated downward once again. As he reached the bottom of the loop, he should have eased off on the stick and leveled off. But he didn't. Instead, he kept the aircraft in full afterburner and jammed the stick back into his lap once again. Four times he pushed the aircraft through a graceful arch, constantly pulling seven Gs, forcing his instructor to groan and strain just to keep the blood in his head. At the bottom of the fourth loop, he heard his instructor mutter through the strain of his mask, "Okay, okay, I've had enough. You can let go of it now." Ammon leveled off and headed back to base. His instructor didn't say a word. He slowly shook his head. The guy had a lot of nerve, pulling such a stunt on him. Cocky little jerk! Arrogant, snot-nose kid!

But inside his mask he was smiling. He loved it! It was just what they were looking for! It was exactly the kind of mentality that a combat pilot would need. From that day on, Ammon's fighter was almost guaranteed.

First Lieutenant Richard Ammon graduated number one in his class. As such, he was entitled to get his first choice of aircraft and assignment. Lt Ammon didn't even have to think.

He selected an F-16 to Bitburg Air Force Base, Germany. Not only would this assignment make it easier for him to be "handled," but he would have access to important intelligence information concerning NATO and the American forces in Europe.

He was in Europe for almost a year before he heard again from the Sicherheit. He was told early to protect his position and not to take any chances that might expose his operation. They would need him later in his career, and they didn't want to take any unnecessary chances at this time. As a result, he was never asked to pass along any information before he was transferred back to the States.

It was then that things had begun to unravel.

Few Americans watched the fall of the Berlin Wall or the breakup of the Soviet Union with as much interest as did Richard Ammon. Over the next few years, he watched in bewilderment as one communist government after another fell, along with their anti-West intelligence machines. During this time Ammon's contact with his handler became less and less frequent. After a while he was not sure any of his former supervisors even remembered he was there. Now it had been years since he had any communication with them, and he doubted they knew of his assignment to Korea.

So Ammon couldn't have been more surprised when, two days earlier, he was contacted. The message was simple. "The train is leaving at two. Gather your luggage." Translation: Expect to be brought in. No more than two days. Gather any classified information that you can and be ready. We will act.

He wondered who had ordered him in? Who were they working for now? What government did they represent, and what did they really want?

But he realized his concerns didn't matter. In such things he had very little choice.

So he gathered what information he could and prepared for the unknown. Although he knew the microfilm he brought with him was worthless, hopefully his superiors wouldn't. And that would buy him their trust, and maybe a little time.

Thinking of the microfilm brought Ammon back to the present. He reached down to massage his wrapped knee, feeling the plastic bag as it rubbed against his skin.

Ammon stared into the darkness as they cruised toward the dim lights of P'yongyang. Amril remained silent, studying oceanic charts that lay on a small table by the pilot's wheel. Ammon glanced at his watch, then returned his gaze to the darkness, his eyes unblinking, deep in thought. But he wasn't considering the possibilities of his future, or even reflecting on the life he had just left behind. The only thing he was thinking about was how hard it would be to find a telephone once he arrived in the communist city of P'yongyang.

OSAN AIR FORCE BASE, SOUTH KOREA

Eighteen hours later, all nine members of the accident board that would investigate the downing of the F-16 met together for the first time inside a cavernous hangar. They watched in huddled silence as a deflated raft was brought through the hangar doors and placed on a stainless steel table in the middle of the floor. Normally, the place would have already been strewn with charred and splintered pieces of aircraft wreckage, carefully laid out, like pieces of a huge jigsaw puzzle. Normally, chunks of engines, computers, and fuselage would have already been placed end-to-end and piece-to-piece in an effort to determine the cause of the crash.

But not this investigation. The Yellow Sea had seen to that.

Air Force Colonel James Wood stared down at the deflated life raft and admitted to himself for the first time that it would likely be the only piece of evidence he would ever have to work with. The Falcon had gone down in more than 1,800 meters of shark-infested water. The initial report from the Navy indicated that the possibility of recovering the aircraft was fairly remote, perhaps impossible. Upon impact with the water, the F-16 would have been blown into a thousand shattered pieces. The fragments would have then been scattered across miles of ragged ocean floor, drifting here and there with the cold water currents.

No, unfortunately, there would be no aircraft wreckage to help them in their investigation. The accident board would be on their own.

Wood ran his hand over his head and let out an audible sigh. He watched the flight surgeon don surgical gloves and carefully spread the raft out upon the examination table. As the accident investigation board president, it was his responsibility to determine exactly what had caused the F-16 to go down. He had spent the past eighteen hours talking to the KC-135 refueling crew and taking their statements, coordinating the rescue effort, searching through Capt Ammon's official flight records, and organizing the members of the accident investigation team.

Together, he, the maintenance supervisor, and the chief flight surgeon had huddled in conference as they tried to put the initial pieces together. But as was usually the case, the early pieces did not fit very well.

Never had he seen anything quite this odd. Never had he heard of a fighter simply exploding in mid-air. The tanker boom operator had described it as a huge explosion—a billowing fireball of blue and yellow flame. He had been very specific. A bright blue and white explosion, followed by a billowing yellow fireball.

The yellow made sense. The blue surely did not. Yellow was within the color spectrum of burning jet fuel. Blue was not. Blue indicated a much hotter flame—a much more powerful explosion than one would expect from burning jet fuel.

Another fragmented piece to the puzzle.

And then there was the most troubling question of all. What had happened to Captain Richard Ammon? What sequence in the survival chain had failed him? Where was his body? Why was he dead?

There had been no radio call. No emergency beacon. No flares or smoke or signaling device of any kind.

And then the rescue helicopter had located the empty life raft floating around in the sea, half inflated and smeared with diluted blood. This would give them some answers. This was where they would begin.

Colonel Wood watched in silence as the flight surgeon and two assistants began to take blood samples on thin cotton swabs and place them in sterile containers. These would be used to make a DNA comparison of Captain Ammon, which would hopefully lead to a positive identification. The blood samples would also be analyzed to help determine the cause of death.

As the Colonel watched the flight surgeon work, a young captain approached him and tapped him lightly on the shoulder.

"Sir, there's someone here I think you should talk to."

The colonel turned and looked at the captain. "Who is it? What do they want?"

"It's one of the tanker pilots, sir. He has something he wants to add to his official statement. Something about seeing a small boat near the crash site. I don't know, sir. Why don't you come and see what you think?"

For the next half hour, the colonel listened carefully as one of the tanker pilots described what he had seen the night before. It looked like a small speedboat, he remembered, heading northeast away from the crash site at a very high speed. He had only caught the briefest glimpse of it in the moonlight while they had been orbiting at two thousand feet. But he was certain it was there. He had clearly seen the splash its bow made in the moonlight and he had even seen its wake spreading out behind it as it ran. There was a boat in the area, he was certain of that. A small craft, but very fast, and it was operating without any lights.

"But that doesn't make any sense," Wood muttered. "A small boat, out in the middle of the night, more than a hundred miles from shore, at the exact location of the downed pilot. It sounds very odd. So think. Think very carefully. What else could it have been?"

The tanker pilot met Wood's eyes with a cold and self-assured stare. "It was a small boat, colonel. I know that. Now who it was, and why it was there, I guess that's something you ought to look into. All I'm telling you is what I saw."

For two days Colonel Wood stewed about what the captain had told him. Three times he interviewed him again, hoping to find some crack in his story, hoping the pilot would rethink what he saw, hoping it would just go away. But the captain held firm, and so, much as the colonel hated to open such a rotten and unpromising can of worms, he felt compelled to follow his instincts. Late in the evening on the third day after the accident, he sent a highly encrypted message to a very small and crowded office deep in the bowels of the USCOM building at Bolling Air Force Base, Washington, D.C.

TO: Director, Internal Counter-Espionage Division (ICED)

FR: President, Accident Investigation Board, F-16-12-21

RE: USAF Directive 99-03

Sir:

We find ourselves in the midst of a class A accident investigation involving a Captain Richard Ammon, 445-78-9321.

Although insignificant and completely unsubstantiated at this time, there are certain factors which lead me to believe that it is at least possible that espionage and/or sabotage may have played a part in this accident. These factors include, but are not limited to the following unusual considerations:

- Captain Ammon's body has not been recovered.
- The sudden explosion onboard the incident aircraft cannot be explained, nor does the eyewitness account of the explosion fall in place with what we would expect from a fuel-feed fire.
- Witness places an unidentified watercraft in the vicinity of the accident at the time rescue attempts were under way.

In accordance with Air Force directives, I am therefore advising you of my intention to seek further latitude in this investigation than would normally exist. If you have any information which could be of any assistance, please advise.

Colonel Wood
Board President

Less than five minutes after Colonel Wood had sent the message, Lt Colonel Oliver Tray, assistant director, ICED, walked over to the huge office vault and pulled out a top secret binder marked:

Ammon, Richard
codename "BADGER"

With the encoded message from Colonel Wood in hand, he returned to his desk and sat down. It had been a very long time since the BADGER file had been opened. Now, here he was, opening the file for the second time in less than three days. Lieutenant Colonel Tray removed the red "TOP SECRET" cover sheet and started to read. Five hours later, he called his wife to tell her he wouldn't be home until long after supper.

FIVE

SEVASTOPOL AIR BASE, SOUTHERN UKRAINE

UKRAINIAN PRIME MINISTER YEVGENI OSKOL GOLUBEV WAS WAITING ON the cement tarmac, standing in front of a dull brick reception building that was used exclusively for visiting dignitaries. Sevastopol was the headquarters for the Ukrainian Black Sea fleet. Because of its location on the southwest tip of the Crimean peninsula, and its proximity to the warm waters of the Black Sea, Sevastopol was one of the warmest cities in the Ukraine.

In the distance, through the smog and haze, Golubev could see the gentle roll of the Krymskiye hills that lined the south side of the peninsula. To the south lay the harbor, with its many huge ports and docks used by the Black Sea Fleet. During the height of the cold war, Sevastopol was one of the jewels of the Soviet industrial crown. But that was long ago. Now, more than a generation had been born and raised in the shanty towns that surrounded the port city. The air, once crisp and clean, now reeked of oily smoke and rusty decay as the smokestacks of the harbor belched forth their gaseous toxins to mix with the humid air that blew in from the Black Sea. Once a favorite vacation spot of Russian Czars, the beaches were now too polluted to be enjoyed.

The day was very warm, especially for this late in the summer, and sweat beaded Golubev's back as he paced the tarmac. As the gusty hot air blew in his face, Golubev wished again that he could have waited in the coolness of his air conditioned car. But the General had been quite specific in his request. "Meet me on the tarmac and come alone." So here he stood, his own car and driver parked some fifty paces behind him. Further back along the fence stood another black sedan. This one contained four security personnel. They watched through tinted windows as their boss walked and fidgeted on the tarmac.

Golubev looked up into the sky once again to watch the Soviet SU-27 make its final approach and landing. As he observed the fighter, it passed over the last of the runway lights. He heard the roar of the engines diminish when the pilot pulled both of his throttles back to idle. The aircraft touched down lightly only eight hundred feet down the runway.

Inside the cockpit, General Victor Lomov extended the speed brakes as he watched the airspeed indicator. Once he slowed below 150 knots, he began to pull the nose of the aircraft back up into the air. This exposed the underside of the fuselage and wings to the wind and helped to slow him down. As the aircraft slowed below 110 knots, he lowered the nose back onto the runway and then gently applied the wheel brakes. The aircraft decelerated rapidly and the general popped opened his canopy as soon as he slowed to taxi airspeed.

Because this was a surprise inspection, no officers from the base had yet come to meet him. Even now, as he taxied off the runway, they were just being notified of his arrival. It would take several minutes before they would have time to assemble the appropriate generals and senior staff. Several more minutes would pass before they could make their way to the operations center to meet him. It was time the general needed and would use.

As the Commanding General of the Ukrainian Forces, General Victor Lomov made frequent surprise inspections. It was not unusual for him to show up unannounced at one of his bases and ask the local commander if he could have a look around. It was both something he enjoyed and an extremely valuable motivational tool. But this inspection was unusual. He had invited Prime Minister Golubev to meet him and accompany him as he inspected the base. It was the first time he had extended an invitation to the Prime Minister to accompany him on an inspection. The story would be that he was so proud of the base's ability to maintain combat effectiveness that he wanted Golubev to see for himself.

The general taxied the small fighter to the tarmac and shut down the engines with his nose facing the waiting Prime Minister. He was pleased to see the man was alone, but he knew that they only had a few minutes to talk before they would be surrounded by insistent aides.

He quickly disconnected his G-suit and oxygen hose and extended the small steps that would allow him to climb down from the cockpit. Although the general was almost sixty, he was fit and agile and managed the narrow steps with ease. After reaching the ground he stretched his arms, cracked the kinks out of his back, then took off his flight helmet and gloves and hung them on one of the steps. Physically, the general was striking. He was tall and slender, with a square jaw, broad cheeks, and penetrating gray eyes. Thirty years earlier, General Lomov had been a poster boy for the Soviet Air Force. His face had appeared on thousands of propaganda billboards and signs, extolling the virtues of service to one's country. As a young captain he had toured the far reaches of the Soviet empire, recruiting young warriors to the Socialist cause. And though the years had passed and softened his features, still the general remained driven by the fires of ambition. He was cold and intelligent, and focused as a laser.

After stretching his muscles, he turned and gestured to Golubev to come over to the jet.

"Have you ever seen such a beautiful aircraft?" he asked as the Prime Minister approached.

"Never!" Golubev replied as he admired the general's fighter. When he noticed Lomov's name painted under the raised canopy, he smiled to himself at the general's vanity. It didn't surprise him that Lomov had his own jet. It fit his character perfectly. The general had the pride of a fighter pilot and over the years, Golubev had come to expect certain things from his ego.

"Does it perform in the air as well as it looks on the ground?" Golubev asked, after walking around the jet.

"Oh, it's a dream you could not understand, Mr. Prime Minister. There is nothing like it in the world. Anywhere.

Come here. Let me show you something."

The two men climbed the tiny steps and crowded together so that they could peer into the cockpit.

"We have recovered the pilot," Lomov whispered as he pointed to the head-up display. "He was brought in last week. He should be in Kiev by Wednesday."

"Is he clean?" the Prime Minister asked as he looked in the direction the general was pointing. "We don't need the Americans asking any questions."

"Clean as snow," the general replied. "It was a perfect break. The Americans aren't asking any questions, aside from the normal investigation after one of their planes go down. They won't find anything unusual. It was a good plan. Simple and with little outside involvement."

"Has he been briefed?" the prime minister asked.

"Not yet. Morozov is out of the country. But he should be back by tomorrow. He will meet with the pilot when he arrives on Wednesday."

Two black sedans pulled through the gate and onto the tarmac, accelerating rapidly across the open cement. Both men turned to watch them as they approached.

"Which brings me to my next point," the general continued. "Morozov feels he has found an additional financier. Someone who can give us all of the money we need to complete this operation. But he may have to be persuaded. I told Morozov he could use some of our people in Cuba, but he seemed to think he could handle it himself."

"After he meets the pilot in Kiev, he is going back to South America to get the money."

"We are running out of time," Golubev muttered.

"Morozov won't disappoint us," Lomov assured his friend. "Yevgeni, haven't you learned that by now?"

"What about the girl?" Golubev quickly asked.

"That news isn't good. We've been watching her apartment, but she hasn't returned. Apparently she just disappeared. It could be hard to track her since we don't want to use any of our official people. Liski is working on it."

Lomov nodded as they watched the sedans approach. The back doors of the second car began to swing open before it even came to a stop.

The two men climbed down from the aircraft. They turned to meet the welcome party, but before they were surrounded, the Prime Minister whispered under his breath. "Keep me informed, Victor. We have come too far to let things start slipping through the cracks. If the pilot is here by Wednesday, I want to meet him for myself. And soon. It would be nice to wait for the perfect excuse, but we can't afford that luxury. Time will not allow it."

"Be ready to go hunting," General Lomov nodded as he walked toward the waiting cars. "I will let you know."

MOSCOW, RUSSIA

The Russian president studied each man in the room, staring into their faces, summing them up, seeking their thoughts through their eyes. Some of the men returned his gaze with equally unblinking and cold-hearted stares, while others, generally the younger ministers, began to fidget in their seats. The Interior Minister seemed particularly anxious as he drummed nervous fingers across the arm of his chair. A few of the men stared off into space, too fearful to even look at Fedotov. The room nearly crackled with stress and only the generals seemed relaxed and at ease.

As the Russian president studied the faces, he almost smiled. Stalin was right. Nothing could be quite so persuasive as fear. The plan was so simple. Kill off the main competition, hit hard and hit fast, then watch the sheep as they flock to your side.

Fedotov sat at the table and gathered his notes. He was a wiry man, with thin brown hair atop a narrow face and pointed chin. Black eyes sat deep within his pock-marked face and his roman nose jutted out above pale, thin lips. Above his left eye was a jagged red scar, his badge from the night on the bridge. Behind his back, his enemies called him "Whorlest"—the "little mink." Fedotov knew of the insulting nickname; but it never bothered him. In fact, he found it somewhat amusing. "Little mink." It wasn't much of title, but it would do.

To most of his subordinates, Fedotov was a mysterious man, shrouded in a veil of paranoia and fear. He was a shadowy figure, a hard and ambitious man who had risen to power with such speed and direction that he left no trail in his wake. His personal life, if he had one, was a complete blank, nothing but a sheet of white paper, and it spoke volumes of the Russian republic that such a ghostlike figure could ever rise to such a position of power.

Unfortunately for the ministers and generals, Fedotov didn't suffer from the same lack of information about his rivals and enemies. There wasn't a single man seated around the table about whom Fedotov couldn't have instantly recited the most intimate personal details—from their habits of personal hygiene to their latest travels, from their political sympathies to conversations they had with their wives while lying in bed. Over the past three years, Prime Minister Vladimir Fedotov and his conspirators had committed enormous resources to collecting such information on the power elite, the most interesting and useful of which was compiled into thick but tidy dossiers and tucked away in his safe.

Fedotov looked up. "Comrades . . . this meeting will be very brief," he began.

"Thirty days ago, Sakarovek was killed, leaving me with the responsibility of leading our nation at a time of its deepest despair.

"Now, for those of you who don't already know, President Sakarovek was nothing but a coward. He brought more misery and suffering to our people than any leader since the Czars. Minister Sklyarov was a thief. And Secretary Moykola. . . . " Fedotov's eyes blazed. "How can I even explain? He was a stooge for the West. A traitor and nothing more. It was my duty to send them to hell."

The Deputy Prime Minister's face remained passive and without emotion. Fedotov's candor didn't surprise him. Everyone in the room knew what was going on. For the past several years they had seen the train coming. All they wanted was to get out of the way.

Fedotov cleared his throat and continued. "Some of you sitting here today were friends of these cowardly men. You know who you are. I know who you are. And while loyalty is an admirable trait, it doesn't change the truth. And each of you . . . if you examine your hearts . . . if you look at the facts . . . you will see what I have told you is true."

Fedotov paused. Absolute silence. No one looked away. "Now, I have called this meeting to make one simple point, and I want to be perfectly clear." A screen behind Fedotov's seat suddenly flickered to life, and the lights in the room slowly dimmed. Fedotov studied the reaction of the men as a picture emerged on the eight-foot screen that was positioned behind him.

It was a picture of a little girl. She was dirty and horribly small. A hollow and frightened face looked up at the camera in hunger and desperation and a terror so real it leapt from her eyes. Tiny arms extended out from underneath a burlap sack of a dress. Her legs, no larger than her bony arms, huddled beneath her bloated stomach. She was reaching out. Reaching out to her mother. Her mother who lay dead and crumpled beside her.

"Her name is Tasha," Fedotov said without turning around. "She is five years old tomorrow." The ministers and generals sat motionless, barely able to breathe.

"Five years old, comrades!" Fedotov cried as he stood and turned toward the screen. "Look at her! She is only a child, and already she has lived through more horror and pain than all of our miserable lives put together!

"She lives in Voroshilovgrad, along the Ukrainian border. Look at her bloated stomach and the horrible rash, the results of the scarlet fever from which she suffers. She has no medicine. She has never even seen a doctor. Every day, like millions of our children, she gets but a few ounces of food. Her life is but hunger and horror. Though living, she is already dead.

"As a nation, we have come to the point where our children are raised in a world of such hopelessness and gloom that it seems they are left with only three choices. Die of starvation. Die of disease. Or live in a world of despair."

"And this . . . ," Fedotov continued, pointing to the mutilated corpse in the picture, "this is Tasha's mother. She and twenty-three of her villagers were killed early this evening in an attack by Kazakhaki bandits. For the past five years, the bandits have been free to roam across our border and plunder our people, all the time knowing they can find protection to the south. The Ukrainian government claims they are powerless to stop them. They claim to have exhausted all available means.

"I, for one, don't believe them. And I think that the time for action has come.

"If there could be a last straw, if there could be one final insult, or one single incident so rending that it changes our lives, then look at this photo and tell me, where will we draw the line?"

Fedotov fell silent. It was as if a massive weight had pressed down on the assembled audience. The room turned oppresively hot. No one moved.

The picture slowly faded out, and the lights in the room flickered on once again.

"Over the next few months, I want you to think of Tasha," Fedotov ordered as he took three steps toward the head of the table. "I want this image forever engraved in your brains.

"Because comrades, I vow to you now. I make you this solemn promise.

"By my life, by my heart, by my soul, things are going to change. You are going to change. I am going to change. Our nightmare has come to its end. It is time to rebuild our nation. It is time to reclaim our power.

"So, remember Tasha, comrades, and know this one thing. Beginning right here. Beginning right now. Things . . . are going . . . to change."

S I X

BOROVICHI SS-18 MISSILE FIELDS,
NORTHWESTERN RUSSIA

FIFTY-SEVEN KILOMETERS SOUTHEAST OF BOROVICHI, RUSSIA, BURIED deep under the rolling hills, lay "Satan's bedroom"—the launch facilities for the SS-18/mod 5 Intercontinental Ballistic Missile. Built very early in the 1990s, the missile complex was comprised of one hundred missile silos and four central launch facilities spread out over a thousand square kilometers of the sub-arctic tundra. The silos extended more than thirteen stories into the rock and soil and were capped by thick steel doors. Enormous bundles of buried wires and fiber-optic cables linked the silos and the launch facilities. The whole complex was an incredible engineering marvel, to the tune of more than a hundred billion rubles.

Yet, to the casual observer, the complex doesn't even exist. The wet tundra extended for miles around, with no buildings or fences in sight. The rolling, treeless hills showed no scars of construction, and a man could walk for days over the complex and never suspect that billions of rubles in technology lay just underneath the wet soil. The native herdsmen, with their goats and their sheep, walked among the unseen missiles every day. There were stories and rumors that tried to explain why they had not been allowed to graze the tundra for several summers, but the theories that the natives came up with were not even close to the truth. The herdsmen never had any idea that they were living atop the most powerful weapons on earth.

Nicknamed "Satan" by western intelligence, the SS-18 was capable of dropping each of its ten nuclear warheads to within just feet of their targets. Each of the ten warheads had the same destructive power as one million tons of TNT. The enormous Sukhoy rockets had a range of over 11,000 miles, placing virtually every target within the Northern Hemisphere at risk. Its sheer potential for destruction, coupled with its pinpoint accuracy and range, made "Satan" the most feared weapon the Soviets had ever developed.

But it wasn't the mass destruction of its cities that the Americans feared, for they knew that the missiles were only pointing at strategic targets. The thing that made the SS-18 so destabilizing was the fact that it could destroy the United States' ICBMs before they could be launched from their silos. It could destroy all of the manned bombers that were sitting alert before they could get in the air, as well the entire fleet of nuclear submarines, even as they sat in their protective pens.

This had the effect of forcing the U.S. to lean forward during an international crisis into a "use them or lose them" mentality.

For this reason, the SS-18 was one of the major sticking points between the U.S. and the Soviets during the START II negotiations. The Russians were unwilling to completely destroy one of their crowning technological achievements, while at the same time the U.S. was unwilling to accept their continued existence.

Finally, an acceptable compromise was reached. It was decided that the SS-18 missile silos would be breached and rendered unusable. Fifteen meters of concrete would be poured into the bottom of the silos, while a 2.9-meter restrictive ring would be placed around the top. This would make the silos' dimensions simply too small to hold the SS-18s, rendering the missiles utterly useless.

But the missiles themselves were never destroyed. The Russians had argued that it would have been prohibitively expensive to properly and safely dismantle the warheads. In addition, it would require money that they simply didn't have. And since the missiles were useless without their launch facilities, it seemed reasonable to give them more time. So the Russians removed the missiles into storage, until such time that they could be "properly destroyed."

But this agreement didn't make everyone happy. Many of the American negotiators were concerned that it would be relatively easy for the Russians to refurbish the silos. But in the emerging era of trust and friendship, their anxieties were altogether ignored. Ignored by everyone, that was, except a very small group of Russian scientists and military leaders. These men didn't laugh at the doubts of the less trusting Americans, for it was their job to secretly ensure that the silos could be used once again.

The restrictive ring that was going to be placed at the top of the silos was never really a problem. A large adjustable crescent wrench and a small hoist were the only tools that were required to remove the ring. And it wouldn't take much time, either. Three men could have the ring out of the silo within just a couple of hours.

The problem that had the Soviet scientists puzzled was the cement that had to be poured into the bottom of the silos. The Russians knew that the Americans would send inspectors to observe when the silos were shut down, so they would have to fill the silos with concrete. But if they used regular cement, the walls of the silos would be destroyed if the time ever came when the Russians wanted to chip the concrete out. So, the question was, how could they save the silos, and yet still appear to comply with the terms of the agreement?

For years they stalled and delayed the SALT II negotiations while they looked for an answer to their problem. Then finally, they hit upon the solution. After years of experimentation a special mix of concrete was developed that initially set hard as rock. This allowed the Russians to pass the treaty verification process, which made both parties to the agreement very happy. But within just a few months of being poured, the special cement began to soften in the silos. Over time it continued to break down. Within a few years, the cement was no more firm than wet sand. This guaranteed that, should the occasion ever arise, the silos could be operational again within a very short period of time.

MOSCOW, RUSSIA

President Fedotov walked out onto the back porch of his living quarters. It was early evening, and a bitter wind had turned the air cold. At the bottom of the steps, a small gray sedan was already waiting, but if Fedotov was in a hurry, he didn't show it. He descended the stairs one by one, then slowly crossed the driveway. When he finally made it to the car, he opened the door with a huff then plopped himself inside.

The car was being driven by General Hrihori Nahaylo, Fedotov's Minister for Defense. General Nahaylo slipped the car into gear, then slowly began to make his way down the long drive and through the security checkpoints until he merged with the light traffic that was circling Kremlin Square. As he drove, he checked his rearview mirror and saw the two black sedans behind him.

Since it was past the dinner hour, General Nahaylo had brought along a small bottle of Kentucky whiskey, a decadent import to be sure, but one Fedotov enjoyed just the same. He waited until Vladimir Fedotov had settled himself back in his seat, then reached out and offered him the bottle. Fedotov lifted it with a smile, then poured a long drink past his dry lips and down his throat. He sucked in his breath and held it as he waited for the warmth to hit his belly.

"Well general, what have we got? Any word from that devil Hussein?"

"I spoke with him only moments ago, sir," General Nahaylo replied. "Taha Ubaisi will be here within two weeks to counter-offer, but at this point, we are only squabbling about the details. The deal is going to go through, of that I am sure. The Iraqis want it even more than we. Three reactors, twenty billion in oil. Another four billion cash for warhead delivery systems."

Fedotov smiled. "Fine, fine. Let's get it done. Let's move along. I want consummation of the deal before the month is through."

"Yes, sir. That can be done, although it would help if you would agree to entertain the Rias here in Moscow. It is important to him, sir. It puts him on equal ground."

The smile quickly disappeared. "Nyet, Nyet!" Fedotov shot back from other side of the car. "I don't have time, I don't have the desire. We're not dealing with the camel-eaters just to agitate emotions in the West. His Sashis can be coddled and soothed sometime later. Let him thumb his nose if he must, but for now at least, I have far more important things to do. Tell him to start pumping the oil and depositing the cash. We'll meet and kiss cheeks later on."

Nahaylo grunted in reply.

"Now tell me, General, what of the nuclear breakout? That is our primary consideration right now. How much longer until it is complete?"

"The initial breakout is complete, sir," Nahaylo announced with some satisfaction. "We finished just minutes ago."

"How many silos have been refitted with their warheads?"

"As of this moment we have sixteen SS-18 missiles ready for service," Nahaylo answered. "That's a total of one hundred sixty nuclear warheads. Another twenty missiles will be placed in their silos within the next five days. It will take about a week to have them fueled and their navigation computers booted and realigned."

"And the Americans have yet to detect any of our activity in the missile fields?"

"Nothing at all, sir. We have no indication that they are even looking." Nahaylo chuckled. Fedotov laughed in response and passed him the bottle of whiskey, which Nahaylo pressed to his lips.

"Stupid Americans," Fedotov sneered. "Trusting a treaty. How could they be so naive?"

WASHINGTON, D.C.

Thomas Allen, the President of the United States, sat stiffly on the edge of the dark sofa, a white bathrobe around his shoulders, and a mug of hot, black coffee in his hand. It was four o'clock in the morning. The President was very awake. He jabbed his finger at Ted Wilson, his Russian specialist, and vented his fury once again. "I want you to tell me," he snapped at his advisor, "with all that has been going on in Russia the past months, as closely as we have been watching those idiots screw things up over there, how could we not have seen this thing coming?"

Ted Wilson's mouth hung open as if he would speak, but no sound emerged. General Gapp, the Chairman of the Joint Chiefs, and Chad Wallet, the Secretary of Defense, exchanged painful glares. The President stared at them, waiting for an answer. The Branson grandfather clock began to chime lightly, then let out four short strikes of its bell.

The four men sat in the President's library, a warm and private little room tucked in a corner of the White House. The library was small and lined with old leather books. A white-framed fireplace adorned the west wall. The wallpaper was soft gray with rose highlights. A gilded wood chandelier hung from the ceiling. The furniture was early American, all original antiques.

Thomas Allen, a relatively young man with deep, brown eyes and broad shoulders, had only been President for twenty-two months. So far, it had been easy sailing. But now he was scared. He had never dealt with anything like this before.

"Gentlemen!" he glared around the room, "I want you to tell me. How was Fedotov able to openly violate the most significant strategic treaty of our time? And right underneath our noses? Those silos were supposed to be utterly useless, yet suddenly he has them on line. How? How did he do it!?"

Everyone started to speak at once. Everyone had an opinion. Nobody had any answers. The telephones started to ring. Voices became even more frazzled. Confusion and speculation soon filled the air.

But through it all, at least one thing remained perfectly clear.

The psychology and politics of nuclear weapons were well established political facts. For more than fifty years, nations had used their weapons of mass destruction to communicate to each other in the clearest of terms. And now, once again, the Russians were using their weapons to send a very powerful message to the West.

"Things are going to change," Fedotov had told them. "And you may not like what you see. But it is none of your business. So stay out of it. Don't interfere. Stay away or risk nuclear war."

SEVEN

P'YONGYANG PROVINCE, NORTH KOREA

IT TOOK AMRIL AND RICHARD AMMON ALMOST THREE DAYS TO GET OUT of North Korea. Amril had been setting up the operation for more than half a year, but still, there were bribes to be made, supplies to be bought, and passports to purchase; all in cash. In addition, he was one of the few Caucasians in the country, making it impossible to move about without being noticed. He had to work very carefully. He had to be very patient.

For three days, Ammon waited in a small thatched farm hut on a rocky knoll. It consisted of one small room with a blackened brick fireplace and a straw mattress on which to sleep. From its only window Ammon could watch the thin traffic that moved along the highway to P'yongyang. He watched peasant farmers working the soil with sixty-year-old tractors and teams of white oxen. He watched thunderstorms build every afternoon, only to blow out to sea before they could drop their much needed moisture on the dry farmland below. He ate whatever Amril brought him; bowls of thin soup, hot noodles, and spiced cabbage. Some of the meals were unrecognizable mixtures of roots and yellow bamboo, but Ammon never complained. He paced the floor, exercised, watched the highway, and worried about Jesse.

Amril was usually gone, but sent him messages through the peasant who worked the rocky soil around the thatched hut. "Stay tight," he was told. "Stay inside. Be patient. Things are going well. We will be out of the country very soon."

Early one morning, Amril shook him awake and led him outside to a waiting truck which had been loaded with small cardboard cartons packed with eggs. Since the eggs were fresh and unrefrigerated, the driver had a permit that would allow him unhindered travel all the way to the Chinese border city of Ch'osan.

Ammon and Amril climbed between the towering cartons. The driver covered them over with boxes of eggs, fired up the ancient truck, and started down the road.

And so began a journey which would take nearly a week. Traveling by truck, airplane, and rail, they made their way across the continent, working their way toward Kiev.

On the fifth day of their journey, Ammon found himself sitting on a train heading west through southern Ukraine, listening to the hypnotic rhythm of the train and watching the dirty towns as they passed by. With every mile that he drew closer to Kiev, Ammon's heart beat a little bit faster. He became moody and sullen. The memories flooded his mind. This was the home of his boyhood. This was his land. His people. His life.

He pushed himself back in his seat and closed his eyes.

He remembered his mother's funeral. He was only four. It had rained and rained, from the day she died, until two days after her body had been laid to rest. It was windy. It was cold. Mud and slime were everywhere as he and his father tracked their way to the graveyard, leading the tiny funeral procession up the barren road to the graveyard hill. Clutched in his tiny hands was a small bunch of white daisies. A gift for his mother. The only way he could think of to say good-bye.

He remembered one night with his father, who, as usual, was very drunk. Ammon was trying to make them both some dinner. He was hungry. Pulling out a huge blackened pot, he began to boil some water. "Father, do we have any rubles for cabbage? If you'll go buy some, I'll make us some stew." His father swore and grunted, then heaved himself out of his chair. Pulling on a coat, he slipped out into the night. Ammon didn't see him again for three days.

Ammon heard his name and opened his eyes. "You seem kind of quiet." Amril interrupted his thoughts.

"I'm the quiet type," Ammon said dryly.

"You should be happy to be going home."

Ammon shrugged and turned back to the window. The train rattled on. The miles slipped by. Ammon slipped further into despair.

It was dark and raining when they finally stepped off the train at a tiny and dilapidated rail station on the outskirts of Kiev. The two crumpled men climbed stiffly down from the train and stood for a moment in silence, waiting under a leaking covered porch as the wind and rain howled around them. The cold drizzle blew through the tall willows that lined both sides of the track and made Ammon shiver.

This was it. He was back. He had indeed come home.

Though he always knew it was possible, he never thought it would actually happen. He never thought he would be back in Kiev. He looked around the tiny station, studying each face in the crowd. Everything seemed vaguely familiar. The weathered clothes. The blushing jowls. The sullen eyes that rarely smiled.

The thick darkness seemed to enfold him, muffling the low voices that ran through the dimly lit terminal. He drew his thin jacket around him and shivered again from the cold. He thought of Jesse, sitting in their California home more than four thousand miles to the west and felt more desperate than he had ever felt in his life.

Before he had a chance to stretch his tired legs, Ammon was shoved into the back of a small sedan and driven to an ancient wood cabin fifty kilometers north of the city. It was near the Dnieper River, deep in a forest of spruce, aspens, and white pines. It was not a luxurious place, even by Ukrainian standards, much more a poor man's hunting lodge than a rich man's summer home on the lake. But it was private and extremely secluded.

Here he was told to stay put. He found a moldy bed in one of the tiny bedrooms and immediately fell asleep.

Fourteen hours later, he awoke. It was late afternoon and the sun was sitting low, sending dim sunbeams horizontally through the window. He heard a truck pull up, its tires crunching the wet gravel until it came to a stop, and then men's voices outside. As he listened, some of the voices faded away, muffled by the thick forest that surrounded the cabin. He listened to the sound of men spreading out through the woods, secluding themselves in the trees as they set up a perimeter security zone. A few of the voices grew louder as they approached the cabin. Ammon sat up in his bed, instantly alert.

After the men entered the cabin, all was quiet. Then the door to the bedroom opened. Amril was standing there, his huge frame filling the doorway, beckoning for Ammon to come.

Ammon followed him into the kitchen. There he found four men sitting around an enormous kitchen table. They appeared to range in age from about forty-five to maybe sixty. All of them were dressed in hunting clothes and covered with mud and muck. He noticed the shotguns stacked against the wall as well as three dead geese that had been stretched out near the kitchen sink. The musky smell of wet fowl filled the air.

The men turned to look at Ammon as he walked into the room. They continued to stare as he approached the table and sat in the only remaining seat. Amril stood near the doorway to the bedroom with his arms clasped behind his back.

For a long time no one spoke. The only sound was the occasional creaking of the old wooden chairs as the men shifted in their seats. Finally the youngest of the men turned to Ammon and spoke in perfect English.

"Do you remember me, Carl?" he asked.

Ammon flinched at the mention of his name. It had been almost twenty years since he had been called anything but Richard Ammon. To be called by his christened name sounded strange and uncomfortable.

Ammon studied the man intently. He was of medium height and stocky. His hands were huge and rough. Short cropped hair spread like stubble across his strangely uneven head. His face was covered by what looked like a week's worth of graying beard. His eyes were pale and green. Almost yellow. His smile was forced and tight.

Richard Ammon had seen this face only once, and it had been many years before, but still he remembered. After a long pause, he replied in a quiet voice, "Yes, Ivan Morozov, I know who you are."

This was the man who had first approached Ammon's father about sending his son to the Sicherheit. This was the man who had come to the apartment early one morning to take him away. After that, Ammon had never seen Ivan Morozov again, though his name had been whispered among the students and instructors at the school. Everyone knew that Morozov managed every detail of the Sicherheit. It was he who directed the lives of his agents.

Morozov hesitated a minute as the recognition spread across Ammon's face. He watched Ammon's eyes flicker and burn. "It has been a long time, hasn't it, Carl? So much water has passed under the bridge. But now, here you are once again. It must be good to be back."

Ammon stared into Morozov's face but didn't reply. After a moment of silence Morozov reached into his jacket and extracted a crumpled package of cigarettes. Pulling out a smoke, he rolled it absently between his muddy fingers.

"It's kind of funny, isn't it, Carl? Life used to be so much simpler. For you. For me. For men such as ourselves. It used to be that we knew who our enemies were. We knew who to fight. We knew who to watch.

"But now, the world has changed. Who would have dreamed. . . ." his voice trailed off. "I mean, look at us, after all these years, both of us finding ourselves back here in the Ukraine."

An awkward moment of silence. Ammon turned to the other men in the room. None of them spoke. None of them even looked in his direction.

Ammon turned back to Morozov. "Who are these men?" he asked abruptly.

Morozov leaned forward in his seat. "If you knew who they were, you would change the tone of your voice." Ammon sat back. He was still unimpressed.

"Why have you brought me here?" he demanded. "You almost killed me with your little scheme. And for what purpose may I ask? I thought our war was over."

Morozov didn't miss the bitter tone of Ammon's voice. Ammon wasn't intimidated. That was good. They would need a man who wasn't afraid, even when he was alone.

"We finally have a job for you," Morozov answered. "With your flying expertise and ability to operate within the United States, we think you—"

"And what if I'm not interested?" Ammon quickly cut in. "What if you have the wrong man?" He folded his arms in silent defiance. "I have always been loyal to my country.

"But what is this? I don't know what your intention is here, but I tell you right now, you have made a huge mistake if you just assumed that, like you, I am for sale."

Morozov's face turned suddenly sour. "I want to tell you something, Carl," he said sternly. "Something extremely important. Since we are going to work together again, I think we should just clear the air."

Morozov inhaled on his cigarette and let the smoke drift lazily out of his nose as he tapped ashes onto the kitchen table. He motioned to one of the Ukrainians and said, "But before I go any further, there is something that we want to know. Victor and I have been talking about the microfilm you gave us. We wanted to ask you. Why is the information outdated and useless? Don't you trust us anymore?"

Ammon instinctively tightened his stomach muscles in an effort to keep the blood from draining from his head. He didn't quiver or flinch or blink an eye as he answered in the same calm voice as before.

"You told me to bring in anything I could, but you only gave me two days. On such short notice, I did the best I could."

Morozov smiled. "Of course. That makes perfect sense," he said, then leaned forward in his chair. "No need to apologize, Carl, but there is something I want to explain. And this is very important, so I want you to listen very closely."

Morozov looked around the room and gestured to the other men as he spoke. "You are one of us, Carl. You are Ukrainian, and have been since your birth. Your father, your mother, your grandparents . . . your people have been rooted in this soil for five hundred years. This place, dark and drab as it is . . . this place is your home.

"And that is not all, my boy," he continued, his lips spreading into a thin and evil grin. "For your commitment doesn't end there. For you are also mine. In many ways you are more my son than your father's. I was the one who taught and trained you. It was I who set the course for your life. I was the one who saved you from a life with a drunk in the gutter.

"You were one of the few who were chosen. Out of the thousands of young men I could have selected, you were one of the very few culled from the crowd.

"And knowing that, did you think you could just walk away from me? Did you think you could just disappear in the West and never hear from me again?

"You'll never be one of them, Carl. While the West may have many things to offer, it isn't you. It simply isn't in your blood. You are a soldier. You are loyal. You will do what I command you to do."

Morozov leaned further across the table toward Richard Ammon. "We need you now, Carl," he whispered. "You're the only one who has the unique talents and training to complete this mission. So we are forced to use you. But I have to be quite honest. Some of these men don't trust you. They suspect that you might have grown soft. Gotten hollow in the middle. So I have had to assure them that you can be relied on.

"I have staked my reputation on you, Carl. So do not let me down. Consider yourself on a sort of probation. If you do well, we will reward you. But remember, I'll be watching you. I will be at your back, watching your every move."

Ammon swallowed hard. Morozov sat back in his chair, waiting for him to reply. But Ammon didn't answer. It was one of the few times in his life when he couldn't think of the right thing to say.

E I G H T

KIEV, UKRAINE

"NOW LET'S GET DOWN TO BUSINESS," MOROZOV SAID COLDLY. "THESE men are very busy, and we have already wasted their time. It is time to get on with the matter. But before I tell you what part you will play, there is something I want you to read." Morozov nodded his head toward Andrei Liski, the weasel-like man who took out a folded piece of paper from his breast pocket and carefully spread it out on the table.

"How well do you remember your native tongue?" Liski asked sharply as he looked up from the paper to Richard Ammon.

Ammon hesitated. Morozov broke in. "He was not allowed to speak anything but English once he entered our training as a child. He has not spoken Russian in more than twenty years."

Liski stared at Richard Ammon, unable to hide his impatience.

"My Russian is weak, but I can manage," Ammon finally said.

"Then take a look at this," Liski said unsmiling, as he pushed the paper across the table. "Tell me if you need help in the translation, for you will need to get this right. This isn't something you want to screw up, or you will never understand."

Ammon picked up the paper and stared at the Cyrillic writing. It seemed so foreign and unfamiliar. He read each word and then translated it in his mind, taking his time as he went, splitting his attention between making a correct translation and understanding the contents of the page. As he read, his face turned pale and the blood drained from his head. His hands began to tremble. His eyes widened and a look of pure disbelief spread across his ashen face. No one spoke, but all watched him intently as he read to the bottom of the page. He looked up at the waiting men, then turned back to the memo and read it again.

1325Z23MAY
WARPLAN OPTION 3
LIMITED TACTICAL NUCLEAR STRIKE

---------------------------   --------------------------

MISSION STATEMENT: THE PURPOSE OF THIS OPTION IS TO CON-DUCT JOINT OPERATIONS AGAINST THE UKRAINE, DETER AN ARMED RESPONSE OR COUNTER ATTACK, SUPPORT OPERATIONS TO ELIMINATE UKRAINIAN LAND/AIR FORCES, SEIZE CONTROL OF THE COUNTRY, ELIMINATE THE CURRENT GOVERNMENT, IMPLEMENT INTERNAL SECURITY MEASURES, REINFORCE AND RESUPPLY RUSSIAN FORCES, SUPPORT KASS SCHEME OF MANEU-VER, INTERDICT FOLLOW-ON FORCES AND ELIMINATE THE THREAT OF WEAPONS OF MASS DESTRUCTION (WMD) AGAINST THE ATTACKING RUSSIAN FORCES, MOTHERLAND, OR OCCU-PIED TERRITORIES, WHILE MINIMIZING OWN FORCE LOSSES.

1. FIRST PRIORITY IS TO PROTECT RUSSIAN FORCES AND MIN-IMIZE OWN COMBAT CASUALTIES WHILE INFLICTING MAXIMUM DAMAGE TO UKRAINIAN FORCES. SREDNEKOLYMSK LABORATO-RIES ESTIMATE MINIMUM 30-37 PERCENT CASUALTY RATE AMONG TARGET FORCES AFTER FIRST WAVE NUCLEAR ATTACK. ASSUMING A CASUALTY RATE OF ONLY 30 PERCENT, 350,000 UKRAINIAN COMBATANTS WOULD BE ELIMINATED WITHIN 48 HOURS. VICTORY WOULD THEN BE ASSURED. COLLATERAL DAM-AGE TO CIVILIAN POPULATION IS ESTIMATED LESS THAN 200,000—CERTAINLY AN ACCEPTABLE RATE. PREVAILING WINDS AND THE LOCATION OF THE SKROVEK HILLS, ALONG WITH THE RELATIVELY LOW YIELD OF THE TACTICAL WEAPONS WOULD LEAD TO MINIMAL LONG-TERM IMPACT UPON THE SURROUND-ING AREA.

2. UKRAINIAN FORCES HAVE NO NUCLEAR CAPABILITY, HAV-ING CEDED ALL NUCLEAR WEAPONS AS PART OF THE START III

AGREEMENTS, SO A RETALIATORY STRIKE IS NOT A CONCERN. HOWEVER, CURRENT UKRAINIAN DOCTRINE CALLS FOR THE USE OF WMD, I.E., CHEMICAL/BIOLOGICAL WEAPONS, AS A LAST RESPONSE OPTION IN THE CASE OF IMPENDING MILITARY FAILURE. ALL UKRAINIAN WMD ARE CURRENTLY STORED IN UNDERGROUND FACILITIES THAT ARE ONLY VULNERABLE TO NUCLEAR ATTACK. THUS, A FIRST WAVE NUCLEAR ATTACK IS THE ONLY WAY TO GUARANTEE THE DESTRUCTION OF ALL UKRAINIAN WMD WHICH MIGHT OTHERWISE BE USED AGAINST RUSSIAN OFFENSIVE FORCES.

3. THE PSYCHOLOGICAL EFFECT OF THE USE OF NUCLEAR WEAPONS UPON THE UKRAINE WOULD BE TWOFOLD:

A. THE SHOCK VALUE WOULD ASSIST IN SUBJECTING THE CIVILIAN POPULATION TO RUSSIAN CONTROL

B. MORE IMPORTANT, IT WOULD ALSO HAVE A DRAMATIC PSYCHOLOGICAL EFFECT UPON WESTERN GOVERNMENTS WHICH WOULD WORK TO OUR ADVANTAGE ONCE HOSTILITIES ARE INITIATED IN THE REGIONS OF THE FORMER WARSAW PACT COUNTRIES. SHOWING OUR RESOLVE EARLY BY USING LIMITED NUCLEAR FORCE AGAINST THE UKRAINE WOULD REDUCE THE POSSIBILITY OF A MAJOR EAST/WEST NUCLEAR EXCHANGE BY AS MUCH AS 70% ONCE THE WARSAW CAMPAIGN IS UNDERWAY. THE FIRST USE OF WMD WOULD UNDOUBTABLY RESULT IN ENORMOUS POLITICAL AND PSYCHOLOGICAL REWARDS THAT COULD EFFECTIVELY BE EXPLOITED ON THE BATTLEFIELD.

4. WE BELIEVE THAT THE UNITED STATES/EUROPEAN UNION WILL NOT—REPEAT——NOT—RETALIATE AGAINST RUSSIA FOR THE USE OF NUCLEAR WEAPONS AS LONG AS SUCH USE IS LIMITED TO ANY ONE OF THE FORMER REPUBLICS.

5. HOSTILITIES AGAINST THE UKRAINE WILL COMMENCE AS PLANNED. RECOMMEND THE USE OF TACTICAL NUCLEAR WEAPONS TO ASSURE A SWIFT AND ACCEPTABLE CONCLUSION.

SUPREME COMMANDER

I CONCUR.
VLADIMIR FEDOTOV

Ammon looked up and swallowed hard, his face a sheet of gray. "How do you know this is real?" he finally asked.

"Oh, it is authentic," Liski responded dryly. "Do you think we would be here . . . would we have brought you here . . . only to stare at forgeries or counterfeit documents? I really think not.

"It is real. We know that. The original document was smuggled to us early last summer by a most reliable source. A source at the highest level within the Russian government. "However, I will have to admit, originally our reaction was identical to yours. We didn't believe . . . we couldn't believe . . . it was actually real. But now we know. It has been confirmed."

Yevgeni Oskol Golubev, the Prime Minister of the Ukraine, put his elbows on the table and leaned forward in his chair. He appeared to be the oldest in the group. He was silver-haired and overweight, with dry, brown skin and an enormous, bloodhound face. He turned to Nicolai and muttered something in Russian, then settled again in his chair.

General Lomov, Commander, Ukrainian Forces, reached into a small canvas bag that lay beside his chair and pulled out a series of eight-by-ten black-and-white photos.

"Take a look at these," he muttered as he placed the pictures down in front of Richard Ammon.

Ammon quickly examined the photos. They were sharply focused, showing what looked to be Russian SS-25 short range nuclear missiles being loaded and fueled on the back of their mobile launchers. He examined the photos more closely, looking for signs of forgery or any other indication the photos might not be real. He studied the launchers along with their protective radar sites. He studied the tending dollies, fuel trucks, and missile loading platforms that accompanied the missile launchers. Everything was there. Everything looked perfectly legit. And the pictures were so clear. He brought one of the photos up to his face to study it in the darkening room. The photos were so good, he could make out the rank of the officers that stood watch over the loading procedures. He could see which men were smoking cigarettes.

He studied the pictures for a full five minutes. As far as he could tell, the photos were real.

"Where did you get these?" he finally asked, tossing them back on the table. He knew the reconnaissance pictures were not taken by a Ukrainian satellite or spy plane. Nothing the Ukrainians had could even come close to this. They were at least two technological generations away from being able to produce this kind of covert pictures.

"The Brits gave them to us. They felt it was something we ought to see." It was Liski who answered.

Ammon looked again at the pictures. Superimposed in the right hand corner of every picture was the date and time that the photo was taken. He checked the date. A little more than two weeks ago.

"But you and the Russians are allies," Ammon muttered.

"No! Russia has no friends," Liski replied. "It has no allies and never has! It only has client states. Do you think that Chechnya considers Russia its friend? Or the Baltics? Or Azerbaijan? Did we volunteer to join the Soviet Union? Do you think we considered Stalin a friend!? Do you know how many million Ukrainians have been killed by Russian solders since the beginning of World War II?

Ammon met Liski's eyes. Liski did not look away.

"I just find it hard to believe. . . ," Ammon stammered.

Liski cut him off at the knees. "Then you're an ignorant fool!" he hissed, waving a bony finger in Ammon's direction. He had now known Ammon for less than an hour, but in that time he had developed a deep dislike and distrust for the man. "Do you think Fedotov considers nuclear war as completely unthinkable? Even the self-righteous Americans have considered going nuclear at times in the past. Don't you remember the threats to Hussein during the Gulf War? I'd say Bush made his case pretty clear. Or what about the Cuban missile crisis? Or Hiroshima? Now, if the U.S. has been willing to use them, don't you think Fedotov would use them as well?

"The man has no moral compass. No internal sense of right or wrong. Already he is an international pariah. By his own choosing. He has isolated himself from the West for this very purpose. He does what suits his own interest. And his interest is perfectly clear.

"He seeks to rebuild the Union. He has been laying this plan for the last several years. And he knows he must move quickly, for only by consolidating his power and rebuilding the union can he create the consensus that will keep him in power. And we, the Ukraine, are going to be his first target."

Liski paused. Picking up the smuggled Russian document, he tossed it in Ammon's direction. "Look at this!" he sneered. "Read the man's own words! Recommend the use of tactical nuclear weapons. I concur. Vladimir Fedotov! It's right there before you. Then consider what the man has already done. Within twenty-four hours of taking power, he declared martial law, eliminated his primary rivals, disbanded the parliament, and shut down the press.

Within two months, he established his own security forces, re-nationalized private industry, expelled half a million foreigners, and initiated a hundred billion rubles worth of nuclear arms sales to Iran, Iraq, Pakistan, and North Korea, all to feed his military machine.

"Now he talks of rebuilding the union. And his people cry out in support."

The room was turning glum as evening came on and the shadows grew. Ammon trembled and ran his fingers through his short hair.

Liski pressed home his final point. "And let's not miss this most important fact. The document you just read makes it clear that Fedotov also has his eye on the former Warsaw Pact nations. Yet his army is weakened and in disarray, which defaults him to the nuclear option. It is the only way he can expand his borders without depleting his troops and reducing his strength. It allows him to control his combat casualties in order to remain strong enough to venture west.

"And west he will go. He will cut through the heart of eastern Europe, in some cases without any resistance. Albania, Bulgaria, Hungary, Romania, each of them right on the edge. Desperate as they are, they are ready, perhaps even eager, to fall under his fold.

"So he will push to the edge . . . right up to the borders of Germany, Austria, and Italy. He will roll his armies westward, striking early, and with such blinding speed that there won't be time to prepare. He will push right up to the point where the United States and NATO will have to respond.

"Then he will pull back and muster his forces while he works to consolidate his power. And when it is over, when Fedotov is finally satisfied, I have to believe that his new Union, whatever he chooses to call it, will be the most dangerous nation on earth.

"Even as we speak, his army is moving into position, supplying and preparing for war. It is now only a matter of time."

The sun had set and the room was growing dark. The cold seeped in. Amril lit a few slender, gray, wax candles and placed them on the table. The men peered at each other in the flickering light.

Watching Amril light the homemade candles, Ammon shivered as he quietly asked, "But what about NATO? What about the U.S.?"

General Lomov leaned across the table and stared into Ammon's face. "Let me ask you something, boy," he said in a low and powerful voice. "Do you really think the Americans will come to our aid? Do you really think they will commit even one soldier to help us protect our homeland, especially if the conflict escalates to tactical nuclear war?

"Of course they won't!" The general slapped the table. "They'll have their quivering tails tucked so far up under their legs you'd have to roll them on their backs to even find it. They'll sniffle and wring their hands. They'll protest and embargo and whine. But they won't lift a finger to help us. Not a finger! They simply won't help us! Not in any real or meaningful way! They will not bloody our soil with the life of even a single American soldier.

"There will be no U.S. intervention. Of that, I am absolutely sure. You know that, we know that, and the Russians know that, too."

The general stopped talking and glared at Ivan Morozov while settling back in his seat. Morozov picked up on the signal and cleared his throat. "This is where you come in, Carl," he said.

Reaching into the canvas bag, Morozov pulled out a set of aeronautical charts and began to spread them out on the table, brushing his hands across the multicolored maps to flatten out the wrinkles. He rearranged the candles on the table to make room for the charts, then produced a small flashlight. The four other men at the table instinctively sat forward in their chairs to get a good look at the charts. Ammon quickly realized he was looking at a map of southwestern Russia. He studied the map for a moment before he saw the eight red triangles. It took him only a second to realize what they were. The Russians' nuclear missiles.

"Oh, no," Ammon said, shaking his head. "It simply can't be done! You're talking about some of the most heavily defended targets in the world."

"No, you're wrong, Carl," Morozov replied. "It can be done. We've studied it out. It won't be easy, we recognize that. But we are convinced, in fact, we are certain, that given the right tools, the mission can be accomplished."

Ammon turned to the charts once again. With his finger, he traced a line from target to target, noting the hundreds of surface-to-air (SA) missile and anti-aircraft artillery (AAA) sites that dotted the way. They were everywhere. SA-6s, SA-8s, and SA-16s sat on nearly every mountain peak. Russian triple A, some of the best in the world, lay hidden in every valley, ready to fill the air with a wall of molten lead and steel. And he hadn't even considered the hundreds of thousands of ground troops that would also be waiting, many of them armed with deadly shoulder-fired missiles.

A long moment of silence. Ammon finally lifted his eyes.

He didn't speak. He didn't have to. The look on his face said it all.

"It's a suicide mission," he said flatly. "The targets are too heavily defended and too far away. Look at this," he jabbed his finger at the chart. "Even the closest target is more than eight hundred miles deep in Russian territory. You just don't have the range. Not with your fighters. The targets are too far away. It's a one way-trip, with no chance of success!

"No, gentlemen, I have to tell you, and I'm just giving you an honest assessment, if this is your only hope, then start packing your bags, because it is not going to work. The simple fact is, you don't have an aircraft. Not for this mission. You will run out of fuel before you hit the first target. And that is to say nothing of the Russian defenses. Thousands of radar-guided missiles and artillery, waiting to blow you out of the sky. And even if your fighters could make it, you don't have the right kind of bombs to find and destroy mobile or hardened nuclear targets.

"No, it would take an incredibly sophisticated, radar-evading plane—one with incredible range and a huge payload—to complete this mission. And that's something that you just don't have."

Richard Ammon looked up, his eyes bright. He straightened his back and squared his broad shoulders. That was it. He wasn't lying. He had simply told them the truth.

Morozov fell silent, his eyes unblinking as he evaluated Richard Ammon. The ancient wooden chairs creaked in the silence. Outside, a night wind suddenly blew, shaking the tattered roof of the old cabin and rattling the dusty windows in their frames. No one spoke. Amril shifted his weight against the wall. Ammon studied each man in the room.

"You're right, of course." Morozov finally said as he pushed the aeronautical charts out of the way. "We know we don't have the right aircraft. But . . . the Americans do.

"You see, my friend, you're going back to the States. You and I. We're going to steal an American B-1 bomber, the most powerful warplane on earth. Then, we're going to use it to take out Fedotov's missile sites. And a few other targets as well. Maybe we'll even head for Moscow! Take out the old man himself! With such a powerful aircraft at our disposal we might as well put it to use!"

Ammon swallowed hard.

"No!" he muttered, his voice softened by fear. "They will know! The Russians will know! They will find the American bomber. And they would have to respond! It would lead to. . . ."

And then he stopped. He finally understood. The blood quickly drained from his face.

Liski smiled and sat back in his chair. Lomov stared down at his hands resting upon the table. Morozov grinned in reply. "Yes, Carl. You now understand. And stealing the B-1 is just the beginning. So believe me when I tell you, once our plan is fully implemented, the United States will be deeply involved in our war."

NINE

KIEV, UKRAINE

AFTER THEY FINISHED PLANNING, AMMON WAS ESCORTED TO HIS BEDroom and instructed to get some sleep. Morozov and the other Ukrainians walked outside into the darkness. Amril remained behind in the cabin to keep an eye on Ammon.

It was cold enough outside that the men could see their breath as they talked. In the distance they could hear a wolf, its lone and mournful howl drifting through the dense trees of the forest. The four men spoke in whispered tones, watching each other carefully in the moonlight.

"What do you think?" Morozov asked General Lomov.

"I think you had better watch him," the general replied quietly. "He's been away so long. After all these years, who knows where he really stands?"

"I don't agree," Prime Minister Yevgeni Golubev jumped in. "He's had his world pulled out from under him. I think it would be asking too much to expect him to climb aboard without some reservations. But I think, given some time, he will come round."

"That may be," Lomov answered. "But still we need to watch him. For one thing, like he said, we are not asking him to work for his country. The country he left no longer even exists. And though he's

Ukrainian, I don't feel that he has a great sense of loyalty or sympathy toward us or our cause.

"Perhaps if we pay him enough, he will go along, but I doubt it. He doesn't strike me as the kind of man who has much interest in money.

"So . . . I think we need to watch him very closely. More important, we need to gain some other form of leverage. I am convinced that the girl may be the only thing that will bring him along to our way of thinking."

"I agree," Morozov said, turning his attention to the last Ukrainian. "We must find the girl." Andrei Liski, Director of State Border Defense, returned Morozov's cold stare.

"We are looking for her," was all he said. Then, when none of the others looked away, he shrugged his shoulders and offered a further explanation. "Apparently she was warned. They must have had something prearranged. We know that he tried to call her the morning he was forced to eject from his plane. He left her some kind of message . . . some kind of code as a warning. By the time we were able to accomplish a voice analysis to confirm it was him, she was already gone.

"But I agree," he continued. "We need the girl. Mark my words, this man will betray us if given the opportunity. I can feel it. I can sense it. Regardless of his training." Liski turned a sarcastic eye toward Morozov. "He is no longer one of our own.

"So, we will find the girl. She isn't trained to survive in such situations. We will have her within a few days."

"You had better," Golubev threatened. "We are sending Ammon to Helsinki soon. There he will begin flying the simulator we have developed. Once he has done that, he will quickly realize just how dangerous this mission really is. If you think he has reservations now, wait until he sees how difficult this mission will be.

"We will need the girl by then. If Ammon should waiver, she is the only thing we have to hang over his head."

General Lomov muttered in the darkness. Liski swatted at some invisible gnat. Golubev nodded, then turned to Morozov to bring up another critical subject.

"When are you getting the money?" he asked.

"I'm leaving tonight."

"Keep us informed. We need to know as soon as it's ready. We are almost ready for action."

Morozov nodded, turned around and walked back into the cabin. The other men watched him leave, then whistling to their guards they gathered their men, climbed into the heavy truck and drove off into the night.

Inside his bedroom, Richard Ammon lay on the moldy mattress. The room was dark and smelled of stale air and moth balls. It was very quiet. He lay there for a very long time.

It was bad. Very bad. Much worse than he had feared.

And one thing was perfectly clear—Morozov and his fellow Ukrainians would kill him if they knew the truth.

He didn't consider himself one of their comrades. He wasn't working for them anymore.

Looking back on it, Ammon realized that the seed of his defection was planted on the day he was taken from his family. Even now, more than twenty years later, he could still picture the inside of his Kiev apartment. It was cramped and dingy, and smelled of urine and boiled cabbage. He could remember the scene in vivid detail: the morning that Ivan Morozov came to take him away.

As Morozov entered the apartment, Ammon couldn't help but notice the whispering voices and sidelong glances in his direction. He watched the yellow-eyed man count out the money, and as his father reached out and took the wad of bills, a great anxiety welled up inside him. Though he was only a child, the arrangement was perfectly clear. His father kissed him lightly on the cheek then picked up his hat and left for work, leaving no explanation.

So it was understandable that Ammon found himself constantly wondering. Why would his father have taken the money? What else had he taken in exchange for his son? A new apartment? A supervisory position at some government office? Whatever it was, it didn't matter. This one fact was perfectly clear.

He had traded his only son for money. He had traded his child to the state.

But of course, that wasn't the way it was explained to Ammon. Such cynicism would have never been tolerated in the Sicherheit.

He was only indoctrinated in the glory of his calling. He was one of the chosen few. His mission was of the highest importance. To be allowed to serve in such a high capacity, and to be selected at such a young age, were honors never to be questioned. But Ammon never fully accepted that explanation. He never resolved the doubts from his mind. And though he never knew to what extent the Party had compensated his father, he knew it wasn't enough. He had lost his entire family. How much money could justify that?

But as the years went by, Ammon learned not to dwell on the past. The Sicherheit saw to that.

Once, when Ammon was twelve years old, he was sitting in a class on moral theory. It was late in the afternoon and the sun was shining outside. As the teacher droned on and on, Ammon grew impatient and began to fidget. For the first hour, he tried very hard to pay attention, but as the time went by, like any twelve-year-old boy, he began to stare out the window and daydream, doodling on the back of his notebook.

Suddenly he was jolted back to the present with a swat. His teacher had slapped him on the side of his head. He looked up in surprise and fear.

"Richard Ammon, I don't think you were paying attention." The pupils and teachers in the Sicherheit always referred to each other by their American names.

"Now you know what happens when you don't pay attention," the teacher continued. "Such a fundamental lack of self-discipline cannot go unpunished. Such a weakness in character cannot be ignored. You know that, don't you, Mr. Ammon."

The teacher began to walk to the front of her class. As she approached her metal desk, Richard Ammon slid out from behind his tiny table and followed her to the front of the room. He knew what was coming, and his head started to pound. He stuffed his hands deep into his front pockets in an effort to protect them from her anger.

The teacher reached into her desk drawer and pulled out a small metal pipe. It was twelve inches long and about as thick as a pencil.

"Hold out your hand," she said slowly.

Ammon lay his hand on her desk. With a sudden snap, she whacked him across his knuckles. Ammon let out a sudden cry. The classroom winced. The room fell very silent.

"Now Mr. Ammon, you may go back to your desk."

Ammon turned away from his teacher, holding his bruised knuckles against his chest. He started to shuffle his way down the narrow aisle. He was hurt and angry. That's what caused him to make the mistake.

"My name is not Richard Ammon," he muttered as he turned away from the teacher. "My name is Carl."

As soon as the words left his mouth, Ammon knew that he had made a colossal error. He immediately froze in his tracks, praying that she had not overheard. But the look on the faces of the two young boys in the front row told him the horrible truth.

He heard the teacher's desk drawer open once again.

"Richard Ammon, turn around."

Ammon turned to face his teacher, his face ashen and white. "Mr. Ammon, why did you say that?" she asked.

Ammon bowed his head in shame. His mind raced for any explanation. But there was none. He just didn't know what to say.

The room remained very quiet. Not a student moved in his seat. Ammon could hear the clock as it ticked on the wall. He could hear a push mower being used to cut the spring grass outside the classroom window. He waited for his punishment, wishing that he could cry.

"Richard Ammon, hold out your hand."

By the time his punishment was over, Ammon's right hand was a broken and bloody mass of meat. It took more than three months for the nerves and tendons to heal. Even now, he had an unusual lump on his first digit, where the bone had mended in a crooked line. To this day, Richard Ammon remembered the beating.

But he learned his lesson. His name was Richard Ammon. Carl Vadym Kostenko no longer existed. He had died long ago on a cold winter morning when a man named Ivan Morozov had come to take him away.

Yes, the Sicherheit had a way of keeping him focused. After years of experience in training young boys, they knew what it took to keep doubts from their minds. And even after he was planted in the United States and began to enjoy all of its pleasures, it never once even occurred to him to defect. He was a soldier. He had been trained to carry out orders. He was intent on serving his state.

Then Richard Ammon experienced two very significant life-changing events.

First, he lost his country.

Beginning with the fall of the Berlin Wall, nation after communist nation seemed to be utterly swept away. The socialist states that had dominated Eastern Europe for more than fifty years all fell by the wayside, a mere historical footnote in the big scheme of things. Then came the collapse of the Soviet Union, a shattering climax to what had already been an amazing few years. And as he watched his nation crumble, as he watched it split into ever smaller, more independent, and ever less friendly states, as he watched a new atmosphere of trust and cooperation develop between the U.S. and Russia, Ammon realized that it was over. He no longer had a foreign master, for his organization in Moscow would surely have been disassembled. He considered it an entirely new ball game. And from that time forward, he believed that he was on his own. His commitment was served. It was finished. He was alone.

And then an even more important event occurred in Ammon's life. He met the most beautiful girl he had ever imagined. She was tall and slender, with shoulder-length, silky brown hair. Her dark eyes could make his legs tremble, her smile could light up the room. She had a perfect voice. Calm and measured, it was the most pleasant thing he had ever heard. It was the kind of voice one imagined cooing to a newborn baby or singing softly in the darkness of a quiet night. She was tall—almost as tall as Richard. And poised. And confident. And smart as anyone Richard Ammon had ever known.

Her name was Jesse Morrel. They met at a military reception for a retiring general, a close friend of Jesse's father. Richard was dressed in his military mess, a dark blue tuxedo with pilot wings and three tiny medals pinned to his chest. As Richard approached his table, he saw her. She sat at her assigned seat beside him, dressed in a shimmering evening gown, her hair brushed back over her shoulders, her dark arms resting shyly in her lap. She was a picture of beauty, a subtle mixture of sophistication and innocence that proved to be completely irresistible. Ammon gulped as he approached the table, suddenly completely unsure of himself. He grinned shyly as he pulled back his chair and sat down beside her. Jesse looked up and smiled as she said hello.

And that was it. From that moment, he was hopelessly in love. Never again would Richard Ammon understand a man's fear of commitment. Never again would he nod in sympathy when close friends talked of their doubts about love. From that moment on, he knew that he wanted to spend the rest of his life with Jesse Morrel.

Ammon sat down beside the dark-eyed girl, rejoicing in his good fortune. For one awkward moment, they both stared quietly at their empty plates. And then it happened. His mind went completely blank. Utterly, hopelessly blank. A perfect white sheet of nothingness. His mouth felt like the Sahara. His heart pattered like a toy gun. He searched desperately for something to say. Anything. Anything that wouldn't sound stupid. He stole a quick glance at Jesse. She smiled again in return. His mind took another vacation. What an idiot! What could he say?

Then he felt a light touch on his arm. He looked up once again.

"My name is Jesse," she said in a quiet tone. "My father is ex-army. They always wear green, but I have to tell you, blue has always been my favorite color."

Beautiful! That was it! Blue! He would talk about the color blue! He knew all about blue. Blue was easy. What a relief. He had something to say.

"Yes, I've always liked blue, too," he said in his most intelligent tone. "In fact, that's why I joined the Air Force. My mom always told me, 'Son, you look best in blue.'"

They both laughed. The awkward silence passed. Ammon's brain returned from Miami. He could actually think of words with more than two syllables. What a relief. It was nice to have it back.

He and Jesse began to talk. About this, about that. They took to each other almost immediately. They talked through the entire meal, leaving cold steaks and melted Jell-O running all over their plates. They ignored the conversation around them, concentrating on only each other. The dessert was served and the retirement presentations were made without either one of them hearing a word. Two and a half hours later, the dinner party was drawing to a close.

"So, when are you flying back to Nellis?" Jesse wondered as they picked at plates of fresh strawberry shortcake.

"I was planning on leaving this evening," Ammon responded slowly, his voice clearly demonstrating his reluctance to go.

Jesse folded her arms across her lap and said nothing. Ammon sat quietly in his chair and watched the steward take their small dessert plates. Jesse and Richard were alone, the other guests having already excused themselves to mingle among the noisy crowd.

"The water in the Santa Monica bay is just warming up," Jesse said softly.

"I've never swum in the Pacific before," Ammon replied.

"Why don't you stay for a few days?" Jesse said as she stared at the table. "We could spend a few hours . . ."

"I'll see what I can do," Ammon immediately replied.

That was Friday night. Sunday afternoon, Richard Ammon called his squadron commander to request two weeks' leave.

"You'll miss our deployment to England," his commander reminded him.

"Yes, sir, I know I will."

"We'll be short a tactics officer and instructor if you don't come."

"Yes, sir. That is true."

"Do you think we have enough time to find a replacement?" Ammon didn't miss the irritation in his commander's voice, though the colonel made an honest effort to hide it.

"Probably not at this late hour, sir."

"Richard, it sounds like I need you here," his commander responded.

"I know you do, sir. But I'm telling you, I need two weeks of leave."

"Okay, Richard . . . I guess you do. I guess you do," his commander finally responded. "Go and enjoy yourself. Take two weeks. Report to me as soon as you get back into town."

"Yes, sir. I will. And thank you, colonel."

There was a quick moment of silence before the colonel said, "Richard, I hope she's worth it. She must be something. Am I right?"

"Sir, if you only knew," Ammon said, more to himself than the colonel as he quickly hung up the phone.

They spent the entire two weeks together. And by the end of the two weeks, they both knew. They would spend the rest of their lives together. Of that, they were perfectly sure.

Four months later, he told her.

It was a bright night, late in August, with a trillion stars and a cool night breeze. The wide wisp of the Milky Way twinkled overhead as they lay on their backs and watched for falling stars. Far in the distance, across the great canyon, Ammon could barely make out the yalp of coyotes as they barked and howled at the moon. The gentle wind blew along the canyon floor and moaned among the towering spires, pushing the sweet musk of juniper and sage up the canyon walls to the desert floor.

Richard Ammon and Jesse Morrel lay against a small grass knoll at Mohave Point, overlooking the south rim of the Grand Canyon. It was almost one in the morning, but neither of them wanted to leave. Jesse had driven from L.A. to Nellis Air Force Base, outside of Las Vegas, to spend the weekend with Ammon. In the morning she had to go back to L.A. Neither of them liked this arrangement, spending only weekends together. It was something that was going to have to change.

But first he had to tell her. It couldn't wait. Before this went any further, he had to tell her the truth.

Richard stared across the darkness of the canyon and swallowed hard. His chest tightened as he practiced the words in his head. He was so nervous. No, more than that, he was truly afraid. What would he tell her? What could he say? How could she ever understand?

She probably would leave him. Just stand up and walk away. He fully expected her to walk out of his life. After all, once she knew the truth about his past, regardless of how he felt now, once she realized that his life was nothing but a sham, how could he hope she would stay?

Jesse wasn't the kind of girl who would accept being lied to. And so far, Ammon's entire life had been a big lie.

Ammon rolled up onto one arm and looked over at Jesse. She lay against the cool grass, less than a foot from his body, her eyes closed, her face illuminated by the pale light of the moon and the stars. He swallowed once again and took a deep breath.

"Jesse," he muttered quietly. She opened her eyes and smiled. His heart pattered and sank into his stomach. A great sadness fell upon him; a great loneliness seeped into his soul. She was there, yet he already missed her. The fear of losing her tore at his heart.

Jesse smiled again. "I'm sorry," she softly said. "I almost fell asleep."

Ammon shifted his arm, rolled onto his back once again and closed his eyes. In his mind, he tried to freeze the picture of her face in the moonlight. Her smile, her hair, her eyes. He wanted to always remember. He might not ever see her smiling again.

"Jesse, there's something I need to tell you."

She leaned closer and lay her head next to his shoulder. He passed his hands across his face, relieved that she wasn't looking as he brushed the sting from his eyes.

Jesse sensed his mood. She lay there quietly, waiting for him to speak.

Ammon took a deep breath and started talking. And soon, like a great bursting dam, it came tumbling out, washing over him with the urgency of years of loneliness and fear and frustration. "I'm not one of them, Jesse," he muttered, praying in his heart she would see that was true. "I never was. I never made that decision. It was forced on me as a child. This wasn't something I sought for myself. I never asked to be put in this situation. I'm not evil, or sinister, Jesse. But once here, I had to be loyal. I couldn't turn my back on my people. I never felt that I had any choice.

"But now I do. Now I do, for I understand things now that I didn't know then. I understand the true meaning of freedom. I know what is real, and I know what was only a facade. I now know what is good and what is evil.

"And even were that not true . . . even were I still to have considered myself a loyal comrade, it wouldn't matter. My nation . . . my homeland

. . . doesn't even exist. My country is gone and nobody owns me. I am free to get on with my life."

Ammon paused and stared at her in the darkness. She had turned her face away, unable to look at him. For the past twenty minutes she had not said a word, just stared quietly off into the darkness. A cold chill ran through Ammon's bones.

"I'm so sorry I lied to you Jesse," he finished sadly. "That's the one thing I didn't want to do. I would do anything to change my past, to deny my existence. To really be able to start over. But I had to tell you the truth."

She lay quietly in the darkness. He waited, always hoping. Were her feelings intense enough now to bind her? Did she feel the same emotion as he? Did the thought of being without him drive her crazy? Or would she turn her back on him and just walk away?

He didn't know. He could only hope.

But as the moments passed, as he looked upon her staring quietly out into the darkness, his faith started to fade.

"I'll take you home now," Ammon finally said softly. "I understand. You don't have to explain."

Ammon started to push himself up.

Jesse turned her face to look up at him. He could see the tears in her eyes. It broke his heart to see her crying. He hated to cause her such pain.

Then, with a quick sweep of her hand, Jesse brushed the tears away. "So, what do we do now?" she softly whispered, reaching out to pull him close once again.

As Jesse gently touched Richard's arm he knew she had made her decision.

Ammon fell back onto the soft grass beside her. A quick shiver ran through his body. His heart heaved and jumped within him. He felt like crying! He felt such relief!

They began to talk. They talked about his past and their future. They looked at all of their options, which weren't very many, then made a decision. And in the end, it wasn't a very difficult thing to do. Because in a world so full of questions and doubts, in a world filled with empty faces and empty lives, in a world of shallow loves and hollow friends, they knew at least three things.

The sun always came up in the east, babies can make people laugh, and, no matter the past or the consequences, they were meant to be together. They needed and wanted each other. Their lives were meant to be one. Beyond that, nothing else seemed very important. Time together was all they asked.

So they drove back to Las Vegas, and at five in the morning, walked the streets of the glittering city until they found an all-night church. It was a small white chapel surrounded by a tiny green lawn.

They paid the Justice of the Peace his fifty dollars, plus an extra twenty for the witness. Ten minutes later, they were man and wife. Bound by love and law, they set out to live their lives together. And nothing could tear them apart.

Except, of course, the Sicherheit.

For there was always the possibility, however small or remote, that Ammon's dealing with the men who once ran the Sicherheit might not be over. One day they might want him back.

And if that ever happened, they wouldn't ask his permission before they brought him in. One day he would just disappear. And if Ammon wasn't particularly happy about that, well, the Sicherheit wouldn't particularly care. He was, after all, their possession.

So, while he and Jesse prepared for that possibility, Ammon had always promised her one thing. He would find a way to get back to her. It might not be easy, and it might take some time, but he would find a way back to his home.

Like his teacher had pointed out, he wasn't Carl Vadym Kostenko anymore. He would never be that person again.

So, as he lay on his moldy mattress and listened to Morozov move around the cabin, Richard Ammon had already made his decision. He wouldn't go along with their plan. At the first chance, he was leaving. He would find a way to escape. He would leave this world of fighters and flying, spies and lying, danger and deceit far behind.

He lay in the darkness and planned his escape.

And prayed they didn't know about Jesse.

LONE PINE, CALIFORNIA

It was still early morning. The sun was just beginning to paint the eastern sky a thin pink as it made its way over the mountains. A heavy dew had moistened the valley floor and left a silvery coat of wet droplets on the maple leaves and thick bushes that surrounded the cabins that looked down on Lone Pine.

Jesse Morrel lay sleeping, her long legs kicked out from under her covers, her brown hair flung across her face. The cabin was very quiet. The bedroom, decorated with framed pastel water colors and light-blue wallpaper, was just beginning to brighten with the morning sun. But still the shadows lay deep and heavy. A squirrel pattered across the roof of the cabin and scrambled onto a tree branch that brushed against the wooden shingles. The alarm clock next to the bed read 6:23.

Jesse's breathing was measured and long. Her eyelids fluttered lightly, then came to rest, motionless and calm. Her hair settled to one side of her face as she buried her head into the pillow. Her lips began to tremble as she dreamed of unseen creatures in the dark. She drew her legs up under the covers and wrapped her arms around herself.

On the night stand next to the bed was a stack of letters, neatly arranged and placed in chronological order in a small silver box. They were the letters she had received from Richard Ammon since he had been away in Korea. They were faded and wrinkled from frequent reading. The top letter read:

Dear Jesse,

Once again I find myself in a foreign land, a new home and unfamiliar surroundings. I suspect at times that it is my ordained lot in life to always be a wanderer, never able to set down any roots, although I now find that is my strongest desire. When I awoke this morning and looked at the sun as it rose over the green hills that surround Osan, I couldn't help but wonder what you were doing. I knew it was early evening in California. I figured you would be out on the back patio, tending your roses, and it comforted me some to know that, though half a world away, we both shared the same spot of light.

I've been in Korea for almost a week now. I suppose I am feeling a little bit homesick. If this letter appears a little melancholy, you will forgive me. It's not that I am unhappy or sad. I guess I'm just missing you.

I had my first flight here last Friday. It was good to be in the cockpit again after almost a month without flying. I flew with a guy named Ken Russell. He is the squadron ops officer, so I will be working for him. A decent fellow, he is one of the few guys here who was able to bring his family, so of course there is a certain envy factor for those of us who go home to lonely Q rooms and empty beds instead of going home to our wives.

More than anything, I have been struck by the pace and tempo of the flying operations. Being this close to the North Korean border has real implications for our day-to-day operations. Everyone takes their job very seriously, and people are wound just a little tighter. That is especially true of the South Koreans. All of the South Korean officers that I have met have been very aggressive and hard chargers. Someone told me the real reason we Americans are here was to keep the south from invading the north, not the other way around. After just a week here, I am beginning to believe that might be true.

My first flight was only a familiarization ride, an opportunity to see the area and get a little bit of my bearings. As I flew along the demilitarized zone, I could look across the border into North Korea and watch the surface-to-air missile batteries as they tracked us across the sky. It was a little unnerving, but Lt Col Russell assured me I would quickly get used to it.

On Saturday, three of us new guys took the train into Seoul. It turned out to be a miserable day, rainy and windy and cold. I did make a couple great buys, though. You should see the solid brass beds you can get here for only a few hundred dollars. And real cashmere is as cheap as cotton. I've ordered you a full length cashmere coat. I really think you will like it. At least that is what I am hoping. It is one of my greatest ambitions to, one day before I die, buy you a piece of clothing that you actually like.

I also had my first taste of authentic Korean Kimchi, an experience I will liken to the explosion of Mount St. Helens. Some of us decided that, should there be a war here on the peninsula and should we ever run out of bombs, we could always drop Kimchi instead.

After spending the day shopping and seeing the sights, we had dinner, then got on the late train for the hour-ride back to Osan. As I was sitting in my seat, I looked out on the platform and saw a pitiful sight. A tiny little girl, she could not have been more than five, was walking through the crowd with an old felt hat, begging for money. She was thin and frail, one of the Cho'Sans, or refugees from the civil war in Burma. The only thing she was wearing was a tattered, oversized shirt that hung down to her ankles. No shoes. No jacket. In one hand she held out her old hat, in the other she was clutching a tiny, worn-out, stuffed-toy rabbit. As I watched, someone brushed her aside, knocking her to the platform floor. Coins spread in every direction, scattering among the crowded floor.

Jesse, if you could have seen her, if you could have watched this poor little girl as she scrambled to find her money, still clutching her old floppy rabbit, it would have broken your heart. I know it broke mine. It was such a sad thing to see. No one could have seen this and not have been touched.

Anyway, I felt I had to do something. I got the two other guys I was with to give me all of the cash in their wallets. Together, we had about fifty bucks. We all started tapping on the window, trying to get the little girl's attention. She looked up and saw us, and I started waving the money around, extending my arms out to her, hoping she would understand the money was for her. She picked up her hat and started to make her way toward us. But then the train started to move. All three of us climbed on our seats, trying to open the windows, but they were never designed to be opened. As the train pulled away from the station, we watched in silence as the little girl faded from view.

It reminded me, Jesse, that many of us are orphans. Some literally. Some figuratively. But for whatever reason, many of us have spent years on our own.

I remember when I was very small, my aunt used to tell me old folk stories; stories with witches and wizards and fairy godmothers. Later, after I was sent to the school, as I lay in my bed at night, surrounded by snoring classmates and fearful for what the next day might bring, I remember thinking, if there is a God, I wish he would send me a fairy godmother. Or maybe even an angel. Either one, it didn't matter. I just remember feeling that, since I no longer had a mother, I needed someone. Someone with magical powers, to make everything all right.

But as I grew, I quit asking. After all, I was a grown man, a soldier, a combat warrior. I didn't need anyone, Jesse. I was trained to be on my own.

But that has changed. And now I do.

I need you, Jesse. I miss you. At times, the memory of the happy moments we have spent together washes over me, and I feel very grateful for the moments that we've had, and I can honestly say, my life's only regret are the times when we cannot be together.

I love you. All I want is to be with you.

Until then.

RA

T E N

BOGOTÁ, COLOMBIA

CARLOS MANUEL SALINAS, ONE OF THE WEALTHIEST MEN IN THE southern hemisphere, lay on the straw mat of his bunk and swatted at the insects that continually bit his legs. Colombia's Harada prison had not only the most aggressive roaches in the world, but also the only ones that were known to bite, burrowing deep into the skin in an effort to find a nest for their tiny eggs. He swatted the flies that buzzed around the open hole that he used for a toilet and listened to the sounds of the prison.

It was past midnight and except for the occasional barking of the guard dogs as they prowled the perimeter fence, no other sound could be heard. So it surprised Salinas to hear his cell door being opened. He had not heard the footsteps coming nor the turn of the key, but the ancient hinges on the huge oak door creaked quietly, and there was the shadow of a guard standing in the darkness.

"Salinas, are you awake?" the guard whispered.

"Yes, what is it? What do you want?"

For a moment Salinas thought it might be Juan, a guard who favored Salinas when it came to sharing a game of chess, but as he studied the figure in the doorway he realized it wasn't. Instead, it was a guard he had never seen before. He immediately became suspicious.

"Quickly sir, come with me. There is someone here to see you."

The guard had already turned and was standing aside, waiting for Salinas to get up. Salinas peered through the darkness and into the hall. He could see that the guard was alone. Usually the prisoners were escorted by at least two guards. And he had never been allowed to leave his cell or see a visitor at night. What was going on?

"Who is it? I am not expecting anyone. Perhaps you have the wrong cell." Salinas replied. He didn't move from his bunk.

"Oh, no Mr. Salinas, I am sure it is you that I need. Please, come quickly. We don't have much time. And be quiet. We don't want to disturb the other prisoners." The guard then stepped back into the cell and pulled out his night stick, beckoning to the open door.

Salinas got up from his bunk and slipped on some shoes. He walked through the door and made his way down the hall, followed by the guard. A few minutes later he found himself entering one of the prisoner conference rooms. It was a dimly lit cubicle of unpainted gray cinder block, the only furniture a small table in the middle of the floor with two wooden chairs beside it.

The guard left him alone, and several minutes passed before the door opened again. In walked a man Salinas had never seen before. He was dressed in a tailored suit, and as he entered the room, he extended his hand to Salinas.

"Señor Salinas, it is a pleasure to meet you," the stranger spoke in English. "My name is Ivan Morozov. You'll have to forgive me, my Spanish is very poor."

Salinas remained seated, and didn't extend his hand to shake. He studied the stranger for a moment, trying to place him. He looked about forty-five. Medium build. Short hair, dark skin, and eyes like a sickly cat, yellow and mean. Salinas studied the eyes and face. He knew he had never seen this man before. If they had ever met, he would have remembered. And he wasn't an American. He spoke with an odd accent that Salinas couldn't place.

"What do you want?" Salinas asked, shifting his eyes away from his visitor to look at the door. He could see through the small glass window, and he noticed that the guard had left them unattended. Never before had he been allowed to talk to anyone, not even his private attorneys, without a guard standing inside the room.

"Señor Salinas, I will ask the questions for now. And please, don't be offended, but I must be brief and get straight to the point."

Morozov pulled back a chair and sat down across from Salinas before he continued. "I have come to make you an offer. It will involve a great deal of money. More than you could imagine, and unfortunately, all of it will come from your accounts.

"But," he continued, "if you agree, then I am offering you something that only we can give you."

"And what is that?" asked Salinas, as he impatiently thumped the table.

"Your freedom," Morozov replied. "You will walk out of this prison with me. Right now. Tonight. And we will provide certain guarantees to ensure your freedom in the future. You will never fear being hunted down and captured by either your government or the Americans. You will be free to go about your business, including your trade in cocaine."

Salinas didn't change his expression. Morozov leaned forward across the tiny table and lowered his voice. "How much would that be worth to you, Señor Salinas? How much would you pay to get back your life? One million, five million, maybe even ten?

"How much is it worth to you not to spend the rest of your life bathing in your sweat? How much would you pay to eat a meal that wasn't prepared by a prisoner with a contagious disease? How much to enjoy the beautiful things of this world?

"Can a man put a price on his freedom? Tell me, Señor Salinas. How much would that be worth?"

COLÓN, PANAMA

Two days later, Salinas walked into the central office of the Banco de las Americas He was dressed in a business suit with a wide-brimmed straw hat. The only piece of clothing he wore that wasn't glaring white was a smooth yellow silk tie that hung below his belt. In tow was his assistant, Mr. Ivan Morozov, carrying his leather briefcase. Salinas walked across the marble floor to a small reception area tucked away in the back of the enormous lobby. Although he had never been here before, he knew this was the office of a Señor Gorge Arellano.

"May I help you?" he was asked by the secretary who guarded the office door. She was a large woman who sat behind an imposing teak desk. She didn't smile as she examined her unwanted guest.

"I would like to wire some money," Salinas replied.

"And the name on the account?"

"Señor Juan Analla Cormona. You'll find it in file eighteen."

The woman keyed the information into the computer. Salinas watched the computer screen as it momentarily went blank. Within a few seconds a single line displayed across the screen: "File eighteen access denied. Dorado account. Return to main menu." was all it said.

The secretary hesitated only a moment, then reached over to her multilined telephone and dialed a two-digit number. Without speaking into the receiver, she replaced the hand piece back onto its cradle and turned again to face Salinas.

"Señor, please come with me," she said as she got up and led the two men back through the office door. There Gorge Arellano was waiting to receive them.

"What can we do for you, Señor Cormona?" he asked as he walked across the office to meet them. He was a short, fat man who looked remarkably like his secretary. They must be brother and sister, Morozov observed.

"As I told your receptionist, I would like to transfer some money," Salinas answered cooly.

"Certainly, sir. Do you have the access number of the required account?"

Without speaking, Salinas passed a folded sheet of paper to Arellano, who unfolded the paper as he walked back to his desk and sat at his own computer. It took him several minutes of typing before he looked up again at the waiting men.

"And the daily code?" he asked with just a hint of suspicion in his voice.

"Dial three two—four five six—three two—two seven eight. Ask for Mr. Dante. Tell him Cormona authenticates Bravo Bravo. He will reply with two seven eight four and today's date."

Arellano scribbled furiously as Salinas gave him the instructions. He dialed the international number and waited for the call to go through.

Nearly four thousand miles away, the phone rang in a small office of the Western Union Telegraph Company. It wasn't answered until the tenth ring. It took several more minutes to locate Mr. Dante. Finally he picked up the phone.

"Mr. Dante speaking. How may I help you?"

"Mr. Dante, I have a Señor Cormona here. His instructions are Bravo Bravo."

Without hesitating Dante answered. "Two seven eight four. Today's date is three September." Then just as quickly he hung up.

Arellano listened to the disconnect tone for a few moments before he lay down his receiver. He then turned to face the two men who were waiting. Suddenly he wanted very much to complete their business and escort them out of his office, wishing all the time he had been more polite.

"What are your instructions, Señor Cormona?" he asked as he picked up a pen to write.

"We are going to transfer money from three accounts in Zurich into one account in Brussels. Don't write any of this down. I will step you through the account numbers and give you all the necessary PINs. It should only take a minute."

Morozov couldn't help but be impressed as he watched Salinas work. It was apparent that Salinas had set up each account so that only he could have access to them. He repeated each account and access code from memory and never hesitated with the required response. In only a matter of minutes exactly fifty million dollars had been transferred into a previously dormant account in Brussels. Salinas had already provided Morozov with the access numbers to the Brussels account. It was now only a matter of waiting to confirm the transfer. That would take some time.

"We will call you in an hour to confirm the transfer," Salinas said as he turned toward the door. "Please don't keep us waiting."

As Gorge Arellano escorted his visitors out, he couldn't help but notice Morozov. The man had not spoken the entire time, which wasn't surprising. But there was something unusual about him. Perhaps it was the way he touched his boss's shoulders to steer him out of the room. Perhaps it was the way he seemed to observe everything, without ever really moving his eyes. Whatever it was, Arellano knew that Salinas wasn't the one to fear.

Salinas declined Arellano's offer to call them a cab. Instead, he and Morozov walked the three blocks back to their hotel. After taking the elevator to the third floor, they entered their sparsely decorated room. They watched television for half an hour, then Morozov picked up the phone. He called the bank and received a transaction confirmation number. Then he dialed an international code and talked to the bank in Brussels. They confirmed the account had been activated, but refused to reveal the new account balance. Morozov smiled in satisfaction.

Twenty minutes later, Carlos Manuel Salinas went down to the restaurant for lunch. He ate alone while he read the paper and then returned quickly to his room.

Five minutes later he was dead.

That night Morozov was sitting comfortably on an international flight bound for Guatemala City. From there he would use three different passports as he made his way back to Europe. His first stop would be in Madrid. From there he would fly to Prague and then finally on to Kiev.

While waiting in the Guatemalan airport for his flight to Spain, Morozov secreted himself in an old wooden box of a phone booth. He studied the ancient telephone for a moment, then began to dial. Once the call went through, it only took a few minutes before he had transferred three million dollars out of the account in Brussels into his personal account in Bucharest. He considered the money as a kind of bonus. An extra tip for a job well done. And besides, since he was the conspirators' bookkeeper, who would be any wiser? Certainly not his fellow Ukrainians. They would never even know it was gone.

After completing his call, Morozov left the phone booth and stopped by a small airport bar and ordered a bottle of Corona. He sipped the beer in silence while eyeing the beautiful, dark-skinned women that seemed to surround him. Ten minutes later, he was on his flight for Madrid.

About the time Morozov's flight was touching down in Spain, a maid entered a hotel room back in Colón. There she found Salinas' body lying peacefully on his bed, his head cocked awkwardly to one side as a result of the three fractured vertebrae in his neck. Protruding from his ashen lips was a crisp fifty dollar bill, along with a handwritten note from Ivan Morozov that apologized for making a mess.

MIAMI, FLORIDA

Less than four hours after the order to transfer money out of the Zurich accounts had been sent from the bank in Colón, Bret Cosner, a senior agent at the Drug Enforcement Agency, had to interrupt his lunch-break game of basketball to answer his phone. He was a huge man, well over six feet five inches and three hundred pounds. His skin was dark, more from his Latino mother than from any time spent in the sun, and his hair was bushy and long. He walked to the sideline, sweating like a pig and swearing under his breath, threw a thick towel over his hairy shoulders, and picked up his cellular phone.

"Cosner here. If this is Kenneth, it better be good."

"Yea, I love you too, babe," Kenneth Murry, Bret's partner at the DEA answered back. "Always good to hear your voice. Now if you're finished playing hopscotch, or miniature golf, or whatever you do during lunch to keep in shape, why don't you come in to work? I've got something you might want to see."

Bret immediately began to head for the shower, waving absently to the guys on the basketball floor to go on with the game. Glancing at his watch, he estimated the time.

"Be there twenty minutes without a shower, thirty with. Which do you want?

"Twenty. With." The telephone went dead.

Bret immediately picked up the pace. He recognized the urgency in his partner's voice; Kenneth wasn't the kind of guy who liked to cry wolf.

Thirty minutes later, Senior Agent Bret Cosner strode into his office at the DEA Regional Center in Miami. He threw his jacket over the back of his chair and sat wearily behind his desk just as agent Murry walked into the room.

The difference between the two men was striking. Murry, a thin man with balding hair and narrow gray eyes, was young and bookish-looking. He always wore a jacket over his white shirt, even on the hottest and muggiest days. His pants were always pressed. His shoes always shined. He was neat and trim and slightly elfish.

Agent Murry closed the door behind him and set himself down opposite Cosner's scratched and worn government desk.

Cosner leaned back in his chair and placed his feet up on the corner of the desk. Murry frowned in disapproval. Cosner reached down and grabbed one of the two double cheeseburgers he had bought for lunch and began to cram food into his mouth. Murry frowned even further. Cosner took a quick swig at his cola, then belched. Murry nearly came out of his seat.

"Geez, you're a pig. You know that, Cosner? Watching you eat makes me want to throw up."

"Hey, cool. That'd be neat."

Murry shook his head in disgust. Cosner belched once again, then shifted in his seat. A noxious fume filled the air. Murry's eyes narrowed and glazed over, but he didn't respond. Cosner laughed. He loved yanking Murry's chain. And after working with him for more than three years, he knew which buttons to push. But it was all just a part of the chemistry—part of what made them a team. Though different as night and day, they liked each other and worked well together. And they liked their work, which was more than Bret could say for most of the other saps that he knew.

Although most DEA agents wore a gun, neither Cosner nor Murry ever did. They had never actually seen a drug deal go down, for they rarely went out on the street. And to participate in a drug bust would be the last thing either one of them wanted to do. Such things were better left up to "street agents," one thing they had never pretended to be.

Cosner and Murry were accountants; specially trained techno-weenies who had become invaluable tools in the international war against drugs.

They worked for a very special and highly secretive office within the DEA. Their job was simple. Track the money. Track the money. Track the money. That was all that they did. From Bermuda to Alaska, from Chile to Moscow, they traced and accounted for the billions of dollars that circled the world as a result of the drug trade.

And they were good. As a direct result of their efforts, organized crime and the drug cartels had had hundreds of millions of dollars confiscated from foreign accounts. Working on the razor-thin edge of legality, Cosner and Murry, and several others just like them, spent their days tapping into foreign bank records, eavesdropping on cellular-telephone conversations, searching Federal Bank transaction accounts, and monitoring the hundreds of thousands of daily financial transactions that flowed through the intercontinental telephone lines, all in an attempt to hit the cartels in the only place they could really be hurt.

As Cosner ate, Murry settled back in his seat, then handed his partner the transcript of the intercepted phone message, along with some handwritten notes describing the general conditions in which the message had been intercepted. Cosner read the transcript fairly quickly.

"You're certain the Zurich accounts are controlled by Salinas?" he asked.

"Yep," was all Murry said.

"That's a little unusual. Much more money than he has seen fit to move around, even before he started his little stay down in Harada."

"Yep. That's a pretty good hunk of cash. I figure it's about thirty percent of everything that he's worth. So, what do you suppose is going on?"

"I'll tell you what I think," Cosner responded between gulps of burger and fries. "It sounds to me like our ol' man Salinas is about to take a fall. One of his boys must be circling around him, setting himself up for the kill. What else could explain it? Somehow, one of his lieutenants must have gotten hold of a few of his numbered accounts and started to figure, with Salinas safely out of the picture, now might be a good time to grab a piece of the action. You know what they say—while the cat's away, the mice will play—and judging what I know about Harada, that's about as 'away' as Salinas can get, at least without crossing to the other side of the veil."

"Yep. You're probably right," Murry replied, then leaned forward in his chair. "Only thing is, based on what we have seen in the past, I don't think it works out that simple. Salinas was no fool, not by any means, and he was always very careful with his money. Never—and I've gone back to check this—never has Salinas manipulated any accounts since he was ordered to prison. The prison won't let him get near a phone. They want him out of the business. So, from the day he was apprehended, none of his accounts has seen any activity at all. No deposits. No withdrawals. No transfers between accounts. I've seen more movement in glaciers. And now suddenly this comes along."

Cosner grunted. Murry went on. "As far as one of his lieutenants taking over, it has always been clear that Salinas had set up the security surrounding his accounts so as to avoid just such an endeavor. Now we find that not just one, but three . . . three numbered accounts have had rather significant withdrawals, to the tune of fifty million dollars, and all the money was wired to some unknown account somewhere in Brussels. Now, does something seem kind of strange, or is it just me?"

Cosner dropped his feet to the floor and sat up in his chair. "So, you think Salinas ordered the transfer? But I just don't see how he could do that, Kenneth. Not while he's rotting in jail. He must have ordered one of his attorneys to take care of it for him. That seems like a pretty simple thing to do."

"Let me ask you something," Murry interjected. "If you were Salinas, if you knew you were looking at at least ten more years in Harada, and if you had surrounded yourself with some of the worst thugs and creeps in the business, would you trust them with your bank accounts and their security numbers? That doesn't seem like a very bright thing to do."

Cosner quit chewing once again. "Okay," he finally said, "let's make some calls."

Twenty-four hours later, the two agents knew the truth. Salinas had indeed paid a quick visit to a bank in Colón, then shortly thereafter was murdered. The details were still sketchy, but one thing was certain. Salinas, the drug lord, was dead.

But that wasn't all. Carlos Manuel Salinas had not visited the Banco de las Americas by himself. He had been accompanied by some kind of advisor.

Cosner and Murry shifted into high gear, for with figures floating in the fifty million dollar range, and with Salinas, one of the most powerful members of the drug cartel, having been popped, something bad was definitely going on. A new guy had obviously come to town. And he was good. He had some connections, that was evident by the way he got Salinas out of prison, then had him killed. The guy had some pretty good tricks. And lots of power.

The real question was, who was he?

Very shortly after the story broke within the drug enforcement community, many people, from the local Panamanian police in downtown Colón to every DEA office in the world, was busy wondering who this special man might be.

The security camera at the Banco de las Americas was quickly confiscated. After several days of behind-the-scenes political wrangling, a copy of the video was sent to the DEA office in Miami, with a follow-on copy to DEA headquarters in Washington D.C. Again and again, the image of Morozov and Salinas entering the bank was run through a high resolution tape machine. Dozens of agents studied the image, racking their brains, searching their memories, trying to figure out who the man with Salinas might be.

Then, some hotshot new agent in D.C. made a suggestion. Why not digitize the image and feed it into the image-processing computer over at the Defense Intelligence Agency? This was just the thing that the DIA computer had been designed for—to take an unidentified image and digitize it so that the computer could search through its files, comparing thousands of known photos in an effort to match the picture with a name. It was a long shot, no doubt, but maybe, just maybe, with the help of the computer, they could put a bead on the man.

Again, there was some behind-the-scenes political wrangling. In fact, the head man, the director himself, had to get involved. A fair bit of begging and maneuvering finally produced an agreement to let the DEA use the image-identification computer.

Six hours later, a "For Your Information" bulletin was sent to every intelligence and counterintelligence agency in the United States government. Ivan Morozov, former head of the Russian Sicherheit was again at work. Last known to have been contracted out to the Ukrainian government, he seemed now to be branching into other things. Keep your eyes and ears open, the agents were told. Based on the amount of money he was now involved with, he was apparently working on something very big.

ELEVEN

BONE 01

THE PASTURES AND DRY WHEAT FIELDS OF SOUTHWESTERN RUSSIA PASSED beneath him in a blur, his shadow sweeping across the empty fields at over 1,000 feet per second. The aircraft's dart-like nose cut through the cold air at just under the speed of sound, the heat and thrust from the four huge engines kicking up faint rooster tails of dust and sand and blowing debris—telltale signs of the enormous aircraft's arrival.

The B-1 first appeared as a tiny dot, a mere pinpoint on the horizon. From a distance, the aircraft didn't have any form, its light-gray paint reflecting back little of the evening's closing light. But as the aircraft got closer, its tapered nose and sharply canted wings quickly became visible, and it was only a matter of seconds before the shapeless dot grew to fill the evening sky.

But for all the speed and commotion, the B-1 approached its target like a whisper. There was no rush of compressed air or roar from its mighty engines to give warning of the aircraft's approach. The B-1 was simply too fast to be betrayed by its own treacherous noise. At .98 mach, the bomber was racing behind the sound of its engines by just a fraction of a second. By the time anyone near the target heard the aircraft approach and turned their eyes upward, it would have already passed overhead.

Dogs were one of the few creatures that knew the B-1 was coming. As they lay on their bellies, they could feel the ground vibrate and shudder as the massive aircraft approached. Their ears could sense the thick wall of compressed air that extended forward from the B-1's nose cone. The canines would raise their heads and look around anxiously, but few of them knew to look overhead.

Sitting inside the cockpit, Richard Ammon heard none of the noise from his engines. The tight steel walls and thick Plexiglas of the cockpit protected him from all of the commotion. But he wasn't oblivious to the power. A small nudge from his throttles was all it took to push him back into his seat. A tiny push with his fingers against the control stick was all it took to roll the aircraft up and onto its side.

The cockpit was tight, every inch of it crammed with computer screens, gauges, and switches. Every inch was designed with some purpose in mind.

In front of Richard Ammon sat his main computer screen, or CRT. This was his primary flight and weapons instrument. Running down both sides of the CRT were dozens of other instruments and gauges. In his left hand were the four throttle controls. Extending up from the floor between his legs was a thick control stick. The top of the stick was also covered with buttons and switches.

Ammon sat in an ACES II ejection seat at the front station, allowing him a clear view of the passing terrain. Immediately behind him, separated by a thick bulkhead, was Ivan Morozov. Morozov's cockpit looked even more intimidating than the pilot's. Before him sat four CRTs, each of them essential to the navigation and defense of the aircraft. Surrounding the CRTs were dozens of keypads, each button superimposed with a series of coded symbols. It was an intimidating maze of computer screens, keypads, and symbols. To someone unfamiliar with combat aircraft, it would have been hopeless. But not to Morozov. Flying, with all of its subtleties and challenges, was something he understood. As a young officer in the Soviet Air Force, before transferring into the intelligence field, he had spent three years as a navigator/bombardier in the Sukhoi SU-24 fighter, flying reconnaissance along the West German border. In addition, for the past several months, he had been studying the B-1's weapon and navigation systems until he knew them like the back of his hand. He knew that someone had to fly the mission with Ammon, and from the beginning, he was determined that it be himself.

As Ammon and Morozov busied themselves in the cockpit, the B-1 continued to speed across the flat terrain, skimming above every obstacle while cruising just below the speed of sound.

This was the B-1's domain. For this purpose was it created. It could cruise at this speed for hours, never tiring, never deviating from its desired course, and always exactly on altitude. With its banks of computers, phased-array radar, low-level terrain following systems, and multiple weapons capability, the B-1 was the most sophisticated aircraft in the world.

But designing and building the aircraft had not been an easy task. For fifteen years the aircraft's designers had wrestled with one engineering problem after another. Many times they had been tempted to quit, for it seemed that they had been given an impossible job. The pieces just didn't fit together. There were simply too many mutually exclusive criteria to bring together in one single aircraft.

To begin with, they had been told to design an aircraft that could penetrate the world's most advanced air defenses to attack a heavily defended target. The aircraft would be required to go against the best surface and airborne threats that the enemy had to offer.

"Okay," the engineers said. "We can do that. We'll build a small and nimble fighter. We'll make it capable of pulling twelve Gs. We'll make it light and extremely maneuverable. And very small. If we are going to send this aircraft far behind enemy lines, we want it to be as tiny as possible. That will give the enemy a much smaller target to shoot at."

But then the engineers were told that the B-1 had to be able to carry up to 50,000 pounds of weapons. In addition to that, it had to have an intercontinental range, which meant it had to carry enormous amounts of jet fuel.

So much for developing a small and nimble fighter. The B-1 would have to be huge—maybe half as big as a football field—to carry such a load of weapons and fuel.

The engineers also discovered that the new aircraft had to be an accurate bomber. Very accurate. It couldn't just scatter a cluster of bombs in any random pattern, hoping a bomb or two would hit the target. Surgical strikes required much more than that. Even dropping a bomb within a few yards of its target wasn't good enough. It had to fall within a few feet. In some cases even inches.

"Okay, we can do that," the engineers muttered as sweat started to bead on their brows.

Then the designers were given the bombshell.

"We want the aircraft to be nearly invisible," they were told. "We want its radar cross section to be one thousandth of the aircraft's actual size. Make this aircraft look like nothing more than a flock of birds that are cluttering up the enemies' radar."

The engineers spent many nights pondering how to make a 400,000 pound aircraft look like nothing but a bunch of speedy sea gulls.

Hey, this will be easy, they used to joke. We can make an aircraft that will do all that. The only problem is, when we are finished, the sucker certainly will never fly.

As the designers wrestled with the problems, they began to realize two important facts that were core to the design of the new aircraft.

First, the new bomber would have to be able to fly incredibly low in order to avoid being detected by the enemy's radar. To do this it would need a terrain-following system that was better than anything yet developed. It would have to enable the aircraft to fly up the steepest mountains and down the deepest, winding valleys, all at treetop level. And it would have to do it automatically, without the pilot even touching the controls. Because the safest time to go into battle would be at night, when it was more difficult to be detected by enemy fighters and missiles. But at night, the pilot couldn't see. So the low-level, terrain-following system had to be completely automatic.

In addition to a low-level penetration capability, the aircraft needed speed. A blinding, shattering, screaming speed. A speed so great that it would leave any attacking aircraft sucking up hot exhaust gases as it watched the B-1 screeching by. The aircraft was too big to play with the fighters. It needed speed so it could run away.

For fifteen years, the engineers worked on the bomber. And when they were finished, not only had they produced the most sophisticated aircraft in the world, but also the most deadly. Rockwell and the Air Force called the bomber the "Lancer". The pilots who flew it called it the "Bone".

Ammon was using the B-1's computers to fly at 200 feet above the trees and telephone wires, hugging the earth like a blanket. This was where the B-1 belonged. This was usually the safest place to be. Usually. . . .

But right now Ammon didn't feel very safe. He was about to be jumped by two Russian Mig-31s. And they were very angry. Their orders were clear. Shoot down the hostile bomber. Kill it before it got away. Although the Mig-31 pilots were never told it was so, it didn't take them long to figure out that the B-1 was after their nuclear assets, and as they realized that their missiles were in imminent danger, their determination increased even more. They would blow the B-1 out of the sky.

It was Morozov's job to keep them alive. It was his job to search the radio spectrum for any hostile aircraft or missiles, then jam their radar if they started tracking the B-1. As such, he should have detected the Mig-31s early, while they still had their radar in search mode.

However, Ammon wasn't the kind of pilot who liked to sit around and hope the other guy would be able to save him. He was looking for the fighters himself, searching the sky ahead and above him as the B-1 skimmed over the ground. He jammed his neck and scanned the horizon, searching for the deadly little fighters.

The Mig-31 pilots detected the bomber on their Hot Light radars at 63 miles. They were approaching the bomber from its four o'clock. They were nearly guaranteed the element of surprise.

Ammon jumped in his seat when the earphones in his helmet came alive. Threat tones cried in his ear, howling and beating like some kind of crazy synthesizer music. The bomber's ALQ-161 defensive system had been designed with a certain degree of artificial intelligence, enough to recognize the fact that it was presently being operated by the hands of a novice. As a result, the automatic features of the system took over, at least to a sufficient degree to advise the crew of the presence of the Mig-31s. The insistent, screeching tone in Ammon's ears was designed to warn him that he soon was going to die. At least he would if he didn't do something. And he had only a few seconds in which to act. Any hesitation would guarantee a tragic result.

"What have you got?!" Ammon screamed, as he slammed all four throttles into afterburner.

"Two Mig-31s!" Morozov yelled back. "One is at three o'clock. Looks like twelve miles. His playmate is right behind him. Okay! Okay! Hang on! Lead is moving in. Now! Break right! Get down in the dirt!"

Ammon threw his stick to the right. The aircraft immediately rolled up on its side. He pushed the aircraft even lower, dishing it toward the fields and trees, searching desperately for somewhere to hide. "Oh, give me a mountain or canyon," he pleaded, as he scanned the landscape surrounding him. But there was nowhere to hide. No valleys or hills to run for. No mountains in which to seek an escape. Only this flat open nothingness.

It would be like shooting fish in a barrel. The Mig-31 pilots could pluck at him at their leisure. He could roll and jam and throw his throttles into afterburner, but they were too close now, and he could not hide.

Still the lower he could get, the better. If nothing else, flying very low would help to clutter up the Mig-31s' radar. Ammon pushed the nose of the aircraft even lower. He sucked in his breath as the B-1 barely skimmed over a tall windbreak of poplar trees. With all four of his engines still in full afterburner, he quickly accelerated through the speed of sound. Behind him, the shock wave and sonic boom blew out the windows of every farmhouse within three miles.

Ammon's eyes never stopped moving. He continued to search the sky around him as he rolled his wings back to level.

"Where are they?" he called to Morozov, searching frantically for the Mig-31s. Instead of turning and running away, Ammon had turned into the oncoming fighters and was now heading straight toward them. Once the fighters had him on their radar, it wouldn't do any good to try and run, and by turning toward them, Ammon had increased the closure rate between the three aircraft to well over 1,000 miles an hour. That would give the Mig-31 pilots only a few seconds to analyze and run their intercept. If Ammon could survive their first pass, they would have to turn around and chase him down. And that was a race they couldn't win. The fighters didn't have the speed or fuel to stay with the B-1 once they got in a high-speed, tail chase down low.

"Where are they?" Ammon muttered again, more to himself than Morozov. The threat tones in his headset told him the fighters were still in search mode. Neither of them had locked him up on radar yet. The Mig-31s' computers were still trying to pick the B-1 out from the ground clutter that dirtied up their radar.

Suddenly the threat tone in Ammon's headset increased in pitch and intensity and became an insistent warble.

"Lead's got us locked up!" Morozov screamed over the interphone. "Break left! I'm trying to jam him!"

Ammon immediately yanked the aircraft into a hard left turn. He felt himself settle into his ejection seat from the G forces that pulled at his body. In the seat behind him, Morozov was constantly hitting his chaff and flare buttons. Chaff, chaff, flares! Chaff, chaff, flares! He punched the buttons as fast he could, spitting them out like a mad man. Bundles of aluminum foil strips were spit out into the slip-stream where they were spread by the wind into a blanket of radar reflecting material. A single flare followed every two bundles of chaff, its phosphorous burning white heat as it tumbled through the sky. In theory, any radar-guided missile would be thrown off by the wall of chaff, while a heat-seeking missile would be drawn away from the bomber by the hot-burning flares. Between the jamming, the chaff, and the flares, no missile should have been able to maintain its lock on the aircraft.

At least that was the theory.

Up front, Ammon was still searching for the fighters. He was focusing all of his attention on finding his attackers, allowing the computers to fly the aircraft.

Because even in a world of radar and missiles and silent death from miles away, one axiom from the aces of the First World War still held true. "Lose sight, lose fight." No one knew that better than Ammon. He had killed many aircraft in simulated dogfights because they lost sight and couldn't see him.

Suddenly a tiny flash of light caught his eye. There they were. Or at least one of them. The lead Mig-31 had followed the B-1 as it made its last break to the left. Now he was abeam them and only a mile out. The fighter began to slide back, moving into position behind them. Once he was behind the B-1 it would all be over. Even if Morozov could jam him, the fighter was close enough now to take a gun shot with his cannon. Ammon jinked the bomber left, then right. No good. The fighter was staying with him and was now nearly in position. Ammon lost sight of the fighter as it slid back behind his tail. He unknowingly tensed his stomach muscles as he waited for the cannon plugs to start shattering their way through his aircraft.

Then Ammon got an idea. It was desperate and risky, but at the time it was all that he had.

With a sudden jerk, he pulled back hard on the stick while simul-taneously slamming all four throttles back into full afterburner. Within three seconds, the aircraft was pointed nearly straight up, climbing skyward at forty thousand feet per minute. The aircraft's speed and momentum carried the bomber skyward. Up into the sky it climbed. Straight up. Up into the sun.

The Mig-31 pilot easily followed them as they shot skyward. But then the unthinkable happened. He lost sight of them in the glare of the sun. He stared and squinted and cursed. He jerked his head from one side of the cockpit to the other as he desperately searched for the bomber. He rolled his fighter inverted in an effort to shade his eyes from the glare. But it didn't make any difference. The B-1 was gone.

The Mig-31 pilot pulled the nose of his fighter back down to the horizon, rolled himself upright, and stared down at his radar. Nothing. He couldn't even find them on radar.

"Lead's blind," he announced in a disgusted tone over the radio, cursing himself as he spoke. He had blown it. He had just lost a year's worth of cool points. His name would be muttered with shame at the bar.

But hopefully his wing man knew where the bomber had stolen off to. The Mig-31 pilot silently prayed that his number two had done a better job of keeping the target in sight.

He swore once again in frustration when he heard two reply, "Two is blind as well."

Fifteen thousand feet below them, the B-1 sped to the east. It was back at treetop level, skimming once again over the fields and trees.

After pulling the bomber up into the sky, Ammon had immediately rolled inverted and pulled back into a steep dive. His evasive maneuver turned out to be nothing more than a modified yo-yo. Kind of a screwed up outside loop. But whatever he called the maneuver, it had worked. The threat tones in his helmet told him the fighters didn't know where he was. Their radars were back in search mode. And even if they found him now, it wouldn't matter. They could never catch him. For now at least, he was safe.

"That was close, fly-boy," Morozov mumbled. "I think you got lucky." His breathing was heavy and hard.

"No, Morozov," Ammon shot back. "I'm not lucky. I'm good. There's a difference. And don't you forget it."

Morozov grunted. "Ok, Carl. Whatever you say."

They pressed on to the target.

"Time to arm the missile?" Ammon asked.

"Four minutes," Morozov replied. "You should start to see the target environment soon after the missile is armed."

Once again Ammon searched ahead of the aircraft. Their first target was the Buturlinovhka-Voerenky nuclear missile site located just north of Khoper River. So far, he couldn't see anything that looked like the target, only the same dusty fields and an occasional farm house. But then they were still more than sixty miles out. He wouldn't be able to see any of the aboveground buildings or guard towers of the facility until he was about fifteen miles away.

In the aft cockpit, Morozov rolled his target radar to the side to take a look at a fix point as they flew by. As the radar looked at the waypoint, it immediately showed up on his center CRT. The point Morozov had chosen to look at was a stop sign at a small intersection near a line of tall trees. "Incredible," Morozov thought as the navigation computer did some quick thinking. "From more than ten miles, I can look out and find something as small as a sign post." Just then, a series of numbers flashed onto Morozov's screen, displaying their new position. They had made a nice correction back to the bomb run course and were now only three hundred feet from their desired flight path. "Truly incredible," Morozov muttered again. They had flown thousands of miles, been intercepted and chased by enemy fighters, and still were able to navigate back to within less than a football field of their desired position. Morozov was truly impressed.

"I'm telling you, Carl, the Americans have made this too easy," he called out to Ammon. "This radar is absolutely incredible. Even at this distance, I can actually make out the air shaft of the facility complex. Now it's just a matter of choosing my target."

After checking the final coordinates, Morozov began to enter the final data into his weapons computer. The Buturlinovhka-Voerenky missile facility consisted of ten hardened silos controlled by a single underground launch facility. It would be a relatively easy target to destroy, for once the central launch facility was taken out, the ten silos would then be rendered useless. Morozov had already determined that, because the command launch facility was "shallow," the M-95 penetration missile would easily destroy it.

One of the most powerful weapons on earth, only about three hundred M-95s had ever been built, for they were incredibly expensive and complicated to maintain in combat order. However, their great expense and high maintenance was easily justified, for they were the best weapons in the world when it came to hitting underground silos or buried bunkers.

The missile owed its great success to three things—its incredible speed, its depleted uranium core, and finally, its small nuclear warhead. As it approached its objective, the missile would pull up into a steep climb, then turn and dive, accelerating to Mach 7 as it bore down on its target. This blinding speed, in conjunction with the ultra-dense uranium core, allowed the warhead to cut through the earth like a bullet through water. Not until then did the nuclear warhead go off, then *baaam!!*, the bunker was gone.

So far as western intelligence could confirm, more than ninety percent of Russia's hardened targets and bunkers could be destroyed if attacked by the M-95 missiles. The Ukrainians didn't have anything that could come close to the destructive capability of the M-95, and in fact, to get hold of these missiles was one of the primary reasons they had devised a plan to steal the Bone. But the M-95 wasn't the only weapon that was stuffed into the belly of the Bone. The bomber also carried other nuclear weapons. But they wouldn't be used. At least not on this target. Morozov was holding them in reserve. For them, he had something special in mind.

After he was finished punching the final target information into his computer, Morozov keyed his microphone switch once again.

"Okay, pilot, I've selected and programmed an M-95 for this target. It is set for maximum penetration before explosion. If we release the weapon at two hundred feet, my systems are telling me we have to get to within . . . thirteen-point-two miles of the target to guarantee the missile is within range. Confirm?"

Ammon did some quick math in his head. "Yeah, that sounds about right," he replied. At twenty miles, Morozov would put the missile in final countdown. At thirteen miles, it could be launched. The missile would then drop from the belly of the aircraft, ignite its ramjet engine in the slipstream, then scream out ahead of the bomber, allowing the B-1 to turn away from the target and proceed to its next destination.

As they closed in on the first target, Ammon searched the sky up ahead of the aircraft. Nothing was there. It appeared they were going to make this a successful bomb run.

Suddenly the aircraft began to violently shake. Two red fire lights illuminated on the panel in front of him as his headset came alive once more. This time it was a constant high pitched tone, warning him of a fire in both of his right engines.

For just a second Ammon pictured himself back in his F-16 as he spiraled down toward the Yellow Sea. The same sick feeling overcame him. He had been in this situation before. He even noted that the fire warning tones sounded the same on both aircraft.

He shook his head and reached up to punch the fire suppression buttons. "I've got a fire in numbers three and four," he said to Morozov, his voice shaking from the violent vibrations.

"I think we've taken a missile!" Morozov shouted back, his voice barely understandable above the cry of the warning tones. "It must have been a heat seeker. I never got any warning on my radar."

At this point, Ammon didn't care what hit him. He only wanted to save the aircraft. He scanned his engine instruments. Engines three and four were definitely gone. They weren't producing any thrust and their exhaust temperatures were climbing through the ceiling. Ammon immediately reached up to select the alternate fire suppression. Just as he was punching the button, a bright light flashed from outside. The aircraft shuddered again, this time with enough force to knock Ammon sideways in his seat. Again another knocking explosion. The aircraft began to settle toward the earth.

The hydraulic legs of the simulator brought the cockpit slowly back down to ground level. Over the intercom system, Ammon heard the voice of the simulator controller.

"You took another fox-one up the tail," he said in a dry tone. "That's the second time you've let that happen. You've got to work together, comrades, or you're never going to make it. We've been doing this sixteen hours a day for over a week now. You should be getting it down. We've got to start seeing some rapid improvement, my friends. It only gets harder from here."

In the simulator across from Ammon and Morozov, the two controllers who piloted the Mig-31s smiled at each other again. So far their job had been very easy.

Ammon heard Morozov throw his helmet up against his console, smashing it loudly against the plastic screen of the simulator. The smoke from Morozov's cigarette began to cloud the tiny cockpit.

BOLLING AIR FORCE BASE, WASHINGTON D.C.

Though the United States Air Force dealt with some of the most highly classified and sensitive information that had ever existed, they had not had a serious internal breach of security in over forty years. All through the '80s and early '90s, while the Navy suffered through the Walker spy case and Pollard scandal, while the CIA tried to estimate how many informants had been killed and how much damage had really been done by Aldrich Ames, while the Army dealt with the sudden embarrassment of the Seymour treason, the Air Force had remained above it all.

This was due in large part to the work that was accomplished in a cramped and busy office buried deep in the bowels of USCOM, an even more cramped and noisy building in the center of Bolling Air Force Base. Located just across the river from the Pentagon, Bolling was near enough to the center of power to know what was going on, yet because it wasn't as convenient to get to as the Pentagon, by and large the politicians and heavy brass left its workers alone, allowing them to do their job without a great deal of supervision or interference.

Located in the basement of the USCOM building was the office of the Internal Counter-Espionage Division, or ICED. Set up in the early '80s, ICED's mission was to monitor, track, observe, and ferret out any spies that might be hiding within the Air Force. Not only did they monitor the whereabouts of suspected spies, they also kept an extensive list of anyone with a TOP SECRET security clearance who they also suspected might be willing to lean in that direction. Young airmen with unusually high burdens of debt, suspected homosexuals, rebellious sergeants, or officers with wounded egos—all of these were people that ICED liked to keep a close eye on.

And through the years, they had had great success on two fronts. First, they had been able to stop several potentially damaging spy rings before they had much success. Second, because they were internal to the Air Force, ICED was able to complete its work without having to look to the outside for help, thus greatly reducing their public exposure. No bad news was ever leaked to the press.

At 6:50 in the morning—at about the same time that Ammon and Morozov were getting shot down in their simulator—Lieutenant Colonel Oliver Tray, deputy director of ICED, was just arriving to work. A slender man with narrow shoulders and sandy blond hair, Tray was dressed in tight bike shorts and a loose fitting t-shirt, having ridden his bike in to work. After hoisting his mountain bike down two flights of stairs, he hid it away in a broom closet and headed down the hallway, through the security doors, to the office lounge. Lt Col Tray bypassed the percolating pot of coffee and trays of glazed donuts and, instead, poured himself a glass of orange juice from the miniature cooler. Gulping the orange juice down, he turned and headed back down the narrow hallway to the men's bathroom to shower.

On his way to the bathroom he passed the director's office. As he strode by the open glass doors, the director's secretary looked up from her tidy desk and called out. "Ollie, if you have a minute, Colonel Fullbright wanted to see you." Tray stopped in his tracks and turned to face Kay, the middle-aged secretary who ran the director's office. Pointing to his sweating clothes he silently mouthed the word "Now?"

"He said to tell you as soon as you came in," Kay responded to Oliver's gesture. "He's on the telephone to General Mann right now. If you hurry, I'll try to cover for you." Tray smiled and gave a quick thumbs up as he hurried down the hall.

Ten minutes later, freshly showered and dressed in a clean blue uniform, Lt Col Tray walked into his boss's office and took a seat by the enormous oak-top desk.

"Have you seen the morning reports?" the colonel asked, throwing a thick red folder across the desk toward his assistant director. He liked Lt Col Tray, but worked him hard. It was just part of their business.

"Uh, no sir. I just got in."

Something must be going on, and as usual, the director was the first one to know. It was to avoid embarrassing situations such as these that Tray usually showed up to work at least thirty minutes before his boss, allowing enough time to take a look at the overnight message traffic before Colonel Fullbright came in. So how was it that Colonel Fullbright seemed to always be the first one in when something was up? Did he have some kind of sixth sense, or was he just lucky? Tray really didn't know, but he hated how it always seemed to work out that way.

Of course, Tray wasn't the first one to sit in wonder at some of the things Fullbright seemed to come up with. Truth was, Fullbright was one of the most intelligent men in the entire Air Force. A graduate of MIT, he had moved up through the ranks with lightning speed, and had already been selected to receive his first star, for many of the nation's top generals had also taken notice of the man. He was young and brash and cool as ice under pressure. And Oliver Tray loved working for him.

Which was the main reason he seemed so embarrassed to tell his boss that he hadn't yet read the morning reports.

Fullbright watched Tray shake his head, then said, as he waved his hand toward the red binder, "Well, take a look at this. It's rather lengthy, so go ahead and take it back to your desk. Give it some thought, then come and tell me what you think."

"Yes, sir. I'll get right back to you." Tray picked up the folder and stood up from his chair and started to walk out of the room.

"I've got to tell you, you're going to love this," Fullbright said with a snort as Tray made his way to the door. "When I read it, it almost blew me away."

"Interesting reading?" Tray replied, not knowing exactly what Fullbright meant.

"Yeah. Do an initial check-out, if you can. See if you think this guy might just be blowing smoke. Bring him here if you need to. I'll get back with you later on this morning."

Tray turned around to leave once again. He was almost out the door before Fullbright called him back. "Oliver, there's one more thing I wanted to ask you."

"Sir?"

"What about BADGER? How does it look?"

Tray wrinkled his nose. "Nothing, sir. Nothing at all. I'm afraid it doesn't look very good."

The colonel swore. "I can't believe that we lost him! How could he just disappear? How did we let him slip through our hands?"

"Unless . . ." Lt Colonel Tray paused, "unless he was actually killed."

"Do you really believe that might be what happened?" Fullbright asked.

After some thought, Oliver replied, "No sir, I don't. Although it's the most likely explanation, still, I don't think it is as simple as that. I'm afraid we might have let him slip away."

Fullbright swore again and frowned.

"Sir, we always knew this could happen. If they wanted him back, there really wasn't much we could do."

"Yes, I know, but still that doesn't make it any easier. We've got two lousy options. Either he's dead, or we let them bring him in. Either way, we didn't do our job."

Oliver nodded his head, but didn't respond. After a while, Fullbright grunted, then turned his attention back to his desk, dismissing Tray with a wave of his finger.

Tray made his way back to his office, shut the door, sat down at his desk, and opened the red folder. The first page was a log which was used to keep track of everyone who had had access to the TOP SECRET message binder. He logged into the file by writing his name, the date, and the time that he had picked up the folder from his boss. Then he began to read.

The first message was from the Defense Intelligence Agency, a short advisory about some Ukrainian intelligence officer who, after many years of inactivity, had recently been sighted in Central America. It was speculated that he was now involved in the drug trade. Lt Col Tray scanned through the single page report. Not much of interest there. He moved on.

The next five messages were from various sources, two from the DIA, one from the CIA, and two from the National Reconnaissance

Office. All five of the classified intelligence reports concerned the recent political tensions between Russia and the Ukraine, particularly the latest movement of Russian troops along the Ukrainian border. In the past few days, eleven Russian divisions had begun to pull back from the border, putting some distance between themselves and the Ukrainian armies that were massed in defensive positions along the common front. However, satellite imagery clearly showed a continued increase in activity of Fedotov's short-range attack missiles. Tray mused over these reports for several minutes. So Fedotov was pulling some of his troops back. Could be good. Could be bad. It all depended on how things went. Either way, the impending war in the former Soviet Union was not his primary concern.

As Tray turned to the last message in the file, he couldn't help but notice how thick it was. It must have been at least twenty pages, which was unusual, for normally the different agencies which passed classified intelligence information to one another tried to keep them very short. It wasn't until Tray read the electronic return address at the top of the page that he realized the message had originated from the ICED detachment out at Wright Patterson Air Force Base in Ohio. The message was addressed only to the ICED director, which was good. That would mean it would not yet have been disseminated out of the ICED agency. As Oliver Tray perused the lengthy report, he became even more relieved that no one outside of ICED had yet seen it.

He read the report several times, highlighting key points with a light yellow marker while jotting down more than two pages of questions and notes, then picked up his STEW III secure telephone to make a few calls.

The first person he contacted was Major Donnald, the author of the report. Tray knew him well enough to know that he didn't have to doubt his work. Still, after getting Donnald on the phone and going through the usual exchange of brief pleasantries, he began to fire off a series of questions. How long had he been working on this project? What first had made him suspicious? Who were his sources? Had he been working alone? How far along did he think they might be in assembling the stolen equipment?

All through the grilling, Major Donnald remained cool. He was obviously very well prepared. As he answered his questions, Tray could hear the major sort through his notes. He remained extremely factual, answering Tray's questions as directly as he could, all the while being careful not to interject his own feelings or personal opinions. He seemed to have done a lot of homework. Tray could just imagine. He tried to picture himself in Donnald's shoes. If he had fired off such a message to his boss, he would have stayed up all night preparing for the arrows of doubt that he knew would soon be lobbed in his direction.

"What about documentation? Where do you stand? Have you got a reasonably good paper trail?" Oliver asked.

"Yes, I think we've got a good start," Donnald replied. "I've got invoices and inventory logs for the missing computers, security police reports of the stolen software, as well as receipts from the contractor and statements from the guys out there in the state department who have been helping me track the destination of some of the illegally exported goods. It's all here. But unfortunately, it still paints a very muddied picture."

"One last question, Major Donnald." Lt Colonel Tray was ready to wrap it up. "Why? Why could they possibly want all this equipment? What are they planning to do?"

A rather lengthy pause. "Sir, I have absolutely no idea. I don't know. You tell me."

"Yeah . . . I wish I could. But we better find out. Listen, what have you got planned for this afternoon? Any chance you could come out and meet with Colonel Fullbright? I'd really like you here. It would save us a lot of time."

"My secretary has already made reservations. I can be at National by sixteen thirty. Can you have someone pick me up?"

"I'll send someone over. And Major Donnald, bring the documentation. We'll want to go through as much of it as we can."

"It's already packed. I'll see you this afternoon."

Oliver Tray hung up the phone and rubbed his eyes.

No wonder the director didn't know what to think. This one was beyond even weird.

All those parts stolen from the B-1 simulator building up at Ellsworth. Whole racks of computers. And an entire bank of missing simulator software from the Rockwell facility out in California. And what about the 28,000 gigs of highly sophisticated computer programs that had been shipped out to Helsinki, all of it legal, but highly suspect?

But why? Who would want all that stuff? It had very little military or intelligence value. It just didn't make sense. If Oliver Tray didn't know any better, he would almost believe that someone was trying to build themselves a B-1.

HELSINKI, FINLAND

That night, Ivan Morozov stalked into Andrei Liski's office and slammed the door shut behind him. He was angry, and his mood showed on his face. Liski looked up from his reading, then leaned back in his chair and gestured for Morozov to sit. Morozov shook his head and remained standing.

"How is the simulator training going?" Liski asked. "Better than expected, I hope, given the deteriorating situation in Russia."

Morozov grunted. "Some good. Some bad. But all in all it is coming along. We're about where I thought we would be."

"How long until you are ready? We have far less time than we originally planned for."

Morozov didn't reply. Liski returned his cold stare.

"Did you call me here to chat about our training, or have you got something else on your mind?" Morozov finally asked.

Liski reached down, opened the top drawer of his desk and pulled out a folded piece of paper. He tossed the paper across his desk with a flip of his wrist.

"Recognize this?" he asked dryly.

Morozov studied the paper and shrugged. "What is it?"

"It's a phone number."

"Okay," Morozov replied. "So it's a phone number."

Liski leaned forward in his chair. "The night we brought Ammon in, he made two phone calls. One to his woman out in California. The other one to this number."

A hint of fear flashed in Morozov's eyes. "Whose number is it?" he demanded.

"I was hoping you could tell me," Liski snapped. "It's no longer a working number. Doesn't have a country code. No area code that matches any within the United States. Nor any other nation, as far as we can tell. So you tell me. You're the intel genius. Who did your boy call?"

Morozov didn't answer.

"Ammon is looking like a total disaster!" Liski announced in a disgusted tone.

Morozov shot Liski a menacing glare. "How did you get this?" he demanded.

"It wasn't hard. A little checking around with the Korea phone company was all it took."

Ivan Morozov swore again under his breath.

"So what do you think, Ivan Morozov? Who did Ammon try to call? What kind of outfit has untraceable numbers?"

Morozov didn't look up. Inside his head, his mind was racing. "That sonofa . . . ," his voice trailed off.

Morozov finally looked up from the paper. "Get the girl!" he commanded in a raspy voice. "Get the girl! No more excuses! No more delays! I want her by the end of the week!"

He turned and stalked from the room.

TWELVE

LONE PINE, CALIFORNIA

JESSE MORREL STARED OUT THE CABIN WINDOW AT THE TOP OF THE Sierra mountains. It had snowed for the first time last night, much earlier than usual, and the highest peaks were blanketed in a deep white powder. But the lower valleys received only a light dusting, leaving clumps of desert wiregrass to stretch their brittle fingers through the thin layer of snow. The morning sun created millions of sparkling prisms as it reflected off the grainy white powder.

It had been more than two weeks since Jesse had come in from her morning walk to find the message Ammon had left her on her answering machine. Within two hours of receiving the message, she was driving the winding mountain roads that led to their summer cabin above the small town of Lone Pine.

As she drove along the highway toward the thin air of the Sierras, she wished for the thousandth time that this was just another weekend getaway. She glanced at the empty passenger seat, remembering the many happy days that she and Richard had spent in the cabin. It had been their mountain hideaway. Every weekend they could, they drove up to the cabin, where they spent the days hiking and swimming and sleeping in each other's arms in the hammock that swung from the back porch.

One morning, just over a year ago, when they had been married for just a few weeks, they had come up to the cabin for Easter break. Early one morning they were hiking along a steep ridge line when they encountered a small black bear. The bear was high on the ridge, about fifty feet up the trail, but still Jesse quickly scrambled back down the trail to safety. While Jesse retreated, Richard stood his ground, insisting there wasn't any danger. Suddenly the furry black bear hoisted herself onto her hind legs and began to swat at the air. She growled and tossed her head around as she glared at Richard Ammon. His evaluation of the harmless bear changed very quickly and he ran for the nearest tree. And that's where Jesse found him, when, half an hour later, she cautiously hiked back up the mountain. Richard sat treed like a coon, perched high in an old white aspen, while the small bear waited patiently below. When the bear heard Jesse approaching, she must have felt outnumbered, because she quickly ran off into the trees. Richard shyly climbed down from the aspen while Jesse doubled over with laughter. From then on, if Ammon ever acted just a little too cocky, Jesse would smile at him, then growl like a bear.

Memories such as these had made Jesse happy to be back in their old mountain refuge. But as time wore on, the rooms seemed to grow more empty and a heavy loneliness began to set in.

The plan had been very simple. If Richard Ammon ever gave her the code, she was to go immediately up to the cabin. He would call her there as soon as he could. It might take some time, he had warned her, but eventually he would get to a phone. For more than two weeks, Jesse Morrel had been waiting, literally living each minute by the phone. She would stay all day in the cabin, then usually sleep in a bundle of quilted blankets by the fireplace, the telephone sitting next to her ear. Once or twice a day, she would pick up the receiver and listen for a dial tone just to make sure the phone was still working.

One morning, very early, the telephone rang. She awoke instantly from a deep slumber and snatched up the receiver with trembling hands. A bright female voice asked if Benny was there. "I'm sorry, you have the wrong number," Jesse muttered. The girl giggled an apology and hung up. Jesse's heart nearly broke. She held the receiver next to her chest and listened to the perfect silence of the room.

Late one evening she called a close friend. She couldn't stand the loneliness anymore. They had only talked for a moment, but since then, Jesse had lived with a constant fear that Ammon had tried to call her while she was on the phone. Her mind knew it was unlikely, maybe one chance in ten thousand. But so many unlikely things had happened. She figured her chances of falling in love with a former spy had been pretty unlikely, too.

The waiting and wondering was driving her crazy. But where could she turn for answers? What was she to do? Drive to Nellis Air Force Base in Las Vegas and walk into the base commander's office and ask if they knew that one of their F-16 pilots was a Soviet spy? Well, not really a Soviet spy, she would explain. The Soviet Union no longer existed, of course. He was a former Soviet spy, former in the sense that he was now a good guy. He wasn't a spy anymore. Never really was. Didn't ever have the chance. And he certainly had never done anything illegal. He was forced into the situation by ambitious and evil men who took advantage of his childhood. Now he considers himself an American. And he is completely loyal. He loves this country and he loves me, too, and he wouldn't leave us voluntarily. He was taken in against his will. Why are you looking at me that way? I'm not crazy! I'm his wife!

Jesse could picture the expression on the base commander's face as he threw her out of his office and had her shipped back to Circus Circus.

Of course he wouldn't believe her. Jesse hardly believed it herself. And that meant she was on her own.

And so she waited. As long as she could. But after two weeks, she couldn't take it any longer. She couldn't stand the loneliness of the cabin or the frustration of not knowing what to do. She was tired of waiting for Ammon, and she wasn't going to wait anymore. Fourteen days after arriving at the cabin, she packed up her small bag of belongings and headed home to Santa Monica.

She arrived late that afternoon. She parked her red Mazda next to the complex pool, then got out and cut through the grass, ignoring the winding sidewalks that led through the maze of buildings. Dressed in white summer shorts, a striped cotton shirt, and white sandals, she walked quickly toward her apartment and let herself in. The first thing she did was check the answering machine. Perhaps Ammon had tried to call her here. Pushing the play button, she tapped impatiently on the counter top as she waited for the tape to start playing. But nothing happened. When she remembered that she had turned the machine off after getting Ammon's code, she let out a long, whispered sigh. It was just another link in a chain of disappointments. She was starting to get used to them now.

It wasn't until then that Jesse noticed the stale, musty air. The apartment smelled like an old tangy sweatshirt. She walked to the sink and saw the spilled orange juice that had been left there for over two weeks. It was now a smelly puddle of brown pulp. She opened the drain and turned on the water to wash it away, then propped open the front door and raised the kitchen window to let the outside air circulate through the room.

Jesse walked through the apartment, looking things over. Everything appeared just as she left it. She grabbed a notebook and pencil, sat down at the kitchen table, and tried to collect her thoughts. You're a smart girl, she said to herself. You can figure this out. After all, this wasn't brain surgery. The problem was where to begin?

She tried to consider every angle. But Jesse was not trained in counter-espionage and one very important consideration never entered her mind. It never occurred to her that Ammon's former master would have any interest in her. And though Ammon had warned her to go to the cabin, she never really thought that her life might be in danger.

Seven miles away, in another rented apartment, a man suddenly sat upright in his chair. For the first time in over two weeks he heard what he had been waiting for. Although he hadn't yet heard any voices, he could make out the distinct sound of light footsteps walking down the uncarpeted hallway. He could distinctly hear the sound of a window being opened and then the faint rush of flowing water.

He immediately picked up the telephone and quickly dialed the number.

"Someone's in the apartment," he said in a cool and even voice.

"Is it her?"

"I don't know, I haven't heard any voices. But someone is definitely there. I can hear them walking down the hall. Whoever it is, they don't appear to be in any hurry. It's not like they're rushing around."

"Maybe it's just the landlord," the voice at the other end of the telephone said.

"Maybe so. That's not my problem, is it? I'm just telling you what I know."

"Has he tried to call her again?"

"No. Nothing but that one time. At least he hasn't left any messages on her machine. Lately it has been very quiet. The phone hasn't rung at all for three days."

"Okay. Keep listening." The line went dead.

Within a matter of minutes, a tall, burly man and his middle-aged wife climbed into an old Toyota. The man threw two canvas bags into the back seat, started the engine, and pulled quickly out into traffic on Southwestern Lane. His name was Clyde. His wife's name was Nadine. They were on their way to Jesse's apartment. They had about five miles to travel. It would take them twelve minutes to get there.

Meanwhile, Jesse Morrel sat at her kitchen table. As she doodled on the notepad in front of her, a plan was taking shape in her mind. She knew that the Air Force would know what had happened to Capt Richard Ammon. They would have to know, or at least have some idea. He couldn't just disappear without some sort of investigation. That was where she would begin.

But she also knew that she had no standing. Her marriage to Richard Ammon had never been reported to the military. She was not listed as a dependent on Ammon's records. She wasn't even a beneficiary on his life insurance policy. The only proof she had was the marriage license that had been issued to them from the Justice of the Peace at the white chapel. That was the way Richard had insisted it must be. He wanted no official ties that would lead the Sicherheit to Jesse.

But that was irrelevant now, and Jesse had already decided that, if she needed to, she would use the paper. She would go in and demand the kind of answers any other wife who had lost her husband had the right to demand. But she wasn't ready to do that yet. Maybe later, if Richard didn't reach her, or she didn't get any answers herself. But she would wait a few more days before she pulled out her trump card.

A slight breeze through the open window blew back the thin curtains, waving them gently. Behind where Jesse sat at the kitchen table, the front door stood slightly ajar, allowing the fresh air to circulate through the stale apartment.

Suddenly, she stood up from the table. She shook her head and shivered with unexpected excitement.

What about the mail? She had asked the apartment manager to check her mail! Could it be that Ammon had been able to write her? Maybe he couldn't get to a phone. Perhaps a letter was waiting for her now.

She grabbed her jacket and ran from the apartment, locking the door as she left. She jogged down the sloping sidewalk, and around the corner of the pool house on her way to the manager's office.

When Jesse entered the tidy, oak-paneled office, she was slightly out of breath from her run. Her brown hair tossed about her shoulders as she walked into the room. The manager, a pudgy man with a shiny, bald head, looked up from his small television and visibly brightened. He was glad to see her. She was one of his favorite tenants. He noticed the flush in her cheeks as she stood behind his desk and asked him if she could pick up her mail.

Without getting up, he rolled his chair across the plastic floormat and pulled out a paper sack tucked behind the counter. He handed the sack to Jesse with a smile. Once again, she didn't notice the look in his eye. She was too used to being admired.

She thanked him politely then, without asking permission, spilled the contents of the sack across the office counter. She sorted through the mail quickly. There was nothing there from Richard Ammon.

The manager noticed her shoulders slump. Whatever she was looking for, it obviously was not there. Jesse made no attempt to hide her disappointment, but the manager didn't offer any encouragement. After all, what could he say? He didn't want to be too nosy. Besides, he had already gone through her mail. He knew it was nothing but junk and bills. Nothing to get excited about.

Jesse gathered the mail up and dropped it in the paper sack, then stuffed the sack under her arm. She turned around to leave, hesitating for a moment while she thought. Finally, she faced the manager once again.

"I guess I'll be out of town for a few more days," she said in a quiet voice, not really looking at the man as she spoke. "Would you mind collecting my mail again? I know it's a bother, but I really would appreciate it."

"No problem, Miss Morrel," he replied. "Anything else I can do to help?"

Jesse shook her head and gave the sack back to him, then turned and walked out of his office. The manager wondered for just a moment why she was leaving town again, then decided it was none of his business. He was about to return to "The Price Is Right," when he suddenly remembered.

"Miss Morrel," he called out after her. Jesse stopped at the door and turned around. "While you're here, would you mind if I come with you into your apartment? We are taking an inventory of all the appliances, and I need to get the serial number off of your stove and fridge."

"Oh . . . huh, sure, no problem," Jesse responded, already lost in her thoughts.

Outside Jesse's apartment complex, a gray Toyota pulled in and parked, taking up two parking spaces right next to the dumpster. The middle-aged couple got out and made their way to Jesse's apartment. The woman carried a black, heavy purse. The man finished his cigarette as they walked, then flipped the butt into the gutter. They didn't hesitate or wander through the maze of identical buildings. They knew where they were going. They had been to Jesse's apartment before.

As they rounded the corner of her apartment building, Clyde and Nadine were a little surprised to see Jesse walking toward them. They both recognized her immediately. They had spent hours studying dozens of pictures of her.

But Jesse was not alone. At her side was a short, chubby man dressed in black slacks and a white shirt. The man hopped and skipped along beside her in an effort to keep up with her. As Jesse and the apartment manager approached, neither Clyde nor Nadine said a word. They looked at each other to avoid making eye contact with the girl and didn't slow their pace. Clyde grunted under his breath and Nadine sniffled in reply as they wordlessly communicated their decision. Without hesitation, they passed by the sidewalk that cut off to Jesse's apartment and continued down the path that led to the next building, where they quickly disappeared from view.

As Jesse and the manager walked up to Jesse's apartment, Jesse pulled out a large set of keys. She sorted through the keys slowly, trying to find the right one, while the manager waited patiently by her side. Finally she separated one key from the others, inserted it into the lock and opened the door. Jesse hesitated, then motioned for the manager to follow her inside.

It only took a moment for the manager to get the information and serial numbers that he needed. While he did his work, Jesse waited patiently by the front door. Five minutes after he had entered the apartment, the manager was gone. Jesse didn't take long to follow.

She picked up her duffel bag and purse. Inside the bag, she had everything she would need, so there was no sense in waiting around.

Twenty minutes later, Jesse was leaving the gray air of the L.A. basin. She drove northeast along highway 15, up through the San Gabriel Mountains and on to the high desert plains. This road would eventually take her to Las Vegas. But she wouldn't stop there. Instead, she would continue to drive for another fifteen miles, until she reached Nellis Air Force base, which lay just east of the glittering lights of the city.

Jesse drove quickly through the desert. The dry miles went by in a monotonous blur. She set her cruise control on sixty-nine miles per hour until she crossed the Nevada state line, then pushed the speed up to seventy-four. Traffic was light. She didn't pay much attention to her driving, and she never noticed the gray Toyota that flickered in and out of her rearview mirror.

THIRTEEN

NELLIS AIR FORCE BASE, NEVADA

ALTHOUGH SHE HAD THE ARTICLE PRACTICALLY MEMORIZED, JESSE READ the tiny news item one more time, carefully mulling over each word.

KOREAN FIGHTER LOST IN YELLOW SEA
By Steven Little, *Air Force Times*

Osan Air Force Base, Korea, — The Fifty-First Fighter Wing lost its second F-16 of the year late Wednesday night when a Fighting Falcon abruptly burst into flames and exploded over the Yellow Sea. The pilot, Captain Richard Ammon, was attempting to air refuel with a KC-135 from Kadina AFB, Japan, when the incident occurred.

Despite an intensive search and rescue effort, the downed pilot was never recovered. Late Thursday morning, rescue forces retrieved a life raft that was floating near the crash site. Further rescue efforts were called off when investigators confirmed the raft was from the missing F-16. According to Air Force spokesman Lt Jason White, the accident investigation board is focusing on the possibility of a fuel leak that may have occurred during air refueling. However, he conceded that, due to the lack of physical evidence, plus the fact that pieces of the wreckage were unlikely to ever be recovered, the Air Force may never fully understand what caused the downing of the F-16.

A final accident investigation report is due within thirty days. Meanwhile, the Fifty-First Fighter Wing continues to fly a normal schedule.

Jesse carefully tore the article out of the *Air Force Times* and placed it inside her purse. She stared at the hole that she had torn in the center of the newspaper, then pushed her finger through the two inch opening and out the other side. Too many holes, she thought. There are too many holes in my life.

She was sitting in a small study cubicle in the library at Nellis Air Force Base. The library was small and silent, with only a few airmen quietly studying for their upcoming promotion tests. The metal building occasionally vibrated and rumbled as combat aircraft took off on the runway that was located just one mile away. For the last two days, Jesse had spent most of her time here, scanning all of the publications that she felt might carry the news of any aircraft accident that happened overseas. Then, on the second day, as evening shadows were forming outside, she finally found what she had been searching for.

The article confirmed what Richard had already told her. It was what she had expected from the day he called and left her the code. No one else would ever believe that, but Jesse knew it was true. She had already accepted his disappearance with at least some degree of inner assurance. Someday he would return. He had promised her he would, and she believed him. Of all the people in the world, Jesse trusted Richard the most.

Now the only question left was, what she should do now? She considered for only a moment, then realized she didn't have much of a choice. She would wait. That's all she could do. She would go back to the cabin and wait. At least for a few more days. She really didn't have any choice.

Jesse picked up her purse and thanked the librarian who had been so helpful, then hastily walked out of the lonely building. As she made her way through the parking lot, she heard an awesome thunder. Looking up into the sky, she saw two F-16s taking off into the evening's darkness, their wing tips almost touching as they flew in tight formation. Their afterburners spewed a hot blue flame behind them as they quickly climbed and turned out toward the north. Ten seconds later, they were followed by two more F-16s. It only took a moment for the four fighters to climb and disappear. Jesse stood and watched them as they faded into the darkness, thinking all the time of Richard Ammon. She pictured him inside one of the fighters, his broad shoulders cramped in the tight cockpit, smiling from the pure joy of flight. As she watched the lights from the fighters blend into the starry night sky, she missed him even more. She turned and walked quickly toward her car.

Passing by an old gray Toyota, she heard a voice. The window was rolled down, and a man stuck out his head. "Excuse me, ma'am, can you help me?" he asked. She studied the man for a moment, then cautiously answered.

"What can I do for you?"

Jesse shivered as she looked into the man's eyes. They seemed to stare right through her. She quickly glanced around. By now it was completely dark. The tall lamppost cast dim shadows through the empty parking lot. She glanced toward the library. Not another soul in sight. Jesse's instincts kicked into high gear. She hadn't spent the past ten years in southern California without developing an acute sense of imminent danger. And right then, her instincts were very clear. Something was not right about this man.

"I'm looking for one of the fighter squadrons," the man continued. "An old friend of mine works there. Can you tell me how to get to the F-16 fighter building?"

"I'm new to base myself," Jesse answered cautiously. "Perhaps the security police can help you." The man watched Jesse very closely.

"Yeah, but if you could just show me where we are, then I could probably find it myself." Clyde said, pointing to a map he had laid out across the steering wheel of his car. Jesse didn't move. Clyde shifted anxiously in his seat. It wasn't working. He swore at her under his breath as he caught a whiff of the soaking rag of chloroform that lay in the seat next to him. He glanced across the parking lot to the blue sedan where Nadine sat watching. He was growing anxious. His eyes darted around. He could be patient, but only for so long.

Jesse took a step away from his car. "I don't think I can help you. As I said, it's my first time on base."

The man grunted. Jesse turned and briskly walked away. Heading back toward the library, she jumped up the flight of stairs, taking them three at a time. Glancing over her shoulder, she saw the man's Toyota start to pull away with a kick and sputter. As she pulled on the thick glass doors, she knew he was gone.

Jesse waited in the library, watching the parking lot carefully for any signs of the old gray car. She didn't know why. She shouldn't have been so suspicious. But over the years she had learned to trust her instincts, and so didn't consider it wasting her time.

Half an hour later, she walked quickly to her car and climbed in, locking all of the doors before even starting the engine. Pulling out of the parking lot, she maneuvered onto the main boulevard that would

lead her off base, merged with the traffic, and headed north on Las
Vegas Boulevard.

Weaving in the traffic behind her, in a rented blue sedan, was
Nadine. She always stayed at least three cars behind the red Mazda,
leaving her enough time to change lanes and follow Jesse off the main
highway if her target ever turned. Steering with her left hand, she
reached down onto the seat and picked up a cellular phone.

"I've got her," she said when Clyde answered.

"Where are you?"

"I'm heading north on Las Vegas Boulevard."

"Okay, I'm about five blocks behind you. Don't lose her. I'm
getting tired of chasing this wench!"

Nadine only grunted in reply.

They followed her all through the night, always keeping their
distance, stopping in the shadows when she pulled over for gas, all the
time expecting her to turn back toward L.A., or check into some hotel.
But she didn't. Instead she headed north, toward central California.
By early morning, she was passing through the town of Lone Pine.
Nadine followed her as she turned off the main highway and onto a
small dirt road that headed off into the pine-covered foot hills that lay
at the base of the Inyo mountains. Once Jesse turned off the main
highway, Nadine didn't follow her any further. She didn't need to. She
knew the road couldn't go very far back into the forest. She knew what
Jesse was driving. She knew they could find her.

FOURTEEN

LONE PINE, CALIFORNIA

THE NIGHT AFTER SHE GOT BACK TO THE CABIN, JESSE STAYED UP AND read until after midnight, then finally forced herself to bed. Several hours later, she awoke with a start. It was very dark. The cabin floors creaked and moaned from the wind. She glanced at the digital clock next to her bed. It was blank. The power must be out, she thought. Funny, there hadn't been a storm. She rolled off the mattress and set her feet onto the bare floor. It was very cold. The gas furnace needed starting.

Then she heard it.

Her heart jumped into her throat. Every muscle in her body grew tense. Her heart beat like a hammer as she peered desperately into the darkness.

Then she heard it again.

Voices.

The hushed sound of whispering voices. And footsteps. Muffled footsteps. Very close. From inside the cabin! From outside her door! Her hands involuntarily shot to her mouth as she stifled a scream. The footsteps tapped once again. Measured, careful footsteps. Then silence. The only sound was the blood pumping in her head. It beat in her ears. It smashed in her brain.

The footsteps were right outside her door!

A gentle night breeze blew outside the cabin window as the mountain air raced to the valley floor. Her window shuddered against the breeze. A pine cone dropped on the cabin's roof and rolled down the eaves, pattering lightly as it fell.

Someone was there! She could hear them! They were right outside her door!

Jesse looked to the window. Twelve feet away. Maybe she could make it. Slowly, carefully, she lifted herself off of the bed.

The door burst open. Flying backward, it slammed against the wall. Jesse screamed in the darkness. At what, she didn't know. She couldn't see. It was so dark!

A bright flashlight beamed through the open doorway. The man from the gray Toyota stormed into the room. Jesse screamed again and pushed herself up against the bedroom wall, the rough logs cutting into the soft skin of her back. The man walked toward her, rope in hand, gun in his belt. The flashlight beamed directly on Jesse, spotlighting her like some kind of trapped animal. She pushed herself away from the wall and tried to run, but tripped and fell to her knees. The man was on top of her in less than an instant, his hands wrapping tightly around her thin neck. Jesse closed her eyes and started to cry.

Clyde pinned her against the wood floor while he pulled both of her arms behind her back and shoved them up toward her neck. Jesse felt a tearing pain which sucked the air from her lungs. She knew he would kill her. She thought she was dead.

Jesse felt the rope twist around her wrists and fingers. Nadine held the flashlight so that Clyde could see what he was doing. He circled her wrists and knotted the rope, then sat back with a huff.

"Go out and turn the power back on," Clyde directed Nadine as he stood up and pulled Jesse to her feet. "And bring the extra rope from the car." Nadine turned and walked out of the room.

Within half an hour, they had unloaded the car and hidden it in back of the cabin. Clyde made certain the place was secure, then after some discussion, they decided to leave Jesse in the second bedroom. Clyde threw her onto the bed and tied her up, then nailed the shutters closed and draped a thick quilt over the window to block out the light. He knew that the constant darkness would leave her disoriented and confused and make it that much more difficult to think of escape.

Then he and Nadine settled in for the wait. They would stay up here in the cabin, keeping a watch on the girl. They would wait until they heard from their client. Then they would do what he told them to do.

Jesse lay in the darkness, listening, her eyes tightly closed. Though she wasn't tied up anymore, she didn't dare move. She hardly even dared breathe. A thin blanket had been stretched across her body, but it left her bare feet exposed, and she was icy cold. Time went by. The cabin was very quiet. Perhaps it was night, and they were asleep. After what seemed like a very long time, Jesse pulled her feet inside the blanket, then curled up into a little ball.

The skin around her ankles and wrists had been rubbed raw from the rough nylon ropes. The tender flesh burned and the nerves flashed in pain. Her wrists, which had taken the worst abuse, oozed tiny drops of blood and clear moisture from the open sores. Purple blotches covered the tops of her feet from the broken blood vessels, a result of the blood flow having been cut off by the tightly cinched ropes.

She shivered again under the thin cotton blanket and tried to think. How long had it been since she had been taken captive? She did not know. Five or six days. Maybe less. Maybe more. She had lost all sense of time. As she lay in the darkness, she was only aware of two things—the terrible pain and the fear.

The door opened a crack. Light filtered into the room. Jesse nearly quit breathing. Despite a violent shiver that ran down her spine, she lay perfectly still. The footsteps moved ever closer. She wanted to cry—cry like a little girl.

"How's the girl?" came the voice from the bathroom.

The man studied her face for a few seconds before he answered. "She hasn't moved in the past ten hours," he finally said.

The man paused as he hovered over the bed. He bent down toward her, studying her closed eyes, watching her breathing. He glanced at the open sores around her wrists.

"She's awake though," he called out after a while. "I guess she wants to ignore me." He reached into his pocket and produced a shiny gold lighter and unfiltered cigarette which he lit with a flip of his wrist.

He walked to the window and studied the thick wooden shutters that covered the double-paned glass. He had used three two-by-fours to nail the shutters closed. He grabbed the thick boards and pulled at them, checking to make sure they were still secure.

Turning back toward Jesse, he took several long drags on his cigarette and held the smoke in his chest. What was wrong with the girl?

She had been laying there for almost two days. She wouldn't eat. She didn't move. She hardly even opened her eyes. Stupid wench. What was she going to do? Just lie there and die?

He took another drag on his cigarette. The glow burned down to his lips, and he tossed the smoldering white stub on the floor and stomped it out, smearing the highly polished wood floor with ashes and spit.

He was bored and tired of the cabin. He was tired of the forest and trees. He missed the noise of the city. He missed his friends and his girl. He was tired of his wife. He was tired of guarding this stupid woman who just lay there and slept. It had been too long. He needed more beer.

He paced across the floor to the bed. Jesse hadn't moved. He glanced at his watch. A couple more days. One way or another, in a couple days this job would be through.

BOLLING AIR FORCE BASE, WASHINGTON D.C.

"Did you read the bulletin we sent out a couple days ago about the Ukrainian named Morozov?" Buddy Spencer asked.

Lt Col Oliver Tray didn't answer as he concentrated on the ball. He checked his back foot alignment and tried once again to relax his grip. Align. Align. Back foot slightly forward. Knees slightly bent. Check displacement from the ball. . . .

"It's weird," Buddy cut in once again. "For six years the guy was a ghost. Absolutely invisible. Now suddenly, it's like he's everywhere. I'm telling you, once we started to track him, he showed up all over the freakin' world."

Left arm straight. Head down. Eyes on the ball. Slow, controlled back swing. . . .

"Have you seen any of the bulletin traffic? It's pretty interesting. You ought to take a look at it if you get a chance."

Tray let it go. The ball sailed off over the trees, cutting the par four dog-leg at a near perfect angle. He squinted into the hazy, early winter sun and watched the ball just clear the last stand of pines and drop out of view. Good shot, he smiled to himself. No . . . great shot. Good distance, no hook or slice, right over the left edge of fairway. It was perfect. He lifted his driver onto his right shoulder and turned back to Spencer. "Just like on the tour," he instructed proudly. "You concentrate. You learn to ignore the distractions. There will always be jerks in the crowd."

Spencer laughed and prepared to tee up. It was only the fifth hole and he was already down by three strokes. It was time for combat rules. Next time he would stand so that his shadow fell over Ollie's tee and dance around the box to distract him.

Tray stood in silence while his friend teed off, placing his ball down the middle of the fairway, a nice but conservative shot.

"You're not going to beat me with balls like that," Oliver prodded. "When you're behind to a master, you've got to play a little more aggressively. Haven't you learned that by now?"

"Yeah, yeah, teach me, Oh Master," Buddy lifted his arms over his head in mock adoration. "Let me walk in your footsteps, Oh Great One. So long as you're buying the beer."

Oliver smiled, picked up his clubs, and began to stride down the fairway.

Oliver Tray and Buddy Spencer had been playing golf together for more than three years. They met at the Bolling golf course every other Wednesday afternoon; rain or shine, heat or sleet, if the course was open, then they played. In that time, Spencer had beaten Oliver only three times, but he no longer let it bother him. He had accepted the obvious fact that, unlike his friend, he would never be a scratch golfer.

Besides, the game was not the main reason he and Tray liked to spend a couple of afternoons a month together.

Passing the ladies' marker, they strolled down a small hill toward Buddy's ball which lay two hundred yards in the distance, a tiny speck of white peeking above the tightly cut grass. "Judging from your ball, it's pretty obvious you weren't listening to me," Buddy observed. "So I'll ask you again. Did you read the general bulletin? It was sent toward the end of last week."

Tray thought for a moment. He remembered something about it, but so many things had been happening the past few days, it wasn't something that stuck in his mind. "Yeah, I saw it in our morning message traffic a couple days back. Didn't pay much attention to it. Something you're working on, Buddy?"

"Me and about three hundred other guys. It's really got the CIA rocking. This guy Morozov has developed a fairly large gathering over the past year or so." Spencer paused as he kicked his way through a small clump of wiregrass and cattails that lined the left edge of the fairway, looking for lost balls as he went. "And there's a little more to it than it would first appear," he continued. Oliver nodded with understanding. There always was.

Buddy Spencer, a big man with piercing gray eyes and a large Roman nose, was an intelligence analyst at the CIA; however, for the past five years he had been on loan to the staff of the National Security Office at the White House. Specifically, he headed the Office of CounterIntelligence and Threat Analysis/European Theatre, or CITA/ Europe, as it was called. His department was responsible for advising the National Security Advisor, and thus the President, of the suspected covert/counterintelligence operations ongoing within Europe. It was CITA/Europe's responsibility to glean, pool, sort, and organize all of the unrelated bits of intelligence information about suspected covert operations, speculate and draw conclusions to determine the threat, then present their observations to the President in a timely and accurate daily analysis. Given the sheer volume of work this involved, anyone with any real knowledge of their operation recognized that it was a hopeless task. The crushing mass of information was nearly overwhelming, and to sort through it all and bring it together on a daily basis was much like sticking a high-pressure firehose down your throat in order to get a drink.

This was one of the reasons Buddy Spencer so much enjoyed his time with Lt Col Tray. Their bimonthly games provided him with an outlet; someone to talk to with a different perspective, someone who could relate to the pressures he worked under, someone who understood the subtleties of the intelligence culture. With both men sharing the same interest, as well as a TOP SECRET clearance, it was only normal that their conversations would center on shop.

"So, who is this guy?" Ollie wondered. Instinctively, he looked around them to make certain no one was within hearing distance. They were alone. Not a soul within three hundred yards. That was the beauty of golf.

"Ivan Morozov. He recruits and trains the guys that you're after. Spies. Traitors. That sort of thing. But his real specialty was deep-seeded moles. Young Pioneers, really just young children, were brought into his organization then trained and provided a cover that would allow them to operate undetected within various Western countries until they were needed. He was the head of the Sicherheit until the Soviet Union broke up. Then he more or less disappeared.

"Until last spring. I guess it was about April when we first started to see him around. Now we see him regularly going into and out of Golubev's presidential palace and—"

"Golubev? Yevgeni Oskol Golubev . . . the Ukrainian prime minister?"

"Yes. Yes. See, Morozov—and I didn't know this until fairly recently—but he's Ukrainian. In fact, both of his parents, along with about two million other Ukrainians, were deported by Stalin to Siberia after World War Two, after they were accused of being German sympathizers. I guess the old man figured the whole of Ukraine was a bunch of Nazi bums, and you know Stalin—never afraid of a little overkill. Fact was, of the two million Ukrainians, maybe one percent of them were actual Nazi collaborators.

"Anyway, apparently nothing could have been further from the truth in the Morozov family, for Ivan Morozov has proven a loyal socialist his whole life through. Now he is home, apparently doing much the same thing he has done in the past."

"Interesting . . . I guess," Oliver replied. "But there must be dozens of guys like him out there. So what is it about this fellow that's driving you all so crazy?"

They were approaching Spencer's ball, and Oliver stepped to one side to watch him take his shot. Spencer stared at the flag that fluttered lightly in the even breeze and measured the distance, then pulled out a six iron and stepped over his ball. Without much further consideration, he pulled back and whacked it toward the rolling green. The ball bounced twice then disappeared into a steep bunker. Spencer swore. Oliver handed him his bag of clubs and the two men set out to Oliver's ball, which lay a hundred and twenty yards short of the green.

"What is it about this guy?" Spencer continued in answer to Oliver's question. "Well, it's several things, really. For one thing, he seems to be working on his own. Like some kind of hired gun. He's not listed in any of the official Ukrainian registries as a government employee. He has no official position. Yet, we see him continually with some of the highest officers within the Ukraine, both military and civilian. And outside of the country as well. He shows up here, he shows up there. Last week he was down in Panama with Carlos Salinas just before the guy got knocked off. And he was involved with the transfer of some huge sums of money. Now, doesn't that seem a little odd? I mean, why would the Ukrainians be popping Columbian drugs kings and stealing their money?"

Oliver Tray didn't answer. It did seem kind of strange, but not horribly out of place. It was obvious the guy was up to something, going about his old trade, but with the situation deteriorating so rapidly between Russia and Ukraine, he seriously doubted it was anything to be much concerned about. If this Morozov guy was working again, his target almost certainly was not the United States. Not with almost two million Russian soldiers camping along the Ukrainian border. They, not the U.S., had to be his only concern.

Tray walked up to his ball and studied his lie, then pulled out his eight iron and practiced a couple swings, cutting his club through the drying grass. It was getting late, and the sun was low on the horizon as he squinted toward the flag. The pin had been placed well back on the uneven green, sloping away from the center. He would have to place his ball right on the forward edge of the green and hope for a reasonable roll.

"And get this," Spencer continued once again, disregarding Tray's effort to concentrate on his ball. "This is the real kicker." Tray gave up trying to ignore him and turned to face his friend.

"We're looking back through some of our old files. Going back over the past year, when we find something that's nearly impossible to believe."

Oliver Tray raised his left eyebrow, only half-interested and less than half-listening. He wished his friend would shut up. He wanted to finish the game.

"We found out that Morozov has been in this country," Spencer said. Tray's ears perked up. That was interesting news. "He was here," Spencer continued. "Maybe as many as three times. All within the past year. We've got pictures of him going through customs in L.A. back in June. And a possible ID from a computer search of passports that have come into Dallas. Can you imagine? The guy was here. Now, why do you suppose that might be?"

Tray could hardly believe it. Here! In the U.S.! Now that was far more than merely intriguing. That was worthy of some real thought. Spencer knew his friend would be fascinated by this little piece of information. It was sure to distract him. That's why he told him before he took his shot.

"L.A. and Dallas, huh?" Tray wondered. "Why do you think he entered the country there? Were those cities his final destination in the U.S., or only his port of entry, and then he moved on from there?"

"To be honest, we don't know. We have a few theories. A few ideas, but nothing set in concrete. I'll tell you this, though. He's after some kind of computer technology. Some of the most advanced and cutting-edge stuff. He was posing as a computer technician when he passed through customs in Big-D. We know that because the customs agent made special note when Morozov insisted on hand-carrying his luggage onto the aircraft and asked that it not be X-rayed through the security machines. So, of course the bag had to be searched. The customs official logged the contents as computer equipment, specifically, hard drives and mass storage devices. We have that on record. Morozov left the country with a bag full of twelve-inch computer drives."

Tray nearly dropped his club. His mouth went suddenly dry, as his heart started to race. "And, uh, I don't suppose you know where he went after he left the U.S., do you?" he stammered. "Did he fly to Europe? Where was his flight going to from here?"

Spencer frowned as he thought. Where had Morozov flown to after he left the United States? He remembered and then answered, "He went to Helsinki. Took a direct flight. We lost him after that. Don't know when or how he got back to Kiev."

Tray's mind started racing. Helsinki! Could it be?!

He thought of the stolen computer equipment. He thought of the missing hard drives. He thought of the State Department's investigation into the request from the rogue computer company in Helsinki who wanted to import the aviation simulation programs. Could it only be a coincidence, he wondered. If it was, it wouldn't have been the first time that a promising lead had suddenly turned sour. After all, it was such a big world. There was so much going on. What were the chances that he and Spencer had stumbled on to something? What were the chances that they each held a piece to the puzzle? Probably not very good.

But then again, maybe he was wrong.

Oliver Tray and Buddy Spencer never finished their round of golf. Instead, at Oliver's urging, they left the course immediately, walked the half mile back to the clubhouse, threw their clubs into the back of Spencer's car, and drove quickly over to the USCOM building where they spent the next eight hours in a secure room, comparing notes. At 12:30, they left Tray's office and went home to get a few hours sleep. By five the next morning, they both were back at work, only this time they met at Spencer's cluttered office at the National Security Office.

By midmorning, they had gone over everything no less than five times. Yet, still, they didn't have any answers, or even know if they were asking the right questions. They were like a couple of hounds in the forest, sniffing here, chasing there, circling around a few trees. The best they could hope for was to shake things up a little bit and see what fell out. That was about all they could do.

"Do you think he's coming back?" Oliver asked as he leaned back and sipped at a warm bottle of spring water. "Would he chance another trip to the states?"

Buddy shrugged his shoulders. "Who knows? Hey, we don't even know why he came here in the first place. I reckon that is the key. If we knew what he was after, we might guess if he'd chance coming back."

"We need more surveillance," Oliver muttered. "We need to have people out watching. Every international flight into Dallas and Los Angeles would have to be monitored. Is that even possible? Or is that too much to ask?"

Spencer only smiled. Apparently Lt Col Oliver Tray was not familiar with the power that the National Security Agency held. He picked up his phone and had a talk with his boss, who then had a talk with the watch supervisor. By five o'clock that afternoon, the surveillance was underway. From that time on, every passenger passing through customs in either L.A. or Dallas was secretly photographed on videotape. The video was then sent to the NSA's main office in Washington, D.C., where it was digitized and compressed for easier viewing. The next morning, two young and eager agency interns, both of them college seniors at George Washington University, began the tedious task of viewing the compressed images on computer, looking for Ivan Morozov.

FIFTEEN

THE WHITE HOUSE
WASHINGTON, D.C.

THE NATIONAL SECURITY ADVISOR, MILTON BLAKE, HANDED THE REPORT to the President (code name Backdog) with trembling hands. Blake had had only three hours sleep in the past two and a half days and it was beginning to show. His face was gaunt, and dark puffy flesh surrounded his eyes.

The President took the report from Blake without any comment and began to read.

TO: Backdog (Eyes Only)
 TOP SECRET HUMIT/SATIT/RADIT/RECIT/WINTEL
 one copy only - Destroy in compliance code A

FROM: Grounder NSA (source copy DIA intelligence report 96-1127)

RE: Analysis of Current Russian Affairs

<u>REPORT:</u>
 1-) The Russians are in the third day of the largest military exercise conducted since 1989. Twenty regular army divisions are massed along the Ukrainian border, with three more held in reserve near Shakhty and Kursk. The 32nd Airborne (Black Hogs) along with two motorized

rifle divisions (light) are currently deployed to Yelets. The entire IL-76 fleet is either on the ground in Yelets, or waiting to fly there from their bases in Saransk and Volgda.

Coinciding with this military exercise is an increase in the level and intensity of diplomatic activity. The Russians continue to press the Ukrainians for guarantees of future grain shipments. They claim to have evidence that the Ukrainian government intends to renege on last year's grain contract. They also fear that the Ukrainians will cut off other shipments of agricultural commodities which the Russians need to feed their population.

Fedotov's government has also accused the Ukraine of gross infractions upon the rights of the eleven million Russian citizens that are currently living in the Ukraine. Fedotov has made it clear that he considers the well-being of his citizens threatened, and that his government will take all means necessary to ensure the safety of its foreign-living citizens. In anticipation of war, approximately five hundred thousand Russians have left the Ukraine over the past seven days.

2-) There are unconfirmed reports of covert Spetsial'noye Naznacheniye (Spetznaz) activity taking place behind the Ukraine border. This includes acts of both espionage and sabotage against Ukrainian command, control, and communications (cube 3). At this time these reports are still unconfirmed, but considered extremely likely.

3-) Satellite imagery indicates that the Russians have fueled and armed as many as twelve SS-25 short-range nuclear missiles. The SS-25 can hit any target within the northern Ukraine.

4-) Yesterday marked the deadline imposed by president Fedotov for the former republics to respond to his invitation to join with Russia in the formation of another Union, to be named "The Union of Russian Republics." As of last night, only three former republics (Georgia, Turkmenistan, and Belarus) have agreed to join the new Union.

5-) The Russian Ambassador to the United States, Evgenii Penza Yaroslavl, was recalled for consultation early this morning. He has refused to leave his post and return to Russia. Fedotov has just announced Yaroslavl's dismissal and will name his replacement by early this afternoon.

6-) Once again, president Fedotov has refused the offer of both the United States and the United Nations to act as mediators in his dispute with the Ukraine. In addition, he has warned the Polish and French peacekeeping units that are presently along the Ukrainian border to leave the theater, or be considered hostile combatants. As of this writing (2100 Zulu, 1600 Local EST), Fedotov has ignored all attempts at communication, through both the American Ambassador to Russia as well as the newly established Direct Military Communication Lines (DMCL).

7-) The Ukrainian Ambassador to the United States has once again asked for guarantees of protection under the "Friends of NATO" agreement. He has also asked the United Nations Security Council to authorize pre-emptive air strikes against the Russian short-range nuclear missile sites, as well as their artillery and rocket positions along the Ukrainian border.

8-) REFORGER (preparations for the Defense of Allies in Europe) has begun. Air Force assets, including five fighter wings and three ground attack squadrons, are currently deploying to their forward operating locations in Germany, Italy, and England. The New Rapid Deployment Force (NRDF), as well as five regular army divisions are also enroute to the European theatre. All military family members and dependents living within any areas considered as "probable of action" have been ordered home. Civilian airline carriers are augmenting the evacuation of dependents from the zone.

ANALYSES:

1-) We expect the Russian forces to move across the Ukrainian border within the next 24–48 hours. The ground invasion will be preceded by an intensive air and artillery campaign to soften the Ukrainian defensive positions. This campaign could begin within the next twelve hours.

In the long run, Russian military forces are strong enough to defeat the Ukrainian forces, although victory is not necessarily guaranteed. DIA estimates indicate Fedotov could have control of the nation's major cities and military installations within 30–45 days, if he is willing to commit to an aggressive frontal assault. Estimated losses to Russian forces under such a scenario are in the range of 25–32%. (See DIA analysis 95-0914:45.)

2-) Fedotov is clearly considering the nuclear option as a way of retaining his forces. A quick, surgical nuclear strike against selected Ukrainian targets and troop positions may be the only way he can reduce his combat casualties to an acceptable level. The refueling and forward deployment of his SS-25s provide him with the short-range capability for just such an attack. If, as we speculate, Fedotov intends to initiate hostilities against the former Warsaw Pact nations, then the nuclear option may be the only way to retain his forces for such a western campaign.

3-) The Black Hogs and their associated light rifle divisions are slated against the Black Sea fleet in Sevastopol. The Black Sea fleet has always been a thorn of contention between the Ukraine and Russia. After four years of intense negotiations, the two countries came up with what would seem to be a completely unworkable agreement. The treaty that was signed last spring not only invited future disagreements, it guaranteed them. We anticipate that the airborne Black Hogs will initiate their attack at Sevastopol and have control of the port city and the Black Sea fleet within seven to ten days of landing. They would then be in a position to push to the northeast, pinching the Ukrainian forces in a piercing maneuver.

4-) The nuclear breakout with the SS-18 and SS-24 missiles was clearly designed to send a message to the West. By bringing the long range SS-18/SS-24 missiles back on line, President Fedotov has given himself a long-range, precision-attack option against targets in the United States and western Europe that was unavailable to him before.

5-) The small peacekeeping forces that are in position to monitor the border between the Ukraine and Russia will not act as a deterrent against a Russian invasion.

6-) The dismissal of the Russian Ambassador and Fedotov's quick action to replace him indicates an ever widening gulf between Fedotov's right wing government and the small number of moderates who managed to survive Fedotov's purge. With Yaroslavl's departure, president Fedotov has silenced the last strong voice of moderation within the Kremlin.

7-) Although Fedotov's claim that the Ukraine is trying to starve the Russian people has zero credibility, the argument has not surprisingly, been embraced by some world nations. Most notably, the North Koreans have offered to ship the Russians rice in exchange for nuclear materials to make additional weapons. China has also tendered offers of trade, as have Iraq, Iran, India, and Japan.

CONCLUSION:

President Fedotov is about to invade the Ukraine. He has made clear his intention to rebuild the former Soviet Union, and we expect that the southern republics will be next, followed closely by the Baltics and then Moldavia and Belorussia.

Fedotov is not intimidated by the West. He sees the conflict between Russia and the near-far republics as a purely internal affair, one in which neither the United States, nor any western country, has any interest or right to interfere. He is betting his future, as well as his military forces', that the U.S. is not willing to become involved in a long and bloody conflict in order to defend a former Russian republic.

That he would consider a limited nuclear strike to preserve his forces is a possibility that must be taken seriously.

In addition, we must seriously consider his apparent willingness to engage in a major East/West nuclear exchange in order to keep western forces at bay. Judging by what we have seen, Fedotov means what he says and doesn't play games.

The current national isolationist mood in which we find ourselves, plus the lack of any historic, cultural, or economic ties to the Ukraine, leave us very little room in which to operate. It would be politically impossible for the United States to intervene directly in a conventional battle. Military action would certainly lack any public support. The Joint Chiefs of Staff have voiced their strong opposition to committing any U.S. forces to an area of little national interest. In addition, they have determined that as many as 600,000 troops would be required to assist the Ukraine in any meaningful way.

And should Fedotov exercise the nuclear option, the above arguments against interference are not eroded, but rather strengthened, for the question then becomes, do we risk geothermal nuclear war to avenge the Ukraine against a limited nuclear strike?

Given the current situation, it is my opinion that there is little we can do to stop the invasion of the Ukraine, and instead, we should continue to focus our efforts on protecting our allies in central and western Europe.

Thomas Allen read through the report once, then turned back to reread the analysis and conclusion. Laying the report by his side, he slumped back in his chair, shoulders sagging, his face taut and strained, his eyes bloodshot, a heavy stubble spread across his even chin. The President remained silent for a very long time, his eyes cast downward as he studied the pattern in the dark blue rug that covered the Oval Office floor.

"Do you really believe Fedotov might go nuclear on this thing?" he finally asked.

Milton Blake's eyes wandered uncomfortably around the room before fixing on the President's desk. He shifted anxiously in his chair and cocked his head to one side as he considered. "Sir, I really don't know. I don't think anyone knows, perhaps not even Fedotov himself. But I will tell you this—it is my gut feeling after watching the man, that if there were any national leader in the past fifty years who seemed willing to use nuclear weapons, Fedotov is that man."

The President grunted and looked at the floor.

"Well then, let's get the remainder of the National Security team in here." The other members had been gathering outside the Oval Office while the President and the National Security Advisor completed their private conference. Blake immediately stood up to open the door.

Three hours later, the United States military was taken to DEFCON BRAVO and its enormous war machine was slipped into high gear. REFORGER was doubled in pace. Across Europe, combat aircraft were put on alert. Reconnaissance aircraft began a constant watch of Eastern Europe. In the United States, B-1 and B-52 bombers were loaded with weapons and pre-positioned to the end of their runways. KC-135 and KC-10 air refuelers were loaded with thousands of tons of jet fuel and also put on alert. ICBM missile crews were advised of the DEFCON BRAVO. The space shuttle Endeavor was quietly loaded with a top-secret payload, and her launch date moved up by two weeks. Five Typhoon-class nuclear missile carrying submarines and four aircraft carriers left their port in Norfolk, Virginia, and began to make their way across the Atlantic. The subs set their course to the northeast, toward the Arctic; the carriers steamed on a more east-wardly heading as they sailed toward the Mediterranean and Aegean Seas. The U.S. Sixth Fleet, based in Naples, sent out two dozen of her own warships to help escort the carrier groups. Meanwhile, back in Philadelphia, tens of thousands of Army and Marine soldiers began to climb aboard the cavernous transports that would take them overseas.

SIXTEEN

McCONNELL AIR FORCE BASE, KANSAS

LT COLONEL TRUMAN SMITH CLIMBED INTO HIS DARK BLUE AIR FORCE staff car and set out for the flightline. He pulled through the restricted area gates and out onto the aircraft parking area. His squadron was about to launch a four-ship formation of B-1s on their way to England for a three-week deployment, and Smith wanted to watch them take off. He pulled his government car out and onto the taxiway and parked on the soft grass that lined it. He was only about forty feet from where the B-1s would taxi by. As he slowed his car to a stop, a security police van immediately pulled up beside him. The two cops eyed Smith suspiciously, then one of them noticed the flightline badge that was hanging from his rearview mirror which authorized Smith to drive his government car anywhere on the flightline. When the cops were satisfied that he wasn't out of order, they gave a quick salute then drove on.

Just then, Smith could see his Thunders begin to pull out of their parking spots. The leader of the formation pulled out first, followed quickly by each of the other three aircraft in the formation. Smith watched the horizontal stabilizer and rudder hinges move on each aircraft as the pilots did a final flight control check. As the B-1s moved closer to where Smith was parked, he could see the pilots through the thick, brown-tinted windscreens. He gave each pilot a thumbs up, but none of them noticed him as they taxied by.

It only took the B-1s five minutes to taxi to the end of the runway and complete their final take off checks. Truman Smith switched his brick over to the control tower frequency so that he could listen to the formation as they took off, turning to the frequency just as the flight was checking in.

"Thunder Flight, check," lead said over the radio.

"Two."

"Three."

"Four."

All of the aircraft in the formation responded with only their number, each of the pilot's voices sounding short and crisp over the radio. That was all flight lead had expected to hear. By responding with only their number, they were telling their leader they were ready to go.

"Tower, Thunder Flight is number one holding short of the runway, ready to go," flight lead broadcast over the radio to McConnell tower.

"Thunder Flight, fly runway heading, climb and maintain the block four thousand to five thousand, you're cleared for take off, change to departure," the tower controller replied.

"Thunder Flight is cleared for take off. Thunders push button three," lead called back. By telling his flight to "push button three," lead had directed them to change their radios over to departure frequency. Lt Colonel Smith switched his radio at the same time.

Flight lead would now have to check in his flight over the new radio frequency. He would want to make certain that all of the Bones in his flight were talking on the same channel. It wouldn't do to have them scattered all over the radio spectrum, unable to communicate with each other.

"Thunder Flight, check," lead said simply.

"Two."

"Three."

"Four."

The other Bones came back quickly. It wasn't until then that the lead B-1 began to taxi out onto the runway. He turned and aligned his aircraft with the runway, then pushed all four of his throttles up into full afterburner. Behind the engines, a light blue flame sprouted and then grew, extending back almost to the B-1's tail. The four GE-101 engines let out an incredible roar as enormous volumes of air were sucked into the engines. Spinning vertices, like miniature tornadoes, funneled out and in front of the huge air intakes and danced along the ground in front of the engines. The tiny tornadoes packed enough power to lift a man and suck him into the engine in less than a fraction of a second. It had happened before. Several years before, some maintenance guy had wandered too close to the engines, got sucked down the intake, and was instantly vaporized into smoke and white ash. All in all, it was a lousy way to die. Painless, but without much glory.

Up in the cockpit, the pilot let his engines stabilize for only a second, then released his brakes and started to accelerate rapidly down the long runway. As he began to move, the second Bone taxied forward, pushing his throttles into afterburner to begin his take off roll behind his leader.

The radios sprang to life.

"Thunder Flight, this is McConnell tower on guard. Abort. Abort. Abort. I say again. Thunder Flight, this is McConnell tower on guard. Abort. Abort. Abort."

Immediately the pilot in the lead B-1 slammed his four throttles back to idle. He was already traveling at over one hundred and forty miles an hour, and now he had to stop the 400,000 pound aircraft before it reached the end of the runway. He extended his speed brakes to full deflection then began to press down on the brakes. Two thousand feet behind him, number two had already done the same thing. The computerized antiskid braking systems immediately slowed the massive aircraft to a comfortable pace. It wasn't until then the pilot got on the radios.

"Thunder Flight, push button two." They all responded immediately, and ten seconds later they had all checked in back on the tower frequency.

"Tower, this is Thunder lead. What the devil's going on? And this better be good." The lead B-1 was just slowing to taxi speed as he turned onto the last taxiway at the end of the airfield. Three other B-1s were following him in tow.

"Thunder Flight, unable to explain at this time. You are directed to return to your parking spot and shut down. Alpha will meet you there." Inside the lead B-1, the pilot muttered and stole a quick glance toward his copilot.

Alpha was the call sign for the wing commander. The head honcho. The big cheese. He was the one-star general who was in command of the entire wing. The very mention of Alpha made every crew member aboard the four B-1s begin to sweat. All of them had to seriously wonder. Whatever was happening, it wasn't something small.

Lt Colonel Truman Smith listened to the tower's explanation, then dropped his car into gear and began to accelerate across the open tarmac. Driving with his left hand, he reached down with his right and switched his radio over to the command post frequency. The squawk of an electronically scrambled conversation immediately filled the air. The command post had turned their radios over to "magic," the secure voice network that scrambled their conversations so that they could talk classified information over the radio. Smith flipped a small switch on the side of his radio, then entered a five digit code on the keypad. The descrambler on his radio was immediately activated, and the noise of the squawking ducks was replaced by an understandable conversation. Smith only caught the tail end of what was being said, but it was enough to let him know that his B-1s had been recalled by Headquarters, Air Combat Command. A stop-launch and general aircraft recall was standard procedure when the Department of Defense went to a higher state of alert.

Racing across the cement airfield tarmac, dodging between rows of parked jets, Smith steered toward the Operations Center. Parking in front of the wing headquarters, Smith ran through the double steel doors of the Ops Center, flashing his security badge as he passed the sentry, and trotted into the battle staff room. There he encountered the chaos. The room was packed with senior officers and rolling with noise. Everyone seemed to be yelling, either to each other or into a phone. Smith stepped to the side and stood for a moment in the semi-darkness, allowing his eyes to adjust to the dim light. Glancing toward the current status board, he read their current war tasking and a quick shiver ran down his spine.

They had been given the order. Preparations had already begun.

Within three hours, all of the B-1s in Lt Colonel Smith's squadron had been towed to the alert parking area, where they were immediately surrounded by men with machine guns and guard dogs. Circling the alert ramp were multiple layers of high-voltage electric fences, laser detectors, and motion sensors, all designed to provide the aircraft with the tightest security in the world.

Then the weapons experts and maintenance crews went to work. For the next fifty-six hours, they scrambled to load each aircraft with a deadly combination of nuclear missiles and the latest generation of smart bombs. By the time their work was complete, the weapons tucked inside a single B-1 represented far more destructive firepower than any other weapon on earth.

SEVENTEEN

PASHITA 87
OVER SOUTHERN UKRAINE

THE ENLISTED MEN INSIDE AIRCRAFT NUMBER 8-0564 WERE YOUNG
and brutal by training and nature. They were Asiatics, hard men from
far eastern Siberia and the northern republics. Human suffering was
no mystery to them, for it had hardened the minds and hearts of their
people for the past thousand years. The officers, culled from elite
Russian units and thoroughly trained for this special duty, were some
of the best warriors Russia had ever produced. They were intelligent
and demanding and, teamed with the brutal Asiatics, they made a
frightening combat team.

The interior of the Russian IL-76 transport was illuminated only by
two small green lights, one on each end of the troop compartment.
Inside the cabin, the seventy-five fully equipped warrior soldiers sat on
the thin nylon-webbed seats that stretched along both sides of the
aircraft, packs at their feet, AK-47 machine guns across their laps.
Tight parachutes were strapped across their chests, and as they flew
inbound to the Drop Zone (DZ), they continually checked each
other's rigging to make sure that everything was in order. The men's
faces had been painted black and gray to merge with the night shadows. None of them wore any rank or insignia on their uniforms. Only

small silhouette of a black hog sewn across each of their shoulders identified the unit.

The Ninth Airborne Division. The Black Hogs. The most battle-hardened troops the Russians had to offer.

If the Ukrainians had suspected that the Black Hogs would be held in reserve to battle across the Ukrainian border-front, they were mistaken. In a brilliant move by Fedotov, the Hogs had been ordered to attack the port city of Sevastopol, home of the Black Sea fleet, prize of the Ukrainian navy. From there, the Hogs, along with six reinforcement divisions, would begin to battle northward toward the main battle group that would then be pouring across the Ukrainian border.

It was 0200 hours. In fifteen minutes, they would be over the DZ. Ural Moon would be one of the first aircraft to fly over the target in a finely orchestrated plan of flying aircraft, falling men, and parachuting machinery and equipment. Two hundred twenty-six aircraft would fly over the exact same piece of earth within just seventeen minutes of each other.

The Russians anticipated a significant number of casualties even before the invasion got into full swing. A midair collision between some of the transports was almost inevitable. Some soldiers would parachute out of an aircraft, only to have another transport fly through the clutter of descending men. There would also be parachute failures. As a statistical average, .05 percent of the seventeen thousand Russian soldiers to jump would have a parachute that failed to open. And finally, there was the possibility of becoming a "buterbrod krovi", or "blood sandwich". That was what the paratroopers called it when a tank or armored personnel carrier descended by its parachute silently out of the pitch black sky to land on an unwary soldier, crushing him into the ground.

As the IL-76 proceeded inbound to the DZ, the two pilots and the radar navigator in the cockpit were carefully watching their radar screens. They were the eighth aircraft in a ten-ship formation that stretched out in a long trail at twenty-two thousand feet. Each transport was stacked two hundred feet above their leader in an effort to ensure that they wouldn't hit any of the preceding paratroopers who had jumped seconds earlier.

This jump was going to be a HALO, or High Altitude, Low Opening. The paratroopers would cast themselves from the aircraft and free fall to 2,000 feet before they would pull on the D-ring that hung at their chest to open their parachutes. This would allow the transports to stay above and out of the range of most of the anti-aircraft fire, while at the same time, allowing the paratroopers to descend very quickly into the DZ. Another reason that the paratroopers would wait until they were very low before popping their chutes was the fact that if they opened their parachutes from a high altitude, the winds aloft would carry them for miles, spreading men and equipment all over the city of Sevastopol.

HALOs had many tactical advantages, but they were not perfect. Perhaps the worst thing about them was that they left the formation of lumbering transports exposed to any surface-to-air missiles or fighter aircraft that might be protecting the target.

But that wasn't supposed to be a problem tonight. Russian military intelligence had reported that the Ukrainians had moved almost all of their fighters and most of their army forward to guard the Ukrainian border. The Ukrainians apparently never suspected that the Russians would make a move for the Black Sea fleet or Sevastopol on the first night of the conflict. Russian intelligence had gone to great lengths to assure the Black Hog commanders, as well as the IL-76 aircrews, that the Ukrainians would be wholly unprepared to defend the target.

When the Ural Moon was three minutes from the DZ, the jump-master illuminated a red light. Immediately, the men stood up and donned their combat packs. Ahead of them, another formation of transports began to drop their load of light tanks, armored personnel carriers, and small trucks. The men of Ural Moon wouldn't jump until all of that heavy battle equipment was safely below them.

Everything was quiet aboard the Ural Moon. They were only two minutes out from the DZ. The pilots concentrated on maintaining their position in the formation. The jumpmaster readied his men.

Suddenly, tiny yellow lights began to flicker all over the radarscope. High-pitched warbles screamed in the pilots' ears to warn them of multiple missile launches. Huge plumes of smoke and fire emanated from the SA-6, SA-2, and SA-10 missile sites as they came to life. The pilots watched in terror as the missiles arched upward at nearly four times the speed of sound.

Something wasn't right. There were far too many missiles. How could their intelligence have so badly underestimated the number of missiles that were protecting Sevastopol? As the pilots watched the spectacular display, they both swore under their breath and vowed revenge upon their intelligence officers.

The navigator didn't have a window, but he watched his combat radar screen as a small dot, very bright and incredibly fast, homed in on the lead aircraft in their formation. The two lights merged and blipped and then disappeared from the screen. For just a second, the navigator wondered what it would feel like to suddenly be falling from the sky. He thought of his good friend, Oleh Demyanov, who was in the lead aircraft that had just been blown to pieces, and in his heart he said a quick good-bye.

Missiles and aircraft were beginning to scatter all around him. Some of the aircraft in the formation were starting to turn away from the target, but the crew inside the Ural Moon were determined to hold their position. They were now only ninety seconds out from the DZ.

Ninety seconds to hold their position. Ninety seconds to maintain a constant heading and altitude, despite the fact that white trails of explosive missiles were tracking in on their targets. Ninety seconds of terror and fire, screaming radios and exploding aircraft, white missiles and falling debris.

The pilots in Ural Moon saw another missile as it impacted the fourth aircraft in the formation. The explosion illuminated their faces with its brazen white light. In the flash, the pilots could clearly see bodies falling through the sky. They watched the stricken IL-76 pull violently upward as it spun and twirled out of control. As the aircraft climbed and turned, it nicked the wing of the transport that was flying directly behind it, sending them both into a fiery dive.

Another missile exploded right next to the third aircraft. And that was it. The integrity of the formation was completely destroyed. Like a huge flock of lumbering vultures, the IL-76s began to scatter in every direction.

The result was chaos. Two IL-76s below the Ural Moon collided as they both turned and dove for the ground. Others began to spit their paratroopers out so early that they had no chance of landing in the DZ. Instead the soldiers would find themselves on the ground, outside of the perimeter of their friendly forces.

The Ural Moon was the only aircraft within the formation that continued to fly in position. It was now only thirty seconds from the DZ. In the back of the aircraft, the jumpmaster was getting ready to open the two huge clamshell doors that would allow the soldiers to jump out in rows of four. The paratroopers were all standing, holding to the sides of the aircraft, ready to jump in a gaggle of flailing arms and blowing air.

Then the pilots saw another missile approach. They watched in terror as it homed in on their aircraft, already climbing through six thousand feet and accelerating upward at an incredible speed. The pilot at the controls reacted instinctively as he threw the aircraft into a sharp, turning dive. He turned the transport toward the oncoming missile, trying to give it the smallest possible radar return to home in on. He pulled his four engines back to idle as his aircraft built up speed in the dive. The nose of the IL-76 was pointed directly at the missile, which was now closing at over 2,000 feet per second. To the pilot, it looked like a flaming telephone pole. Just as the missile was about to impact the transport, the pilot pushed over once again and then pulled back hard on the yoke. The aircraft's nose tracked violently down and then up, forcing the aircraft to porpoise through the cold air.

But it worked. The missile sped on by them, arching upward into the night sky before its rocket engine depleted its fuel. The warhead exploded harmlessly in the air, six thousand feet above its intended target.

The pilot let out his breath, and relaxed his death grip on the control stick. They had defeated the missile. He could hardly believe it was true.

They were now only fifteen seconds out from the DZ. Although they were much lower than they were supposed to be, they were still in a position to drop. In his headset, the pilot heard the jumpmaster counting down to his paratroopers. In seconds they would be falling from the sky.

Suddenly, there was a shattering explosion as the air boiled around them, then the noise of metal wrenching apart. A tearing sound filled the air and penetrated the cockpit, emitted from the bowels of the aircraft with a long and terrible groan. The pilot instinctively screamed. He knew he was dead. Another surface-to-air missile, this one unseen, had exploded just thirty feet from the left wing. The Ural Moon immediately rolled onto her back, a result of the enormous aerodynamic forces that were exerted upon her as her left wing shattered and then abruptly separated from the fuselage. For just a fraction of a second, the aircraft flew backward and upside down before it began to roll and spin violently toward the earth.

Inside the troop compartment, most of the seventy-five soldiers were thrown against the walls and ceiling of the aircraft by the centrifugal force. Their knees buckled and their arms were pinned to their sides. They could hear and feel the structure of the IL-76 bend and twist as the aircraft tumbled through the air. A gaping hole was ripped along the left side of the aircraft where the wing root used to be. A violent wind filled the cabin with a horrible noise. Discipline and order were quickly replaced by a dark despair.

A handful of lucky soldiers were sucked out of the aircraft and into the night sky where they could safely descend in their parachutes to the marshlands below. A few more pushed themselves out of the already open door, fighting against the centrifugal G-forces that were trying to pin them inside. But most of the paratroopers rode with the Ural Moon as she spun to the ground, howling and scratching at the darkness as they fell.

The Ural Moon impacted the side of a small hill and burst into flames. Within minutes, the only recognizable part of aircraft number 8-0564 was the core of its four jet engines. Everything else, from the composite structural spines to the pilot's seats, was melted into a semi-fluid aluminum goo. Eighty-thousand pounds of burning jet fuel would do that to an aircraft. Inside the wreckage, only a few skeletal remains and charred weapons would ever be recovered.

No accident investigation board or review panel would ever be convened to determine what had caused the deaths of so many men. No one would ever try to identify the human remains or give them a proper burial. Instead, the wreckage was bulldozed into a large pit and then covered up, along with a burned-out tank and some unexploded ordinance that was discovered nearby. The exact location of the pit was forgotten. Such was the indignity of death during war.

Huge searchlights illuminated the sky over Sevastopol as thousands of Russian paratroopers descended onto the airfield. White and blue tracers arced upward to meet the descending paratroopers, making them easy targets for the Ukrainian forces. Although there was some question in the minds of a few of the Ukrainian officers as to the legality of firing upon an enemy soldier who was still descending in a parachute, none of them considered withholding their fire.

So the Ukrainian ground forces continued to light up the sky as they fired upon the descending paratroopers, while their missile batteries sent salvo after salvo of missiles up into the darkness. An occasional explosion encouraged them onward as they fired upon the transports that flew four miles above their heads.

But in the end, it didn't make all that much difference. The Ukrainians were wholly unprepared, and thus were outnumbered, out-trained, and outgunned. Within twelve hours, seventeen thousand Russian paratroopers were on the ground in Sevastopol. The Russians quickly secured a defensive parameter around the airfield. Further reinforcements were quickly flown in. Within a day, more than thirty thousand Russian soldiers, along with their armor and equipment, were grouping into squads and regiments along the outskirts of the city. Within fifty-six hours, the Ukrainian port commander was forced to surrender what remained of his defensive forces. The Sevastopol operation would go down as one of the largest and most successful aerial assaults in the history of modern day war.

The Russians soldiers continued pouring in—the line of holding Russian IL-76 transports stretched through the sky for twenty miles as the aircraft waited their turn to land at the captured base and unload their troops and equipment. The Black Hogs began to fan out through the city, taking control of the area's major communication lines, power supplies, radio and television stations, industrial centers, and military facilities. Terror fell upon the port city like a dark winter snow—heavy and bitter and cold. The streets ran red with the blood of cowering civilians and poorly trained home-soldiers who were hopelessly attempting to protect their families and homes. The captured Ukrainian troops, what few there were, were taken to the rusty docks that lined the Black Sea and loaded onto transport ships, which acted as POW holding facilities. There, the officers were separated from the enlisted. Late in the night on the second day of the invasion, the officers were loaded into the back of transport trucks, taken out to the country and shot twice in the head. Their bodies were then burned in mass crematoriums made of huge pits of burning oil.

Throughout the city, Russian soldiers began to enjoy the spoils of war. Russian officers looked away as their men raped and plundered with abandon, a reward for a job well done. The Hogs knew that they only had a few days to pillage the city before they would battle again, and they sought to take advantage of the opportunity in a violent and brutal way.

Soon, they would begin their long and deadly march northeastward—toward the mass of Ukrainian soldiers that were waiting for them along the five-hundred-mile stretch of Russian front. Moving across the unprotected belly of the Ukraine, they would attempt to meet up with other divisions of Russian ground troops that were even now battling their way across the heavily defended border. Approaching from the enemy's rear, they hoped to pin them from two sides, wedging the outgunned Ukrainian forces in a crushing vice.

As the Hogs were landing in Sevastopol, one thousand kilometers to the north, along the Ukrainian border, the war raged in full force. Twenty Russian divisions, along with their tanks and field artillery, hacked at the Ukrainian forces in a coordinated land-air attack. Supported by waves of supersonic fighters and thousands of crushing 120 millimeter guns, the Russian soldiers pounded soft spots along the Ukrainian front. Batteries of deadly, multiple-rocket-launchers and hundreds of laser-guided rockets fired from attack helicopters rained exploding metal upon the hunkered-down defensive forces. Thirty kilometers behind the front, two thousand Russian T-80 tanks waited for any opening, prodding for any hint of a weakness, pushing at every fracture, in hopes of punching a hole through the enemy lines.

E I G H T E E N

HELSINKI, FINLAND

ANDREI LISKI, THE UKRAINIAN DIRECTOR OF STATE BORDER DEFENSE, opened the door into Richard Ammon's room without knocking, then walked silently over to sit on a black metal chair. The room was a small cubicle built from gray cinder block and white cement. Besides the black chair, the only other furniture in the room was a short bed and the small wooden desk where Ammon sat reading.

Ammon immediately recognized him as one of the four Ukrainians he had been introduced to that first night in the cabin. He was so frail. So droopy and thin. Ammon remembered him well.

Neither man spoke for a moment as Liski surveyed Ammon's sparsely furnished room. From where he was sitting, he could touch the foot of Ammon's bed, and he reached over to push on the bed springs, as if to test them for comfort and strength. After compressing the bed several times, he smoothed out the covers, then turned to Richard Ammon.

"Have you found everything to your liking so far?" he asked. "We want you to be as comfortable as possible."

Ammon couldn't tell if Liski was serious, or just trying to make light of his obviously uncomfortable living conditions. Ammon studied Liski for a moment before he answered. The expression on Liski's face didn't change, and Ammon decided he probably wasn't the kind of man who sported a great sense of humor. He decided to keep his answer simple. "Everything is fine," was all he said.

Liski pointed to the huge manual that was laying on top of Ammon's desk and then asked, "Do you feel that you have enough information now? Or is there something else we could get you?"

Richard turned back to the manual and thumbed through the pages as he considered the question. The book was almost three inches thick, and full of charts, graphs, and very small print. It was the manufacturer's flight manual for the Rockwell B-1 bomber. It told the pilot everything he needed to know in order to safely fly the B-1 and use all of its systems. There were more than two thousand pages in the manual, and everything in it was critical. Ammon flipped the book closed with a heavy thump, then turned back to face his unwelcome visitor.

"I think you have given me what I need," he said. "But I'll tell you right now, it's apparent you guys haven't done your homework on this one. I have found a problem that was obviously overlooked, and it isn't some insignificant detail. It could cause a real kink in our plans."

Andrei Liski continued to stare at Ammon, his eyes unblinking, his face revealing nothing as he thought.

"What do you feel is the problem?" Liski asked.

"Very simply, we won't have enough fuel," Ammon replied. "I've been going over the fuel charts and it just doesn't add up. Even if we assume that we get a B-1 that is fully loaded with fuel, including an auxiliary tank in the forward weapons bay, that still isn't enough gas to make it to Russia. Now if you consider the high fuel burn rates that we will use in combat, lighting our afterburners and maneuvering down low, I figure we will flame out just about a thousand miles short of the Strait of Gibraltar. That's a long way from our targets in Russia. It would appear that your planners have screwed this one up."

For the first time Liski smiled.

"Mr. Ammon," he said, pushing back a strand of hair before rubbing his hands on his pants, "do you really think we could have made such a critical mistake? I think you should give us a bit more credit than that." His voice was sarcastic and hard.

Ammon realized that Liski had taken his remarks as a personal insult. He also realized that it wouldn't help him to anger this man.

"Will you tell me then how we will get enough fuel for the mission?"

Liski's response was immediate. "Yes, Mr. Ammon, I will tell you. But not now. Just be assured, we do have a plan and we know what we're doing. We have been in this business a very long time.

"And keep this in mind as well, Mr. Ammon, because it is important for you to understand. I personally couldn't care less whether you live to see the light of day. Your personal safety is of no concern to me. Still, I will be praying for you to succeed. You see, we have to have the aircraft. We absolutely have to have it. If you die, we all have failed. The whole thing is over for us, too. So peace to your mind, Mr. Ammon, we haven't screwed up the plan."

After a short pause, Liski continued. "When will you and Morozov be ready?" he asked intently.

Richard turned back to his desk. Once again he thumbed through the two thousand pages of his flight manual. He considered the lack of success that he and Morozov had been having so far in the simulator. He thought of his old buddies flying F-16s, and how easily they could blast a B-1 from the sky unless it were flown by a highly trained and experienced crew. He thought of the Migs and the other Russian fighters, some of the best in the world. He thought for a very long moment before he answered Liski's question.

"Three months," Ammon said matter-of-factly. "If you want us to have a better than fifty-fifty chance, you've got to give us at least three months. Anything less, and you'll never see your B-1 over Russia. We'll never even make it out of United States' airspace. All you'll have is wreckage scattered across the west Texas prairie, because that is as far as we'll get without time to prepare."

Andrei Liski pushed back his hair once again.

"It has started in Russia," he said calmly. "You only have a few days left to prepare."

Ammon's jaw dropped.

"We won't be ready," he said matter-of-factly while looking Liski straight in the eye.

"Be ready," Liski said. His face was as expressionless as before.

Ammon rose up in his chair. "No!" he said. "No! We will not be ready. Do you think that just by saying the words, suddenly everything changes? Do you think this situation is that much under your control? Look at what you are saying! Look at what you want us to do!" Ammon reached beside him to pick up a set of flying charts and threw them toward Liski, dropping them square in his lap. "Look at these charts!" he commanded. "You are sending us into the very heart of Russia! Novomoskovsk, Razayevka, Buturkinoovka! We must penetrate thousands of kilometers behind enemy lines! It would be like the Russians attacking St. Louis. And good as the B-1 is, it isn't invisible. Nothing is. They will know we are there. They will be chasing us down. After all, that is the thrust of your plan. For us to be seen. For the Russians to know they are under attack so they will be forced to respond.

"So don't sit there and pretend that by just saying 'Go,' suddenly things will just drop into place. We need time. We need more training, or simply put, this mission is screwed."

Liski watched Ammon settle back into his chair. "Sometimes, Mr. Ammon, we do what we're told, even though it may not be what we like. And, yes, I think that I do have control, for when I say go, you will go. I thought that was something which you understood?"

Ammon didn't reply. He sat speechless, his mouth dry, his throat too tight to swallow. Liski stretched against his chair, arching backward, then stood up as if to leave. He walked to the door and stepped out into the hallway, then paused and poked his head back into the room.

"I have a message for you," he said. Richard slowly looked up from his chair. "It's from a mutual friend of ours," he continued. "Someone who seems to care about you very deeply." Liski paused. Ammon's heart began to pulse wildly. He knew immediately he was talking about Jesse.

"You know, Mr. Ammon, I don't believe you ever mentioned the fact that you were married. I've got to say, if my wife looked anything like Jesse, I surely wouldn't keep it a secret." Liski watched Ammon's face grow pale, his chest tremble, his eyes narrow with anger and fear. Liski smiled again. It was things like this that made his job fun.

Liski paused for a moment, then stepped back into the room.

"In fact, Mr. Ammon, I've got something I've been wanting to show you. I've been waiting for just the right time, and I guess that time has come." Liski reached into his breast pocket, pulled out a small envelope and tossed it onto Ammon's bed. Ammon stared at the envelope for a long time, swallowing the bile in his throat. Liski did not move. With great effort, Ammon pushed himself back from the desk and slid over to the bed where he dropped himself onto the soft mattress. His hands trembled with fear as he picked up the envelope and tore it open, spilling a collection of color pictures onto the bed.

The pictures were very poor quality from a color fax. Ammon began to sort through them. With each photo his heart thumped more violently inside his constricted chest.

Every photo was of Jesse. There were pictures of her standing outside their Santa Monica apartment, her brown hair blown back by the wind, a small duffel bag strapped over her left shoulder. She was glancing to her side, her eyes unknowingly staring past the unseen photographer. Another photo was of her driving her Mazda. There were pictures of her in a dark and empty parking lot, talking to a man in an old gray compact car. Ammon slowly sorted through the small stack of photos, his arms turning into great weights, his stomach a block of ice.

Then he got to the last picture. Tears of frustration and rage swelled his eyes. Liski, still standing by the open door, watched him very closely, his body tense and ready, his hand ready to go for his gun. Ammon glanced at the picture for only a second before crumpling it up in his hands.

It showed his wife very clearly, laying on a wide bed, her hands tied together above her head, loops of rope stringing her tightly to a thick headboard. Her bare feet were also tied together and strapped to the foot of the bed, her legs drawn against the thick rope. She was dressed in jeans and a white t-shirt. She had a black rag stuffed in her mouth. Her eyes were open wide in terror and fear, her hair pushed to one side to ensure a clear picture of her face. Seated next to the bed where Jesse lay bound was the man from the gray car. He was staring directly into the camera, smiling, holding a glowing cigarette just inches above Jesse's head, having flicked gray ashes onto her face.

Ammon crushed the picture in his white knuckles. Darkness smothered him. His mind went completely blank. Instinct and rage took control. He let out a low, animal groan and hurled himself toward Liski, his feet sliding on the slick linoleum floor, arms ready, fist tucked to his side.

But the Ukrainian was ready. Stepping catlike to one side, he grabbed Ammon by the shoulders and pushed him down, pitching him against the cinder-block wall. Ammon's head hit the cement with a sickening thump, and he slumped to the floor. Reaching quickly under his jacket, Liski pulled a blunt handgun from a leather holster. As Ammon pushed himself up to his knees, Liski threw back his arm and struck him over the head, sending a splatter of blood against the wall. The rough, beveled grip of Liski's pistol caught the soft flesh behind Ammon's right ear and tore away a small piece of the scalp. The cold steel jammed into his skull. Ammon fell to the floor once again, moaned once, then rolled onto his back. His eyes glazed over with pain, his hands began to twitch at his side. His breathing became suddenly shallow. He didn't move, and as Liski stared down at the body, watching the skin turn grayish-white, he began to regret that he hit him so hard.

Ammon started to stir. Liski knelt down beside him and forced his knee into his chest. He pushed his pistol into Ammon's ear and shoved his face so close that Ammon could feel the heat from his breath.

"We've got your girl, Ammon!" he sneered. "She is mine! I hold her life in my hands! Now, I think you know what will happen to her if you fail us or attempt to get in our way." Liski lowered his voice and pushed himself even closer to Ammon's face. Richard stared up at him with unfocused eyes. A knot of bruised bone and tissue was already beginning to bulge from the side of his head.

"Just do what we say," Liski commanded. "Do what we say, and she lives. Do as you have been trained to do. Follow orders. Your little girl is going to be just fine, if you do what we tell you to do.

"But, my fly-boy friend, screw up just one little thing, cause me even one hint of concern, and we turn our boy loose on your wife. It won't be pretty for her, Ammon. And you'll never know what he did with the body. You'll never even find a grave to say good-bye. Now that's no way for this all to end."

Ammon lay there motionless, the short barrel of the gun crushing into the tender flesh of his ear. Liski twisted the barrel and pushed a little harder.

"Do you understand what I'm saying to you?" he muttered, twisting the barrel once again. "Or do you want me to show you more pictures? I could order something special, just for you."

Ammon moaned, but didn't say anything. Liski pushed his knee deeper into his chest. "Say it, Ammon!" he sneered. "I know you can hear me. Now tell me that you won't let us down!"

"I understand. I know what you want." Ammon finally muttered, his voice heavy with pain.

Liski smiled. It was enough.

He pulled the gun from Ammon's ear, stood up, holstered his weapon and straightened out his clothes. Without another word he left the room, closing the door behind him.

As he began to walk down the hallway, he looked up and saw Ivan Morozov leaning against the wall, waiting. Liski gave him a nod, but didn't say anything as he passed by.

Inside his room, Richard Ammon lay on the floor, his head propped against the cement wall. The room swirled and spun all around him. His stomach twisted into churning knots. His head pounded in pain as blood seeped from the wound behind his ear and rolled down his neck. He closed his eyes and covered his head.

Never had he felt so ashamed. Never had he felt so afraid. His stomach turned and he started to gag, heaving wads of spit and crimson bile onto the floor.

For a long time he lay in a heap. The room grew very dark. Richard rolled over and rested his head against his right arm. He couldn't think. He couldn't focus. All he knew was the pain in his head.

Three hours later, he finally pulled himself up and staggered into his bed, still holding the crumpled photo of Jesse in his fist.

NINETEEN

RICHARD AMMON STARED OUT THE SMALL OVAL WINDOW AND WATCHED as the eastern coast of the United States slipped into view, thirty miles off in the distance. The sun was just coming up, chasing the airliner as it flew to the west and casting long shadows across the dark, open ocean as it climbed its way upward on the horizon. The North Atlantic air was cold and crystal clear, and Ammon estimated the visibility to be at least seventy miles. He could make out the tiny lakes, rocky shores, and green rolling hills of northern Maine as the Boeing 767 entered United States' airspace. He stared out on the horizon, looking south toward Boston and the Massachusetts Bay. From thirty-eight thousand feet, he could just make out the slight curvature in the earth.

Turning away from the window, he sighed and leaned back in his seat, then glanced over at Morozov, who sat two seats over, sleeping. A steward passed by and asked him once again if he needed a pillow. Shaking his head, he abruptly sent him away.

He couldn't sleep. He couldn't think. He couldn't eat. He couldn't even close his eyes without an image of Jesse's tortured face filling his head. He wanted to strike! He wanted revenge! He wanted to kill the man who had done this to him!

He opened his eyes and looked over at Morozov once again. As he stared at the sleeping man, he realized he had vastly underestimated Morozov's resolve. How could he have not seen it coming? How could he have let her down so? At the time he first had met Jesse, he didn't think that the secret Russian intelligence organization was even still in existence. And even if they were, what was he to them? It had been years since he had heard from them in any fashion. And so much had changed. The whole world had changed. Surely they must have forgotten.

But he had been wrong. At least partly wrong.

The Sicherheit may have forgotten. But Ivan Morozov had not.

Ammon shook his head once again, trying to shake off the despair. He wiped his hands across his eyes and tried to concentrate.

His options were really quite simple.

Number One. He could refuse to help them. And Jesse would die. Even the thought made him icy and weak.

Number Two. He could go along with their plan. And die in the process. Or worse yet, start the next world war!

Ammon ran his fingers through his hair and took a deep breath. He felt so . . . compressed. It was a horrible feeling. Like a thousand tons of sand had been poured on his shoulders. It was pushing him down. It was crushing his chest.

He felt hopeless and alone and utterly trapped.

The sun broke through a low line of morning clouds and began to shine through his oval window. He reached up and pulled down the shade, settled back in his seat, and tried once again to get some sleep.

But as he lay there, one thought, one desperate glimmer of hope, kept rolling round in his mind.

"Don't you guys let me down!" he silently pleaded. "We had an agreement. Now please, don't let me down!"

The aircraft continued southwest for another three hours until it finally began it's descent into the Dallas-Fort Worth airport. As the pilot throttled back his engines, Ivan Morozov stirred. Stretching to rouse himself, he reached his husky arms skyward, then looked across the empty seat that separated him from Richard Ammon. Ammon was finally sleeping. With a grunt, Morozov reached over and pushed against Ammon's shoulder. Ammon immediately bolted awake.

"We're almost there, my boy. Back to your home. Must be good to be back in the States."

Ammon turned his head and looked out the tiny window at the dry prairie that was passing below him, but didn't respond. Morozov leaned forward to check the duffel bag which was stuffed under his seat. He pulled the bag out and rooted briefly through its contents, then, satisfied that all was in order, carefully shoved the bag back.

The aircraft continued descending and, twenty minutes later, was taxiing off the runway toward its arrival gate. The passengers began their usual stir. It had been a long flight, almost eleven hours, and everyone seemed very grateful to be on the ground. Ammon and Morozov had been seated toward the rear of the aircraft and it took some time before they could exit the plane. As he walked up the ramp and began to mix with the crowd, Ammon stifled a quick urge to run.

He and Morozov departed the gate and walked to the line that had formed to clear customs. Neither of them had anything to declare. Their carry-on luggage was inspected and their passports closely scrutinized—more so than in the past Morozov observed—then they were waved on through.

After passing through customs and collecting their bags, they walked the considerable distance to the long-term parking area, where Morozov found the car. It was a mid-size, black sedan. The doors were unlocked.

"Throw the bags on the back seat," Morozov instructed.

"Don't you want them in the trunk?"

"No, the back seat," Morozov replied.

Ammon did as he was instructed while Morozov searched under the dash for the key, which he found stuffed up under the glove box, right where he told them to leave it. Five minutes later, they left the noise of the airport behind them as they headed out on their way.

DALLAS–FORT WORTH INTERNATIONAL AIRPORT, TEXAS

Chuck Robertson, watch supervisor, DFW Airport Security, walked into the dim room without turning on the light. The two security cameras were mounted on the far wall, their lenses pointing through a one-way glass and out onto the immigration and customs floor. Both of the low-speed, high-resolution cameras were recording the passengers as they made their way through the whole process. Usually, Airport Security was required to use only one camera at a time. But Robertson's instructions had been very specific, and for the past several days he had kept both of the cameras running. He couldn't afford to have something go wrong.

Robertson walked over to the special video cameras and checked the tape indicator readouts. The right camera was almost out of video-tape. Reaching behind him, he pulled a fresh cassette from out of a small box and ripped it open, letting the torn cellophane drop to the floor, then turned the camera off, extracted the recorded cartridge, and replaced it with the new one. Leaning over, he checked the indicator on the other camera. It had another hour left on it. He checked his watch and decided he would return after lunch.

As he walked out the door, he placed the recorded cassette tape in a purple and white Federal Express envelope. It would be sent to D.C. on the evening flight and delivered before ten the next morning.

GUTHRIE, OKLAHOMA

That night, Richard Ammon and Ivan Morozov sat in a small booth at the back of the Wooden Spoon restaurant, a greasy tin and glass cafe.

The orange vinyl bench in which Ammon sat made his back sweat. His skin stuck against the torn plastic seat. Although they were in the nonsmoking section, Morozov constantly kept a cigarette going. The waitress would give him an occasional look of displeasure as she refilled his thick mug of coffee, but she never considered asking him to quit smoking. Richard Ammon had no doubt that, had they been in Los Angeles, the waitress would have taken Morozov's cigarette and stuffed it in his coffee.

But they weren't in L.A. The ocean and hills that surrounded the Los Angeles basin were over one thousand miles to the west. Where they sat, they were surrounded only by wheat fields and dust and an occasional line of trees that had been planted to break the wind. They were nearly in the center of the country. Small town, U.S.A.

For the past seventy-two hours, Ammon and Morozov had been world travelers. Using four different passports, they had made their way across Europe, first from Helsinki to Copenhagen, then across the ferry into Germany, and finally by train into Brussels. The nonstop from Brussels to Dallas had left them both cranky and tired, jet lag fouling up their natural circadian rhythm. After leaving the confines of the metro airport, Morozov had headed north along Interstate 35 toward Wichita, Kansas. Or, to be more specific, McConnell AFB, which lay just outside the Wichita city limits.

All through the day they drove, always traveling just the speed limit, until they came to the small town of Guthrie. There Morozov had turned off the highway and pulled into the tacky pancake house. The two men walked inside and, though it was night, ordered the breakfast special. It didn't take the waitress long to bring them a heaping stack of hot pancakes with a half dozen links of tiny, greasy sausage on the side. A smaller plate with diced ham and fried potatoes was set down next to the plate of pancakes. Both men dug into the food like they hadn't eaten in a week, neither of them talking until they had cleaned their plates.

Then Morozov ordered a refill on his coffee while Ammon sipped at the lemon slice that floated in his ice water. While he waited for Morozov to finish his coffee, Ammon looked around the restaurant with a renewed appreciation for the States. There were so many things here he had learned to enjoy. So many little things that made life here pleasant and easy. He also loved the feel of the air. Not just the smell, but the feel. It was dry and brisk and smelled of fresh wheat. It raced along the prairie and touted its freedom. It stood as a symbol and seemed to remind him of what this country was about.

Ammon leaned back on his bench and stretched his arms while he yawned. He stared across the table at Morozov, then glanced at his watch. Morozov noticed him check the time, but gave no indication that he was ready to leave. Instead, he asked for another refill on his coffee and struck a match to light a fresh cigarette. While the waitress filled Morozov's cup, she asked if they wanted their check. Morozov waved his hand to send her away, all the time keeping one eye on the door.

It was then that Ammon noticed the man staring at him from the counter. The stranger had turned on his rotating stool to rest his right elbow on the counter while he inspected Richard Ammon. He made no effort to hide his interest, never turning away, eyes defiant and unblinking. Ammon tried to ignore him, avoiding his stare. The stranger was obviously not a local boy. He was dressed in tight blue jeans, thick steel-toe work boots, and a tattered black t-shirt. His head was shaved clean, except for a narrow band of six-inch hair that protruded from the back of his head and dangled down the nap of his neck. Three gold earrings protruded from his left ear. A diamond stud highlighted his pierced nose. He had enormous shoulders and arms, the obvious result of long hours pumping weights. On his right bicep was a long, black tattoo of a slanted dagger which pierced his own skin, red blood dripping from the tattered wound. He had narrow eyes, a square face, and eyebrows so heavy they connected over his flat nose. He looked to be about Richard's age, maybe a little bit older.

Moving slowly, he placed his coffee cup on the edge of the formica counter, stood up, and approached Ammon and Morozov. Richard nervously looked around the crowded room. The stranger pushed his way into the booth, ignoring Ammon's look of displeasure as Morozov slid across the plastic bench to make room for him to sit down.

"You don't remember me, do you?" the stranger asked, directing the question to Richard Ammon. Ammon looked up to study the face. He stared into the water-blue eyes. They were cold and unfeeling. Pale as haze and reflective as glass. He knew those eyes from somewhere. Sometime long ago. He studied the face, taking in the shaven head and bulging neck. It, too, was familiar. But from where, he didn't quite know.

"I don't know who you are," he finally said, sounding very vague.

"Oh? You don't? Come on, Carl. Think. Think back on your past." the stranger prodded.

Ammon still shook his head.

"Well, we were both much younger then. Really no more than children.

"But I know all about you, Carl Vadym Kostenko. I know where you come from. I know why you're here." The stranger stared intently into Ammon's eyes and frowned. He challenged him, willing him to look away, a cold burning in his eyes. Ammon returned his cold stare, his mind racing, searching his past to place the stranger's face. The waitress approached their table again, pot of hot coffee in hand, a check protruding from her apron string. Upon observing the two men, she changed her mind and quickly turned to the side and passed their table by.

"Let me see your hand," the stranger said, reaching across the table to examine the top of Ammon's knuckles. Ammon did not pull away. With rough nails, the stranger traced the thin white line of a scar that ran between Ammon's third and fourth knuckles. He tapped lightly on the ring finger, still knotted from the long-ago beating.

"Good ol' Mrs. Downer," he sneered. "That ol' wench could sure swing a pipe." He let out a husky laugh. Ammon pulled his hand away.

Morozov's lips spread into a thin smile and he raised his left hand to cover his face.

And then it hit him. "I remember you now," Ammon said. "Back at the school. You were a little bit older. I competed against you once in boxing. Broke two of your teeth. Everyone laughed. You were already the ugliest kid in the school. Made you look even worse."

The stranger faked an exaggerated smile, exposing two crooked front teeth. "One day, I'll give you another chance," he breathed. "We'll go at it again, you and I. See if you can take me out twice. I don't think that you can. From what I've heard, you're turning soft and pink in the middle."

Ammon didn't reply. The stranger coughed and looked away. Under the table, he reached into his front pocket, pulled out a tiny bundle, and hid it inside his fist. Leaning forward, he grasped the back of Ammon's neck. He pulled Ammon's head across the table until their foreheads nearly touched. Ammon reeled from the smell of his breath and pushed himself back. He felt the man's enormous fingers tighten around the muscles of his neck. His bones and tendons crunched together. He felt as though the stranger would pull off his head.

"Do the right thing," the man commanded in a hiss. "Do what's right for the girl." Tiny drops of spittle splashed across Ammon's face. "Finish the mission, and don't let us down." He squeezed once again to emphasize his point.

Ammon's eyes flickered. He reached out and grabbed the man's chin in his hand, forcing him to look in his eyes. "Touch her," he breathed, "and I'll kill you. It will be my only reason for living. To find you and tear out your heart."

The stranger's lips curled up in the corners. "You do that, Carl," he whispered. "I'll be waiting for you. Pretty Boy."

The stranger released his grip and leaned back in his seat. Tossing something across the table, he got up without another word, placed his baseball cap upon his head, turned, and walked away. Several people, including the waitress, watched him warily as he left, his patch of dark hair curling out from under the back of his cap.

Ammon turned to look down at the object which lay before him. As he stared at the bundle, his heart sank into his chest.

There sat a four-inch lock of silky hair, tied in a tight knot around a simple gold ring. Jesse's hair. Jesse's wedding ring.

He reached out and, ever so gently, raised the ring and hair to his face. He could smell the soap and cream rinse. The hair smelled of Jesse.

He lifted his eyes to Morozov. He burned with murderous rage. His shoulders shook. He swallowed hard. He fingered the hair with trembling hands, then closed his eyes.

Morozov watched Ammon for a moment, then smiled and said, "Let's go," as he slid across the booth and stood up. He dropped a fifty dollar bill on the table and walked casually out the front door.

After a very long time, Ammon followed him outside. They climbed into the car, and Morozov pulled out of the parking lot, turned onto the interstate, and headed north. After accelerating up to seventy, Morozov set the cruise control, then turned on his wipers to their lowest setting. It was just barely starting to mist, but ahead of them a long line of rain clouds loomed. Ammon stared at the dark shadows that passed by on his side of the car. Blackness filled his soul. The lonely miles melted by.

After driving for a long time in silence, Morozov suddenly turned to Ammon. "Carl, I'm going to ask you something." he said. His voice was very direct. He made no attempt to hide his bitterness or impatience. "I want you to think about this before you answer. And I want you to tell me the truth."

Morozov paused. Lightning flashed in the distance. A huge semi-trailer sped by, washing their car in a spray of dirty mist. Ammon waited.

"Where does your heart lie?" Ivan Morozov continued. "What is important to you now? Do you feel any allegiance to your past or this mission?" The wipers stroked the windshield at an even pace as Morozov leaned across the car toward Ammon and asked in almost a whisper. "Carl," he said, "can I trust you?"

Richard Ammon didn't respond. He continued to stare into the distance, watching the shadows from their headlights. His mind flashed back to the picture of Jesse tied to the bed, cigarette ashes specking her face. He thought of the ropes and terror in her eyes. He thought of the thug in the diner. He reached up and gently touched the tender bruise on the side of his head.

Morozov already knew the answer to this question. Ammon really had nothing to say.

Morozov turned his attention to the road ahead. "I want you to know something, Carl," he said after a while. "I want you to know where you stand. I want to be very clear about the seriousness of your situation.

"I want you to realize that it was you. You are the one who brought in Jesse. It was your disloyalty that dragged her into this mess.

"You forced us to do that, Carl. I want you to know that. I would have preferred to not get Jesse involved. But as we watched you over the past few weeks, as we started to do a little digging, it became very obvious that you couldn't be trusted. So we had to use Jesse. It wasn't something we wanted to do. It was you who forced our hand."

Morozov glanced over at Richard Ammon, his yellow-green eyes darting between the road and his passenger. He could see that Ammon was furious. Morozov drummed on his steering wheel for a few seconds, then continued. "Ammon, your personal feelings about this job are irrelevant. And you know what I have told you is true. You would have taken off and run before I could even have stepped off the plane back in Dallas, except for the fact that you now have to worry about Jesse.

"But as I considered your loyalties, I started to wonder. If you could be so disloyal to me, was it also possible you would walk out on your wife. I had to ask myself. What if the coward leaves me, too? What if he doesn't really care about Jesse? What if he cares more about his thin hide than he cares about that poor little girl?"

Ammon didn't respond. It was such a startling thought. Leave Jesse! He had to be kidding! She's my life. The only reason I breathe every day.

The two men rode in silence. Lightning continued to dance in the distance, flashing from cloud to cloud. A few miles passed before Morozov slowed down and took an isolated ranch exit. The exit ramp quickly narrowed into a roughly paved road. After a few hundred feet, the pavement came to an abrupt end and a dirt road took over, winding its way into the darkness. Not another car was in sight. Morozov drove down the dirt road for about a mile, to where it suddenly made a sharp cut to the right. There he let the car coast along until it rolled to a stop.

"What are we doing?" Ammon asked in an urgent voice.

"There's something I want you to see."

"In the middle of this field?"

Morozov grunted. "Follow me." He jerked open his door and stepped out into the night.

Richard Ammon reluctantly followed him into the cool, misty air. He watched Morozov walk a short distance out into the open fields. Morozov's body soon turned into a faded outline as he kicked and paced through the dirt. He seemed to be looking for something. Suddenly Morozov stopped and bent over. After a short pause, he yelled, "Come over here."

Ammon began to walk slowly out to where Ivan Morozov was now standing, stepping carefully through the muddy soil. He stopped for a moment about ten feet from Morozov. From this distance he could recognize what lay at his feet.

"Come here," Morozov commanded.

Ammon inched forward until he was standing next to Morozov. There on the ground, illuminated by the reflected light of the head-lights, lay a woman's body. It was curled up into a fetal position. A dark pool of blood had collected around the figure's head and short brown hair. A thin arm lay sprawled across the face, hiding her identity. Ammon could see that the face had been horribly mangled. A skeletal grin stared up from the darkness. The eyes were round and gaping and dried over in a thick film. Ammon instinctively recoiled.

In a rage, he turned on Morozov. Grabbing him by the collar, he twisted his head and spun him around. "What have you done!" he screamed in his face. "Who is this? What have you done?"

With surprising strength, Morozov pushed him away. Ammon slipped in the mud, then caught himself before he fell. Ammon turned and brought up his fists, only to find himself facing a Colt 45, the muzzle just inches from the center of his eyes. The polished steel glistened in the semi-darkness. Ammon heard a click and froze.

"You want to know who this is?" Morozov asked, waving the center of the barrel in front of Ammon's face, moving the tip from his nose to each of his eyes in a taunting, rotating circle. "I'll tell you who this is. I'll tell you anything you want to know. I'll give you all of the details. Like how did it feel? What did we use? How long did it take her to die? You name it, and I'll spill my guts. I'll tell you anything you want to know."

Ammon shuddered, then looked away. Morozov kept the gun at his head. Ammon ignored it. Morozov pulled back on the hammer, locking it in the fire position.

"This is you, you stupid fool," Morozov said coldly, his voice suddenly calm and even as glass. "So take a good look. This is your future! This is you if you don't go along.

"You know who this is, Ammon? This is the airman who planted the bomb in your jet. We thought we could trust her. But look at her now. Look what my boy did to her face. And all because she got a little sloppy. Came home on leave. Had to impress her old friends. Started flashing her money. Started talking too much. Couldn't control her loose lips.

"And if you think this looks ugly, keep this thought in mind, for I swear to you, for every throb of pain that I cause you, I will make things even worse for your girl!

"So walk softly, you snot-nose little fly-boy. Walk softly. And don't piss me off."

Ammon glared up at Morozov. Morozov smiled. Ammon choked on his rage and frustration, then passed his hands over his eyes. Turning away, he stumbled into the darkness and made his way back to the car.

WASHINGTON, D.C.

Buddy Spencer held the color photos up to his nose to get a close look. His hands shook.

"When did these come in?" he demanded.

"Yesterday, sir," the aide replied. "We got the tape from Dallas in this morning. It took us until noon to digitize it so that we could manipulate the pictures for better observation. One of our interns made a match late last night. I think we got lucky. It looks like a good pick to me."

Spencer held the photos close once again, then set them down on the top of his desk and picked up another picture, this one a glossy black and white. It was a clear shot of Ivan Morozov. He held the pictures side by side. He was a little unsure. He wasn't very good at such things. But it looked like a match. He punched the intercom switch to buzz his secretary.

"Get Oliver Tray," he said abruptly.

Forty minutes later, Lieutenant Colonel Oliver Tray walked into the office, escorted by an Agency security guard. He wore a visitor's pass around his neck and carried a brown leather briefcase. As he walked into the office, Spencer nodded to his desk and Oliver immediately picked up the pictures and started sorting through them. There were eleven photos in all. Each of them had been enlarged and cropped to zoom in on Morozov's face. They showed him from several different angles as he had made his way through customs in Dallas.

"That's him!" Oliver announced with no hesitation. "No doubt about it. He's a little older, and his hair is cut short, but that's him."

"Are you certain?" Spencer prodded. "I think you're right, but we have to be sure."

Tray didn't hesitate. "It's him. Look at the eyes. It's him. I'm perfectly sure. I can't believe he's back in the country. This is wild, Buddy! Incredible, really! Now, where were these pictures taken and when?"

Buddy looked at his watch. "About forty-five hours ago. In Dallas. I've got people standing by."

"What else do we know? Where did he go from the airport? Did he take a connecting flight, or rent a car? Did somebody meet him? Did he have any unusual or oversized luggage? Did he enter the country alone?" Tray was talking so fast, Spencer had to concentrate just to follow what he said.

"Nothing," Spencer answered. "We don't know nothing. Or at least very little. And to a large degree, it is leaving our hands. The FBI has already been notified. Once Morozov stepped foot on U.S. soil, he became their man. Of course, we'll continue to work with them, and other agencies have been notified as well, including the state and local police. However, we don't think that he flew on from Dallas. At least no ticket was made under the alias he used to enter the country. And he wasn't alone. He was traveling with this man." Buddy Spencer tossed another photo across the desk. "We don't know who he is. Got nothing on him at all."

Oliver reached down and picked up the photo. The color immediately drained from his face. His eyes opened wide. His body visibly tensed and a look of pure astonishment and shock spread across his face. Spencer watched his friend in surprise.

"Oh my . . . ," Oliver muttered. He swallowed hard, then reached for the phone, ignoring Spencer's attempts for some explanation.

Tray dialed as quickly as he could. "I've got him, Colonel Fullbright!" he yelled into the receiver. "I've got him! He's here in the States!" He paused, listening.

"BADGER, sir!" he replied. "He's here! He's with Morozov!"

Another pause.

"Yes, sir. I'll be right there!"

TWENTY

KREMENCHUG-CHERKASSY, UKRAINE

THE UKRAINIAN PRIME MINISTER'S BLACK SEDAN CAME TO A BRIEF STOP under the canopy of swaying pine trees. Yevgeni Oskol Golubev stepped quickly from the car, not waiting for his driver to come around and open his door. A light smog still hung in the morning air, a mixture of frozen ice particles and smoke from the burning fires that raged in Poltava, a hundred kilometers to the west.

Golubev's driver sped off as soon as he shut his door, leaving him alone to walk the asphalt path that wound its way up the side of the mountain. Most of the trail was covered by the natural canopy of pines and huge red oaks, but in the few spots where it wasn't, a camouflage netting had been strung up to make the path invisible from the air.

Seventy meters up the side of the hill, the path suddenly ended in a very small clearing. There, several guards were waiting for Golubev to appear. They stood at attention as he approached and when he raised his eyes to meet theirs, they each offered a crisp salute. As Golubev closed in on the group of soldiers, the tallest guard turned and led him to a heavy metal fence which surrounded a large hole that had been cut into the side of the mountain. The two men passed through a small gate and walked back thirty feet into the man-made cave.

There they came to a huge metal blast door. It was six feet high and three feet thick. The guard picked up a yellow telephone that was attached to the front of the steel door and spoke in a hushed voice. As he spoke, both he and Golubev looked up into the two security cameras above them. After a few seconds, they could hear the tumblers inside the door roll over, then a gentle warning tone rang out as the door began to swing open on its huge hydraulic pistons. Yevgeni Golubev slipped through the opening and disappeared into the dimly lit hallway. The guard watched him for just a moment, then stood back as the door began to close once again.

Golubev walked briskly down the busy corridor. The hallway was wide enough to accommodate a large truck, but dimly lit, illuminated by only a few small, yellow light bulbs that hung from the cement ceiling. The floor sloped gently downward, sinking deeper into the side of the mountain. Guards with small machine guns and squawking radios paced slowly along the sides of the hallways, eyeing each man that they encountered with equal suspicion.

The Prime Minister turned down a red hallway and walked until he came to another large steel blast door. This was the entrance to the Tactical Command Center. Again, a guard was waiting to let him through. After Golubev passed through the door, he tromped across the "fly paper", a five-foot mat of sticky tape that had been stretched across the floor. The thick, tacky paper pulled the dust and dirt from off of his boots, helping to keep the air free from contaminants that might gum up the hordes of sensitive computers that were jammed into the enormous command center.

As Golubev entered the Tactical Command Center, he looked around in admiration once again. He loved the glowing lights, the huge display boards, and the hustle of the officers that filled the room. He took a deep breath of the purified air while he listened to the sound of the humming computers.

The Tactical Command Center, or TCC, was shaped like a steep indoor theater. The room was dark, illuminated only by the back lighting from the huge display board and small table lights that sat at each of the control centers. Tiny aisle lights illuminated the steep walkways. Rows of control boards sat in a tight semicircle around the main tactical display board, a twenty-foot screen that was the focus of the room.

As Golubev stared at the screen, he noticed a dog fight in action. Two blue triangles, signifying Ukrainian SU-27 Flankers were about to engage three Russian Mig-31 Foxhounds, represented by three bright red stars.

Every eye in the room turned to watch as the air battle began. The two Ukrainian Flankers sped along the ground at low level, coming up from behind and below the Russian fighters, who were orbiting in a wide circle at 20,000 feet. It appeared that the Foxhound's radar had not yet detected the low-flying Flankers.

As the two Flankers approached their targets, they pulled their aircraft into a steep climb and fired off two AA-11 air-to-air missiles at the lead Foxhound. From each blue triangle, two small white dots began to track toward the closest red star.

It wasn't until then that the three Russian aircraft began to maneuver. The lead aircraft immediately banked over into a steep dive. Although the display board didn't show it, Golubev knew the pilot would also be spitting out white-hot flares, interspersed with small bundles of radar-reflecting chaff. Golubev's stomach muscles tightened as he watched the two missiles track in on their target. It was going to be very close. He silently coaxed the missiles onward, cheering for them to pursue.

The two small dots converged on the fighter and merged into one. The room exploded into cheers as the Russian aircraft disappeared from the screen. The two Ukrainian fighters turned and ran to the south. The Russian fighters did not pursue.

Golubev watched his cheering men, then turned his attention to the latest update of his combat losses. He scanned down both sides of the display board, hoping to find some good news. But nothing had changed. His army was still mired along the Ukrainian border and taking heavy losses. It was going poorly, and getting worse. He started to count the number of army units that now had a red line slashed through their name. There were so many. The board was bleeding red.

But the losses were not entirely one-sided. The Ukrainians were beginning to inflict heavy casualties upon the invading Russian forces. His intelligence estimated the Russians had lost at least three of their army divisions and a hundred and forty aircraft, including three Mainstay airborne radar observers and thirty-seven IL-76 transport loaded with combat troops. The Russians were winning, but the battle was bloody. Which was the only reason that Golubev was here.

The prime minister turned and walked into a small conference room at the back of the TCC. The front wall of the room was nothing but a huge pane of glass; a one-way window which allowed its occupants to look out onto the floor of the command center without being observed. From here, Golubev had a clear view of the entire TCC. He could easily read the control board and watch the bustle of activity on the floor.

Three minutes later, General Victor Lomov walked into the room. He was wearing a formal dress uniform. Combat ribbons and silver pilot wings hung from his chest. His pants were starched into a tight crease and his shoes glistened with a mirror-like shine. But his face was unshaven and his hair lay matted down to one side. His eyes were bloodshot and tired. He entered the room cursing Golubev for the interruption.

Golubev waited for the general to settle down, then walked to a small icebox and poured them both a strong drink. He knew that General Lomov had been working around the clock in the constant twilight of the TCC, sleeping when he could and eating only when one of his aides put a plate down before him.

So despite the early hour, he poured out the liquor. They raised their glasses to one another. "To our success," said Yevgeni Golubev.

"To our brothers," Lomov replied.

The two men drank in silence as they watched the TCC floor. They watched as the latest movements of their army units were updated on the board. They watched as another combat regiment was declared combat ineffective, its name slashed through in red.

Golubev got straight to the point.

"He's getting ready to use them. I'm sure that you've seen the reports."

"Yes, I've seen the pictures. I've read the reports."

"He's already fueled his missiles. He's pulling back his forward battalions to offer them a little protection. Last night we had two mock air attacks against the chemical weapons storage facility at Kirghiziahn. They were testing our air defenses, all in preparation for the real thing. I don't think that we have but a few days. It might already be too late."

Lomov nodded and rocked on the balls of his feet but didn't respond.

"It's time we did it," Golubev demanded. "You know that we don't have a choice. Let's just do it. It makes no sense to delay."

Victor Lomov glanced up at the display board once again. He had spent so many hours staring at this board over the past seven days. He leaned his forehead against the one-way glass for a second. His head seemed so heavy. He felt so tired, he closed his eyes.

After a few moments, he opened his eyes and turned to face the prime minister.

"Let's do it then, Yevgeni," was all he said as he turned and walked from the room.

Three hours later, Golubev had a message sent to a Ukrainian agent in Northern Russia. By early the next morning he had already completed his job.

PSKOV AIR BASE, RUSSIA

One thousand miles to the north of Golubev's command center lay Pskov, home of the Tu-160 Blackjack bomber, the newest and most sophisticated long-range bomber that the Russians had ever developed. Roughly equivalent to the American B-1 in both size and shape, the Blackjack was a highly capable and very threatening aircraft.

Each of Pskov's twenty Blackjack bombers lay hidden in a cement bunker. Inside the bunkers, an armed guard stood watch over each aircraft. Security was very tight.

Sergeant Boris Kozyrav was one of the security policemen whose responsibility it was to guard the Tu-160. For eight hours a day he would stand idly by the huge bomber, endlessly trying to find new ways to keep his mind occupied. Boredom and fatigue were a constant battle, especially since he had been transferred onto the night schedule. From ten at night until six in the morning, Sgt. Kozyrav was alone in the bunker. By two in the morning, he was usually sleeping in a corner of the maintenance bin, his pack stuffed under his head as a pillow, his hat pulled down over his eyes.

For Sgt. Kozyrav, the night that Golubev and General Lomov had decided to initiate their plan was just like any other. He made his rounds, read for a while, then promptly fell asleep.

He didn't hear the soft footsteps as they approached the aircraft from the rear of the bunker. He didn't stir when a small black box was attached to the underside of the main landing gear. The box was placed under the main brake lines, where it would never be seen, even when the ground crews did their normal preflight inspection.

The aircraft that Sgt. Kozyrav was guarding was scheduled to fly the next day. When the aircraft lifted off from the runway and the main gear were retracted into the belly of the aircraft, the black box would only be three feet from the 27,000 pounds of jet fuel that was stored inside the Blackjack's main fuel tank.

TWENTY-ONE

DAGGER 34
OVER THE NORTHEASTERN
COAST OF MAINE

TWENTY HOURS LATER, TWO TU-160 BLACKJACK BOMBERS WERE FLYING down the eastern coast of Canada. Although they would stay in international airspace, they intended to press the edge of the twelve-mile Air Defense Zone that surrounded the United States. After flying south along the coast of Maine, they would turn slightly eastward to clip the edge of Cape Cod. Not until then would they turn around and head back north, flying the same route back to their home in Pskov.

The purpose of their mission was twofold. First, they would once again test the United States air defense response and capabilities. They knew that Vermont Air National Guard F-16s would scramble from their alert shelters to intercept the Blackjacks just after they passed south of the coast of Maine.

But there was another purpose for this mission. Their presence was intended to be a political show of will. It had been several years since the Russians had regularly run their bombers down the eastern coast of the United States, and President Fedotov thought this might be a good time to remind his American friends of his long-range bombing capability.

The Blackjacks didn't show up unannounced. American early warning radar had been tracking them since they passed over the southern tip of Iceland. As the American radar operators tracked the bombers on their southern route, they kept expecting them to turn around. They were more than a little surprised when the Blackjacks continued south along the Canadian coast.

When the Russian bombers were fifteen minutes from the United States border, two F-16s were scrambled to intercept and escort them along the coast. As the F-16 pilots flew out to intercept the bombers, they talked over their have-quick secure voice radio, reviewing the rules of engagement that they would follow against the Russian Blackjacks.

The rules were fairly simple. Don't act in any hostile, aggressive, or threatening manner. Don't intimidate the bombers in any way. As long as the Russians remained in international airspace, the fighters could only observe them from a safe distance.

But the fighters would definitely make their presence known. They would fly to the side of the bombers, occasionally flashing on their acquisition radar as a little reminder to the Russians that they weren't alone up there in the sky.

Inside the lead F-16 was Captain Les Harris. Les spent most of his days running his father's computer service store. Most weekends were spent inside the cockpit of an F-16. Les had been flying the F-16 Falcon for more than nine years, and it had been a long time since he had felt uncomfortable with a mission. But this one had him just a little bit rattled. Any time the Americans ran an intercept on a Russian aircraft, there was the potential for small things to be blown into international incidents.

As Captain Harris and his wingman flew north, they were receiving vectors toward the two Russian bombers from Darkhorse, the ground radar controllers. Captain Harris's call sign was Dagger three-four. The Blackjacks were referred to as Unknown Cowboys.

Harris listened on his radio as the female controller was giving him directions. "Dagger three-four, turn left heading zero-four-zero. Your bogey is now one-two-zero miles, twelve o'clock and closing. Call when you have him on radar."

"Roger, heading zero-four-zero for the Daggers," Harris replied.

The Darkhorse controller's voice was very calm and even. Husky and low. Confident and cool. It was a voice that made Harris wonder what the controller looked like. He could picture her as she sat at the console, legs crossed, arms on the table as she leaned forward and stared into her radar screen. He imagined her to be a very smooth and self-assured girl.

But the truth was, Darkhorse was also a little bit nervous. Running intercepts like this could be tricky. It was her responsibility to vector the pilots until they were within range of the F-16s' radar. If she didn't give the pilots a good intercept heading, they might not ever find the two Russian bombers. So she was concentrating as much as the pilots as she guided them northward to the oncoming Blackjacks.

After responding to the controller, Harris looked back at his wingman to make sure he was still in position, then glanced down to check his safety switches one more time. He had to be certain that his weapons were not armed, but instead were in the "safe" position. Harris was carrying two AMRAAM missiles, as well as a case full of 20mm shells for his cannon. It would be a very difficult thing to have to explain if he were to accidentally shoot down a Russian bomber.

So he checked his switches one more time. "Safe" and "Locked" appeared on his head-up-display.

Then Harris checked his airspeed indicator and did some simple math in his head. He figured the four aircraft were now closing at nearly 1,000 miles an hour. In a few seconds he should have the Unknown Cowboys on his AN/APG-66 radar. Then he would challenge them over the radio.

Once again Harris looked at his wingman, then squinted his eyes into the distance. They were flying above a broken layer of clouds, but here at 30,000 feet the visibility was nearly unlimited. Harris figured he should be able to see the Cowboys when they were about twenty miles away. Once he got a good positive visual identification, he could move in for a closer look.

"Dagger, I now have you eight-zero miles from the Unknown Cowboys, twelve o'clock and closing. They are riding at two- three thousand feet. Call visual on the Cowboys."

Les acknowledged the controller with a simple "Rog," then focused his attention back to his radar. The Cowboys were just beginning to show up on his screen. He confirmed their position, altitude, and airspeed, then pumped on his control stick several times. His wingman noticed Harris's horizontal stabilizer as it fluttered up and down in the air. This was the signal for him to move out and away from Harris to a tactical position three hundred feet behind and slightly above his leader. From there, the wingman could monitor his own radar while still protecting his leader.

Harris then switched his transmitter over to guard frequency and clicked the button to his radio.

"Unknown Cowboy, Unknown Cowboy, this is Landmass Dagger broadcasting on 243.0. How do you read?"

By adding "Landmass" to his call sign, Captain Harris had identified himself with the internationally accepted term for U.S. air defenses. He waited several seconds for the bombers to respond, then broadcast the same message again. After a short pause, the Russian pilot replied in broken English.

"Landmass Dagger, Landmass Dagger, this is Losko six-six-seven. Go ahead."

Harris quickly looked down at a small notebook of classified code words that was strapped to his leg. He thumbed through it very quickly until he found the call sign "Losko." According to his notebook, "Losko" was the call sign for the Russian Blackjack bomber. That was what Darkhorse had told him the bogeys were. So far, so good, he thought.

Harris keyed his microphone switch once again. "Losko, you are approaching United States airspace. Recommend you turn left, heading one-eight-zero. Copy?"

"Negative, Landmass Dagger. We are in international airspace. We have not penetrated your Air Defense Zone. Do not attempt to interfere."

This time Capt Harris didn't reply. Instead he rocked his wings several times. Within seconds his wingman had moved back into a tight position, his wing tip just three feet from his leader. While Harris was waiting for the other F-16 to move back into position, he checked his radar once more. The Blackjacks were now less than thirty miles away. They appeared as two small boxes, moving down from the top right-hand corner of his screen. They had not changed their altitude, but they had picked up their airspeed. They were now cruising at over five hundred knots.

Harris turned his head slightly to look at his wingman. The two fighters were so close that Harris could read the letters on his wingman's name tag. Harris raised his hands into a fist, shook it slightly, then extended three fingers toward the sky.

Almost immediately his wingman banked his fighter up and peeled away from him, then rolled into a dive. Harris watched for a moment as the other F-16 accelerated earthward, then leveled off just above the tops of the clouds. Not until then did Harris pull back gently on his stick. His own F-16 began to climb, and he was soon level at 36,000 feet.

He and his wingman had now sandwiched the Russian bombers between them. They would continue on this heading, flying straight toward the Blackjacks. Once the two bombers had passed underneath him, Harris would roll inverted and pull into a dive, at the same time reversing his course. As he was doing this, his wingman would be pulling into a steep climb. When they had both rolled out and leveled off, they would be at 23,000 feet, the same altitude as the bombers. They would also be heading in the same direction. The F-16s would then move slowly forward until they were abeam the Blackjacks, one fighter on each side, five hundred feet out from their wings.

From here they could monitor the bomber's intentions. This was the standard intercept position. It was designed to provide for the safety of all of the aircraft while at the same time allowing the fighters to defend their country's borders.

As the four aircraft quickly closed the remaining gap that separated them, Captain Harris got on his radio to Darkhorse. "Daggers are turning on railroad," he said as he watched the targets on his radar.

"Roger, you're cleared on railroad. Call when bingo fuel," the ground radar controller replied.

By "turning on railroad," Harris had advised Darkhorse that he and his wingman were going to maneuver in on the bombers. Once "railroad" was initiated, the controller then accepted the responsibility of clearing any civilian air traffic that might be in the way of the intercept. This would allow Harris and his wingman to change their altitude and airspeed without prior coordination with Air Traffic Control. It basically gave them carte blanche to go where they wanted, when they wanted, and at any speed they required. The controller would vector other traffic away, allowing the fighters to focus on the target.

"Bingo fuel" meant the controller wanted to know when the fighters were running low on gas. That way she could begin to coordinate for other F-16s to come out and continue to escort the bombers, assuming that they hadn't turned around by that time.

Just then Harris caught a glimmer in the distance. He scanned the airspace in the general direction of the flash that had caught his eye. Then he saw them, two dark shadows in close formation, 14,000 feet below him. They were still about twelve miles out. He kept them in sight as they closed the distance between them. When the Blackjacks had passed underneath, he rolled his fighter inverted and watched the bombers for just a second while he hung upside down in his seat.

Then with a short, "Daggers push . . . now" he declared the intercept on. Pulling back on his stick, his fighter began to pull down into a steep dive. He allowed the F-16's nose to track earthward for a few seconds, building up speed in his dive.

At 520 knots he began to pull back hard on his stick. He felt his G-suit compress tightly around his abdomen and thighs in an effort to keep as much blood as possible from draining from his head. Harris strained against the force of the Gs as he pulled the nose of his fighter back up to the horizon. He glanced at his radar once again to check the position of his wingman, already in his climb.

Harris rolled out level, not more than four hundred feet from the bombers. He glanced over to see that his wingman was already in position, directly across from his leader.

"Landmass Dagger, we have you off our wing. Push back. I say again, push back. You are violating our space."

Harris didn't acknowledge, but he did pull out a little on the bombers. He positioned himself 1,000 feet off of their left wing. He pulled up twenty feet above the Russian aircraft so that he could look across at his wingman, who had also pulled back slightly from the Blackjack's right wing. This was where they would stay.

They didn't plan to converse with the bombers any further. So long as they continued to maintain this distance from U.S. airspace they would just hang out, watching them as they plodded along.

It was only a few minutes later that the bombers were ready to turn around. They had seen what they wanted to see. There wasn't much use in pressing any further now that they had a chance to evaluate the Americans' air defense capabilities.

So, without announcing their intentions, the bombers began a gentle left hand turn to the north. The F-16s stayed in the same position on their wing all through the turn. They would stay with the Blackjacks as they tracked up the coast until they had passed north of the coast of Maine.

As the Russian bombers began to fly to the north, Harris and his wingman faded back in their positions until they were a little more than a mile behind them. From here they would watch the bombers retreat.

Harris glanced down to check his fuel. He had just under 2,300 pounds of gas. Plenty to stay with the Blackjacks for another eight or ten minutes, then they would have to head back to base. But he wouldn't call for any other fighters to come and escort the bombers. By the time Les was out of fuel, the Blackjacks would almost be out of U.S. airspace. It wouldn't be worth it to scramble two more fighters to escort the bombers for less than one hundred miles.

Harris then took a glance at his wingman as they both faded back from the bombers. They dropped back to two-mile spacing. With two miles between the two formations, Harris felt comfortable enough to take care of some paper work. He knew that when he got back to base his commander and the intelligence branch would want a full report on the intercept. He would need to have good notes if he wanted to remember the details. He reached down to write a few quick lines on the kneeboard that was strapped to his leg.

He was just beginning to write when a blazing flash of yellow caught his eye. He dropped his pencil into his lap and looked up very quickly. The flash was extremely bright and he knew immediately that something was wrong.

As Harris looked forward through his canopy, he sucked in a short gasp of air. A knot of fear began to tighten in his throat as he searched the sky up ahead.

A thick cloud of black smoke and a rolling ball of fire was billowing up through the sky. Tiny black pieces of metal composites were beginning to bounce off of his canopy as he flew through a thin cloud of debris. He frantically searched for the two Russian bombers. He peered through the cloud of black smoke and scattering wreckage to see a single Blackjack as it began to frantically jink and dive through the air.

"Landmass Daggers, hold your fire! Daggers, Daggers, hold your fire! We pose no threat. We are retreating. We are unarmed. Withhold your fire!"

Captain Les Harris reached up and tore off his oxygen mask as he watched the falling debris. He swore and cursed and screamed at the empty air. He knew that somewhere in the scattering pieces of metal were the remains of four Russian aviators. He began to circle the wreckage as it tumbled through the air, hoping against hope that he might see a chute. But nothing was there. Only the smoke and falling debris.

Three minutes later, black and charred pieces of the Blackjack bomber finally began to splash into the North Atlantic.

TWENTY-TWO

KIRGHIZIAKN, UKRAINE

THE LARGEST MILITARY SUPPLY CENTER IN THE UKRAINE WAS VERY BUSY. Thousands of tons of war-fighting equipment was being prepared for shipment to the Ukrainian border, now simply referred to as the "Front." Seven thousand men worked under the blanket of darkness, packing the pallets of the food, ammunition, medicine, clothing, tents, paper, and weapons that were desperately needed to assist the Ukrainian army in their efforts to repel the Russian invasion.

Because these supplies were so critical, Kirghiziakn was the most highly defended target in the Ukraine. No less than thirty-seven anti-aircraft guns surrounded the massive complex. Nine different surface-to-air missile batteries formed a protective ring around the center. This protective bubble extended outward from the heart of the complex for eighty-six kilometers and reached skyward to 70,000 feet. The SA-10 and SA-12 surface-to-air missiles were capable of shooting down everything from fighters to cruise missiles.

Six SU-27 Flankers circled over Kirghiziakn in combat formation, ready to repel any Russian attack. Tucked inside their tiny cockpits, the Flanker pilots were nervous. Their eyes were constantly moving, darting from their cockpit to the sky, to the ground. But it wasn't the fear of Russian fighters that had them scared. So far, the Russians had chosen to leave Kirghiziakn alone. It was the fear of their own missiles and anti-aircraft guns that made them jumpy. Over the past twelve hours, two Ukrainian fighters had been shot down by friendly fire, one by a Ukrainian surface-to-air missile, another by a barrage of 57mm anti-aircraft shells.

Two combat kills upon their own forces were far too many. But that didn't mean it couldn't happen again. So the Flanker pilots were very alert. None of them wanted to be kill number three.

The night was very dark. The little light that did reflect from the quarter moon was completely absorbed by a thick overcast of snow clouds well before it could begin to illuminate the frozen ground. The city of Kiev, thirty kilometers to the east of Kirghiziakn, was completely black. Every exterior light, from street lamps to front porch light bulbs, had been turned off in an effort to make it more difficult for the Russian bombers to find their targets.

Winding through the darkness was a four-lane highway. It extended west from the center of Kiev to Kirghiziakn, then turned northeast and made its way through the flat grasslands of northern Ukraine toward the Russian border.

A long stream of supply trucks drove along the highway in the darkness. They, too, had turned off their lights in an effort to be less of a target. Nothing would tempt the Russian fighter-bombers like a convoy of supply trucks on their way to the Front. So the trucks drove in complete darkness, their drivers peering through their night vision goggles, watching the tail of the truck up ahead, hoping that no one came to a sudden or unexpected stop.

Kirghiziakn was a huge complex of mile-long warehouses, narrow alleys, and squat administrative offices. High razor-wire fences and guard towers surrounded the complex to protect its cache of food, medicine, and military supplies from the outside world. Most of the materials were stored in long wooden warehouses. Some were kept in more modern brick storage units. But a very small percentage of the materials that were stored inside Kirghiziakn required much tighter security than a simple warehouse had to offer.

This was where the bunkers came in. Inside the wire fences that surrounded Kirghiziakn were twenty-three semi-buried bunkers, their thick cement frames protruding just a few feet above the ground. At one time, these bunkers had been used to protect nuclear bombs and missiles. But the Ukrainian military had ceded their nuclear weapons to the international community several years before. Since then, the contents of these bunkers had been kept a very well-guarded secret.

At 2100 hours, a small covered truck pulled up to one of the bunkers. As the truck coasted to a stop, the bunker's huge steel doors began to roll open. Three soldiers emerged from the bunker, their submachine guns flung across their backs. They wore white winter overcoats on top of thick, white woven pants. On their feet were Liata, very expensive winter boots that could only be purchased in Italy. The men were all Ukrainians, though most of them were Russian by birth. None of the men wore any rank or insignia. None of them carried any identification.

The men helped to guide the two-ton truck as it backed down the narrow incline that led into the bunker. When the truck was safely inside, the doors were rolled tightly closed.

The men worked quickly. Setting their machine guns aside, they stripped off their heavy overcoats and began to don their gear; heavy insulated pants, long rubber gloves, thin latex hoods, and alien-like face masks with dark protruding eyes.

In the back of the bunker was a single pallet loaded with eight small blue drums. Working together, the men started to load the drums on the back of the truck. Their pace was agonizingly slow. Every movement of the drums was very deliberate. Very careful. Every move was planned and calibrated to ensure that the drums weren't knocked or jostled in any way.

The drums were placed onto a special platform that had been installed in the back of the truck. It was suspended above the bed on a complex series of springs and shock absorbers, isolating the platform from the bumps that it would encounter along the road.

Within an hour, the drums had all been loaded. One of the men started the truck's engine while two others rolled back the bunker doors. The truck pulled out of the bunker and into the cold night air. Ten minutes later, it had joined another convoy of supply trucks that were making their way to the Front.

AKHTRYKA, UKRAINE

Boris Yershov switched on his landing light as he searched through the fog and darkness for his landing pad. But the bright light couldn't cut through the fog. Instead, it spread and reflected around him, engulfing him in a billowing world of white clouds and wispy darkness, making it even more difficult to see.

Yershov quickly reached up and turned his landing light back off. He gently tugged up on his collective while at the same time pulling back on the stick. His helicopter stabilized in a hover above the high and blowing trees. The downdraft from his rotors stirred the treetops into a constant dance of motion, pushing their branches outward and washing the snow from their bristled leaves.

Directly below him, Yershov could barely make out the shape of a huge inverted Y. It was made up of a string of small lights and was suppose to direct him downward as he attempted to land in the clearing that had been cut through the trees.

But the clearing was small. Very small. He stabilized the helicopter in high hover directly over the clearing, then pushed against his right foot pedal. The helicopter began to slowly spin, giving Yershov a chance to survey the site.

The clearing was probably big enough—but barely. Yershov aligned his helicopter with the hole, then slowly lowered the collective and began a gentle descent, slipping downward through the blanket of fog.

After settling onto the thin layer of snow, Yershov brought his engine to idle and looked around him. Not a soul was in sight. He began to wait. His rotors created a dull *woop, woop* as they slapped through the cold, dense air.

Someone should have been here to meet him. He checked his watch once again. As he held his wrist up to the faint lights of his cockpit, he noticed his trembling hands. It had been a long time. Not since his combat days in Afghanistan had he felt the strain and excitement of a mission.

Yershov peered through the darkness once again to see three distinct shadows moving toward him through the trees. Billowing ponchos flapped in the wind. Dark masks with huge, bug-like eyes glinted in the darkness. Yershov recoiled at the sight. Chemical warfare suits! That was bad. Very bad. Something deadly must be floating through the air. Something evil and painful. Something silent, yet toxic. The invisible death. A gas that could suck the breath from his body, or a slimy film whose smallest touch would poison his blood.

A knot of fear immediately grew in the pit of Yershov's stomach. His mind began to scream to him, "*Run!*"

Boris Yershov had a very special fear of chemical weapons. He had seen first hand what chemical agents could do. He had watched men writhe through the dust in pain, begging for someone to shoot them as they heaved and choked on their own blood. He had watched men pierce their bodies with half a dozen five-inch needles in a desperate effort to inject themselves with the proper antidote. He had listened to the cry of suffering soldiers as they wailed in a deathbed of despair.

Yes, Boris Yershov knew the power of chemical weapons. And that fear drove him to make a quick decision.

He was leaving. He didn't care how good the pay was, it could never be enough. He would wind up his engine and climb back up through the trees. If chemical agents were here, he was gone.

Yershov rolled up the throttle on his engine. The helicopter began to vibrate as his rotors picked up speed. As soon as he was at full power, he would yank up on his collective and blast upward through the trees.

His rotors were just coming up to full power when one of the men began to walk up to his chopper, motioning for Yershov to shut down. Yershov shook his head. The man pulled off mask. Yershov relaxed his grip on the throttle. The man set his mask to one side and pulled off his gloves while motioning once again for Yershov to shut down his helicopter. This time Yershov complied.

Forty-five minutes later, all of the three holding tanks that were strapped to the side of Yershov's helicopter had been filled with the contents of the blue drums. Yershov had been issued his own chemical agent gear, along with some very detailed instructions.

For the next fourteen minutes, Yershov flew over very specific portions of the battlefield. He flew under the cover of darkness. His small helicopter was never picked up by anyone's radar. No one even knew he was there. Using the wind, he sprayed his cargo over an area twenty miles square.

When he was finished, he came back to land in the same spot as before. His job was finished. He would collect his payment and go home.

It was one of life's ironies that Boris Yershov, who harbored an enormous fear of chemical weapons, was more than happy to spread them all over the battlefield, protected in the bubble of his own chemical suit. And now that his duty was over, happy to have served his country one more time, he was ready to go home.

Once again, Yershov allowed his helicopter to settle down through the trees. After landing, he shut down his engine and sat in the cockpit as his blades slowly rolled to a stop. He was waiting for someone to bring him his money. But, once again, it appeared that no one was here. He sat and listened. The silence became almost eerie as his rotor blades coasted to a stop.

Then Yershov saw a sudden motion. A quick shadow darted from behind one of the trees. Yershov peered into the darkness. He turned on the battery to his helicopter, then flipped on the searchlight. It shined through the trees, casting long shadows outward from the helicopter. Then he saw it again. Another shadow, this time much closer, moving catlike through the brush.

Yershov felt his heart quicken. Something wasn't right. He could feel it. Once again his instincts screamed to him *"Run!"*

The last thing Boris Yershov saw was the flash from the muzzle. It cracked the night like lightning, strobing the trees. But Boris was dead from a shot between the eyes long before the sound of the gun echoed through the forest to his ears.

KREMENCHUG-CHERKASSY, UKRAINE

The Ukrainian prime minister watched from the TCC's conference room. Below him, most of the soldiers and controllers in the center sat in a horrified stupor as casualty rates were posted on the control center board. Seven thousand Ukrainian soldiers killed. Nine thousand more were contaminated and not expected to live. In one night. From one biological attack.

Golubev looked over at Andrei Liski, who sat at the back of the room, eating a fresh orange, one slice at a time. Between slices, he occupied himself by doodling on a white piece of scratch paper, writing notes to himself. He seemed completely unaffected by the casualty rates. The simple truth was, so far at least, they were much lower than he had expected. The Nertrav must have been nearly out of date. Secretly, he had expected at least three times the number of casualties. He just hoped the numbers were impressive enough to have the desired effect.

General Lomov sat at the opposite end of the table, slouched down in his seat, his head supported against the wide headrest. His haggard face was a perfect blank, his eyes staring unseeing at the far wall. He looked corpselike, with his mouth slightly open and his flesh drained of its natural color. The night had already become his own private nightmare, and deep in his skull, he considered an old German proverb.

"In times of war, Satan makes more room in hell."

Certainly that was true. He knew it was true. And his fate was now guaranteed.

WASHINGTON, D.C.

The President of the United States awakened very slowly. The soft buzzer that sat on his nightstand sounded for several minutes before he finally rolled over. The President yawned and stretched and pushed his head against his pillow. He shut his eyes tightly, wishing the buzzer would just go away.

But it didn't, and after a few seconds he finally reached over and pressed a small button on the side of the alarm.

"Mr. President, I'm sorry to wake you." It was Milton Blake, his National Security Advisor. "Sir, we have a problem. Could I come up for a moment."

President Allen stretched once again, then rolled his feet to the floor and sat up on the side of his bed. "What time is it?" he asked.

"It's almost four, sir," Milton Blake responded.

The President rubbed his hands through his hair and pressed his palms against the side of his head.

"Come on up, Milt. I'll be waiting for you." The President spoke in a rough and congested voice. He reached over and turned on his lamp, then rubbed his eyes to help them adjust to the light. He sat on the bed for a minute or two before standing up and pulling on his bathrobe. He then stumbled into the bathroom and splashed some water on his face.

About that time, Ken Labrems, his personal secretary, knocked gently on his bedroom door. Ken walked into the room without waiting for the President to answer, followed by the President's National Security Advisor. Both of the men were freshly showered and dressed in dark suits.

President Allen caught a glimpse down the hallway as the two men entered the room. The upper floor of the White House was very quiet. Only one small light illuminated the hallway and no one else was in sight.

The President walked over to a huge leather couch that sat against the far wall of his bedroom. He plopped down on the soft leather and put his feet up on the oak coffee table, then motioned for Blake to sit down beside him. Meanwhile, Ken Labrems went into the President's closet to begin to lay out his clothes.

"What is it, Milt?" the President began in a weary voice. "And don't tell me the Russians have lost another bomber."

"No sir, it's nothing like that," Blake quickly responded. "Though I only wish it were so. I'm afraid this is much worse. Something has happened in the Ukraine. It has enormous implications, and it may prove very complicated for us to work through."

Blake paused and then continued. "It's Fedotov, sir. Last night, portions of the Ukrainian Army were attacked with a chemical weapon. The number of casualities is unknown at this time, but it might be enormous.

"We have reason to believe it is Nertrav, the Russians' newest blood agent. If it is, there will be no doubt that the attack was precipitated by Fedotov, for the Russians are the only country that have Nertrav in stock. We should know in a few hours when the final analysis comes back from our lab."

As Blake spoke, he leaned forward in his seat to study the President's face. He couldn't help but notice that the strain from the past few weeks was beginning to show. Only a handful of men in the entire world would ever understand the burden that the President carried. And of those, only one or two were close enough to President Allen to see how the stress had carved deep lines in his face.

The President stared straight ahead in a horrified stupor. He didn't know what to say. Finally, Milton Blake broke the awkward silence.

"Mr. President, there is going to be enormous pressure for us to do something. And maybe we should. I mean, how far do you let a man like Fedotov go? When do we take a stand? How long can we stand idly by?

"Mr. President, I understand that in times of war, the bounds of human decency are sometimes vague and ambiguous. I mean, when your objective is to kill and destroy, it is easy to fall into a mode where one means of death is the same as another.

"But sir, there have been, and always will be, some things that are clearly unacceptable. Some actions scream out to be punished. Some lines were not meant to be crossed."

The President slowly shook his head. How could he ever disagree?

That afternoon, after hours of urgent meetings, the President authorized his National Security Team and the Pentagon to draft a contingency plan calling for limited air strikes, using forward deployed F-117s, against carefully selected Russian targets, primarily chemical and biological weapon storage facilities.

Three hours after the planning cells were assembled, an anonymous source called the *Washington Times*. By early the next morning, the entire country had been notified that the United States was developing its military options against Russia.

The press reports alarmed many people. The country seemed to be bracing to enter the war. And the news didn't go unnoticed in the Kremlin. By late that evening, Fedotov's people were making contingency plans of their own.

BOLLING AIR FORCE BASE, WASHINGTON, D.C.

Lieutenant Colonel Oliver Tray stared once again at the map, with the city of Dallas at the center from which concentric circles expanded. Tiny pins noted the various reported sightings, though none of them had yet born any fruit. They were scattered from Houston to Oklahoma City. From Baton Rouge to Pacos. It was such a huge area they had to cover! More than two hundred thousand square miles! Simple old fashioned police work would not be the answer. They didn't have time! They needed him now!

"When will the National Reconnaissance Organization decide on moving the satellite?" he demanded.

"Hopefully by the end of the day." Colonel Fullbright replied.

Tray rocked on his feet as he studied the map and cursed to himself. What was taking so long?

Fullbright read the look on Tray's face and said, "Keep in mind what we are asking for, Oliver. You know that moving a satellite takes direct approval from the National Security Advisor himself. As you can imagine, he is extremely busy. This isn't the only pile of worms on his plate. Not only that, but we are requesting one of the K-23s. The K-23s, Oliver! There are only two satellites in the entire world that are capable of doing what we want it to do—detecting and locating a microburst transmission. Do you have any idea how difficult it is going to be for us to convince Blake to move one of them out of the combat theater to monitor the States? We'll be lucky if he doesn't throw us out of his office!"

Tray nodded. He understood.

"But still," Fullbright continued, "I have ten minutes on his schedule at five this evening. General Mann is also going with me, and as you know, he can present a very hard sell. If we can get Blake to relocate the K-23 for just a few days, that might be all we need. If he approves, the satellite will be moved overnight. It should be in place to monitor the southwestern part of the U.S. by early morning."

Oliver turned to face his boss. "We've got to have it, sir. We've absolutely got to have it. We can't count on anything else. They will be getting and receiving messages. They have to. Of that I am sure. And if we can just get the satellite in position to pinpoint their location, if we can get it there before it is too late, assuming it isn't too late now, then we will get them. As soon as that bloody Morozov so much as peeps on a satellite broadcast, we'll nail his hide to the wall!"

Fullbright grunted, then turned away from the wall map and strode around to sit down at his desk. Oliver Tray turned back to the map.

As he stared at the wall, a funny thought kept rolling around in his head. It had popped in his mind when he had first woken up, and now he couldn't seem to get rid of it. It was a line from *How the Grinch Stole Christmas*, a perennial favorite among his three kids.

"He puzzled and puzzled until his puzzler was sore."

That was how Oliver felt. His brain actually hurt. Deep in his skull, it actually hurt. A result of the stress and constant worry. And three nights without any sleep. The frustration was boiling inside him! The answer was there, but he couldn't see it! It all fit together, but he didn't know how!

What was going on with Badger? It just didn't make any sense! Why had Morozov suddenly called his man back? And now, here they were, the two of them back in the country! That was the absolute last place Tray thought Morozov would be. With the Ukraine about to be overrun by a million Russian soldiers, why on earth would he be here in the States? And what about the stolen computers? It all fit—it had to—it's just that he hadn't yet figured out how.

He shook his head and reached into his pants pocket to take out a tiny package of aspirin, popped two in his mouth, then chewed on them without any water.

"Any news on Jesse?" he finally wondered, with genuine concern in his voice.

"Nothing yet," Fullbright replied. "I talked with Pearson, one of the deputy directors, yesterday noon. Those guys over at FBI are ready to pull out their hair. I think they are even more stressed out than we are. It's like she just disappeared. Normally, I wouldn't be too concerned, but with the way things are going, I see a negative trend, which makes me believe that it might not look so good."

Tray replied, "Yeah . . . but you know, I was thinking, late last night as I was driving home from work. He said something to me long ago. It didn't mean much at the time . . . but I wonder. Now I know it's a long shot, but I think we should try. I mean, at this point, what else have we got?"

Fullbright looked up from his work.

Tray glanced quickly around the room, scanning the cluttered desk and the disorganized bookshelf that filled the far wall. "What I really need is a Rand McNally," he finally said. "Have you got a map of California anywhere in this mess?"

TWENTY-THREE

WICHITA, KANSAS

RICHARD AMMON LAY IN HIS BED AND LISTENED TO THE SOUND OF
the aircraft as they took off and landed at McConnell Air Force
Base, located just outside the Wichita city limits. The cheap motel
that Morozov had chosen for them was situated directly underneath
the departure routing for the airport, and Ammon tried to identify the
different aircraft by the sound of their engines as they flew overhead.
The KC-135 tankers sounded like any jet airliner, while the F-16s
lifted off with a high-pitched scream.

Then there were the B-1s. The sheer size of their engines made
them impossible to miss. The walls of the motel vibrated and rattled as
the B-1s took to the air.

Ammon glanced at the alarm clock that was sitting on the fake
cherry nightstand next to his head. It was almost 10 A.M. He couldn't
remember the last time he had slept in so late. It had been three days
since he and Morozov had checked into this truck-driver dive, and so
far, laying in bed and watching television was about all he had been
allowed to do. Once he had walked to the window and pulled back the
blinds, but Morozov had quickly pushed him away. But still, Ammon
had had enough time to see him. He was walking from a dark blue
Camaro toward his hotel room. The goon from the diner. Morozov's
main man.

For three days Ammon had not been allowed to leave. No maids ever came in, for the "Do Not Disturb" sign was always left hanging from the outside doorknob. The only thing he had eaten was Domino's pizza and the soggy coffee cakes that Morozov brought him from the corner vending machine. He was never left alone. Morozov had always stayed with him, except for quick walks to the lobby for donuts, colas, and the morning paper. And whenever Morozov left for even the shortest amount of time, the goon from the diner, who was apparently staying in the room next to theirs, was invited in first. The goon would sit in the corner and play with his nose ring while drinking beer and watching television. He would swear at the television and complain about Morozov while spitting black chew into a plastic hotel cup. He always seemed anxious and very impatient.

It had been three very long days.

Ammon listened to the sound of Morozov sleeping, then rolled onto his side and stared at the clock once again. For the thousandth time he looked at the tan telephone on top of the night stand. It was dead. Morozov had pulled out the cord and cut it in half the night they had checked into the hotel.

How long had Richard been trying to get to a phone? From P'yongyang to Kiev to Helsinki, he had only one thing on his mind. It wasn't a huge undertaking. It shouldn't have been a big thing. All he wanted was three minutes of time with a telephone and an international operator. But he now recognized that had been one of his biggest mistakes. He had never realized how closely Morozov would control him, once he had him back under his wing. He had assumed that he would be trusted. And given a little leeway. A little freedom.

How wrong he had turned out to be.

Come on you guys, where are you? he thought, as once again he stared at the phone.

LONE PINE, CALIFORNIA

It was early morning when Nadine pulled Jesse from her bed, dragged her by the hand into the cabin's tiny kitchen, and sat her at the kitchen table. After three days of lying on her bed in the darkness, without eating, without responding in any way to their presence, Jesse was worrying Clyde and Nadine. If things didn't go well, if anything happened to Jesse on their watch, they would pay a terrible price. The foreigner had been very specific. Keep track of her. Keep her in the cabin. And don't hurt her in any way.

But something wasn't right. For the past seventy-two hours, Jesse had done nothing but toss in a restless sleep. Her skin appeared cold and clammy, her hair drenched in sweat. Clyde had been wakened at four in the morning to the sound of her retching. Huge, gasping, dry, wrenching heaves.

They needed to keep her alive. And to keep her alive, she needed to eat. Clyde was in the small kitchen, waiting, already sitting. As Jesse was shoved up to the table, she noticed the 9mm pistol holstered over Clyde's left hip.

Jesse sat down. Clyde pulled out a long, black nightstick and placed it on the table next to his plate, just out of Jesse's reach. Its thin leather wrist-strap dangled over the edge of the table. On the chair, between him and Jesse, was a long cord of rope. Jesse recognized it immediately. She could see faint smears of blood smattered throughout the length of the rope from where they had tied up her wrists. With a barely perceptible motion, Clyde caught Jesse's eye as she glanced down at his gun. He nodded his head toward the stick and rope while raising an eyebrow. The meaning became very clear. "Make any moves, do anything funny, and I'll whack you on the head with my stick. Then I'll tie you back up to your bed. It won't be fun. It will be painful. So sit still, girl, and do what I tell you to do."

Jesse looked at the floor.

The woman had made an enormous breakfast; ham, eggs, pancakes, blueberry muffins, toast, and hot cereal. The kitchen smelled like a House of Pancakes. A huge plate of food was set before Jesse.

"Eat something, you idiot!" the man ordered. Jesse sat without moving. The man made a sudden motion toward her, lifting up in his chair, raising the back of his hand, his face a picture of contempt. Jesse flinched.

"Stupid woman. Why won't you eat?"

Jesse turned her face away, shielding it with her shoulder. The man sat down with a huff. Jesse looked down at the food. Her stomach ached from hunger. Her arms felt heavy and weak. Her mouth started to water. Oh, how she wanted to eat! The pit in her stomach began an insistent growl, begging to be nourished, reminding her of the many hours since she had eaten anything of real substance. The smell of ham and maple syrup overwhelmed her. It smelled so good. So sweet and warm.

It had been three days since Jesse had eaten. Although the man had brought her a small tray of cold cereal and toast every morning, she would only pick at the food. She never ate more than a mouthful, keeping her hunger at bay. She would take the glass of water, and when Clyde wasn't looking, pour it onto her pillow. The foam pillow soaked up the water like an enormous sponge. Later, she would use the trapped water to moisten her face and hair, making herself look matted with a clammy sweat.

Jesse looked down at her food and rolled her eyes. Clyde stared at Jesse for a moment. Nadine busied herself at the stove, preparing her own breakfast plate. Jesse sat motionless at the table, her face pale and emotionless, her eyes glued to the pancakes on her plate. Clyde looked away, paying her no more attention as he focused on his own breakfast.

Jesse's heart was beating wildly. Her nerves were wired, tight as steel, raw as bone. This might be her chance. Her only chance. She couldn't wait any longer to act.

Very slowly, Jesse lifted her left hand from her lap and began to explore the underside of the kitchen table. It was made of rough pine and square nails. The top of the table had been sanded smooth. The bottom had not. It was rough as newly timbered wood, splintered and uneven. It bristled with sharp and tattered edges. Jesse carefully felt around with her fingers, running them along the edges of the wood until she found what she was looking for. She touched a sharp piece of wood, pointed and jagged, but fairly strong. This would do.

She took a quick glance at Clyde and Nadine. Neither of them paid her any attention. Clyde poked at his ham with his fork.

Jesse took a quick breath and held it. Her heart raced. The muscles in her chest drew tight. Her mouth went dry. Another quick look at her captors. She touched the splinter of wood once again.

With a jerk, she jammed her finger against the sharp spur. She smothered a wince of pain as she felt thick drops of blood forming on the tip of her finger. She took another deep breath and held it, then rolled her eyes back into her head, moaned once, and bit down hard on the inside of her cheek.

She rolled off the kitchen chair with a groan, her body shaking violently, uncontrollably, her eyes wild. She chewed on her cheek once again as red spittle dripped from the corner of her mouth. She quickly jammed her bleeding finger into her left ear, squeezed it tight, then dropped her hand down to her waist, shaking with a violent seizure.

Clyde watched her fall to the floor. For a fraction of a second he remained unimpressed. Then he saw the blood. It spat from the corners of her mouth. It dribbled from out of her ear. It smeared all over her face as she jerked around on the floor. He saw the gaping, unseeing eyes as they rolled back. Jesse's neck twitched violently and she smashed against the corner of the kitchen table, causing a gash across the right side of her forehead.

He stared down at the quivering and moaning girl, completely confused. He had no idea what to do. It was Nadine who finally sprang into action. Bounding around the kitchen table, she threw herself onto the floor next to Jesse and wrapped her arms around her shoulders and neck in an attempt to keep her from bashing her head against the hard wooden floor. "Don't just sit there," she screamed. "Do something!"

"What! What should I do?"

"I don't know . . . get a pillow!" Nadine screamed again. Jesse pushed and pulled against the woman's weight. She moaned and wailed and cried. Bloody spit flew everywhere. Her teeth began to chatter and her eyes rolled back again, leaving only the whites exposed under the eyelids.

Then suddenly, just as quickly as it had began, she went perfectly limp. Her arms dropped to the side of her waist, her legs flopped out across the floor, her head dropped to the side. Every muscle in her body turn to liquid. Her dark eyes stopped rolling, but didn't close. They stared, unseeing, perfectly blank, brown and tearless. She didn't move. She hardly breathed, her chest rising in desperate and shallow gasps.

Nadine released Jesse. "What do we do? We can't just take her to the hospital!" she cried.

Clyde stood and ran from the room. The cabin's only telephone was in the living area, on the other side of the huge rock wall that separated the two rooms.

"I'll call Morozov. I'll call the foreigner. He's got to know. We've got to tell him. Let him decide what we should do."

Nadine reached down and placed her face next to Jesse's nose and mouth. She was still hardly breathing. She felt for her pulse at the side of her neck. She couldn't find it. She didn't really know where to look.

"I think we're losing her!" she called out to her husband. "Stupid, stupid, girl!" Nadine sobbed in frustration as she sat herself up on the floor, wiping the spit and blood from her arms against her denim blouse and brushing her hair from her eyes.

From the next room Clyde began to yell. "Where is his number? Where is it? How do I get a hold of Morozov?"

"It's by the phone. No, wait . . . it's in my purse. I think. He called two nights ago and gave you the number. You idiot, I think you put it in my purse."

Jesse lay perfectly still on the floor, her breath coming in short, gurgling gasps. A tiny dribble of red saliva still dripped from the corner of her mouth. Every few seconds, her left foot would twitch. Nadine was genuinely scared. Not that she cared about Jesse. Her life wasn't worth a flying wad of spit. But they had been told that they had to wait before they could kill her. He had been very explicit. Keep her alive until I tell you otherwise. And based on what little she knew of the man and his friends, Nadine had a very good idea what the foreigner would do to them if they let her die before it was time.

"Did you find the number?" she called into the other room, fighting the fear in her voice.

"No! It's not here! You've got half a million pieces of junk in your purse. You come find it! I'm telling you, it isn't here!"

Nadine pushed herself up from the floor and ran from the room.

Within two seconds, Jesse was out the kitchen door. She leaped over the patio railing, dropped the four feet to the forest floor and raced off into the woods, cutting across the hillside, dodging behind thick pine trees and white aspens, wiping the tears and blood from her eyes as she ran. She slanted her path slightly upward, knowing neither Nadine nor Clyde had the physical ability to follow. Not through the brush and trees. Not uphill. Not in the thin mountain air. Under the best of conditions, neither one of them could have kept up with her for more than twenty yards. In the forest, they didn't stand a chance.

But then again, they both had guns. That was worth far more than a few extra yards.

By the time Jesse was thirty paces into the forest, she had already faded from view. Ten seconds later, she had completely disappeared. Only the distant crack of an occasionally broken branch gave any indication of where she had run.

Clyde and Nadine spent only ten seconds looking through Nadine's purse before Clyde ran back into the kitchen to check on the girl. He scrambled around the huge stone wall and stopped dead in his tracks. The girl was gone.

His eyes darted around the kitchen. He started to scream as he pulled his 9mm from his shoulder holster. He ran out the screened patio door and onto the patio, gun in hand, held in the ready position. He would kill her before he would let her go! He searched wildly through the thick forest of trees that surrounded the cabin. Nothing. He ran down the patio steps and began to scramble through the trees, running left and then right, jerking his way through the forest.

He stopped to listen. Nothing. No sound at all. He ran deeper into the woods, peering through the trees. His heart pounded like a sledge-hammer, his head beating with every pump of his heart. Perspiration dripped into his eyes. He stopped to listen once again, leaning against a small tree.

Forty yards behind him, he heard the screen door slam open and shut. "What have you done?" he heard Nadine screaming. "You idiot, what have you done?"

"*Shut up! Shut up and listen!*" Clyde cried out. Nadine fell silent. Clyde peered through the brush.

There it was. A brittle snap from a tree limb. Then the quiet rustle of leaves. He turned to his right and headed up the side of the mountain. She was there. She couldn't be far. He only had left her for just a few seconds. He ran another twenty yards, then stopped again to listen. Another quick rustle of leaves. He turned and waved his arms, beckoning Nadine to follow, and ran another thirty steps up the hill.

Then he saw her. Forty yards into the forest and directly off to his right. She had crawled up under a thick mulberry bush. She was laying down, her head facing the top of the mountain, her back toward Clyde, her body completely obscured by the leaves. Only her shoes and bare ankles lay exposed on the downhill side of the green, leafy bush. But they were plainly in view. The sweat poured down his back. Glancing around, he looked for Nadine. She wasn't there.

He lifted his 9mm pistol to the fire position, holding it steady with both hands, his arms fully extended out before him. He carefully aimed, then slowly pulled on the trigger. His hands bounced into the air, still clasped together, as the force of the recoil made its way through his arms.

The silencer uttered a muffled *thong*. A tiny explosion of dirt and dry leaves bounced into the air, barely twelve inches from Jesse's exposed feet.

"I see you, Jesse," Clyde called out.

He raised his pistol and fired off another shot. It too impacted the dirt with a quick and silent *thump*, just a fraction above Jesse's ankle. The leaves of the mulberry bush rattled and shivered, but still, Jesse didn't come out.

"I see your feet." Clyde took a few steps toward the shaking bush. "I see your feet. You're too tall to hide them. Now watch as I blow one of them off. You're not going to run away from me, Jesse. You'll never run or walk ever again!"

Clyde raised the pistol for the last time. He was completely serious. He would shoot off one of her feet. He was tired of screwing around with the girl. This job was over. He was going to kill her and be done with it. Screw Morozov. Let him take care of his own problems. He had already been paid half of the money. That was enough. This job was done.

He aimed the pistol, placing Jesse's left ankle in the center of the sights. He held his breath and began to slowly squeeze on the trigger. From under the bush, he could hear Jesse sob.

With a sickening thump, he felt the bullet pass through the back of his left shoulder and out the front side, exploding blood and muscle and cartilage through the air in front of his face. A searing pain and burning sensation cut through his back and made its way up his spine. Every ounce of breath was knocked from his body, and he immediately slumped to the ground, his face mashing into the dry and rotting leaves. He gasped and rolled and cried for breath as the blood spurted from a splintered hole, just half an inch above his left collar bone.

The agent had fired through the trees from just over two hundred yards. But clearly, it was a near perfect shot.

TWENTY-FOUR

WICHITA, KANSAS

IVAN MOROZOV WALKED BRISKLY THROUGH THE PARKING LOT. THE HOOD of his coat was pulled down tight around his face as he sought protection from the bitter cold and freezing rain. He jumped over small puddles of brown water that covered the rutted asphalt, then walked into the Wichita Mall and shook off the sleet from his coat. He stood before the mall directory for only a moment while he searched for his destination, then turned and walked toward a small coffee shop that was located in a deep corner of the food emporium.

He looked around quickly as he entered the restaurant. It was not very crowded. At least not yet. Ten-thirty was too early for the lunch traffic to begin. He ignored the sign that asked him to wait to be seated and walked deliberately back to a corner booth. The man was already waiting.

He didn't look up as Morozov pushed into the booth, but continued to run dry pieces of toast through the dripping egg yolks, stuffing them into his mouth. Morozov made himself comfortable, then reached over and picked up the newspaper which lay rolled up next to the man's plate of eggs. As he flipped it open, he was surprised to see that it was two days old.

"You're a little behind in your reading," he muttered.

The man stuffed another piece of dripping toast in his mouth. "Been busy," was all he replied.

Morozov scanned the headline, which was two inches high, bold and black. Headlines like this sold a lot of papers.

RUSSIAN BOMBER SHOT DOWN
U.S. BLAMED FOR AIRCRAFT'S LOSS

The United States Government denied any involvement in yesterday's apparent downing of a Russian Blackjack bomber, despite Russia's claim that one of two U.S. Air Force fighters shot down the Tu-160 aircraft twenty miles from the coast of Maine.

The Russian aircraft was flying in international airspace when the incident occurred. Russian president Vladimir Fedotov denounced the downing of his bomber, calling it a "calculated, cowardly, and deliberate act of war."

Although the U.S. military continues to deny any involvement, the incident has heightened the current crisis to an explosive level. Right wing members of the Russian parliament have demanded an immediate and unconditional apology from the United States. President Fedotov has threatened a retaliatory strike against U.S. military aircraft that are currently operating in the Mediterranean Sea as a part of NATO war game exercises.

"We cannot let such aggression go unpunished," Fedotov said in a hastily called news conference. "We had an unarmed Russian aircraft, operating in a perfectly legal manner, with no hostile intentions, suddenly shot from the air. It was a completely unprovoked attack. But I will say this. We know now who is an agent for peace, and who is an agent for war. We now have a clearer idea of who is an enemy to the new Russian state. And knowing that, we will respond. Beyond that, I will say no more."

Morozov scanned the story, then folded the paper and smiled. It was a pleasure to see a plan come together.

Fedotov's friend looked up from his eggs. He was a large man, middle-aged and serious-looking. His skin was lily white. His eyes were a pale brown, like dry winter leaves, and just as lifeless. They spoke of painful days and long winter nights and were a perfect complement to the cold smirk that marked his face.

Ivan Morozov studied him for a moment, then spoke in a harsh whisper as he looked around the near-empty restaurant.

"What's the official count on the Nertrav incident?"

The man answered with an expressionless face. "The Ukrainian press is calling it twenty thousand, give or take. Officially, the U.S. Defense Department refuses to say. Liski thinks it is not quite that high, maybe fourteen thousand by the time the Nertrav has run its full course. But really, what does it matter? Ten . . . fourteen . . . twenty . . . what's the difference? Either way, it had the desired effect."

Morozov smiled once again. "Hear about Korea?" he asked. The man shook his head.

"CNN is reporting that North Korean troops are beginning to mobilize along the South Korean border. They have promised their support to Fedotov, should he be the victim of any NATO air attacks.

"I'm sure they are praying the United States enters the war," Morozov continued. "What with all the condemnation they have come under over the past year for their nuclear build-up, the diversion of attention and resources away from the Korean Peninsula would be just what they need. In addition, Libya and Iraq have promised concessions to the Russians on their oil. And with yesterday's announcement that both Moldavia and Kazakhstan have agreed to join the new Russian Union, it would seem that Fedotov's allies, few and brash as they are, seem to be falling in line."

The man grunted. "Yeah, that's great. But now let's get down to business." Morozov's eyes narrowed as he leaned slightly forward.

"Okay, Volodymyr. What have you got?"

"The air refueling tanker has been set up. Our people got onto the network early this morning. It was just about like you said. We got a receipt message from Torrejon, and it has all been confirmed."

"Yes . . . okay . . . that is good," Morozov said. But he knew there was more. He could tell by the look in Volodymyr's eyes.

"And . . . ? Is that all?"

"No," Volodymyr said. "We are having a little problem with the girl."

Morozov glared and waited while stuffing a Marlboro between his dry lips.

"It goes like this. One morning last week, everything is cool. Clyde and Nadine have her safe and sound in the cabin. I went there myself. Everything looks good. I check things over. Have a little talk with them. Everything was under control.

"Two days later, they call and say she is sick or something. Won't eat. Sweats a lot. Throws up stuff in her sleep. Refuses to get up and walk around. You know. Typical sick hostage crap."

Just then a young waitress came up to their booth and pulled out a pencil and ticket pad. Morozov pushed his coffee mug over so that she could pour him a cup, then shook his head when she offered a menu. She left quickly. The two men waited until she was out of earshot before they continued their conversation.

"Yeah, yeah, so what's the story?" Morozov asked in an irritated voice as he took a small sip from his coffee. "You didn't call me out here to tell me she's got the twenty-four hour flu. So what's going on?"

"Don't really know. Which is the main problem."

Morozov put his coffee aside and looked up.

"I called out there this morning," the man continued. "Got no answer. Called every fifteen minutes for the past three hours. No one is home."

Morozov swore under his breath. "You idiot! You stupid fool! You better not have screwed this thing up, my friend, or I'll cut off your hands and feed them to my dogs!

"What do you mean that no one is there!? Didn't they have their instructions? They were supposed to keep her at the cabin! You'd better find out what's going on! And you better not bring me bad news."

The man didn't blink as he stared at Morozov.

"May I remind you, Comrade Morozov," he sneered, "the man and his wife were your idea. Not mine. So you crap all over the place, then send me in to clean up the mess. I don't think so. So don't be telling me how to do my job.

"Now, I've sent some people out there to take a look. They'll be in position in another hour or so. I'm certain the girl is still there. I'm sure that there is some explanation. The phones are down. They had a bad storm. Whatever, she's got to be there. Unless you think she took out both of your people. Chopped them to pieces with a butter knife or something. Possible, but not very likely.

"So let's not overreact just for the thrill of a good panic. It seems like we've done that before."

Morozov stared silently at the man and grunted. The man stood up. "I'll be talking to you," he said as he threw a twenty dollar bill on the table and left. Morozov took another sip at his coffee, then picked up the money and slipped it into his shirt pocket. He pulled out two fives from his own wallet and left them on the table. Then he followed the man out the front door.

Outside the coffee shop, Morozov watched the back of the man's head as he made his way through the maze of plastic tables and morning shoppers that were beginning to crowd into the food court. The man soon disappeared in the throng. Morozov then turned in the opposite direction and walked back toward the same doorway in which he had entered the mall. He put on his overcoat as he walked quickly back out to his car.

It was cold. The freezing rain had turned to a light snow, and the temperature had dropped into the twenties. Ivan Morozov studied the sky for a moment as he stood by the side of his car. It wasn't flying weather. Low clouds and fog hung over the trees, and the visibility looked to be less than a mile. He had noticed that there weren't many B-1s that had taken off from the base this morning. He understood why. It was a lousy day to be in the air.

Morozov shivered from the cold, then ducked into his car and started it up. Pulling out of the mall parking lot, he headed back to the hotel. As he drove, he kept the heater turned off. The interior of the car began to fog over. From time to time, he would reach up and clear a round spot on his windshield with the back of his hand, wiping away just enough condensation so that he could see to drive. By the time he pulled into the empty parking lot that surrounded his hotel, his windows were completely fogged over. He parked in the far corner, thirty yards away from the next closest car. He rolled to a stop, but kept his engine running.

Reaching under his seat, he pulled out a tiny laptop computer. As he opened the lid, the pale gray screen came to life. "PASSWORD" was flashing in bold letters.

Morozov typed very carefully, very slowly, using only one finger to enter the twelve digit password. He knew that a single error would instantly trigger the computer's self-destruct program. And all it would take was one simple mistake. So he punched the keys very deliberately.

After typing in the twelve numbers, Morozov reviewed them in his mind, then hit "Enter." The screen immediately went blank. His heart skipped a beat. For just an instant he thought he might have blown it. Then a white cursor appeared and began to flash on the left side of the screen. Morozov breathed a quick sigh of relief.

He reached into his shirt pocket and pulled out the twenty dollar bill that had been left at the table. Turning it over in his hands, he found the serial number that was printed on one side. He reached down and typed in the first digit.

The screen began to roll and tumble with a random mixture of letters and numbers. After several seconds of this, the letter "T" appeared at the top of the screen. Then the cursor returned once again.

Morozov typed in the second digit of the serial number from the twenty dollar bill. Again the screen rolled with a maze of numbers and letters. Again, after several seconds, another letter appeared on the top of the screen, next to the original letter "T."

And so it went. After a few minutes, Morozov had a complete message. It was very simple.

TUESDAY 23, 1415 Z -PLAN CHB- GO

It was the final approval for their mission. On Tuesday morning, at 1415 Zulu time, they would be taking off.

Morozov studied the message, then deleted it from the screen. He looked at his watch and did some mental calculations. In less than twenty-four hours, he and Richard Ammon would be in the air on a one-way flight to Russia in a B-1 bomber, the most sophisticated aircraft on earth.

Now there was only one thing left to do.

Reaching down, he plugged the computer's AC adapter into the cigarette lighter, which connected him to a maze of secret electrical equipment in the trunk of his car. Typing quickly, he wrote his response.

"In receipt of message. Plan Change B. 23/1415. We are ready and now in position. The timing will work. Proceed as per plan."

He quickly reviewed his acknowledgment of the message, then hit the "F6" key.

The computer screen went momentarily blank before "SENDING MESSAGE" appeared on his screen.

He held very still and listened very closely. He could barely hear the tiny electrical motors in the trunk of his car as they moved the eighteen-inch satellite dish around on its thin steel mounts. The laptop computer interfaced with the Global Positioning System, which was also hidden in the car trunk, to determine his exact location, then used that information to move the miniature dish around to align it with the Ukrainian satellite that spun 21,000 miles overhead. Once the dish was in sync with the satellite, it sent a one second data burst to test the connection. After receiving the test data, the Ukrainian satellite responded back to Morozov's system with a one second burst of its own. Not until then did Morozov's computer send up his message, which was then bounced off another satellite before being beamed down to a station in Kiev.

Morozov shut the lid on the computer and turned off his car. Walking to his motel room, he glanced once again at his watch. Eleven o'clock. Not much else to do now, but wait. Tomorrow would come soon enough.

He entered his room and nodded to the diner man, who frowned, then immediately left. Morozov fell down on his bed. Ten minutes later, he was fast asleep.

Ninety seconds after Morozov sent up his signal, the Cray super-computer onboard the K-23 satellite had finished its final computations and downloaded the information to the National Reconnaissance Organization center in western Virginia. It had a good fix on the source of the data transmission. The target area that the computer came up with was much less than twenty feet square. Twenty minutes after that, a military C-21 transport took off from Andrews Air Force Base, just outside of Washington, D.C., enroute to Wichita, Kansas.

The door exploded open as seven armed and helmeted men burst like lightning into the dimly lit room. Morozov awoke with a start, then instantly rolled off his bed and went for his gun. Ammon stood at the bathroom doorway without moving.

"*Get down on the floor!*" someone screamed. "*Get your freaking face down on the floor!*"

In a daze, Morozov reached for the 9mm which was stuffed under his left armpit. But before he could even get his hand around its beveled grip, he found himself sailing backward and crashing into the wall. Three men were instantly on top of him, pushing him to the floor and smothering him with their weight. A thick, black hood was immediately pulled down over his face. And then he felt the jabbing pain of the needle as it was shoved deeply into the meat of his thigh.

Six feet away, Richard Ammon found himself in an identical position, covered with black-uniformed bodies and pressed unmercifully onto the floor. He also felt the sharp sting of the needle and almost immediately passed away into a deep and foggy sleep.

As the two men stopped struggling and drifted away, a husky voice spoke into a cellular phone. "We've got them," he said without introduction. "Yeah, they're both alive. No shots were fired. We're bringing him in."

BOOK TWO

Simply put, it comes down to this.
You have to drop steel on the target.

TWENTY-FIVE

WICHITA, KANSAS

RICHARD AMMON WAS ALONE. HE LAY ON HIS BACK ON A HARD MATTRESS, staring at a bare cement ceiling. It was dark and cold and very quiet. His mind was swimming, he couldn't think, and it hurt to focus his eyes. His tongue felt numb and swollen and his mouth was thick and dry. His arms felt like heavy weights and there was a soft buzzing in the back of his head. It would take another twenty minutes for his kidneys to completely wash the heavy sedative from his blood. Not until then would his arms quit tingling and the feeling move back into his legs.

He closed his eyes and smelled the urine and cleanser as he tried to figure out where he was. With a painful strain, he rolled over, pushed his feet onto the floor, and sat up. Looking around him, his heart sank. He was in a prison cell. A dank, dark, cold prison cell. He rubbed his eyes and glanced around the room, taking in the stainless steel toilet and tiny wash basin, the cement bed and the shiny, flat, metal plate that served as a mirror. He studied the huge steel door, with its tiny slot to pass through plates of food, and the windowless, gray cement walls.

And then it hit him. And as he remembered, he took a quick breath, paralyzed for a moment in fear.

Morozov had sworn he would kill her. He could hear his cold voice and could see the green eyes.

"If this mission fails, for whatever reason, Jesse will certainly die."

Ammon's heart raced. Pushing himself up, he stumbled to the door. Pressing his face against the tiny, grate-covered window, he peered out into the hall. Nothing. He couldn't see a thing. He stopped and listened. Nothing. Not a sound. He called through the window. No one was there. He glanced at his watch. It was gone. How long had he been here? How much did they know? He called out through the window once again.

"Is anyone there?" He listened as his voice echoed down the empty, steel hallway. He called again. No response. Far off in the distance, he could hear a fan turning, an eerie and lonely sound.

Thirty yards away, at the end of the hallway and behind two thick, double-locked doors, three guards sat behind a bulletproof window and watched on their remote controlled monitor as Ammon pushed his face against his prison cell door. One of them immediately picked up the phone.

"Yeah, he's awake. No, not more than a minute ago. Yes . . . yes. . . . Okay, we'll be waiting." He placed the receiver back in its cradle and motioned to one of the other guards.

"Open her up. They're on their way down." Another guard pushed a series of codes on a computer keypad, and they listened to the quiet buzz as the internal locks inside the first door retracted into the cold steel.

Ammon swallowed hard to fight down the panic. Morozov would kill her! He was running out of time!

He stumbled back to the bed, fell onto the corner and pressed his eyes with his fists. A mighty shiver ran the length of his body. Folding his arms across his chest, he rubbed his biceps until the skin burned.

Like a cold slap of thunder, the sudden clang of a metal door sounded from the end of the hallway. He looked up and listened and waited. Footsteps approached from the far end of the hall. He sat on the edge of the bed. His own door buzzed and then clicked as the internal locks rolled open.

For the first time in weeks, a flicker of life burned in Ammon's eyes. He pushed himself to his feet as Lieutenant Colonel Oliver Tray walked into the musty cell.

Ammon stumbled forward. "Tray! They got Jesse," he muttered through a thick tongue and chattering teeth. "They got Jesse. Please, you've got to help me!"

Oliver Tray grabbed Ammon by the arms and turned him back to the bed. "Richard, it's okay. It's okay. We got her."

Ammon slumped onto the mattress and looked into Oliver's face with unbelieving eyes.

"I swear to you, she's going to be okay," Tray assured him.

Ammon's eyes glistened. He wiped his hands across his face and through his short hair. Was it really over? He just couldn't believe it. He looked up at Tray, pleading. Oliver read the pain in his eyes. Kneeling in front of his friend, he said slowly, "Richard, listen to me. We got her. I wouldn't lie to you. Everything is going to be fine. We brought her in a couple days ago, and I swear to you, she's doing just fine."

Ammon dropped his eyes to the floor, then buried his face in his hands. She was alive! She was okay! He was so grateful. Words could never explain. It was enough. It was all that he needed. He would ask for nothing ever again.

Three hallways over, in a cell of his own, Ivan Morozov was still suffering from a heavy and continuous dose of Pentothil. He was proving to be a good patient, very receptive to the mind-intrusive drug. He was talking up a storm, spilling his guts, seemingly willing to reveal every classified thing he had ever known. The Air Force intelligence officer was having a hard time keeping him focused, keeping him on track and off of the superfluous details of long-past intelligence operations. But Colonel Fullbright, who was supervising the whole interrogation, kept prodding him on, pushing the intelligence officer to keep the prisoner on the matter at hand.

By the time the interrogation was over, Colonel Fullbright's face was as gray as an old tombstone. It was an incredible operation! An absolutely incredible plan! Whoever had conceived the whole thing, well . . . just think of it . . . attack Russia with a stolen U.S. bomber— at the height of a bitterly renewed Cold War. With U.S. bombs exploding all over Russia, who could expect them not to retaliate? And in the midst of the missiles and anger, who would even remember the war with the Ukraine?

Fullbright shivered again as he considered what might have been.

And they had nearly made it work. They were within hours of completing their plan.

Fullbright leaned against the cell wall and stared at Morozov, who was now in a deep sleep. He stood for a very long time, shifting his weight from one foot to the other, deep in thought. And as he stood there, watching Morozov sleeping, an idea emerged in his mind.

They could use him, this slimeball Morozov. They could use him.

It was a very promising thought. No, more than that, it was a downright brilliant idea. It was bold and daring and the potential pay-off was hard to comprehend. However, it was peppered with danger, and there wasn't much time.

But still. . . .

Turning to the Army physician, he asked, "How much will our patient remember, once we bring him around?"

The doctor looked up, expressionless. "How much do you want him to remember?"

"How 'bout nothing. Let's bring him around in the morning, thinking that he just fell asleep watching television. Can that be done?"

"Easy as making a pancake."

Fullbright smiled. Morozov would never even know! Never have any idea. Not a clue, until it was already too late.

Turning toward the cell door, Fullbright called out over his shoulder. "Okay, do it," he commanded the doctor, then quickly walked out.

He glanced at his watch. Time. Time. He needed more time. He had to talk with Milton Blake. And Oliver Tray. And Ammon. . . . What about Ammon? He was the key.

Col Fullbright left Morozov in his cell, under the watchful eye of two guards and the Army physician. He nearly trotted down the hall-way to where the sheriff, a willowy man in a brown uniform and gray cowboy hat, was waiting. The sheriff followed Fullbright down a barren corridor, through another set of guarded, double doors, down a wood-paneled hallway, and into a tiny office where two of Fullbright's staff sat, unsure of why they were there or what they should do.

"How long you going to be here screwing around with my operation?" the sheriff asked as he followed Fullbright into the office. "I'm not running some secret military training camp here, ya'll know. This is the Harvey county prison, not some CIA headquarters. You've already caused me a lot of trouble. So why don't you just tell me what the sam hill is going on? I think I deserve some kind of explanation."

Fullbright cocked an eye toward the sheriff. The colonel was wearing a white shirt and tie, as were all of the other members of his party. They had shown no identification. No papers to use the prison had ever been served. A quick e-mail message from the Justice Department in Washington, D.C., was the only authorization the sheriff had ever received.

But of course, inside his shiny, bald head, the sheriff's mind was already racing. Who were these men? What were they doing? Whatever it was, it had to be big. Direct orders from Washington, D.C.! Had to be CIA. Or some kind of paramilitary operation. This was so cool. He couldn't wait to get home and tell his wife. And maybe even his brother-in-law, Jake. There were a few people he just couldn't keep a secret from.

Fullbright didn't waste time with the man. "Yes sir, sheriff. You certainly do deserve some answers. But don't expect any. Now if you'll just leave us alone, we'll soon be out of your hair. Then, I promise you, we'll never bother you again."

The sheriff started to protest as one of Fullbright's aides stood up and opened the door. Then, changing his mind, he shrugged his shoulders and walked from the room, shutting the door quickly behind him.

Turning to a captain who stood by his side, Fullbright commanded, "Get Oliver Tray in here! Now! And you," he turned to another captain, "get Milton Blake on the phone. Then all of you, clear out of the room."

A guard brought Ammon a tray of corned beef and mixed vegetables, and Ammon dug into the food. He was feeling much better. His head was clear, and the feeling was rapidly returning to his arms and legs. He was famished. And very thirsty. He felt like he hadn't eaten or drunk in days. Col Fullbright disappeared and came back with a couple of Cokes from the machine at the guard station on the other side of the double doors.

"How did you know about Jesse? How did you find out about the cabin?" Ammon asked. He avoided looking into Oliver Tray's eyes. It was a very uncomfortable question. But still, he needed to know.

"Really, we got very lucky," Oliver answered. "It was just a shot in the dark. I remembered you telling me about spending weekends up in some cabin together, but I didn't have any idea where it was. I knew it was somewhere in eastern California, but that was about all. We finally found it through tracing the deed. The FBI is pretty good at such things. But to be honest, even once we found out the location of the cabin, I still wasn't very optimistic. It was my own feeling that we wouldn't find Jesse there. Fortunately, it turned out I was wrong."

Tray thought back on the scene of Jesse hiding in the bush, while Clyde took pot shots at her through the trees. It had been very close. Two minutes later, and Jesse would have been dead. Someday, he would have to tell Richard Ammon. But not now. There were more pressing matters at hand.

"You know, Richard," Tray continued, "it would have helped if you had told us about your plan. If we had just known what you had intended to do, we could have helped. You should have trusted us to take care of her."

Ammon stared at his plate. He knew that now. But that wasn't the only harsh lesson he had learned over the past few weeks. And it wasn't the last time he would feel guilty for what had happened to his wife.

He scooped up a forkful of meat and shoved it into his mouth, wanting to move on from the subject.

"You know, Oliver, I called the number you gave me. On the day that they brought me in. I called and left you the code. Do you think that Morozov might know? If he had my lines tapped, could he have traced the call?"

Tray thought about that for a moment, then shook his head in reply. "Perhaps, but I really don't think so. Even if he were to trace the call, it wouldn't lead him to our organization. We are very careful about that. Having an untraceable number might have caused him to be suspicious, but it would give him nothing concrete to go on. Nothing he could point to with any degree of certainty.

"So, no. I'm certain that you are still clean. I don't believe that Morozov knows that you have been working for us. Now, he might have suspicions, but that would be all. You and I both know that if he did know for certain, you would already be dead."

Ammon looked up and shrugged his shoulders, then turned back to his food. "What about the drugs? Why did you have to drug me up? Had you decided I couldn't be trusted?"

"No. It was nothing like that. It's pretty simple really. We were running out of time. We knew that we had to take you fast. It had to be an extremely clean operation. No mess and no fuss. And we wanted everyone alive. But we figured Morozov to be very unpredictable. Not the type to go down without a big fight. And we didn't have time to do a thorough examination of the tactical situation inside your hotel room. We didn't know how many were in there. We didn't know who. We weren't even certain you were still with Morozov. So we made a sweeping generalization that everyone would go down the same way, then, when everything had settled down, we would sort the good guys from the bad."

Richard Ammon nodded again, then sat back and smiled.

He was feeling as good as he ever had in his life. His nightmare was over. Jesse was safe. Even now, she was sitting out in California, protected from Morozov and his goons by a detail of FBI agents. It was over. And Morozov was had.

He sat up and squared his shoulders. "So, when can I leave?" he asked. "When can I get out to California? What else do we have to do to button this thing up? I know the debrief will take some time, so let's get on with it."

Tray looked uncomfortably over at Col Fullbright, who cleared his throat and said, "Well, Richard, there's something that we need to tell you. And the truth is, you won't like what we have to say."

Ammon looked up with a start. His eyes clouded over and his face shaded just a hint as suspicion began to burn in his eyes. Fullbright continued, "You see, we need you now, Captain Ammon. We really need you. More than you ever could know."

"Oh, no," Ammon pleaded. "Please don't say it. Don't tell me this thing is not over!"

Tray shook his head and jumped in. "We can't tell you that, Richard. I guess that will be up to you. We can't promise you protection. We can't promise you safety. But for the first time in your life, we can offer you this: a real opportunity to do the right thing."

Ammon looked into Oliver's face. There was no way to miss the look in his eyes. Ammon's heart leapt into his throat and his stomach dropped to his knees. "Oh, no," he mumbled. "What are you guys thinking? What do you want?"

Oliver lowered his voice and told him.

When he was finished, Ammon sat back and swore. He leaned against his seat and stared up at the ceiling, shaking his head. He hated them for even asking. All he wanted was to go home. He hated Morozov and all of the Russians. He hated the danger and risk of the mission. He hated his deep sense of honor. He hated the Air Force. He hated it all.

But all of these feelings didn't change one simple fact. He had to do something. And he knew he could never say no.

WASHINGTON, D.C.

Ninety minutes later, the President of the United States folded his arms across his chest and rocked back in his chair.

"So, you're telling me that this is our only option?" he asked with suspicion. "That this is really what you think we should do?"

Milton Blake shifted uncomfortably in his seat. Weber Coy, the director of the CIA, stared off into space, as if he didn't want to answer the question.

"Sir, it isn't our only option," Blake replied. "There are other things we are looking at, some of which we have already discussed with you. But this is a new and radical development. The heavens just seemed to have opened and dropped this thing into our laps. Now what we do with it is left up to you.

"But sir, I urge you, in the strongest of terms, to seriously consider our recommendation. As I see it, and I think that I have considered every angle, it is our best hope, perhaps our only real hope, to eliminate the threat of a nuclear war. Fedotov is taking significant losses— much more than we ever expected. And he won't allow the Ukrainians to wear his army down. They are his one golden asset. His ticket to the big show.

"Our satellites show him to be in the final stages of his preparations. He has already fueled and positioned his missiles.

"As it stands, we have to do something. Unless . . ." Blake paused for a moment, "unless we are willing to let him start lobbing around his nuclear weapons."

The President frowned. "Perhaps that's exactly what we should do." he mused. "Let the idiots fight their own battle. Ugly as it is, perhaps there's nothing we can do."

Blake shrugged his shoulders.

"Sir, two days ago, I might have agreed with that contention. I have never pushed for us to defend the Ukraine, nor argued that we should involve ourselves in the war. We have always drawn the line of our interest along the borders of our NATO allies.

"But everything has changed. In light of Fedotov's recent actions, in light of what has been given to us out in Kansas . . . well, I think it would be cowardly to just sit on our hands. In my mind, it would be nearly an act of treason to just pretend that there's nothing we can do. Sir, I know you have no military training, but it doesn't take a warrior to see. . . ."

Blake immediately caught himself and shut his mouth. Weber Coy visibly bristled in his chair. Allen raised an eyebrow and straightened his back. Blake lowered his head in regret. He knew that he had just struck a nerve. He should have been smarter than that.

He swallowed and looked quickly around the room, hoping the moment would pass, then continued in a low and cautious tone.

"Sir, just for the sake of the argument, let's assume that I'm wrong. Let's say that he doesn't go nuclear. I think that it is highly unlikely, but let's say that it turns out that way. Now let me ask you. Where would that leave us? With a nuclear madman barking at our door. A maniac in control of all of Eastern Europe. And where will he stop? What next will he do? It's like a global game of Russian roulette. Someone will die. We just don't know when. We just don't know who. But the possibility of carving out a long-term peaceful existence with Vladimir Fedotov is absolutely zero."

The President pushed himself away from his desk. For a long time no one spoke. Then the President said, "Do you want to know what I think?" The two advisors sat forward in their chairs.

"I think it's a stupid idea," he said in a sarcastic tone, pointing an accusing finger toward Milton Blake. "Milt, I can't believe you are sitting here, proposing this plan. I think that it is absolutely crazy. It fails every logic test that I know.

"Look! We were lucky to have stopped the Ukrainians in the first place. There is no doubt in my mind that, had their operation been a success, we would be facing all-out global war! The Russians would have thought we had attacked them! Fedotov would not have hesitated to respond. And how could we have blamed him? With an American bomber roaming around the heart of his country, he would do the only thing he could do.

"Now, maybe I'm not as smart as you gentlemen are, but I fail to see how your plan is so different. How does it keep us from starting a war?"

Blake was very quick to respond. "Many things are different for us, sir. First, keep in mind, the primary objective of the Ukrainians was to provoke the Russians. To force them to respond, hoping to thrust us into the war.

"With that goal in mind, they designed the mission, not based on sound tactics and military doctrine, but to guarantee a Russian response. They selected targets deep within Russia to ensure that the B-1 was eventually detected. They selected targets other than the missile launching facilities—like armor rally points, troop concentrations, and Russian command bunkers—all designed to look like the first wave of a major attack. And they made everything time-critical. Very time-critical. The Russians would see the missiles and bombs exploding, and only have a few minutes, maybe only seconds, to decide how they were going to respond.

"But," Blake continued. "we have a very different priority, and I promise you, they'll never even know we were there. Unlike the Ukrainian mission, we will never penetrate their radar coverage. It's one missile, one shot, and we're gone. One quick *baaam* and we're out of there and heading for home. Ammon only has to get eighty miles behind the enemy . . ." Blake stopped and corrected himself, "excuse me . . . the Russian border, at which point, he would be within range to launch the missile and then turn and run. And although we do penetrate the border for a very short time, we have designed the mission to take advantage of the gaps in the Russian coverage. If Ammon stays low, if he takes advantage of the terrain to hide from the Russians' radar, if he lets the B-1 do what it was designed to do, then he will remain always hidden, hunting between holes in the Russian radar sites. And they'll never even know he was there."

"What about the missile itself?" Allen asked. "Won't they see it coming? I mean, its target is in the very heart of Moscow. How could it penetrate so deeply without being detected?"

"Sir, this new missile is one fabulous thing. It is extremely fast. It cruises at seven hundred knots and thirty feet. It is very small. And stealth was its primary design goal. From radar-absorbing paint to absurd and angular lines, it has it all. Nothing can pick it up. Nothing. Not even us. On its initial flight test, we couldn't even find it, even when we knew it was there. So, no sir, the missile will never be seen."

Allen stood up from his chair and began to pace around the room, stretching his arms out behind him and cracking his knuckles in his hands.

"How will you target him?" he wondered aloud. "That seems an impossible task. Think back on the Gulf War, my friends. How many Air Force sorties, how many missions did they send after Hussein, hoping to kill him in one of his bunkers? Fifty? Sixty? A hundred? And still, we never found him. Never even got close. Despite dozens of sorties from the world's greatest Air Force, he was never in danger at all.

"Now, you tell me we can get Fedotov with one missile. How? He adheres to the same security measures. His movements are always top secret. He never sleeps in the same place. He spends a lot of time inside hardened bunkers. He only moves around late at night.

"Given these facts, how in the world will you find him? How do you program the missile? It has to have target coordinates. It has to know where to go. But how do you program a missile to hit the target when you don't know where the target will be? Now, unless this missile is a lot smarter than we are, I just don't see how this mission can be a success."

Weber Coy, the director of the CIA, smiled and leaned forward in his chair. "Sir, do you remember the KY-400 satellite?"

The President frowned.

"The new EYE, sir. The reconnaissance bird. You were briefed on it last week at the SPACECOM conference."

The President nodded his head.

Coy cleared his throat and began to explain. The President sat back and listened.

President Allen looked at his watch. Four-thirty in the afternoon. He was tired. He needed a nap. He hadn't yet eaten any lunch. His head pounded at the base of his skull.

So much had happened in the past ten days. The invasion of the Ukraine. The Blackjack. The Nertrav with its eleven thousand Ukrainian soldiers killed. Since then, the U.S. and Russia had done nothing but pound their chests and rattle their swords. His life had taken on a nearly surreal edge, with middle-of-the-night meetings, a panicking press, endless military and intelligence briefings, preparations to defend Western Europe, while at the same time trying to keep the hawks in Congress at bay. It had stretched him to the absolute limit.

The President pushed himself back in his chair and propped his feet up onto the desk which had once belonged to James Madison and had been used to pen a large portion of the United States Constitution. Milton Blake winced as Allen's shoes scuffed across the antique desk, perhaps one of the most valuable pieces of furniture in the world. The President ignored the look on Blake's face as he brought his fingers up and gently rubbed his forehead, then spoke without opening his eyes.

"Okay, I think you've convinced me. I think there's a chance it could work. But now let me ask you, if this is such a great idea, then why don't we use our own men? We have B-1 crews sitting on the end of the runway, all loaded up and ready to go. We have the assets. We have the objective. Why not give them the mission and let them go?"

Blake glanced over at Weber Coy, who cleared his throat. This was, after all, his area of expertise. He had some experience with this question before, although years ago and with another administration.

"Sir, I know you already understand why we can't do that," was all Coy said.

The President raised an eyebrow. "Yes, Weber. I think I do. But why don't you go ahead and explain, just in case one or the other of us might have missed the point."

Coy answered in an even tone, as if reciting the lines from rote memory. "Sir, during peacetime operations, it is now, and has been for more than a generation, illegal for you, or I, or anyone else within our government, to order the assassination of a foreign leader, regardless of how unpleasant or dangerous they may be. In this matter, our hands are tied. It is simply illegal." Coy paused and then added, "Sir . . . as you already know."

"So what you are suggesting is we disregard our own law," Allen sneered. "Take matters into our own hands. Just say screw the Congress and our Constitution. It's cowboy time! And we're running the show."

Coy shifted uncomfortably in his seat. He hated the President's sarcasm. As long as he had known him, he still wasn't used to it. Blake glanced over to Weber Coy. Their eyes met quickly, then Coy looked away.

"What we're suggesting, sir," Blake finally replied, "is that we avoid a nuclear war. Yes, it is a highly controversial solution. But let me put things into perspective by asking you this question. Years from now, when you are seventy-five, and lying awake in your bed, which action will make it more difficult for you to sleep? To remember how you ordered the elimination of an insane tyrant who was preparing to use nuclear weapons? Or how you sat on your hands and did nothing while thousands of people were sent to their deaths?"

The President leaned forward in his chair and shook his head. His eyes were drawn and tired. For a while he stared off into space and said nothing. "This is indeed a lousy business that we find ourselves in," he finally commented.

Blake and Coy nodded their heads in agreement.

Allen remained silent for some time, and then said, "One more problem. Let's say that, by some freak of nature or unforeseen circumstance, let's say that someone finds out. Be it the Russians, or God forbid, our own press. There's so much that could go wrong. What if this Ammon fellow gets shot down and captured? Or what if the Russians detect the missile and somehow trace it back to us?" Blake opened his mouth to speak. Allen lifted his hand to cut him off. "Now I know that you say it is impossible, but let's face it, in the fog of war, anything can and will happen. So, let's just go ahead and plan for the worst. How do you propose we respond?"

Blake didn't hesitate to answer the question. "In the first place, sir, should the Russians ever even hint that we had anything to do with eliminating Fedotov, most of the entire civilized world would simply stand up and applaud. If we are successful in stopping a nuclear war, then who could argue that the means didn't justify the end? But, should the Russian government insist on taking it further, should it ever appear that the Presidency or our nation is implicated in any way, then we simply tell them the truth. It was a Ukrainian operation. Flown by two Ukrainian agents. They stole our weapon. They precipitated the whole attack. We wash our hands of the whole operation. It will be as simple as that."

"Deny any foreknowledge of what happened?"

"Yes, sir. Of course. We have absolute deniability. It's the most beautiful part of this plan."

"And what about our man, Richard Ammon?" the President asked in the softest voice he had used during their entire conversation.

Blake shifted around in his seat. "Sir, I know what you're asking," he answered. "And we have considered how best we can help him. We can divert a few of the fighters. Send them north when they need to go south. And we can thin out the Naval defenders as he makes his way across the Mediterranean Sea.

"But the hard truth is, there isn't a lot we can do. By and large, we have to let the thing play itself out. We can't just hand them a bomber with its nuclear missiles, then send them merrily on their way, while we clear a path for them to go and bomb Russia. And to help him out, in even a small way, would take a great deal of planning and coordination. It would involve far too many people. And we have to be very discreet. Very, very discreet. No one must ever know what we've done."

"Besides," Coy broke in, "it would be highly illegal. As we have already discussed."

Allen glanced at Coy with a look of contempt.

Blake saw the look on the president's face. "In addition, sir," he quickly continued. "If we made things too easy, Ivan Morozov would become suspicious."

President Allen turned away from Coy and pulled at his chin. A smoldering fire began to burn in his eyes. "And does Ammon realize we won't be there to help him? Does he understand he will be on his own?"

"Sir, to my knowledge, it has never been discussed. But it is something he would have to understand. He is a soldier. There are certain things we don't have to tell him. There are certain things that he knows on his own."

"And what about Morozov? Do you think he will go along with the plan?"

"No, sir, he won't," Blake said matter-of-factly. "While killing Fedotov would be a good thing to him, we fear it would not be enough. For one thing, it leaves the Russian military completely unharmed. And the Ukrainians are determined that they be destroyed, especially their nuclear weapons. The only way to do that would be to carry out their plan and instigate a major U.S./Russian confrontation. In addition—and this may be the most important—it would appear that Morozov is seeking revenge. Revenge upon Fedotov. Revenge upon the whole nation! He will settle for nothing less."

"So where does that leave us, then," Allen wondered, "if Morozov won't go along with our plan?"

"Sir, the thing is, he doesn't have to know. The physician out in Kansas has assured us that he won't remember a thing about being taken captive. As far as Ivan Morozov is concerned, he will awake in the morning, thinking everything is on track and going according to schedule. And it won't be until they are just beginning to cross the Russian border that he finds out. Then, Ammon fires the missile, and it's over. There will be nothing Morozov can do."

The President settled back, closed his eyes and raised his hand to silence them both. Coy remained cocked and loaded on the edge of his seat. Blake glanced around the room and loosened his tie. The Oval Office was always too hot. As they had talked, he couldn't help but think back on President Nixon and his White House full of bugs. He prayed that Allen would never be so foolish. Nor any President ever again.

"Okay, then," Allen said after a while. "Let me think about it. Something like this is going to take some time."

Allen started to push himself back from his desk, a signal to his men that the meeting was over. But before he could stand up, Milton Blake interrupted.

"Sir. Actually, that's not quite true." The President looked down with a scowl. Blake glanced over to Coy and then continued.

"We need an answer, sir. This afternoon. Really, right now. For if we don't move within the next few minutes, if we don't begin to make our preparations, we will ruin our cover." Blake thought of what Morozov had told them. Tuesday. 1415 Zulu time, 0915 D.C. time, 0815 local time in Wichita. He glanced at his watch. Less than sixteen hours to prepare.

"Sir, I apologize," he continued. "You know how I feel about bringing this to you with such short notice. But we really have no choice, sir. It's something that came up really just a few hours ago. And unfortunately, it's either now, or we come up with some other plan, for by nine fifteen tomorrow morning, if we don't act, the whole option will just go away."

The President swore and sat back in his seat. "Okay," he said, "tell me once again. Complete deniability? Right? No threat of exposure? Right? Fedotov will not have any warning? He'll have no chance to respond?"

"Sir," Milton Blake was quick to reply. "I promise you, he'll never see anything coming. One second, he's there. The next second, he's gone. Without any notice or warning. We strike like a bolt from the blue."

WICHITA, KANSAS

Fullbright walked quickly into the room. Ammon and Tray raised their eyes from their charts and their pencils. "It's a go! Everything is falling in place!"

Ammon nodded his head as his stomach tightened up. Tiny drops of sweat began to trickle down his ribs. He turned away from Tray and stared off into space. So that was it. He was on his way. But he wasn't surprised. What other choice did they have? He knew it would go all along.

"The CIA has a few of their very best people working on the matter," Fullbright continued. "They are also sending out the materials that you asked for. We should have it in less than an hour."

Neither Ammon nor Tray replied. Turning to their charts, they went back to work. They still had an enormous amount of planning to do. Tray picked up the laptop computer and silently tapped in the next coordinates of the flight plan.

Three hours later, they were on their way back to the motel. It was dark. Morozov was slumped over in the back of the van. He wouldn't wake up until morning. And when he did, he wouldn't remember a thing. Not so much as a whisper in the back of his mind. Beside him was his friend from the diner. He too had been laced with enough drugs to guarantee that he slept through the night.

Oliver Tray rolled among the light traffic, switching lanes to pass a small trailer. As he drove off the freeway and down their exit ramp, he turned to Ammon and said, "It's going to work, Richard. I really believe that it will."

Ammon stared ahead in the darkness. The success of the mission was not his only concern. After several minutes, he quietly asked Tray, "Have you ever killed a man, Oliver?"

Oliver winced. Of course, the answer was no.

Ammon waited, then nodded his head. "Neither have I. Never thought of myself as an assassin."

Oliver didn't respond. There was no time now for moral discussions. They both knew what they had to do. And to him, it wasn't even an issue. Killing Fedotov to avert nuclear war? He'd pull the trigger in less than a heartbeat. Never think twice. It wasn't even gray. It was straight black and white.

But then again, he wasn't the man flying the mission. He wasn't the man launching the missile. And it wasn't he who was putting his life on the line. So he didn't respond. He had nothing to say. Nothing that hadn't already been said. Except for maybe one thing.

"You know, Richard, if you can pull this thing off, if you are successful, though forever untold and forever anonymous, you will be one of the few men who have ever lived who actually changed the course of human events."

McCONNELL AIR FORCE BASE, KANSAS

The B-1 was silently towed back into the hangar and the enormous doors rolled shut again. After chocking the wheels and grounding the aircraft with static-dissipation lines, the weapons specialists went to work. Opening the mid-bay internal weapons door, they downloaded a B-93 nuclear bomb. Then, very carefully, another weapon was loaded up in its place, a large, black, dart-like cruise missile. Five hours before, the missile had been sitting in a test hangar out at Edwards Air Force base. Now here it sat, in the belly of the Bone, awaiting its first operational mission.

CAPE CANAVERAL SPACE CENTER, FLORIDA

The space shuttle Endeavor's launch date had already been moved up by more than two weeks, at a cost of more than eight million dollars and an additional twenty thousand man-hours of labor. And now, by order of the President himself, the launch time had been moved up again.

Inside the Endeavor's cargo compartment was an enormous satellite, one of the largest and heaviest payloads the shuttle had ever lifted into space. It was thick and white. And extremely expensive. Even more so than the shuttle itself. It was also one of the most highly classified satellites that the Department of Defense had ever developed. Its true capabilities were astounding, and if it lived up to its expectations, it was sure to become one of the most significant pieces of equipment ever launched into space.

WICHITA, KANSAS

Colonel Fullbright listened as the phone patch was put through to the White House. The line clicked and then buzzed as the voice encryption system kicked into gear. A small, red light on his mobile transmitter turned green, signifying the line was now secure. Three seconds later, Milton Blake picked up the phone.

"They're back in position," Fullbright said.

"Okay. Good. I'm seeing the President in about ten minutes. I'll tell him everything is ready and in place. Now, what else can we do?"

"Nothing. We've done all we can."

For a moment, Blake didn't respond. The secure phone line buzzed in the background. Then he finally said, "Okay, then. Now I want your final appraisal. What do you think are his chances of success?"

Fullbright didn't hesitate. "Seventy-five to eighty percent, sir. And that's a consensus from all of the planners. The Russians will never even see the B-1 coming. All they'll see is a sudden explosion. A hidden bomb, I'm sure they'll suspect. And by the time the confusion is over, the Bone will be safely back in our midst. Our appraisal of the mission has not changed. Ammon's chances are still very good."

On the other end of the line, Blake smiled and nodded as he wrote the figure down. Seventy-five to eighty percent. That was what he would brief President Allen. The mission was looking very good.

T W E N T Y - S I X

WICHITA, KANSAS

RICHARD AMMON PUSHED AGAINST MOROZOV'S BARE SHOULDER, AND Morozov finally rolled over to stare at the clock. Five A.M. It was still dark outside. The motel was deathly quiet. It had seemed like a very short night. Morozov stretched and pushed himself up. His brain came slowly to life. He felt groggy and tired.

Ammon stared at him for a moment. "You feel okay?" he asked.

Morozov coughed and shook his head to clear it. "Let's go," was all he said.

The two men began to dress in the semi-darkness, the room illuminated by one small bedside light. Neither of them spoke. They pulled on black leather flight boots and Air Force flight suits, complete with name tags, rank, and B-1 squadron patches. Over the flight suits they wore brown leather jackets. They packed what little they had into two small duffel bags, and then they were ready to go.

Before leaving, they parked their car in front of the motel and walked through the tiny lobby to the smoky diner. They sat down in a corner booth and ordered breakfast, then ate in silence.

After a few minutes, Morozov leaned across the table. "Do you have any final questions?" he asked.

"No. I know the plan."

"Any concerns about our route of flight, or the threats we expect to encounter? What about the fighters out of Florida, any problem with them? Or our routing through the Ukraine?"

"No, no, no. We've been through it all a thousand times. I know the plan better than you do. It isn't perfect, but nothing is. Given the time constraints and the limited amount of intel that we have had to work with, I'd say we have a reasonable plan."

"So you think we are ready?"

Ammon considered the question. "I think it doesn't matter. We both know we are going to go."

Morozov studied Ammon for a moment, shook his head in a barely perceptible nod of agreement and then said, "I hope this goes well for us, Ammon. For Jesse's sake."

Ammon swallowed hard and fought to control the look on his face. Morozov was doing his best to play out his cards. But Ammon knew. And it made all the difference.

A tiny smile spread across Ammon's lips. He stood up from the table and turned and walked from the restaurant, leaving Morozov somewhat perplexed.

After a few minutes, Morozov got up and paid their bill. He went outside and saw Richard Ammon standing by the car, watching the morning sky.

For the past three days, it had been miserable. Overcast and cold, with a nearly constant freezing drizzle. But now it appeared to be clearing up. The eastern sky was just beginning to glow with the rising sun. They could see patches of deep blue and purple surrounded by a brightening pink. A south wind was beginning to blow, bringing the promise of warmer weather.

"Looks like a beautiful day," Morozov said as he approached the car.

Ammon studied the sky for a moment longer, then slipped into the car without responding. Morozov climbed in and started the engine. Within a half hour, they were driving north on highway 15, which would take them to the front gate of the base.

As Morozov drove, Ammon retrieved one of the canvas duffel bags from the back seat and pulled out a small plastic container. He reached inside and pulled out their fake identification, two laminated plastic cards for each of them. One was a standard military identification card. It was embossed in light green, with their pictures prominently displayed in the center. But it was the other plastic card that was the most important. This was their flight line identification. It was this card that would allow them access to the flight line and the B-1s that were now sitting on alert, fully loaded and ready to fly.

Morozov took his identification cards and shoved them into a pocket of his flight suit. But Ammon hung on to his. He studied them for a moment, staring at his picture. Finally he pulled out his wallet and slipped the two cards inside.

It only took a few minutes before they were approaching the main gate to McConnell Air Force Base. Standing at the gate were two guards. One of them held a burly German shepherd at bay while the other stopped the oncoming cars to inspect their occupants and check them for proper identification.

When it was Morozov's turn, he pulled up to the gate and rolled down his window. The guard bent down to look inside. Ammon didn't look in his direction but stared straight ahead, trying to appear as uninterested as he could. The guard was the first one to speak.

"Good morning, sir," he said to Morozov. "May I see your ID, please?"

Morozov pulled out his military identification card and handed it to the guard. The sergeant inspected both sides of the card, then looked a little closer at Morozov; holding the small card up to the light that shone down from his guard house, pulling it close to his nose, absorbing every detail. Then he bent over and peered back into the car.

"Sir, there appears to be a problem with your identification," he said.

Ammon's heart nearly stopped. What was going on? Surely Morozov's people hadn't screwed up such a simple thing as forging an ID card? Surely they hadn't come this far, just to be arrested by some nearsighted sergeant? After all the preparation, it couldn't come down to this. As Ammon turned to the guard, he tried to look bored and tired, but inside he wanted to scream.

Morozov didn't even flinch. He reached out and took the card from the security policeman, as he replied in an innocent voice, "What seems to be the problem, Sergeant?"

"Sir, your ID needs to be updated. It is printed on the old Air Force Form 215. We started converting to the new Form 311 last month. I'm surprised that no one has pointed this out to you. You really need to get a new ID card issued. Especially in light of the current situation. Security has got to be tight."

"Well Sergeant, I believe that you are right," Morozov replied. "The problem has been that for the past few months I have been out of the country. You know how it is. Temporary duty always calls. But now that I'm back, I'll get this thing updated. Thanks for the reminder. You are doing an excellent job."

"Thank you, sir," the guard replied. "Now you get that taken care of, will you? Then I won't have to stop you in the morning."

"Roger," was all Morozov replied.

With that, the sergeant stepped back from the car and offered a quick salute while motioning for Morozov to pass through the gate. The guard needed to keep things moving along, for the morning rush of cars onto the base was already beginning to flow. Morozov returned the salute with a smile, then accelerated through the gate and onto the base.

They began to drive down the main boulevard that would take them to the flight line. It wasn't until then that Ammon let out a huge sigh of relief. He turned around and took a quick look at the guard house that was receding behind them.

"I can see that your people do quality work," Ammon sneered. "Yes sir, it is obvious that you guys have thought of everything. There is nothing to worry about now."

Morozov didn't respond. Ammon was right. His people had nearly screwed it up. To a large degree the success of their mission would depend on strict attention to detail. And someone in his organization had nearly blown it. He would have to find out who it was.

They drove along in silence. As they got closer to the flight line, Ammon started to look for the aircraft. He was anxious to get his first glimpse of the Bone. But from where they were, the aircraft parking area was still hidden by a long row of enormous brown hangars.

Morozov followed the road for almost a mile, past the row of hangars to where the road made a sharp turn to the west. As they came upon the last set, Ammon could start to see F-16s, KC-135 tankers, and even a couple of transports. But he couldn't see any B-1s. He looked all the way down to the far end of the flight line.

And then he saw them. Across the runway; black, lean, and menacing, like enormous fighters they stood. Their canted wings and sharp tails gave the impression of coiled tigers; hunched down and leaning forward, ready to spring through the air. Their sharp noses stretched toward the runway as if they were anxious to fly.

What a beautiful sight, Ammon thought as he watched the B-1s come into view. For a moment, he almost lost himself in the excitement. In a short time he would be at the controls of this beautiful aircraft. He was now reacting instinctively to the challenge. The challenge was just too much to resist.

But before he and Morozov even got close to the B-1, they had one more obstacle to overcome. The security that surrounded the B-1 was always tight. It was significantly easier, and far less dangerous, to rob a bank in midtown Manhattan than it was for an unauthorized person to get close to a Bone.

Everything from razor wire to laser detectors surrounded the Bones as they sat on alert. Armed guards were on a constant watch. It wasn't possible for a bird or a rabbit to get within 200 feet of the B-1s without being detected. If any intruders tried to penetrate the area, they would quickly be surrounded by the cops.

And then there was the "Zone," the final line of defense that surrounded the B-1s.

Painted on the cement, fifty feet out from the bombers was a thick red line. This designated the Zone. The Zone had its own very special set of rules, and every person who worked around the B-1, whether they were pilots or maintenance specialists, knew the rules of the Zone very well. The Zone offered no room for excuses. Inside the Zone there was no room for error.

The rules were very simple. Any unauthorized persons caught within the Zone would be immediately shot. If they were alone or didn't appear to be threatening the bombers, then they would probably be shot in the legs. The security police were all excellent marksman, and they were trained to fire at the knees. But if there were more than one intruder, or if they appeared to be armed, or if they acted in a hostile or threatening manner, then the use of deadly force was automatically authorized. The security police would shoot three times. One shell at the heart. Two at the head.

No questions would be asked. No warning would be given. It was that simple. It was a harsh and unforgiving policy, but when it came to nuclear weapons, the security forces didn't feel a need to be nice.

With all the laser motion detectors, noise sensors, razor wire, men, dogs, and machine guns, it was easy to understand why tiny beads of sweat began to roll down Morozov's back as he stared at the Bones.

GULF OF MEXICO

Twelve hundred miles to the south, a Ukrainian naval cruiser cut through the warm waters of the Mexican Gulf. The Chernova Ukraina was one of the largest surface vessels that was still operated by the Ukrainian Navy. Completed in 1988, she was a "Slava" class helicopter cruiser that was equipped with a variety of surface-to-air missiles, torpedo tubes, and attack helicopters. Although she was very capable of attacking surface vessels, her primary purpose was to hunt and kill enemy submarines. And given the chance, her skipper had no doubt that she would have been very good at her job.

But so far, she had never been put to the test. Such was the irony of modern-day weapons. The more powerful and capable they were, the less likely they were to be used.

So it was not surprising that, when the Chernova had been ordered from her port in Sevastopol, her commander was one happy man. A war was brewing in the north, and he was very anxious to play in the game.

But when he got his orders, his excitement was quickly replaced by confusion and anger. The Chernova would be nothing but a messenger. Hardly more than an expensive errand boy. It was a humiliating task for a warship. Nothing to attack. Nothing to be gained. No medals or glory to be won.

But being a military man, as always, the captain did exactly as he was told.

And that is how he found himself cruising through the Gulf of Mexico, one hundred and seven miles from the white sands and high-rise hotels that lined the beaches from Galveston to Corpus Christi.

It wasn't long after Morozov and Ammon had driven through the main gate at McConnell that the Chernova turned and began to cruise to the northeast, paralleling the Texas coast. The captain ordered one-half power, then gave his communications officer the nod to proceed.

On the aft deck of the cruiser, just below the helicopter landing pad, was a huge drum filled with a long, thin, copper wire. As the Chernova cut through the four-foot waves, an electric motor on the drum began to turn, pushing the end of the wire from the drum casing. A two-foot canvas basket was attached to the wire and then dropped into the sea. The basket immediately filled with the warm salt water, pulling the wire taut against the side of the ship.

Not until then did an electric brake on the drum release with a click and a thump. Immediately the drum began to rotate as the basket pulled the wire from the drum.

As the Chernova cruised along at 19 knots, the wire fed out behind it, streaming from the cruiser like an enormous tail. It only took a couple of minutes for the basket to pull out the entire contents from the drum, stretching the huge antenna for two kilometers across the rough sea.

When the captain had been advised that the antenna was deployed and in position, he looked at his watch and said, "Stand by to broadcast message. Broadcast will begin in twenty minutes. After broadcast, stand by to run."

Using the ship's Ultra-Low Radio Transmitter (ULRT) and the long copper antenna, the Chernova would transmit a short message, a simple code of seemingly random numbers. The ultra low radio waves would hug the contour of the earth, traveling for almost 5,000 miles before they weakened and began to disperse. But it would take a little time to send the whole message, for the ULRT was only capable of transmitting a single character every few seconds. Several minutes would pass before the message transmission was complete.

Once the message was sent, the Chernova would immediately cut the thin copper wire. Then she would turn to the east and push up her speed. By early morning she would be safely docked in Havana, Cuba.

LOS ANGELES COUNTY, CALIFORNIA

Jesse looked out on the calm morning sea. The moon was low on the western horizon. The planet Venus was clearly in view, the brightest star in the early morning sky. A pale of light blue was just beginning to tint the eastern skyline, though sunrise was still at least fifty minutes away. A warm wind blew in from the ocean and pushed her hair back from her face.

She looked down at the gauze pads, which had been wrapped around both of her wrists and felt a sudden shiver of pain. But it wasn't real. Only a vivid memory, though the overall effect was the same. She reached down and gently pulled at the bandage, then glanced quickly back over her shoulder, to see if the agent was still there. He nodded as she looked for his presence.

Turning away from the ocean, Jesse left the balcony and moved back into the safe house. They had told her today was the day. By tomorrow, the whole thing would be over. Then maybe they would tell her where Richard was and when he would be coming home. The worst part was not knowing. And not knowing what next to expect.

For the past two days, they had tried to assure her. The agents had been gracious and friendly and kind. But the truth was, they had no knowledge of the real operation. They had no idea what was really going on. All they knew was it was something very big. Their instructions came right from the top. So they would shrug their shoulders and ask for her patience, and assure her it was going to be all right.

But Jesse could feel the crisis arising, a bitter feeling she just couldn't describe. It was there, brittle and cold, like a frozen pit in the center of her heart. A feeling of doom seemed to settle upon her, leaving her lonely and desperate for hope. And try as she might, she couldn't push it aside.

An ugly voice seemed to whisper from the corners of her mind, "Say good-bye, Jesse. He's not coming home!"

TWENTY-SEVEN

McCONNELL AIR FORCE BASE, KANSAS

MOROZOV LOOKED AT HIS WATCH. TWELVE MINUTES TO GO. THEY WERE running late. He looked across to Richard Ammon who was still staring in wonder at the B-1s. He could tell from the look on his face that Ammon was excited at the prospect of flying the Bone. That was good. That was very important. Perhaps they had chosen the right man after all.

Morozov was parked on the side of a road that ran around the north end of the runway. From here he had a good view of the entire alert area. He studied the ten-foot electric fence that surrounded the B-1 parking ramp. He could see the small disks of motion detectors that ran parallel to the fence. He looked up at the guard towers, then down at the armored security vehicles that circled the parked B-1s. There must have been at least a hundred security policemen, all of them armed with machine guns. He squinted and peered at the white cement. Yes, there they were. He could see them. The red lines that depicted the Zone.

He looked at his watch once again, then slipped their car into gear. It was time to go.

He turned around and headed for the alert facility. Four minutes later, he and Ammon pulled into the parking lot that was just outside the facility gate. From there, they did one final scope of the fence.

"Everything looks good," Morozov observed.

"Yeah, looks good to me. You go first," Ammon suggested.

They climbed out of the car and started walking toward the high fence, Morozov leading the way, carrying a small black duffel bag under his arm. Ahead of them were two huge barbed wire fences, one inside the other. Ten feet separated the two fences. Each fence had only one gate, which was a steel revolving door. Two armed security policemen, each of them with a German shepherd, watched as the two men approached.

The two fences were designed as a trap. Both Ammon and Morozov would have to show their identification before they would be allowed through the first gate. There they would be confined between the two fences. In no-man's-land.

Once inside no-man's-land, they would be challenged once again. But this time not only would they have to show their ID, but they would also have to give the proper code word. The code words were classified TOP SECRET and they could change as frequently as every few hours. If either Ammon or Morozov didn't give the proper code, they would be thrown to the ground and arrested.

It was the code procedures that had Morozov the most worried.

The problem was in the master code books. New code books were issued in a completely random manner. A code book might be used for several weeks or several hours, so Morozov could never be completely sure that he had the most recent edition. Morozov's code book was only fifty-six hours old, but it could very well be that a new edition had already been issued. Maybe even two. Maybe even three. There was no way to know. But he soon would find out.

As they walked toward the gate, Morozov checked his watch once again. Eight minutes to go. They would have to hurry, for they couldn't be even a second late. He gave Ammon a gentle nod and then picked up his pace just a little. When they were still twenty feet from the fence, one of the guards held out his hand and yelled, "Halt!"

GULF OF MEXICO

The Chernova Ukraina continued to cruise effortlessly through the four-foot troughs. Inside her Command Center, the captain was staring at the radar screen. An unidentified aircraft was approaching. It looked to be a U.S. Navy P-3 Orion. The turboprop aircraft was approaching from the east at 320 knots and heading directly for the Chernova. No doubt, the P-3 had been sent to check them out. As the Orion flew toward her target, she would have on all of her "ears," or radio signal detectors, so that she could hear what the Chernova was up to.

That was very bad. If the Chernova tried to transmit her encoded message on the ULFT, the Orion would certainly detect it. Then the Americans would know that it was the Chernova that had sent out the message.

And the captain of the Chernova Ukraina had been given very specific orders. Take any means necessary to avoid being detected as the source of the ULFT transmission.

But the Orion couldn't home in on their transmissions until she got to within two hundred miles of the Chernova.

The captain looked at his watch once again. Six minutes, thirty seconds to go.

"Is the message ready to send?" he asked his communications officer sharply.

"Yes, sir. We are awaiting your word," he replied.

"How long will it take to broadcast the entire message?"

"Three minutes and eighteen seconds, sir. The ULFT is very slow. It can only transmit one character every seven seconds and—"

"I know the limitations of the ULFT," the Captain snapped. He turned and looked at the radar screen once again. The Orion had picked up her speed just slightly and was now approaching at 340 knots. She was charting a course that would bring her to within seven miles of the Chernova's starboard bow.

"At this speed, how long until she is within homing range?" the captain asked.

The radar operator pushed two buttons next to his screen. The radar's computers did the calculations within a fraction of a second.

"Six minutes, twenty-two seconds, sir."

The Captain scowled as he did the math in his head. Six minutes until he was suppose to send the message. A little over three minutes to send it. That was nine minutes. The P-3 would now be within range in six minutes and twenty seconds.

It wasn't going to work. That would leave the Orion with almost three minutes to home in on their transmitter. That was about sixty seconds too long.

The Captain considered his options for only a moment before he made up his mind.

"Stand by to broadcast message. Commence broadcast in . . . ," he paused to look at his watch, "three minutes. That will ensure the message broadcast is complete before the Americans get into homing range."

The Chernova's communications officer glanced at the Captain for just a moment. He was one of the few men on board that had been authorized to read the orders that had sent them here to the Gulf of Mexico. He understood the importance of not being identified as the senders of the ULFT transmission.

But he also understood something else. Their mission was very urgent. And the timing was critical. Absolutely critical. They were to begin their transmission at a very specific time. Not a second early. Not a second late.

The communications officer considered arguing this point to the captain. Then he changed his mind. The captain knew what he was doing. He would trust him to do the right thing.

McCONNELL AIR FORCE BASE, KANSAS

Ammon and Morozov stopped in their tracks. The guard closest to them swung his M-16 down from his shoulder.

"Approach the gate one at a time."

Morozov looked at Ammon, then turned and walked up to the gate. He stood just outside the revolving steel door. The guard spoke to him through tiny slots in the steel.

"May I see your identification please, sir?"

Morozov reached into the breast pocket of his flight suit and extracted his military ID and his line badge and slipped them through a slit in the door.

The guard reached through and picked up the cards. He began to study them as Morozov looked at his watch. Six minutes.

"Sir, will you step back as we rotate the gate?" the guard asked. Morozov stepped back two paces and the gate began to revolve. He judged the timing so that he could walk through the swinging arms. As he passed through the gate, the first guard returned him his ID.

"Sir, please proceed to the next gate." Morozov stepped by the first guard, whose German shepherd sniffed and strained at his harness as Morozov passed by.

Morozov walked up to the second gate. Again the guard spoke to him from a slit in the door.

"ID," he said curtly.

Morozov passed him the two pieces of identification. He looked back at Richard Ammon, who was still standing outside the first gate. He glanced at his watch, trying to make his preoccupation with time as unnoticeable as possible. Five minutes, twenty seconds.

"Bring the other one in," the second guard yelled. The first guard motioned for Richard Ammon to step forward. Ammon proceeded on up to the gate and quickly passed his identification through the slit to the guard.

Within a minute he was standing next to Morozov, trapped between the two fences. He passed his ID to the second guard, who studied them as carefully as he had Morozov's.

When he appeared to be satisfied with the ID, he motioned for Morozov to step forward. On the side of the gate was a simple keyboard with a small computer screen. Morozov would have to type the code word into the computer before he could pass through the gate.

"Sir, are you ready to type in the code word?" the second guard asked through the fence. Morozov nodded in reply.

"Type in the code word then, sir. Time now is 1409 Zulu. The code will change again in fifty-one minutes."

Morozov reached out and began to type in the code.

GULF OF MEXICO

"Commence broadcasting," said the Chernova's Captain. His communications officer nodded, then turned back to his console. He punched a series of buttons on his keyboard and the ULFT began to transmit. The communications officer checked his watch and noted the time of transmission into the ship's log.

As the transmission began, long radio waves in the ultra low frequency began to spread out from the enormous antenna that trailed from the Ukrainian cruiser. The radio signals extended out in all directions. They spread across the ocean waves until they hit landfall, then continued to roll across the terrain. It was only a few seconds until they had reached the wheat fields of southern Kansas.

McCONNELL AIR FORCE BASE, KANSAS

The former Soviet Union was never shy about their intention to take advantage of what they perceived as one of the United States' key weaknesses; their unregulated environment in matters of defense. This enabled the USSR to commit various acts of sabotage and subversion, many times without the Americans even knowing what had been done.

One example of this was the McConnell Air Force Base new fuel storage facility. Millions of gallons of JP-8 jet fuel were stored in eight huge tanks sitting on a small hill at the north end of the runway. The tanks were just three hundred yards from the B-1 alert parking area. Huge pressurized underground fuel lines carried the JP-8 to the fuel pits where hoses could be attached to the B-1s. This made refueling the thirsty aircraft very easy and efficient. It also made the transfer of the fuel much more secure.

At least that was the theory. But there were a few things that the Air Force didn't know. For example, they didn't know that one of the civilian contractors who helped to build the storage facility was a paid Soviet informer, controlled by a Ukrainian officer from the KGB. One day, just as the construction project was being completed, the contractor walked by one of the tanks and dropped in what looked to be a large black lunch box. The box immediately sank to the bottom of the tank where its presence was never detected.

Now, as the ultra-low-frequency radio transmissions rolled across the McConnell flight line, the black box suddenly came to life. A tiny computer inside the watertight box began to decode the message. When the complete message had been received, it would be verified against the black box's computer files. If it confirmed to be valid, the black box would go into a countdown. Ten seconds later it would explode.

Morozov finished typing in the code. He looked at the screen on the side of the fence. He studied the code word for just a moment to check his spelling. There was a policy of zero tolerance for spelling errors. It was the same thing as having the wrong code. When Morozov was satisfied, he reached up and pushed the "send" button.

A small screen on the other side of the gate immediately illuminated the code word that Morozov had typed in. The guard read his screen then looked over at Morozov. Morozov was looking around, trying to appear bored by the whole affair, scratching at his head. The guard glanced at the screen once again and then said. "Sir, will you stand back while I rotate the fence?"

That was it. Morozov was in. The code word was right.

Morozov stepped back and the door began to slowly rotate. Again he timed it so that he could pass through the swinging arms of the gate. After passing through the gate, Morozov turned around to look at Richard. Ammon was watching Morozov with a slight smile on his face. So Morozov's people had gotten the right code word. Ammon was almost surprised.

"Sir, will you step up and type in the code?" The guard was now looking at Richard Ammon. Ammon walked over to the keyboard and began to type. Morozov looked down at his watch. Two minutes, ten seconds. They were back on time.

Ammon finished typing. He, too, stepped back and looked up at the screen to check his spelling before he sent it to the guard. He reviewed the code word carefully. Everything was right. He reached up to hit the send button.

With a sudden burst of heat and light, an enormous explosion rocked the air, knocking them all to the ground. Even from three hundred yards, the heat and shock wave blew them over, searing their skin and burning their eyes. Morozov looked up to see a huge rolling ball of fire climb into the sky. Long arms of darting flames seemed to reach up and push the fireball skyward. Black smoke billowed up from underneath the rolling inferno. A rush of air was sucked inward to feed the hungry flames.

Three million pounds of fuel was gushing from a ruptured fuel tank. It streamed from the bent and crumpled metal like water from a high-pressure hose. Most of the fuel ignited immediately, sending waves of fire in every direction. But some of the fuel shot out from the base of the tank with such pressure and speed that it gushed underneath the flame, sending it spouting all over the hill before it had a chance to ignite.

A burning river of fuel began to stream down the side of the hill toward the B-1 parking area.

The fuel tank right next to the explosion began to molder from the heat and explosion. Flames reached out to melt its sparkling white paint. Its thick metal ribs began to expand and glow from the heat of the inferno. If it wasn't watered down and cooled within the next ninety seconds, it, too, would explode, spewing another three million pounds of jet fuel out to feed the rolling fire.

Next to the fence, Morozov and the others lay stunned on the ground, covering their faces with their arms. Morozov was the first to sit up.

The area around the alert facility became a swarm of chaos and confusion. Warning horns sounded from all directions as the security forces stormed into the area. Armored jeeps and security vehicles squealed toward the B-1s, forming a protective parameter around them. Fire trucks raced in, sirens and horns blasting, lights flashing, men in fire gear clinging to the sides. Huge klaxons blared as the loudspeakers came to life.

"All aircrews, report to aircraft! All aircrews, report to aircraft! Prepare for emergency taxi! Prepare for emergency taxi!"

A river of fire, smoke, and heat was gushing down the side of the hill. Even from this distance, the heat was nearly unbearable. The Bones that were parked inside the alert gate were soon going to be engulfed in a pool of burning fuel. Teams of pilots and navigators began to swarm from the alert facility, racing against the stream of fire that was rushing toward the B-1s.

Morozov watched the wild scene that surrounded him for only a second, then scrambled to his feet. Ammon was already standing.

"Let me in!" Ammon screamed to the guard. "I am a pilot. My aircraft has got to be taxied. I've got to get it away from those flames!"

For a moment the guard only stared in confusion. Then he looked to his computer screen to check the code word that Ammon had typed in.

The screen was blank. No, it was black. The explosion had cut the electricity off.

Ammon could tell by the look on the guard's face that there was some kind of problem. He sensed what it was and immediately began to yell.

"*Stallion Red! Stallion Red!* The code word is *Stallion Red!* It's still a valid word, now let me in!"

The guard stared in utter confusion. That was the proper code, but was it still okay to let this guy in? Whenever there had been an emergency within the alert facility, they had always shut down access through the gates. Always. When there was an emergency in progress, the gates were always closed and locked.

But the captain did have the proper code. And he did need to taxi his aircraft. So what should he do? Nothing in his training had prepared him for this.

Meanwhile, nearly all of the aircrews had made it to their aircraft. The ramp was utter chaos. Fire trucks, ambulances, humvees, security cops in big four wheel drive pickups. They all were squealing across the ramp. Morozov heard the slow whine of the first B-1 as its four engines started to wind up. He and Ammon should have already been in an aircraft.

This was supposed to have been Ammon and Morozov's chance to get inside the B-1. They had about a twenty second window. And the window was beginning to close.

Morozov took two steps toward the guard, then squinted his pale green eyes.

"Let the captain in!" he said cooly. His voice was very determined. "Our time is running out, Sergeant. Let the captain in."

The guard continued to stare in utter confusion. He made no effort to open the gate.

Then Morozov made a decision. He would give the guard just three seconds to act before he shot the man in the head.

Streams of fire were now starting to pool across the cement taxiway, approaching the B-1s at an unbelievable speed. The first fire truck had arrived at the top of the hill, its lime-green paint a stark visual contrast to the blackness that seemed to surround it. The firefighters were spraying their high pressure hoses on the fuel tank that sat next to the fire.

The first B-1 was starting to taxi. Morozov glanced over to see it roll down the taxiway, building up speed as it went.

"Let the man in!" Morozov said one more time. Then he reached for the weapon that was strapped to his chest.

Ammon's heart nearly stopped when he saw Morozov slip his hand under the open fold of his jacket. His face froze with a cold look of terror. He knew immediately what Morozov was going to do.

Both guards had their weapons drawn and were ready to fire. If Morozov pulled out a gun, he might get off one shot. But that would be all. He would never be able to kill both of the guards before the other one mowed them both down with a long burst from his M-16.

Richard Ammon was about to die, cut in half by a stream of flying lead. Muscle and tissue and bone and sinew would be splattered across the cement. His blood would spill and then pool as it ran onto the flight line. He would take his last breath as he fell against the razor-embedded fence. A great darkness would envelop him. And then he would die as he whispered her name, staring skyward with glazed-over eyes.

TWENTY-EIGHT

McCONNELL AIR FORCE BASE, KANSAS

MOROZOV REACHED INSIDE HIS FLYING JACKET. HE SLIPPED HIS FINGERS around the cold metal of his gun, pushing the beveled handle into the palm of his hand. Taking another step toward the guard, he estimated the distance between them. Ten feet of cracked concrete separated the two men. Killing this guard would be easy. Morozov could send him to the ground in less than an instant.

He stole a quick glance back through the fence. The other guard already had his machine gun trained on the two men in the flight suits. He alternately pointed the end of his muzzle between Morozov and Ammon, jerking the weapon back and forth in sudden and erratic motions. His finger was pressed against the trigger, just a hair's width from firing the gun. He looked scared and confused and was ready to shoot. The blazing fires illuminated the fear in his eyes.

The guard knew that the situation was growing dangerous. Something wasn't right. These men were far too anxious to enter the compound. There was too much noise. Too much confusion; the heat, the flames, the scrambling pilots, and screaming klaxons. He had to get the situation under control. Something had to give.

And then it did. And just in time. The guard was just drawing his breath, ready to command Ammon and Morozov to hit the dirt, when the second guard reached up and slammed a handle on the side of the fence. The door immediately rolled back on a huge set of well-greased hinges, its emergency retraction mechanism pushing it out of the way.

"It's open," the guard screamed over the noise and confusion. "Come on in, man! Come on, let's go!"

Ammon ran through the gate to the inside of the fence.

By then Ivan Morozov had withdrawn his hand from his jacket and was already sprinting toward the waiting Bones. Richard ran after him.

There was only one B-1 that wasn't already surrounded by a hurried crew. Aircraft number 68-347. Reaper's Shadow was her name. She was the last aircraft in the row of bombers, the closest aircraft to the gate, only 175 yards from where Ammon and Morozov had started running. It was also the only aircraft that had been loaded with the new top secret cruise missile. The fact that it was parked closest to the gate had been no accident. It had been placed there by design.

As Ammon ran, he looked over his shoulder to the alert facility door. There he saw the last crew emerge from the building, the pilot half dressed, his hair frothing with a cap of shampoo. His navigator pushed him along the tarmac as they sprinted to the B-1.

Ammon judged the distance between them. It was going to be very tight. The other crew was slightly closer, but not as fast, scrambling to get dressed as they ran. He and Morozov would be the first ones to the aircraft. They might beat the other crew by only five or six seconds. But that would be enough.

Ammon was thirty yards from the bomber when suddenly an armed security guard appeared from behind the main wheel gear. He had his M-16 drawn to his side and his radio pressed to his ear. He was trying to follow the panicked conversations on the radio as he watched Ammon and Morozov approaching the aircraft.

He put out his hands and started to yell. "*Stop! Halt!* I need to see your ID!"

Ammon and Morozov completely ignored him. They didn't even hesitate as they ran into the Zone. Let the guard shoot them if he would. The real crew was now only fifty yards behind them. Ammon and Morozov had to get inside the aircraft and shut the hatch before they could be stopped.

They ran right past the guard. Morozov yelled at him as he passed by. "Pull the intake covers! And hurry!"

The guard hesitated for a second, glanced at the oncoming river of fire, then ran toward the four big engines and began to pull the red square plastic covers that protected the engine inlets.

Morozov and Ammon ran up the ladder that led into the cockpit. Ammon slammed a switch beside him as he climbed inside. He heard the electric motors start to retract the ladder, just as the other crew ran underneath the aircraft's belly.

Ammon climbed past Morozov and slipped into the forward cockpit and started flipping switches to start the engines. In less than ten seconds he could feel the aircraft gently vibrate as the four GE-101 turbofan engines began to wind up. He reached up and put on the helmet that was already pre-positioned by the side of his ejection seat, pulling it down over his ears and dropping its dark eye shield to cover his face.

He looked around the cockpit. In front of him was his main computer screen. Several smaller displays were set off to the side. He was surrounded by hundreds of switches, gauges, and knobs. It was an intimidating sight. He was immediately grateful that he and Morozov had spent so much time in the simulator. Without that training, he wouldn't even know where to begin. But as it was, everything seemed very familiar.

The only thing that caught him by surprise was the sound. The simulator had been very quiet, but inside the actual aircraft there was a constant muffled roar, a reminder that they were sitting on one hundred and forty thousand pounds of thrust and power. And the air from the air-conditioning and pressurization systems hissed through the cooling vents, blowing like a tiny storm.

The first thing Ammon did was strap a thick plastic book of checklists around his left leg and secure it with a stretch of velcro-covered elastic. Then he began to strap himself into his ejection seat. It required nine different connections; five chest harnesses, two waist straps, and finally two leg restraints. By the time he was all strapped in, Ammon almost felt claustrophobic. The thick harnesses and restraints made it very difficult to move around in the seat. But that's the way it had to be. Otherwise his arms and legs would be shattered if he ever had to eject from the Bone.

After strapping in, Ammon set about to bring up the aircraft's systems, while Morozov went to work in the back. Ammon worked through his checklist very quickly, setting the various switches to their proper positions, taking time to complete only the most critical items that would be necessary for immediate flight. Once they were in the air, he would go back and check the aircraft's secondary systems, but he didn't have time for that now.

Ammon was ready in less than sixty seconds. He checked his watch, then pressed his intercom switch and talked into the microphone in his mask.

"How long?" he asked abruptly.

"Two minutes, thirty-five seconds," Morozov answered. That was how long it would take before Reaper's Shadow's computers would be up and running. And the Reaper wasn't going to take off until its computers were ready to go.

Everything on the Bone was controlled by one of the eleven central computers. The official name of the computer system was Main Avionics Central Computer System, but everyone just called it the MACCS. Without the MACCS, Ammon wouldn't be able to raise his gear, sweep the wings, transfer fuel, or control his radar. Without the computers, he couldn't move any of his flight controls. Everything, from dropping his bombs to flushing the toilet was commanded, controlled, and monitored through the MACCS. So they were at the mercy of their computers. They couldn't take off until the MACCS was ready to go.

Which wouldn't happen for another two minutes and thirty-five seconds. That would be just barely in time. Ammon looked down the airfield at the other bombers. Almost all of them were already on their way to the new parking spots. After a moment's hesitation, he spoke again into his mask. "I'll start to taxi," he said over the intercom. "I'll go slowly out to the alternate parking area. Most of the other Bones are already on their way. We will be the last in line. Tell me when you're ready to go."

"Yes, yes. Just get going," was all Morozov replied.

Ammon pushed up on his throttles. The Shadow hesitated for just a second. It took a significant amount of power to break the aircraft free from the 400,000 pounds of weight that pressed down on its tires. But finally it began to inch forward, slowly at first, but building up speed as she went.

Ammon steered the aircraft toward the alternate parking area that was situated at the end of the runway. Most of the other B-1s were already pulling into the parking ramp. They began to line up in a long row, facing the runway.

Ammon would taxi as if to follow. Once he approached the parking area, he would push up his throttles and pass it by. It would only take him a few seconds to taxi onto the runway. Seconds later, they would be in the air.

More than seven security police squads, hunkered down inside squat armored personnel carriers (APCs), had been following the progression of the B-1s as they made their way across the airport. They covered the movement of the aircraft from start to finish. As the Bones began to line up in the alternate ramp, all of the APCs pulled back and formed a protective circle around the bombers.

Except for one.

One of the APCs was sitting in the way. Hidden from view behind the last bomber, the three-ton truck, complete with a 50 caliber machine gun and multi-shot grenade launcher, was now situated at the end of the runway, positioned so no aircraft could take off.

The security police were no fools. They knew that the B-1s were only doing an emergency taxi. Fire or no fire, explosions or no explosions, none of the Bones were suppose to get on the runway. It would have been a disastrous breach of nuclear security if one of the bombers took to the air. So, as a final precaution, they stood in the way, a steel barrier to block off the runway.

Inside Reaper's Shadow, Ammon was busy preparing the aircraft for his takeoff. Morozov began to help him with the checklist.

"Flaps and slats," Morozov called out.

"Extended and down, set for takeoff," Ammon replied.

"Wings."

"Fifteen degrees. Set for takeoff."

"Fuel panel."

"Fuel panel set, sequence initiated."

And so they went, going through some fifty-seven different items in less than two minutes. As they worked through the checklist, they continued to taxi out of the alert parking area and down toward the end of the runway. By the time they had finished the pre-takeoff checklist, they were only a hundred yards from the turnoff that would lead them into the alternate parking ramp.

"How much longer for the MACCS?" Ammon asked once again.

"Another thirty seconds," Morozov replied.

"Come on baby, be a sweet little girl," Ammon spoke to the aircraft in a gentle tone, trying to coax her to life. In less than fifteen seconds they would be on the runway. After that, he wouldn't wait. He couldn't wait. MACCS or no MACCS, he was going to take off.

Ammon taxied past the long row of bombers. Every eye on the airfield immediately turned in his direction as his intentions became very clear. Ammon pointed his nose to the runway as his aircraft began to pick up speed.

"How long?" Ammon demanded, his voice sounding squeaky and strained.

"Twelve seconds. That's close enough now. Let's go!"

Ammon didn't need to be prodded. He immediately shoved his throttles up to fifty percent power. His aircraft pushed itself forward. He passed the last bomber. The APC finally came into view.

Ammon's stomach churned in acid. His heart, already up in his throat, began to beat with the force of a hammer. He scanned the taxiway ahead of him, judging the distance, hoping that there might be enough room to slip by the APC that stood in his way.

It wasn't going to happen. There simply wasn't enough space. Not by a long shot. Ammon wasn't getting onto the runway.

He reached up and slammed on the brakes, throwing himself forward in his seat as the B-1's computerized anti-lock braking system brought the aircraft to an abrupt stop.

"What are you doing?" Morozov cried out over the interphone. "What's going on?" From the back cockpit, Morozov had no view out the front of the aircraft.

Ammon didn't take time to respond. He was sitting just fifty feet from the APC. Ammon could see the driver of the armored truck. They stared at each other with equal displeasure. The driver began to frantically wave his arms, gesturing for Ammon to turn around. At the same time the top hatch of the APC popped open. Two wide-eyed soldiers stuck their heads through the hatch. One of them turned the 50 caliber machine toward the Bone, while the other began to load six grenades into his launcher.

There was just a fraction of a second's pause while Ammon considered what to do. Morozov yelled into his microphone once again. "Ammon, what is going on!?"

"We've got an APC in our way," Ammon called back.

"Go, man! Just go! Run it over if you have to. Push it off the taxiway. But don't stop. What are you going to do, just sit here and surrender?"

But Richard Ammon had a better plan. Kicking in the nosewheel steering, he slammed the throttles forward. The aircraft began to shudder as it lurched ahead once again, turning sharply to the right, spinning around on its center axis. Ammon pushed up the outboard engines to a higher throttle setting and touched lightly on the inside brakes. The bomber began to swivel even tighter, spinning on its inside wheels. Ammon felt himself swinging sideways as the nose of the aircraft cut sharply through the air. In a very short time, the aircraft had turned completely around on the taxiway.

"What are you doing, you stupid fool!" Morozov screamed. *"Ammon, I swear I will kill you! You coward! Why are you turning around?"*

Ammon reached down and turned off his intercom switch, then pushed up his power. He began to quickly accelerate down the taxiway once again. It looked as if he were going back to his original parking spot. One hundred yards ahead of him, the taxiway turned. From there it extended for 13,000 feet, all the way down to the other end of the runway.

Inside the APC was Staff Sergeant Kevin Cutter. He was the squad leader and driver of the armored vehicle. Above him were his gunners. One of them manned the carrier's grenade launcher, while the other one trained his 50 caliber machine gun on the Bone. Everyone inside the APC was agitated and confused.

When they first noticed the B-1 pass by its intended parking spot and head toward them on the runway, they had all assumed that the aircraft had simply missed its turn off. Some pilots were smarter than others, they had joked. This suspicion seemed to be confirmed when Reaper's Shadow had came to an abrupt stop and immediately turned around. The soldiers inside the APC tensely laughed. What an idiot! They watched as the aircraft begin to taxi back, fully expecting the bomber to pull quickly back into the parking area.

But what was it doing now? Even as they watched, Reaper's Shadow was rolling by the other bombers once again. Sgt Cutter watched the nozzles on the back of the Reaper's engines swing closed as the pilot pushed the throttles forward. The aircraft accelerated quickly. In a few seconds, it would make a right turn down the main taxiway that led to the other end of the runway. What was this idiot pilot trying to do?

Cutter got on his radio and began to bark instructions in a hurried voice. "Break. Break. All sky cops. We've got a rambling bomber. I say again, we've got a rambling bomber. Looks like he's heading for the other end of the airfield. Initiate stop gag. I say again, initiate stop gag. Do it now."

Inside the cockpit, Ammon could see a half dozen security vehicles converging on the field. They came from all directions, racing toward the lone bomber in an attempt to cut him off or box him in. Half of the

APCs were rushing toward the other end of the airfield. There they would form a line to block Reaper's Shadow from getting onto the runway.

Meanwhile, the other APCs were following the aircraft as she taxied south. With an APC on each wing, and two right behind her, they would force her toward the barricade at the other end of the runway. There they would shoot out her tires. Then, if the bomber didn't come to an immediate stop, a grenade would be sent up one of her engines. They all hoped that didn't happen, but either way, they intended to see that the bomber never took to the air.

Ammon watched from the cockpit as the security forces gathered around him. He could see their flashing lights as three of them accelerated to the opposite end of the field. He knew they would be there waiting. He glanced out his window to see another APC following him on his right side. He watched as the driver of the truck pulled right under his wing.

As he approached the right turn on the taxiway, he tapped on the brakes to slow down, then steered abruptly to the right, following the long taxiway that led toward the other end of the runway. He glanced out his side windows once more. Two APCs were staying right with him, tucked tightly up under each wing. Ammon stared ahead, down the long taxiway that lay before him, a narrow ribbon of white cement. It was bumpy and thin, and was never designed to be used as a runway. But that's exactly what he would use it for now.

As soon as he had his nose pointing down the taxiway, Ammon pushed all four of his throttles up to maximum power. Four small green lights illuminated each of his engine instruments, telling him that his afterburners had all come to life.

Behind him, a huge blue flame extended out from each of his engines as massive amounts of fuel was dumped into the hot engine exhaust. The engines were now burning fuel at a rate of 300,000 pounds an hour. In a burst of power, thrust, and heat, the Reaper's Shadow accelerated down the taxiway.

Inside his APC, Sgt Cutter watched as the B-1's engine nozzles swung closed once again. He was following directly behind the huge bomber, so it was easy for him to see the bright blue flame as it began to sprout from the back of the engines.

He knew immediately what the pilot was trying to do. He frantically pulled on his steering wheel and slammed on his brakes in an effort to get out of the way.

But it was too late. Within two seconds of lighting his afterburners, Ammon's four engines were producing more than 140,000 pounds of thrust. A massive blast of superheated air shot backward from the tail of the four engines. The blast hit the APC at over 2,000 mph, blowing out all of its windows before sending the vehicle tumbling like a leaf in the wind. After rolling three times, the vehicle came to a stop. Sgt Cutter and his gunners slowly crawled out of the broken vehicle and sprawled on the ground, happy just to be alive.

Frantic voices filled every radio channel as the bomber accelerated down the taxiway.

"He's taking off! He's taking off! He's using the taxiway. Stop him! Shoot his tires. Stop him now!"

Inside the Reaper's Shadow, Ammon was concentrating on his takeoff. He swiveled the massive aircraft back and forth on the tiny taxiway, trying to keep himself pointed down the narrow strip of concrete.

He was accelerating very quickly now, pressed against the back of his seat. He watched his airspeed indicator for an indication of when it was time to rotate and pull his nose into the air.

To his left side, an APC began to fire its 50 caliber machine gun. The gunner ran a stream of blazing shells along the ground in front of the bomber's eight main wheels. Two of the outboard tires were shot out. They spun themselves off of their aluminum wheels and blew to pieces in less than a second. But by then, the Reaper was at 115 knots and her wings were producing enough lift that she was starting to get light on her wheels. This reduced the amount of weight that the remaining six tires had to carry. The tires held out, supporting the weight of the aircraft with the help of the partial lift from the wings.

One hundred and twenty knots. Ammon heard a click and a buzz as his MACCS finally came to life.

One hundred and thirty knots. All of the armored vehicles had been left far behind.

Ten seconds after lighting his afterburners, Ammon was accelerating through 160 knots. Decision speed. He was committed to the takeoff.

Ahead of him, in the last APC, sitting on the end of the runway, the machine gunner got a good bead on the bomber. It was still seven thousand feet away. About one and one-quarter miles. In another few seconds it would be within four thousand feet. Then he would start to fire.

To his side, one of his buddies manned the grenade launcher. He was not very thrilled at the prospect of trying to shoot down a flying bomber. His launcher was never intended for this purpose. It was designed to kill men on the ground, not shoot a high performance aircraft from the air. But still, he stood there waiting. He figured he would only have enough time to fire two shots at the approaching bomber. All he could do was aim for the engines and hope that he got lucky.

One hundred and sixty knots. Ammon began to pull back on the stick. His nose rotated upward and he felt his wheels drop as the aircraft lifted into the air. He breathed a huge sigh of relief. He reached down and lifted the gear handle. They were fast approaching the end of the runway. There was no way to stop them now.

Then he saw the blaze of smoke as the gunners on the last APC began to fire. He watched the tracers from the 50mm cannon reach upward like long, bony fingers, stretching out to touch the fleeing aircraft with their pellets of steel. He subconsciously winced at the sight of the grenade launcher as it fired off three shells in a fury of smoke.

Ammon screamed into his oxygen mask as he pulled back on the stick.

TWENTY-NINE

REAPER'S SHADOW

REAPER'S SHADOW HURTLED SKYWARD, LEAVING THE THREE ROCKET-propelled grenades to fall harmlessly back to earth. But the 50 caliber machine gun shells continued to arch upward, following the Reaper's Shadow as it climbed like a wild dart up into the sky. The gunner ran the tracers forward, tracking just ahead of the B-1's flight path in a long and continuous burst. The cannon's muzzle began to glow a faint burnt orange and the smell of burning powder filled the air. But still the gunner pressed against the trigger of his cannon, never once thinking of holding his fire. The aircraft was climbing too quickly. Very soon it would be out of range.

Richard Ammon began to jink and roll in an effort to throw off the gunner's aiming solution. He kept the throttles in full afterburner and the aircraft continued to accelerate while she climbed. He yanked his stick to the right. The B-1 rolled onto its side and began to pull away from the APC's blazing gun. By then, Reaper's Shadow was over the end of the runway and climbing through twelve hundred feet, her nose pulled up at an impossible angle. Any other aircraft would have stalled and fallen from the sky. But the B-1 continued to climb, her four engines thrusting her skyward.

In the end, it was sheer power that saved the aircraft. The gunner had anticipated that the Bone would fly directly overhead. But he didn't realize that she had the ability to climb so far, so fast. He had never seen what 140,000 pounds of thrust could do. The bomber came at him far too quickly. And then she started to maneuver, turning and rolling, pushing and pulling, it was like shooting at a drunken mosquito, and although he tried, the gunner just couldn't quite keep up. His window of opportunity was only eight or ten seconds long. And it wasn't enough. He fired his last shell as Reaper's Shadow accelerated away, becoming an ever smaller dot on the horizon, leaving the gunner to stare in amazement as the black form of the aircraft melted into the haze of the Kansas morning.

As soon as he was out of range of the gun, Ammon pushed the nose of the aircraft back toward the earth, leveling off at at a mere three hundred feet. He set a course of 160, almost directly south toward Texas. As soon as he could, he went back through his checklist to clean up any items which he might have missed. He knew that he only had a few minutes before the fighters moved in.

WICHITA, KANSAS

Three miles from the runway, a deep blue pickup was parked off to the side of the road. Inside the pickup sat Morozov's friend from the diner. He continually checked his watch, counting the minutes until the appointed time. Beside him sat a Minolta 35mm camera, with autowind and a 100mm telephoto lens.

The man stared into the distance toward the base. He was growing anxious. He fiddled with his radio, trying to find some country music. He checked his watch once more, then flipped the radio off and rolled down both of his windows. He wanted to hear the explosion if he could. He thumped against the steering wheel, beating out the seconds as they passed.

Then he saw it. A billowing fireball rolled into the air, growing for a moment, then collapsing in on itself. It was quickly followed by a thick black column of smoke. The ground shook and trembled and then the air groaned as the noise from the explosion made its way across the flat grasslands. The smoke rose into the sky, pushing north-ward as it caught the prairie wind. Six and one-half minutes later, a B-1 roared into the air, passing two miles in front of the parked pick-up truck. As it flew in front of the man's window, he took a series of pictures with his camera.

Forty minutes later, he was on his way to Kansas City International airport. On the way he stopped to make a phone call to a small hotel room outside Washington, D.C.

"Looking good," he said when the connection went through. "We're closing down, and I'm coming in. I'll see you back in Kiev." The line went dead.

LANGLEY AIR FORCE BASE, VIRGINIA

TSgt Barney G. Rolles sat at his desk in the command post, Headquarters, Air Combat Command (ACC), Langley AFB, Virginia. As the duty controller, it was his responsibility to monitor all of the message traffic that was input to the Commander of ACC. The command post received many different types of reports, some as routine as tracking the flights and operational status of each of the fighter and bomber wings under ACC. Some were a little more intriguing. Daily intelligence updates were filtered through the command post, as well as status reports from around the world. Through the command post, the generals of the world's best fighting Air Force could monitor current events—from troop movements along the Ukrainian border to weather patterns off the English coast, from satellite photos of Russian missile batteries to the position of American submarines under the Arctic icecaps. If it was happening, and if it was important, the information was there to be told.

For the past several months, the command post had been a very busy place. The pace of operations had been constantly frantic, bordering on panic at times.

But not today. Since he had reported to work at seven in the morning, Rolles had seen very little message traffic that would demand any immediate attention. So, for the first time in months, he sat and drank a cup of coffee while browsing the morning edition of the *Daily Press.*

If the command post had any windows, TSgt Rolles could have passed the time by staring out onto the Virginia wire grass that dotted the Chesapeake Bay. He could have watched a small flock of osprey as they hunted for fish in the shallow-briny water. He could have watched a four-ship of Langley's F-15s as they rolled along the taxiway before taking off for some combat training with Navy Norfolk fighters.

But the ACC command post, like most good military command posts, didn't have any windows. It was dry and cold and perfectly sterile. It had purified water and purified air. The lighting was always dimmed, creating a feeling of constant twilight. The computers, paper shredders, status boards, and encryption machines perpetuated an artificial feeling of urgency that kept its occupants strained and on edge.

Along one wall were three huge walk-in safes. These were used to store the War Orders and Operation Plans that would be implemented in times of a national crisis. Opposite the safes were a bank of computers and telephones that were used to connect the command post with the rest of the world. A row of clocks hung overhead, displaying the time in such fascinating locations as Diego Garcia, Indian Ocean, and Incirlik AFB, Turkey.

A bank of printers sat in an orderly row beside Rolles' desk. They were arranged in a descending order of message priority. Those that carried only highly classified and urgent material were placed on the right. Those that carried routine, unclassified junk mail were arranged on the left.

To the far right of the printers was a large, clear plastic box with red hash lines painted around each of its corners. Inside the clear plastic box was a rarely used machine. It was a printer that was reserved for messages coded FLASHDANCE, the highest priority of message there was. When the printer had first been connected to its communication's bank, its black ribbon had been ripped out and replaced with a bright roll of red tape. Tiny electrodes monitored the paper feed of the printer, sounding a gentle alarm whenever the printer kicked on.

TSgt Barney G. Rolles was just beginning to doze through the classifieds when a soft buzz jolted him to attention. He immediately walked to the FLASHDANCE printer and anxiously watched the message as it was typed across the white paper in deep red ink. The words printed out very slowly, for it took time for the STU VI decoder to unscramble the incoming code.

```
ZZZZZZZZZZZZZZZZZZZZZZZZZZZZZZZZZZZZZZZZZZZZZZZZZZZZZZZZ
-----------------------------------screen  on-----------------------------------
ZZZZZZZZZZZZZZZZZZZZZZZZZZZZZZZZZZZZZZZZZZZZZZZZZZZZZZZZ
```

TO: HEADQUARTERS, AIR COMBAT COMMAND/IMMEDIATE PRRITY/DMQ
RE: CODE FLASHDANCE SECURITY VIOLATION/US ASSET WHISKEY
FM: 27 WG/CC, MCCONNELL AFB, KS/MGRTS/1424Z/101596***

MESSAGE FOLLOWS:
AT APP 1417Z, A CODE NATIONAL ONE SECURITY VIOLATION TOOK PLACE. WE ARE IMPLEMENTING SHATTERED BONE. REPEAT: SHATTERED BONE PROCEDURES HAVE BEEN IMPLEMENTED.
REQUEST AUTHORITY TO SEEK AND DESTROY. THE TARGET MUST BE CONSIDERED HOSTILE. INTENTIONS UNKNOWN. NUCLEAR ASSETS INVOLVED.
AWAIT CLEAR TEXT INSTRUCTIONS. STUIII 567-1111

TRANSACTION COMPLETE
RECORD UPDATED

ZZZZZZZZZZZZZZZZZZZZZZZZZZZZZZZZZZZZZZZZZZZZZZZZZZZZZ

Rolles stared at the paper in puzzlement as the printer kicked it out. "Shattered Bone." That was a new one. He quickly reached for the small leather code book that lay chained to the corner of his desk by a thin steel cord. Rolles flipped through the top-secret book, scanning the words that were listed in alphabetical order until he found what he was looking for:

SHATTERED BONE: the code word used to signify the theft, hijacking, or unauthorized flight of a B-1B bomber loaded with nuclear weapons. Such activity should be considered a class "A" security violation. The incident aircraft will be destroyed using any and all means available. Its destruction is the highest priority.
Follow notification procedures appendix three.
Follow command and control procedures appendix ONE HELP JULES.
Implement Emergency War Tasking Operations Plan "SPLINT."

TSgt Rolles swallowed hard, then read the instructions once again. Class "A" violation! Emergency War Tasking "SPLINT!"
"Major!" he cried to senior controller. "Major, get over here *now!*" Dropping the codebook, he reached for a yellow telephone that sat near his desk and picked it up with trembling hands.

WASHINGTON, D.C.

Twelve minutes later, three Air Force generals were escorted into the office of Chad Wallet, the Secretary of Defense. For the next five minutes they stood in a humble stupor, shooting quick glances among themselves as the Secretary carried on in a rage. They winced as the Secretary cursed and threatened the generals.

The Secretary slammed his fist on the table. "How on earth am I going to explain this? And what is going on? Three days ago, we shoot down a Russian Blackjack bomber! But you claim our pilots never fired off a single shot! Now one of our bombers—with nuclear weapons—has been stolen and was last seen heading south!" The secretary cursed and raged again.

Then, suddenly, Wallet stopped and passed his hands over his face as he tried to think. He needed to calm himself down. He could crucify these officers later. For now, he needed to attend to the matter at hand. He needed to get a firm handle on the situation. And there were some things he didn't understand.

"Okay," he said. "So, why didn't you send another B-1 after the renegade? They were right there! Why didn't they go bring him down?"

The Air Force Chief of Staff quickly rolled his eyes in his head. He sometimes forgot that the SecDef had spent thirty years in the academic profession and zero time in a uniform of any kind. Besides, he was still new to his job. And he had a huge amount still to learn, as was evident by this stupid question.

"Sir," the general said, trying his best to be patient. "The B-1s are not fighters. They carry no missiles or guns. They are bombers, sir. They drop bombs. They kill things on the ground. They don't go after other airplanes. There was nothing the other B-1s could do."

"Okay. Okay. I understand that." Wallet said "okay" a lot when he was under stress. "The other B-1s are out. So, what do we have to bring him down with? What fighters do we have in the area? This should be no big deal, right? We have the entire Air Force. Let's just go find the traitor and shoot him down!"

"Sir." It was the Chief of Staff once again. "We will do that. I'm certain we will. But I don't want to pretend to you that it will be easy. The fact is, since the end of the Cold War, the United States has maintained only a handful of fighters to protect our entire East and West coasts. So, it's not like we have a hundred fighters out there on alert and waiting to intercept the stolen bomber. In numbers, I would say there are only eight aircraft available and standing by that could fly this mission. Four on each coast. So you see, we are spread very, very thin.

"And the bomber will not be easy to find. The B-1 is one of the stealthiest aircraft ever built, so I won't pretend to you that we won't have trouble bringing her down."

"But isn't there some type of beacon?" Wallet wondered. "Some kind of tracking device on the bomber that we can use to find out where it is?"

The general shrugged his shoulders. "Sir, this was never supposed to have happened. We never thought . . . We never dreamed . . . a violation could ever get so far. The security measures around the B-1s are the best in the world. Better than any security on the earth. So, no. We don't have any internal tracking mechanism. We never thought such a device would ever be required."

Walking from behind his desk, the SecDef positioned himself directly in front of his generals, looking them square in the eye. He swallowed hard and produced a fresh handkerchief to wipe the sweat from around his lips. He stared at the men for a long moment, then gave them his final instructions.

"Gentlemen, we don't know what this pilot's intentions are. Perhaps he wants the bomber for money. Ransom it for what he can get. Maybe he intends to sock it to the Russians. Finish the war by himself. Or far worse, perhaps he's some kind of insane traitor and he plans to use the weapons against one of his own!

"But either way, whatever his motives, I don't care. We will deal with this problem all the same.

"Down the bomber. Blow it out of the sky. Find it. Kill it. Gut it. Smash it. Wherever it is going, track it and scatter its wreckage for a million miles across the earth. Do whatever it takes, take any measure or step, but do not allow the aircraft to escape."

The Secretary paused to swallow.

"Gentlemen, I want you to end this Shattered Bone," were his final words. "Have I made myself perfectly clear?"

Every man in the room had a very clear understanding of what the SecDef wanted them to do.

The Secretary nodded his head toward the door, dismissing the men with a nod. They turned and began to make their exit, anxious to get out of the office and down to the business at hand. The last man to leave the room was the Air Force Chief of Staff. He paused at the doorway, then turned back to face the SecDef and said, "Mr. Secretary, do you want me to alert the President?" His voice was strained, but calm.

"Let me worry about the President. You go find your stolen bomber. I want him dead within the next hour. Now get going. You know what to do."

The general turned and slipped from the room.

For a long moment, the SecDef stared at the door as it swung closed on its massive hinges, then, reaching down, he picked up the secure telephone and punched in the number to Milton Blake's office over at the NSA.

"Blake, its me, Chad Wallet. Yeah, listen, I need to see the President. And you better meet with us, too. No, it can't wait. I need to see him now. We got ourselves a little problem over here."

Inside his office, Milton Blake checked his watch. 0942. Exactly on time.

"Okay, Chad," he replied in a calm and knowing tone. "I'll set it up. Meet us in the basement as soon as you can."

THIRTY

SOUTH OF BELGOROD, RUSSIA

SGT SERGEI MOTYL SMILED, HIS CROOKED TEETH AND SPOILED GUMS poking through his chapped lips. He tasted the bile at the back of his throat and suppressed a deep urge to cough. The Russian soldier concentrated, listening to the wind, smelling the air, feeling the night breeze as it blew against his neck. The moon had drawn itself behind a thick bank of dark winter clouds. Soon it would be snowing. That was good. The snow would help cover his trail.

Glancing around, Motyl found his pack were he had left it, leaning against a small tree. He hoisted the pack onto his back, then turned and walked away from his camp, leaving his fellow soldiers behind him.

Inside Motyl's pack were eight warheads for the SA-18, the Russian's newest hand-held, shoulder-fired, surface-to-air missile. The SA-18 was an exceptional piece of equipment, capable of bringing down virtually any aircraft that was unfortunate enough to get in its sight. It contained technologies that were years ahead of anything developed by the West. So it came as no surprise that certain parties were very anxious to get their hands on a launcher. To tear one down and look it over. To study it and see what it really could do.

If Motyl could deliver an SA-18 launcher to the right people, it was worth an enormous amount of money. 270,000 rubles to be exact, seven years' worth of army pay. Then, for an extra 200,000 rubles, Motyl had agreed to bring eight warheads for the launcher as well. One launcher, eight missile warheads for 470,000 rubles.

From where his squad was camped, it was only 17 kilometers to the Ukrainian border. If he left right now, when there were no guards posted, he wouldn't be missed until morning. By then he would be across the border. Motyl planned to hike almost due south, cutting over the tops of the tree-covered hills where he knew it would be easy to evade the thin line of Ukrainian troops, then on toward the Ukrainian city of Khar'kov. There his friends would be waiting.

In eighteen hours, Sergei Motyl, formerly of the Russian Fourth Army, would be a very wealthy man.

He hiked silently down the trail for thirty meters before stopping by a low growth of dead brush and leaves. Bending over, he rummaged through the debris and pulled an SA-18 launcher from its hiding place under the dry thistles and dead leaves. With a huff, he hoisted the five-foot launcher onto his back. Motyl then turned and put the moon to his back as he left the trail and set off through the trees.

THIRTY-ONE

TYNDALL AIR FORCE BASE, FLORIDA

Lt Dale Peterson coaxed the contestant on. It was a phrase. Three words. The second word was "the."

"Buy a vowel. Come on, don't be stupid. Buy a vowel," he yelled at the television. The contestant reached down to spin the wheel once again. Lt Peterson watched the numbers spin, clicking as they went. He already had the puzzle figured out. If the dimwitted woman would just buy another vowel. He sat back in his chair and took a sip from his Coke while he watched the wheel clatter around, winding slowly to a stop.

"I'll take a W."

"Sorry, no W," the host replied. A groan went up from the crowd.

"Idiot!" Peterson mumbled in frustration, as he lifted his right leg and placed it up on the small formica table.

Suddenly the alert facility dining room was splintered by a deafening bell.

Lt Peterson jumped way from the table, spilling his Coke as he ran. He sprinted down the brightly lit hallway and out into a cavernous hangar. The hangar's huge steel doors were already beginning to roll open on their steel wheels. Peterson ran to the side of his aircraft where his crew chief was waiting. The chief helped Peterson climb up the tiny ladder that was attached to the side of the F-16. Peterson dropped into the narrow cockpit. The crew chief began to strap the pilot to his ejection seat while Peterson ran his engine-start checklist.

Three minutes later he was in the air, following his flight lead through the overcast layer of clouds that hung over the Florida panhandle. Lt Peterson concentrated on staying in tight formation as they passed through the low clouds. His leader's wing tips cut through the moisture-laden air. At three thousand feet, they broke out above the cloud deck and Peterson backed off to a loose trail formation, twenty feet out from his leader.

Above the clouds, the sun was shining brightly, forcing Peterson to pull his dark visor down over his eyes. He also dropped his oxygen mask, letting it hang to the side of his face. All the while, he never took his eyes off of his leader. As he stared through the orange-tinted Plexiglas, a white sheet of compressed air formed over his leader's wing tips and washed back over his tail.

It was so beautiful. These practice scrambles could be so much fun.

"Tyndall Departure, Blade six-four, a flight of two F-16s is with you climbing to two-one thousand," the pilot in the lead F-16 broadcast over the radio.

After a short pause the controller's voice came back. "Blade six-four, you are radar contact. Climb and maintain flight level three-two-zero. Turn right heading two-six-zero. New Orleans center request you contact them now on 122.4."

"Blade flight is continuing up to three-two-zero, right turn heading two-six-zero," the lead pilot replied.

He sounds so smooth, Peterson thought. Confident and cool. Like he really knows what's going on.

Fresh out of pilot training, twenty-three-year-old Dale Peterson knew that a good radio voice was one of those intangible assets that all pilots prided themselves on. Because so much happened on the radio, it became a very important, though subtle, source of information. Every voice was evaluated for stress, anxiety, or fatigue. Every radio transmission said a lot more than mere words.

Some new pilots would sit and practice their radio voice, much like a broadcast announcer or a television star. They would force their voices lower as they practiced their radio lingo. All of this emphasis on radio technique came from an old pilot saying. "It's better that you sound good, than look good, because at twenty thousand feet, no one can see you looking good."

Lt Peterson was still young and inexperienced. And green. Green as an Irish golf course. But there was nothing that a few thousand hours in the F-16 couldn't teach him.

Peterson followed his leader as they made a gentle turn out to the west. When they were rolled out on the appropriate heading, he heard his leader say, "Blade flight, push 122.4."

"Two," was all Peterson said in reply, then reached down to set in the new frequency on his radio.

This was kind of weird. Departure had turned them in the wrong direction. This heading would take them straight to Texas. They always did their practice intercepts out over the coast. Always. But then again, this was only Lt Peterson's second intercept. Maybe he didn't know quite as much as he thought.

But there was something else rather unusual. Why were they being sent over to talk to New Orleans Center? New Orleans was completely out of their sector.

Yeah, something was definitely up. And with everything that had been going on, with Russia going at the Ukraine, and now, sending Blackjacks and Bears down the coast of Maine, who knows what it could be? But they were being sent west? Toward New Orleans? Didn't make much sense. Peterson listened intently while his leader checked in with New Orleans Air Traffic Control Center.

"New Orleans Center, Blade six-four is with you passing nine thousand for three-two-zero."

"Blade six-four flight, Night Hawk is active. I say again, Night Hawk is active. Dragonfly is going to control you. Contact them on 251.6. They want you to report up on magic." The controller sounded hesitant, almost unsure of himself. Even Peterson recognized the uncertainty in his voice.

There was a long hesitation before Peterson's flight leader responded to the controller's instructions.

"Center, confirm Night Hawk is active?"

"That's affirmative, Blade. Night Hawk was initiated approximately seventeen minutes ago. Suggest you contact Dragonfly without further delay."

Again a long pause. Lt Peterson carefully watched Major Perry, his flight leader in the other F-16. The Major looked over in his direction. He was close enough that Lt Peterson could see the worried expression on his face. For a long time Major Perry did not respond to the controller's instructions. Finally, he turned back to face the empty space that lay before him and replied, "Roger N'Orleans, Blades are pushing to Dragonfly. We'll talk to you guys on our way back home."

The controller did not reply.

Peterson could feel a small bead of sweat begin to roll down his side from under his arm, tickling his ribs as it went.

Something was wrong. Perhaps terribly wrong. This was no longer a routine exercise in air defense. It was obviously much more than that. By using a few special phrases and carefully selected code words, the controller had made that quite clear.

For one thing, the southern sector of the United States had been declared a "safe passage" area. That was accomplished when "Night Hawk" procedures had been initiated. This meant that every aircraft in the southeastern United States would now be considered hostile unless they were able to correctly implement their safe passage procedures. This was not a problem for the hundreds of civilian airliners that now dotted the sky. They all were squawking the appropriate computer generated codes that had been given them before they took off. But if any aircraft did not squawk appropriately when they were interrogated by Air Traffic Control's computers, they would immediately be considered a Bogey, or unidentified aircraft. If they then did not immediately and exactly comply with the controller's demands, they would be considered a Bandit.

And it was Lt Peterson's job to shoot Bandits from the sky.

Which brought them to the Dragonfly. Dragonfly was the common call sign for an AWACS airborne radar controller. AWACS was an aircraft that was used to communicate with airborne strike packages during a time of war. The E-3 AWACS was a highly modified Boeing 707. On the back of the aircraft sat an enormous rotating radar disk. The huge onboard radar could see for hundreds of miles. Using its radar, the AWACS could do it all, from directing an attack, to finding enemy aircraft, to leading a thirsty bomber into its tanker for gas. And there was one other thing that they were very good at—vectoring fighters to intercept and attack incoming targets.

Never before had Peterson heard of a practice intercept that was run by an AWACS controller. Usually the AWACS were reserved for special training exercises, and, of course, times of war.

Finally, there was the fact that the controller had directed the F-16s to come up "magic." This meant that he wanted them to contact the AWACS on their have-quick secure voice radio. All of their conversations would then be scrambled and free from unwanted listening ears.

This intercept was not for practice, Lt Peterson realized. This one was beginning to look very real.

Peterson carefully eyed his leader as they flew to the west and continued to climb through the sky. They were now passing through 18,000 feet. Peterson reached down to reset his altimeter and did a quick scan of his instruments and weapon systems. He tuned in Dragonfly's frequency on his have-quick radio just in time to hear his leader check in.

"Dragonfly, Blade six-four is with you." Lead's radio sounded slightly garbled from being scrambled and encoded for broadcast.

"Blade flight, say number and status," the AWACS controller replied.

"Blade six-four, flight of two F-16s. Sixty-nine hundred on the gas. Two Heaters, four Rams." The controller made a quick note in his log. Two F-16s, each armed with two heat-seeking and four radar-guided missiles.

"Roger, Blade six-four. Turn right heading three-three-five. These are vectors to your Bandit. He is two-hundred-ten miles at your one o'clock. Altitude three hundred feet. You are cleared to engage."

A very, very long pause. Peterson watched and listened intently. Sweat now poured down his back. Suddenly he felt very thirsty. He felt for the small water bottle that he kept in the calf pocket of his G-suit and gulped down a quick drink of water before he heard Major Perry respond.

"Dragonfly, did you say Bandit?! What the—" he cut himself short. Peterson could see his shoulders rise as he took a deep breath, then continued. "Dragonfly, what's going on?" Major Perry demanded. "Who is the target? What do you mean we are clear to engage? Are you telling me we have a Bandit over the middle of the United States? Now, what's going on?!"

The controller responded very quickly. His voice was hard. "Blade six-four flight, your instructions are as follows: you are being vectored to your target. Your target is an American B-1 bomber. I say again, your target is an American Bravo-One bomber. The target is considered extremely hostile. The aircraft has been stolen. Its crew is of an unknown origin, as are their intentions. It is loaded with Category Alpha weapons. That's category Alpha, Blade flight.

"The renegade bomber is presently flying in a southeastern direction, six hundred knots at three hundred feet. You will engage and destroy by any means available. Do not attempt to make contact with the target. Do not attempt to force the target to divert. Do not try to force it to land. Your mission is simple. To seek and destroy. I say again, to seek and destroy."

Inside the AWACS, the controller paused and looked up once again at the two-star general who sat in the observation chair overlooking his controller display. The general nodded his head, giving his approval once again. The controller waited for the Blade leader to reply. After fifteen seconds of silence, he queried the pilot.

"Blade six-four, did you copy your instructions?" His voice sounded stern and directive. Again he waited. Ten seconds later, Major Perry shot back.

"Dragonfly, authenticate Bravo, Zulu."

A young sergeant at the next console quickly flipped through the code book for the correct reply. She hurriedly pointed to the proper response. The controller glanced at the code book and then said, "Dragonfly authenticates Whiskey, Delta. I say again, Whiskey, Delta. . . . Now Blade, do you copy your instructions?"

This time there was no hesitation. "Blade flight copies all," the fighter pilot quickly replied.

"Now listen, Blade," the controller continued. "We've only got one shot at this, so we've got to make it good. The only other air-intercept aircraft are your friends up in Vermont, and I don't think they're going to make it to this party. So, it's all up to you.

"Your target departed from McConnell approximately thirty minutes ago. It has tracked on a southeastern direction since then. You are the only chance that we have to get him now. You are the only thing between him and the Gulf of Mexico. At the speed he is flying, you're only going to get one shot, so let's keep things good and tight, okay guys?"

As the AWACS controller spoke, Lt Peterson began to slowly shake his head, rocking his helmet against the back of his headrest. He was nearly numb with disbelief. An American B-1! How could that be? Some terrorist group must have stolen one. Probably Hamas. They were always involved. Now, with a bay full of nuclear weapons, who knows what the rag-heads would do?

Peterson looked over at his flight leader. Underneath his mask was a determined frown. He watched as the lead F-16 cut through the moisture-laden air. He scanned his eyes down the wing line, examining his leader's six missiles. Between the two of them, they had twelve missiles and more than eight thousand 20mm shells for their cannons. Two of the world's best fighters, fully armed and ready for combat. Against a single B-1. Piloted by a couple of raghead terrorists.

They would blow the B-1 into a thousand smoking pieces of fine dust.

Peterson reached down to fine-tune the contrast on his APG-68 radar, then looked at his leader once again.

It was then that he saw the smoke begin to trail from his leader's exhaust.

"Blade lead, this is two," Dale Peterson said, his voice sounding squeaky and shrill. He swallowed hard before he continued. "Uh, Rick, it appears that you have some smoke coming from your tail."

"Yeah, yeah, I know. I've been fighting a light compressor stall for the last couple minutes. Every time I adjust the throttle, it stalls again. Could be one of those new fuel controls we've been testing."

"How's she doing?" Dale asked as he surveyed his leader's aircraft, looking for telltale signs of a problem. All the while he was silently pleading to himself. "Come on, baby, hang in there." He coaxed the other aircraft along. "Falcon, heal thyself," he commanded, while he made a quick sign of a cross. Lt Dale Peterson was finding a sudden deep need for religion.

Then he saw it again. Another thin wisp of smoke. This time he could also see Major Perry's F-16 shudder as its engine sputtered and churned. Peterson started to move forward on the other Falcon, an indication that Perry's F-16 was slowing down. He pulled back on his own throttle so that he could stay in the proper position.

"Blade flight, come up squadron common," he heard his leader command.

Peterson quickly changed his UHF radio to their squadron's common frequency. This would allow the two falcons to talk without being heard by the AWACS controllers. As soon as he had the frequency dialed in, he heard Major Perry's voice.

"Dale, it looks like you got this one on your own, you lucky dog."

"What's the deal, Lead?" Surely he must be kidding. Major Perry wasn't going to leave him out here by himself? Dale had only been checked out in the F-16 for three weeks. He wasn't even checked out in dissimilar air combat tactics. This wasn't the time, and he wasn't the pilot, to go chasing a B-1 on his own.

"This baby just ain't gonna make it, my boy," his leader continued. "I've got my engine set at eighty percent now, and that's all that it will give me. I think I can make it back to Biloxi, but that's as far as I can hope to go."

Lt Peterson did not reply.

"Now listen, buddy," his leader said. "This is a piece of cake. No big thing at all. You just let Dragonfly drive you into the target. Then set up for the AMRAAM shot while he's still in your face. Remember, shoot, shoot, look. Fire two missiles and see what they do. That will probably do it. If it doesn't, give him two more. If the guy is really lucky, he might get through your missiles, but then you always have your guns. "Man, I'm telling you, this is going to be great," Major Perry continued in an effort to buck up his young wingman. "You are one lucky guy. You'll be the youngest lieutenant to ever log a combat kill.

"Now go get her, ol' boy, and I'll get your autograph when you get home. Just take it easy and follow the book. You'll do fine. I know you will."

Peterson clicked his microphone twice in reply. His mouth was too dry to form any words.

The major took a quick glance back at Lt Peterson to see the lieutenant wipe his glove across his face. The major figured he had about a fifty-fifty chance of getting the bomber. Maybe. If he was lucky. Or a little more experienced. Perry turned back and studied his engine instruments, which had continued to gradually decay. He was starting to lose altitude. The cockpit shuddered and rumbled as the wounded engine roared. He cursed once more at his jet, then jammed down hard on his microphone switch.

Peterson listened as Major Perry coordinated with the AWACS for a clearance and heading to an emergency landing field, then watched in sheer fear and amazement as his flight leader peeled off and turned to the south, heading toward Biloxi, Mississippi.

Blade six-four was now a flight of just one.

"Blade two, you still with me?" It was the AWACS controller. Peterson blinked twice and cleared his throat. He took a deep breath as he mustered his voice.

"That's affirm, Dragonfly. Blade is with you."

"Blade, target is now one-five-zero miles, straight ahead, heading one-three-zero. He must know that we are tracking him, but so far he has made no attempt to jam our radar. He will be breaking your bubble in the next two minutes."

Peterson reached down and selected range-while-search on his radar, then adjusted the range out to eighty miles. He pulled back his power to begin a descent, then reached down and armed all of his weapons while he waited for the Bone to appear on his radar screen.

REAPER'S SHADOW

Richard Ammon let out a long and weary sigh. His hands trembled. His back knotted into taut strands of muscle. He felt exhausted. Ammon knew he would have to pace himself. He had a very long mission. He shook his shoulders and tried to relax as he studied the terrain up ahead.

After taking off from McConnell, Ammon had initially steered the bomber south toward Texas. After two hundred miles he turned forty-five degrees to the east and took a heading that would steer them toward the Gulf of Mexico. His intention was to get away from the many military installations that dotted the southern States. He was flying at three hundred feet and 550 knots, just under the speed of sound. At this speed and altitude, it would have been impossible to have been tracked by any ground-based radar. They were too low. Virtually invisible to any radar on the ground.

Unfortunately for Richard Ammon, eight minutes after taking off he had flown directly underneath the nose of an AWACS airborne control aircraft.

At the time, the AWACS was on a routine training mission and was completely unaware of the crisis. But soon after the bomber had passed unobserved under its nose, the AWACS began to receive a series of urgent commands. At first, there was total confusion as the airborne command center scrambled to understand the scope of the crisis. It took the controllers several minutes to decipher their codes and authenticate all of the messages that had begun to pour in. Precious time was lost as they scrambled through their checklist. But once they got past the initial confusion, the controllers set about to track the low-flying bomber. They immediately tuned the huge orbiting radar that sat on the aircraft's back and concentrated its electronic energy toward the south. They had little trouble finding the fleeing bomber. It was only sixty miles off its right wing.

So much for Ammon's stealthy escape.

By then, the B-1 was passing through central Arkansas. The Mississippi coast was just four hundred miles to the south. Forty minutes away. Once the fleeing bomber went "feet wet" out over the water, it would simply disappear into the huge expanse of the Gulf of Mexico and its thousands of miles of aqua blue sea.

Inside the B-1, Ammon was busy as he concentrated on making their escape. He knew the fighters were coming. He knew that by now they would already be airborne, their radars tracking in search mode, hunting the sky, snooping along the terrain in an all-out effort to find him.

But there would only be a few of them—thank heaven for Cold War military cutbacks—and they wouldn't know where to look. From Texas to Tennessee, the B-1 could be anywhere. There was simply too much terrain for the fighters to cover. Like a needle in a haystack, the Bone could just slip away.

BLADE 64

Lt Dale Peterson leveled off at twenty thousand feet. He pushed his throttle back up to ninety-two percent to hold his airspeed at four hundred knots and reached down to adjust the tracking file on the target.

The bomber was now seventy-five miles away and closing very quickly. His radar told him that the two aircraft were approaching head on at over one thousand miles an hour. Over eighteen miles every minute. One thousand five hundred feet every second. Either way you looked at it, the distance between them was closing very quickly.

Which was good. Peterson's Doppler radar needed a fast rate of closure in order to pick the low-flying B-1 out from the clutter of the ground and the trees. Speed was the only thing that allowed the Falcon's radar to see the incoming B-1.

Peterson stared through his Head-Up Display (HUD) at the terrain that lay below him. Rolling hills heavily forested with tall pine and birch trees. An occasional lake sped underneath his nose, its surface frothing and white from the twenty-knot wind that was blowing at the surface. The towns were scattered and widely dispersed, but Peterson was also getting a very large return on his ground-mapping radar at forty-six miles. He knew that would be the mass of buildings, highways, and homes of Little Rock. Peterson did some quick calculations and realized that he would encounter the bomber as it passed just south of the city.

"Dragonfly, say bearing and range to the target," Peterson said to the AWACS controller.

"Bearing three-five-eight. Range six zero miles. Have you lost the target on your radar?" The controller's voice sounded alarmed.

"Negative Dragon. Just checking." Peterson was tracking the target very easily. It showed up as a solid dark square that was making its way down his screen at a steady and predictable rate.

Which was the reason that he had asked the AWACS to confirm its location. The Bone was flying very low and very fast, but it was holding true to its original heading as it flew across the rolling hills of central Arkansas.

Which caused the Lieutenant to wonder. Why wasn't the bomber maneuvering away from the fighter? Why wasn't it trying to hide behind some of the higher terrain? So far it had made no attempt to jam his radar. It was as if the B-1 didn't even know he was there.

WASHINGTON, D.C.

"We have contact with the bomber," Chad Wallet said to the President in a whisper. "It is flying southeast, toward the Gulf. We have two . . . I mean one . . . of our F-16s out of Florida inbound to the target."

Allen looked up from the huge conference table in the White House situation room with a blank face. The room was cramped and very noisy. Surrounded by the banks of telephones and computer screens, he felt awkward and out of place.

As Wallet strode up to him to give him the news, Milton Blake stood by the President's chair, anxious to hear every word. Weber Coy, the CIA director, was also standing nearby.

"How did they find him?!" the President asked, turning toward Milton Blake. "You told me he would just slip away. So how did they find him so quickly?"

Wallet glanced around the room to make sure that no one could hear them, then answered the question. "Apparently there was an AWACS radar plane that happened to be on a routine training mission near the bomber's planned escape route. When the Shattered Bone message went out, the AWACS was brought into the loop. As luck would have it, they were almost directly on top of the bomber, and they have continued to track him as he's flown to the south."

"'As luck would have it,' huh? That is so much B.S.," Allen replied. "I don't believe in tooth fairies, and I don't believe in simple luck. So, what's the deal with this bomber? This . . . the cutting edge of our military technology . . . the best warplane that we have, and already, it's being tracked by an airborne radar?"

Allen frowned at his security advisor. "Milton, you told me you had considered every angle. So I'm wondering, what do you plan to do now?"

REAPER'S SHADOW

"Ammon, we've got a small problem," Morozov broadcast over the intercom. Richard Ammon immediately began searching the sky, expecting Morozov to announce an incoming fighter.

"What do you have?" he asked, not taking his eyes from the sky.

"The airborne threat warning computer seems to have taken a hike. It's giving me all sorts of sporadic and wild indications. I've tried several times to reset it, but so far no luck. I'm not sure if I know how to straighten out its logic."

Ammon's mind raced. That was the computer that searched the sky, looking for any sign of a hostile fighter's radar. Without it, they were blind. They would never see what hit them. They could have a whole squadron of F-16s flying right on their tail and never even know they were there.

"Come on Morozov, that system is our baby! Do something. Do anything. Just get that thing back up on-line."

Ammon continued to search the sky up ahead, his eyes darting from cloud to cloud as he searched for American fighters. He racked his brain, trying desperately to think of how to reboot the defensive systems computer. But he had no idea. None at all. That was supposed to be Morozov's area of expertise.

Morozov continued to flip through the operator's manual for the ALQ-161 defensive system computer. He scanned his fingers down the trouble-shooting guide. He read quickly and tried everything he could think of, but nothing seemed to work. The computer continued to bounce around, giving spurious and incorrect information.

For a long time, Ammon didn't say anything as he frantically searched the sky for incoming fighters. He craned his neck from side to side, looking for a contrail or the quick flash of a wing. He paid particular attention to the bright haze that circled the sun, knowing that was where the fighters would most likely come from. He squinted into the sunlight, fully expecting to see the white tail of an incoming missile.

But he saw nothing but hazy, gray sky dotted by an occasional cotton-white cloud. In the distance, on the horizon, he could barely make out the dark shapes of a few high-rise buildings. Little Rock lay directly ahead.

BLADE 64

Peterson watched the target track down on his radar. How could this be? It was almost too easy. It almost didn't even seem right.

The bomber was now fifty-two miles away. It was still heading southeast. Same speed. Same altitude. If this kept up, it would be like shooting a blind deer with a machine gun. Not very sporting, but a kill just the same. The boys in his squadron were going to be very proud of their newest pilot.

Peterson flicked at the coolie hat on the top of his stick. A small cursor glided over his radar screen toward the target. When the cursor was superimposed over the black square, Peterson pushed up a small switch on the top of his throttle. His HUD immediately indicated that two AMRAAM missiles were armed and ready to fire. A light growl in his headset indicated they had locked on to their target. The bomber was just moving inside of fifty miles. From this altitude, that was nearly an optimum range. Peterson listened to the missile trackers for just a second to ensure that they had a good solid lock, then cleared his voice and said, "Dragonfly, confirm Blade is cleared to fire?"

The controller inside the darkened AWACS looked up at the general once again. The general nodded his head at the controller without taking his eyes off the radar screen. The controller keyed his microphone switch and replied, "Blade, you are cleared to engage."

Lt Peterson pressed the "fire" switch with his finger. He felt the two missiles as they dropped off of their rails. His eyes narrowed to a slit as the powerful missiles ignited their motors, filling his cockpit with a dazzling strobe of white light. For a fraction of a second, the missiles hung in midair, suspended. Then they began to pull ahead of the fighter as they quickly accelerated away, leaving a trail of white smoke and turbulent air.

THIRTY-TWO

OVER ARKANSAS

THE MISSILES ACCELERATED TO MACH IN LESS THAN TEN SECONDS AND tracked straight to the target. Steered by a miniature radar within their nose cones, the missiles honed in on the low flying bomber, seeking the scattering protons of radar energy that reflected and bounced back from the aircraft's wings and tail.

Every second that passed brought the missiles 5,600 feet closer to Reaper's Shadow. The missile's onboard computers were constantly updating the geometry that made up the intercept solution. It was beginning to look like a near perfect tracking scenario. No rough terrain for the target to hide from. No blazing sun reflecting off white hot desert sands. A huge rate of closure to home in on. And the target was not even attempting to maneuver away.

In the Reaper's tail lay an extremely sophisticated radar-detecting antenna. Its purpose was to detect and gather any radar signals that were beamed onto the bomber. It quickly sensed the energy from the AMRAAM missile's radar and sent a signal to the ALQ-161 defensive system's computer. The computer received the signals and began to process the information. It analyzed the wavelength, frequency, and strength of the signal, then sorted through two and half million bites of information in its attempt to identify the source of the radar.

In less than a second it had its answer. The radar in question was classified as non-threatening. Its source was more than 93 million miles away. The bouncing protons were nothing more than scattered energy from enormous sun spots. Nothing to be concerned with at all.

As part of its redundant safety features, the computer was programmed to analyze the signals once again. The whole process started over. Gather data, send to computer, analyze features, compare against memory banks. Conclusion. The source of the energy was a Russian Bad Dog acquisition radar, found only on the newest Russian Naval destroyers.

This conclusion obviously failed the computer's logic test. The process began once again. Sometime during this third and final circuit, the computer realized that it could no longer tell the difference between a radar signal and a piece of Swiss cheese.

Three seconds later, the computer shut itself down.

Which is why the threat warning tones were not screaming through the earphones in Ammon's helmet as the missiles tracked in on his bomber.

On the panel in front of Morozov's face, a caution light flickered on. "Ammon, we've lost the system!" Morozov shouted. "It just completely shut itself down!"

"Come on, Morozov, you're supposed to be the expert. Do something! Get it back on-line. We need that system. Do something, *now!*"

Morozov continued in his desperate attempt to reset the defensive systems. But all to no avail.

The two missiles were now only thirty miles away. Passing through twelve thousand feet, they looked down on their target. They were twenty-eight seconds from impact.

The bomber flew over a small lake. For just a second the missiles lost their radar return as the radar signal was bounced and scattered by the swelling waves. But still they continued to track downward, their computers analyzing the bomber's last known position and airspeed to predict where the aircraft should be. Four seconds later, the Bone passed over the U-shaped earth dam that formed the lake and proceeded down a small valley of tall birch and white pines. The AMRAAM missiles immediately picked up their target once again, only eighteen feet from where they predicted it would be.

Just fourteen miles to go. The missiles were now passing through five thousand feet. At this angle, the first missile would impact the root of the bomber's left wing. The second missile would impact on the top of the bomber, directly behind the cockpit. Of course, the AMRAAMs wouldn't wait until they impacted the bomber to detonate. Their fifty pounds of high explosives would explode as soon as they got to within eighty feet of the bomber.

Inside his F-16, Lt Dale Peterson was screaming into his mask as he coached the missiles on.

"Go, my sweet little ladies!" he cried. Oblivious to everything around him, he stared at his radar screen as the missiles tracked in on their target. "Come on . . . come on . . . go and get her!" he screamed into his mask, as if cheering a football team on.

Inside the AWACS, the controller was doing much the same thing. The two-star general leaned forward in his seat, his hands clutching his armrest, his expression firm as granite.

Ten seconds. Fifty-six thousand feet lay between the bomber and the missiles. The controller pushed back against his seat and waited for the impact.

REAPER'S SHADOW

Ammon saw the missiles when they were still nine miles away. They burst through a steel-gray cumulonimbus cloud, their white-hot engines condensing the air that trailed them into a thin contrail, giving the effect of a long, thin arrow that was pointing directly at the bomber. Even at this distance, Ammon could see the glint of the twelve-foot missiles. They were directly before him, closing at an incredible speed.

For nearly a full second, Richard Ammon stared in a stupor of fear. It took a while for his mortal brain to comprehend the threat.

The warheads began their final fusing countdown.

Adrenalin pulsed through Ammon's body. His heartbeat tripled in an effort to flood his brain with oxygen. Time seemed to slow and stretch itself out. When he finally began to react, his actions were purely instinctive, born from years of intensive training, for there was simply no time now to think.

"*Missiles, twelve o'clock!*" he screamed while rolling the aircraft up onto its side. "*Chaff! Jamming! Flares!*"

Morozov immediately began dispensing silvery bundles of chaff and kicking out streams of red-hot flares. At the same time, he selected manual on his electronic countermeasures display and began to radiate white electronic noise in every direction. No sense trying to be discreet about his jamming. It was obvious the Americans knew where they were. So he filled the electronic spectrum with random bursts of energy, hoping to destroy the incoming missiles' tracking solution.

Meanwhile, Ammon continued to roll away from the missiles, doing everything he could to put some distance between them and his Bone. He pushed the aircraft even lower, hand flying the machine to tree-top level as he screamed across the rolling hills. He kept his throttles in full afterburner, pushing through a thick wall of compressed air and accelerating through the speed of sound. He thrashed across the forested terrain in a howl of fury, the thrust from his engines blowing the branches off of trees and scattering their limbs in a thin trail of splintered wood and toasted leaves.

But still the missiles closed in on their target.

For a fraction of a second, Morozov's jamming started to work. The missile's guidance systems lost track of their target as Morozov filled their receivers with a huge burst of electronic noise. But the AMRAAMs were not easily fooled. Their receivers immediately attempted to burn through the thick wall of electronic jamming as their tiny guidance computers sorted through banks of logic algorithms in an attempt to keep locked onto the target.

The missiles made several attempts to burn through the jamming. No good. The radar noise was simply too thick. There was nothing to see but a huge blanket of electronic clutter that obliterated their radar return.

The guidance computers then made a quick decision. Since the target was jamming their radars, they would target the jamming instead. It was that simple. The computer's logic was very straightforward. The target had disappeared. An electronic transmitter had appeared where the target should be. The transmitter was jamming their radar. The transmitter was now the new target. The transmitter would be the thing they destroyed.

Through it all, the countermeasures and jamming, the chaff and the flares, the missiles never deviated more than ten feet from their desired course toward their target. They were now flying level at three hundred feet, closing in on the bomber from its left side.

BLADE 64

Lt Dale Peterson suddenly fell silent. The missiles and the target had begun to merge upon his screen. He lifted his eyes and looked out into the horizon. Even from this distance, he expected to see the rising fireball. He strained his neck and pushed forward in his seat to get a better view down the nose of his F-16. He stared across the rolling hills, with their tree-lined rivers and highways, as he waited for the seconds to pass.

Inside the AWACS, the controller reached up and adjusted his screen. As the Bone threw out multiple bands of electronic noise, his screen became blotchy with intermittent patches of sparkling fuzz. In addition to the jamming, the B-1 was also approaching the edge of his radar coverage. The controller keyed in a series of instructions at his console to command his computer to try and filter out and clean up his radar picture. He desperately hoped that he could keep a good radar return for at least a few more seconds. It was the only way he would have to confirm whether or not the Bandit was really destroyed.

REAPER'S SHADOW

Ammon was giving up hope. The missiles loomed larger than ever. Like blazing poles of fire they pursued him, matching his every pitch and roll with considerable ease. They were almost upon him. Only seconds to go.

Then he saw them. Directly ahead, little more than two miles, there stood a huge set of high-tension, high-voltage power lines. At least a dozen of the wires were strung across the small valley on their way toward the substations that lay on the outskirts of Little Rock. They glistened from their silver towers, thick and shiny, suspended seventy-five feet in the air. Ammon was flying a little lower than the wires and he had to look upward through his windscreen to keep them in sight. Big red balls were suspended from the middle of the silver threads to warn low-flying aircraft of their menacing presence.

Richard Ammon threw his stick to the right. The aircraft immediately banked to ninety degrees as he pulled around to parallel the wires. The strands of high-voltage wires slipped under his wing as the aircraft bellied up to the towers. Ammon knew that his only hope lay in putting the wires between himself and the missiles.

But he was going too fast. At this speed his turn radius would swing him past the set of high-voltage wires and into the path of the missiles. He had to stay on his side of the wires. He immediately yanked his throttles back to idle and extended his speed brakes in an attempt to slow down. The aircraft decelerated quickly, throwing Ammon forward against the harness of his ejection seat.

"Keep jamming!" he screamed to Morozov as the aircraft turned and slid up against the wires. *"Light up the sky!"* he cried as the B-1 rolled out and flew past one of the steel-framed towers, missing it by less than a wing span.

Morozov reached up and slammed the power switch on his jamming computer. The computer immediately increased the jamming. Enormous bursts of energy emitted in every direction. The Bone was illuminating the invisible radio spectrum with a hundred thousand watts of flashing power. It blazed and strobed and flashed and burned, coaxing the missiles forward, beckoning them on, pulling them toward the aircraft, the only possible source of such amazing electronic power. The electronic haze spread for miles, immediately turning both the AWACS' and the F-16's radar screens to little more than round scopes of white strobing fuzz.

As Morozov threw his power switch to maximum, Reaper's Shadow was just beginning to fly down another small valley. It paralleled the high strands of wire. Ammon turned away from the wires to put some distance between himself and the cables.

The missiles sped along, cutting toward the bomber from its left side, oblivious to anything but the aircraft. They flew directly into the strand of three-inch cables. The copper wires immediately cut the missiles into fractured pieces, detonating the high explosive warheads in the process. There was an enormous explosion. The cables fell, strobing the air with arcing bolts of white lightning as the missiles exploded around them. A burst of vaporized metal and plastic filled the air, sending a billowing cloud of black smoke skyward to be dissipated by the southern winds.

A bright flash reflected into his cockpit from the blazing explosion. *"Stop jamming! Stop jamming!"* Ammon cried into his mask. Morozov flipped his jamming switch to off.

Ammon pushed the Bone back into the wires, flying as close as he dared. He snugged in tight to the strands of high cables, nearly scraping his wings along a copper-tipped tower. It took all of his concentration and mental ability to mask so close to the wires without getting caught in their web.

Ammon knew that the fighters were still out there. And they wouldn't know for sure if he was dead. So they would still be searching; sweeping the ground with their radar from their perch up at twenty thousand feet. They would attack again if they found him. And this time he couldn't count on being so lucky.

He only had one hope of getting away. And the next thirty seconds would be the most critical. If the fighters could be distracted for just a moment, thinking they had already gotten their kill, then they might not begin a secondary sweep with their radar. If he could just get some distance between them, it was possible he might get away.

An experienced fighter pilot would not have fallen for such a simple deception. Even after seeing the impact on his radar, a good pilot would have immediately begun another sweep, knowing that it was possible that his missiles did not get a kill.

Fortunately for Richard Ammon, he was not being pursued by an experienced pilot.

The AWACS controller still stared at his screen. He had seen the whole thing. He had watched as the missiles tracked in on the bomber, then the wild gyrations as the aircraft attempted to maneuver away. He had watched as the B-1 attempted to jam on the missile, his screen filling entirely with white fuzz from the intensive electronic noise. Then, just as the missiles should have impacted the target, his screen had suddenly cleared.

Then there was nothing. No missiles. No target. No jamming. Only a few clutters of ground return as his radar continued to sweep through the area, searching for the bomber from high in the sky. But he didn't see any target and he had to assume the target was dead.

"Blade, it appears that you have a good kill," the controller finally said. His voice sounded stressed and fatigued.

"Yeah, I blew that sucker out of the sky!" Peterson cried. His enthusiasm was perfectly clear. "Did you see that, Dragonfly? I thought he was going to burn out my radar from all that jamming. Unbelievable, eh? But I got him. Did you see that? That sucker is dead!"

The AWACS controller didn't smile as he listened to the pilot congratulate himself. After a few seconds he pressed his microphone switch to interrupt.

"Yeah Blade, you did a wonderful job. But listen, we may not be finished here yet. We are at the outer envelope of our radar. We're getting lots of clutter in our low-level return. I don't think we could see the bomber any more, even if he was there.

"Now we need you to take a few good sweeps with your radar. Check it out real good and tell us what you see. Meanwhile, proceed to the detonation site and get a confirmation on the kill. This is something we need to be sure of. We also need to know where the wreckage is. Someone's got to get out there and clean up all the mess."

Lt Dale Peterson shrugged his shoulders and began a few half-hearted sweeps with his radar. But what was the use? He had seen the explosion. He had seen the flash of white light and the rising pillar of black smoke. And then the aircraft jamming had suddenly dropped off of his screen.

So where had the bomber suddenly gone to? Just disappeared into thin air? I don't think so, Peterson thought to himself. Man, that sucker is gone.

So he took a few quick sweeps with his radar, then concentrated on finding the crash site. The smoke was beginning to dissipate, so he marked the site on his navigation computer. It shouldn't be too hard to find the wreckage, he thought. It must be scattered across the countryside for more than a mile.

For the next ten minutes Peterson flew atop the Arkansas forest, looking for a smoking hole or burning fields. By the time he realized there was no wreckage to be found, Reaper's Shadow was more than one hundred miles away.

WASHINGTON, D.C.

Milton Blake turned toward President Allen and wiped the sweat from his brow. The president returned Blake's look with a cold stare of his own.

"That was pretty close, now wasn't it, Milton? We almost killed our own man."

Blake looked up, but didn't respond. It was Weber Coy who finally said, "Yes, sir. That was far too close for our comfort. But it should be smooth sailing from here. He's within a few minutes of hitting the coastline. Getting away from our own fighters may prove to be the most difficult part of this mission. At this point, I feel that we have every reason to be optimistic."

Once again, Blake reached up to wipe the sweat from his forehead and nodded in agreement. Then, stuffing his hand into his enormous pants pocket, he fished around for a small tube of antacids and popped four of them into his mouth.

Allen studied his men for a moment and then said. "No. I think that is wrong. The toughest part is yet to come. He still has to fight his way through the Med and across the Ukrainian border. That will be much more dangerous than this. So I've come to a decision. We can't just sit here, watching like fools, when there is something that we can do."

"But sir," Blake replied. "You know that we can't get involved. We can't expose ourselves to—"

Allen cut him off. "I know that, Milt. But still, there is something that we can do. Something that may prove very important for Ammon if things suddenly turn bad. And I think it's the least that we owe him.

"Now tell me, what helicopters do we have in the area?"

Milton Blake looked puzzled. "In the area?"

"In the Med. Something near the Ukraine."

Blake thought for a moment and then said, "The U.S.S. Ticonderoga is on duty in the Med. She has a small contingent of choppers. She is probably the closest thing that we have."

Allen smiled. The Ticonderoga. He was familiar with the ship. "Okay, here's what I want you to do. . . ."

THIRTY-THREE

REAPER'S SHADOW

RICHARD AMMON WAS STARING THROUGH THE THICK PLEXIGLAS, OUT the right side of his windscreen. From this altitude, he could just barely make out the dim lights that dotted the Azore Islands, fifty-seven miles to the south. The bright white lights were dimmed to a soft yellow glow as they filtered through the water-soaked atmosphere. They looked comforting and inviting as they twinkled in the distance.

Ever since passing over the forested beach line of southern Mississippi and out into the Gulf, Ammon had seen nothing but deep water and hazy gray skies. Just north of the Bahamas, he had counted six or seven tiny islands beneath him, but since then, he had seen no land at all. For seven hours he had watched the endless waves and open nothingness, feeling more lost and isolated with every mile that passed beneath him on his way out into the enormous Atlantic Ocean.

His day was short, flying east as he was, and it wasn't long until the blue water and white-capped waves began to darken into a deep black of shadowy water. Then, in the late evening, as the sun slipped rapidly down behind him and darkness settled in, he lost even that much of a view, leaving him only an occasional glimpse at the moon as it broke from behind the high stratus clouds.

When he finally caught a view of the Azores, the tiny island chain that dotted the Atlantic almost 1,000 miles west of Portugal, it seemed like he had been over the open ocean for a very long time. After hours of empty water, it seemed good to see at least a reminder of dry earth.

He raised his eyes and glanced at the glistening moon as it shimmered above the deep waters of the North Atlantic. It had been dark for nearly an hour and the moon was now high on the eastern horizon. At this altitude, the sky looked like a huge platter, round and full, sparkling and blinking with stars.

He looked down at his navigation computer and read its digital display. 28.15.10W 41.12.07N. Without referring to his chart, Ammon mentally plotted his position in the North Atlantic. It was only a rough guess, but he figured they were at least nine hundred miles from the closest shore.

For the hundredth time he checked his total fuel remaining readout. His pulse quickened again. Six thousand pounds of jet fuel! Six thousand pounds! They had started out with just over two hundred thousand. Now they were down to just six!

Another twenty minutes of flying. Maybe twenty-two minutes. If he was careful. And if they were lucky.

And landfall was almost two hours away.

He sucked in a chestful of air and held it, trying to calm himself down. He reached down and pulled on his parachute harness, making certain it was strapped tightly to his back. He stared outside, forcing himself to look away from the fuel readout. He listened as Morozov called out desperately on the radio.

"Wolf five-three. Wolf five-three. Do you read? Do you read?"

Nothing. No response. The radio was deadly quiet.

In the rear cockpit, Morozov fiddled with the radio squelch. He positioned the switch for better long-distance reception, then pressed his radio switch once again.

"Wolf five-three, Heater four-one."

Again he waited. Nothing came back. Morozov checked for the third time to make sure that he had dialed up the proper frequency. It was the right one. His voice thickened and a heavy sweat beaded across his upper lip.

Ammon listened for as long as he could stand it, then shaking his head, he finally said, "Okay, Morozov. Less than six thousand pounds."

Morozov didn't respond. The radio remained very quiet.

"Less than six thousand pounds, now ol' buddy. Less than twenty minutes. Let's see . . . just about nine hundred miles to landfall. How far do you think you can swim?"

"Shut up!" Morozov commanded. "I haven't got time for your mouth!"

"Okay, okay," Ammon replied in his humblest tone. "Sorry, I'll try to be a bit more discreet."

Morozov slammed his microphone switch down once more.

"Wolf, Wolf, how do you read?"

Ammon listened intently to the radio, hoping like he had never before. But still, there was only the static. And his four jet engines continued to suck down the fuel.

WOLF 53

Three hundred miles to the east, and cruising toward the B-1 at its highest speed, was an enormous KC-10 refueling tanker. The tanker crew had taken off late, for most of the entire northern coast of Spain was socked in with horrible weather, and they were now more than thirty minutes late for the air refueling. In fact, they were lucky to have made it at all. But the weather had broken just enough for them to get off. Now they needed to make up some time. They were scheduled to refuel a B-1 that was being deployed from the States. And the bomber would be very thirsty. So they hurried to get back on time.

The pilot pushed at his throttles once again, adjusting them to just below his max-limit speed. The copilot looked at his watch, then, nodding his head to the pilot, reached down to dial up the air refueling frequency on his UHF radio.

"Twenty minutes now to air refueling," he said. "We're still a few minutes late."

"The bomber shouldn't complain," the pilot replied. "Not with the weather we plowed through to get here. I've never seen so much lightning in my life. And I'm telling you now, if he gripes even once, I'll make him beg us before we pass on any fuel."

The copilot smiled and agreed. "Yeah," he laughed. "It's kind of cool when you're the one with the gas."

Three days earlier, a forged message had been sent from Headquarters, ACC, to the Tanker Task Force that was deployed at Torrejon Air Base in Spain, requesting them to refuel a B-1 thatwas going to be enroute to a forward operating location, somewherein Germany. The message gave a time and a refueling location. It appeared to have been run through the appropriate channels. It appeared to have the appropriate codes.

But the message had originated not from any Headquarters office, but from a home computer that had hacked its way into the Department of Defense's message network.

It hadn't been a complicated process. The message network that carried such routine requests as asking for air refueling support had never been very well-protected, and hackers had broken its code dozens of times. But because the network only dealt with routine and unclassified information, the Department of Defense had never felt it a high priority to spend the money to upgrade the network's security systems.

Morozov's people had broken into the system twice before, and although it had been several years, still, nothing had changed.

So, four hours after putting the request into the computer, Morozov's people had his reply. The Task Force would support the B-1 deployment. They would refuel the B-1 in the air, just northeast of the Azore Islands. The times, headings, altitudes, coordinates, and pre-assigned radio frequencies all checked out.

And that was it. Everything was set.

REAPER'S SHADOW

Morozov shook his head. It had been a very good plan. It was going to be tight, he knew that from the very beginning, but it should have worked out. They had burned a lot more fuel than he had ever planned on, thanks to that F-16 episode back in the States. But even still, he had expected to meet the tanker with just enough fuel.

Of course, he had assumed the tanker was going to be on time.

He tried another channel as he swore into his mask. In the front cockpit, Ammon stared out the side of his canopy and watched the cold sea down below.

WOLF 53

The KC-10 pilot nodded to the copilot, who then switched the radio frequency over.

"I hope they're up on this freq," the copilot said. "With all that weather going on back to our east, we really can't afford any delays."

"Yeah," the pilot agreed. "I'd really like to get this thing going, then head on back home." The flight engineer in the aft seat nodded his head. They were all anxious to start heading back toward Spain. No one liked these mid-Atlantic air refuelings. Especially at night. Especially with bad weather at home base.

The copilot dialed up the frequency. Almost immediately, an anxious voice filled his headset.

"Wolf five-three, Wolf five-three, this is Heater four-one. Wolf five-three, do you read?"

"Heater four-one, this is Wolf five-three," a man's deep voice boomed through Morozov's headset. "We got you loud and clear. You're a little early tonight, aren't you?"

Morozov breathed a short grunt into his mask. Wiping his flight glove across his upper lip, he spoke into his microphone once more.

"Oh, yeah, that's a roger. It looks like we are going to be about twenty minutes early. Big tail wind crossing the pond from the jet stream. And we're running a little bit low on gas. Any chance you could meet us at the rendezvous point a little early?"

"Stand by, Heater," the tanker replied. Then after a short pause, the voice crackled back.

"That's a negative, Heater four-one. In fact, we'll be lucky if we get there on time. We got socked in back at Torrejon. Thunderstorms everywhere. Best we can do would be a rendezvous time of twenty-one eleven. How will that work for you?"

Morozov glanced at his watch. That was still twelve minutes away!

"How much fuel we got?" he called out tersely to Ammon.

"Forty-one," Ammon replied.

Morozov did the math in his head. Forty-one hundred pounds . . . about eighteen minutes of fuel. It would take them twelve minutes to the rendezvous. Couple minutes to hook up with the tanker. That was fourteen, maybe fifteen minutes total.

They would only be running on fumes!

He never intended to cut it so close.

"No, Wolf," Morozov finally replied. "That's still too late. We are almost running dry here. Starting to suck on our cushions, if you know what I mean. So just tell me, what is the soonest you can be at the point?"

Inside the tanker, the pilot glanced over at the copilot who did some quick math on a portable air-data computer. After several seconds, the copilot lifted the small display up to the pilot so that he could read the numbers, while shrugging his shoulders.

The tanker pilot keyed his microphone switch.

"Sorry, Heater. That is about as early as we're going to make it."

A short pause.

"Heater, how much fuel do you have?" the tanker pilot asked.

"Twenty thousand pounds," Morozov lied.

"Uh . . . that's not much now, Heater." Inside the B-1, Ammon almost laughed as he wished it were true.

"Okay, Heater," the tanker pilot continued, "you still have the option of turning back to the Azores, just like the emergency air refueling plan says."

The tanker pilot was right. No aircraft was ever sent across the Atlantic without always being in a position to make some kind of emergency landing, just in case their air refueling tankers couldn't meet them to pass off fuel. But he didn't want to give the impression that he knew more about their situation than the B-1 pilot did. So he was careful about what he said. And, as always, the ultimate decision was left up to the bomber crew.

The tanker pilot listened for a moment, then said, "Did you copy, Heater four-one? Do you need to turn back to the Azores for an emergency landing? If twenty-one eleven will not work for you, maybe that's what you should do. I'm sorry, that's the earliest that we're going to be there."

Morozov swallowed hard and stared at his watch, then said, "No. No, Wolf. Plan on meeting us then. Twenty-one eleven will work out."

Ammon could hardly believe it. How close was it going to be?!

Ammon glanced at his fuel gauge once again. Under 4,000 pounds. He slowly shook his head as he figured how quickly they would burn 4,000 pounds of fuel.

It was going to be tight. Very tight. There was no room for error. Not the slightest edge for mistakes. If his fuel gauge wasn't exactly right, if the tankers were even a little bit slow, or if they had any trouble finding or linking up with the tankers, then it was over. And they were taking a swim.

As Ammon looked out ahead for the tanker, he heard Morozov talk to the tanker once again.

"Wolf five-three, Heater four-one."

"Go ahead, Heater."

"Yeah, ahh . . . we are receiving some static on this frequency. Might be some bleed over from one of the carrier groups off of Lisbon. Any chance we could change over to another frequency? How about two-forty-seven point nine five?"

"Sure, no problem, Wolf. We are switching over now."

The radio had seemed very clear to Ammon. He hadn't noticed any static at all.

TORREJON AIR BASE, SPAIN

Twelve hundred miles to the east, at the Torrejon Air Base, the command post was going crazy. On the far wall, illuminated red lights strobed the semi-darkness, and a buzzer sounded gently overhead. Telephones were ringing from all over the world. Printers clacked and spit out long rolls of white paper. The senior controller and communications officer were eyeing each other across the padded floor.

"What do you mean, you can't get them up on the radios?" the communications officer shouted.

"The storms have created some interference on the High Frequency," the senior controller responded. "We've been trying for the past two hours, almost since the tanker took off, but we haven't been able to raise them."

"Sonofa . . . ," the communications officer muttered. He thumped on the table and stared up at the map, thinking, then turning to his controller, he said, "Okay, forget the HF. Try getting ahold of Atlantic Radio. They track all of the transatlantic aircraft. They should be able to get through to the tanker.

"I want you to do whatever it takes. Call them on the land-line. Use the satellite communications if you have to. But get through to Global Atlantic and tell them to turn that tanker around!"

The controller nodded and turned back to his console. Picking up one of the phones that hung near his rolling chair, he too began to yell at whoever was on the other end.

The communications officer shook his head, turned back to his desk, and read the message once again. It was very short and to the point.

ZZZ

TO: Butter 46
FR: Chief of Staff, USAF
RE: "SHATTERED BONE"
Message follows.

ZZZZZZZZZZZZZZZZZZZZZZZZZZZZZZZZZZZZZZZZZZZZZZZZZZZZZ

1- Reason to believe your Tanker Task Force has been unlawfully tasked to refuel Atlantic crossing B-1.
2- DO NOT . . . repeat . . . DO NOT allow your tanker to refuel B-1. Abort refueling by any means.
3- Acknowledge receipt of message with follow-on actions.
4- Message complete

ZZZZZZZZZZZZZZZZZZZZZZZZZZZZZZZZZZZZZZZZZZZZZZZZZZZZZ

The communications officer leaned back in his seat and sucked on his tongue. "SHATTERED BONE"? Code Alpha messages from the Air Force Chief of Staff? Unlawfully tasked tanker orders? What was going on?

REAPER'S SHADOW

Six minutes later, Ammon found the tanker's lower rotating beacon as the enormous aircraft made its final turn back toward the Bone. Two minutes after that, the tanker rolled out directly ahead of the B-1, one thousand feet above it. Richard Ammon quickly punched off his auto pilot and began a swift climb up to the tanker. As he climbed, he watched his fuel readout click down through 2,500 pounds. A bright yellow light continually flickered in his face, warning him of his critical fuel state. It had been on for the past sixty minutes. He was able to ignore the light now.

He began to concentrate on the tanker that lay up ahead. He was closing very quickly. It would only be a matter of minutes before he would be taking on fuel.

"Tanker is at twelve o'clock, four thousand feet," Morozov announced from the back cockpit. He was monitoring Ammon's approach to the tanker on his radar.

"Rog," Ammon replied, keeping the tanker in sight. He was just beginning to see the outline of its huge wings as they were illuminated by the underbelly floodlights. He glanced at his airspeed indicator as he continued closing. He had almost fifty knots of closure speed on the tanker. That was way too fast. But he didn't pull back on his throttles. He didn't have time to slow down and make a nice, smooth approach to the tanker. Instead, he stole another quick glance at his fuel gauge. One thousand nine hundred pounds.

Tight. It was going to be tight.

Ammon was still five hundred feet from the tanker when his number four engine flamed out.

THULE, GREENLAND

"Wolf five-three, this is Global on eleven-forty-six HF. How do you read?" the Global Air Traffic controller transmitted for the fifth time. Again no response. The controller, sitting in a warm office in Thule, Greenland, turned to his supervisor and shrugged his shoulders. The supervisor then spoke into a phone.

"No contact. Yes, yes, of course we'll keep trying. But it doesn't sound like they're there. Now that could be because of two things. They could have turned their radios off. Or switched over to another frequency. Either way, if they aren't listening to us, there isn't much we can do."

REAPER'S SHADOW

Caution lights flashed all over the cockpit when Ammon lost his number four engine. He quickly extinguished them by hitting the master caution light reset button on his forward instrument display. He could live without the engine for now. What he needed was to get up to the tanker and get some gas.

The KC-10 loomed up before him, filling the front of his windscreen as he moved in closer. He could now see the air-refueling boom as it hung down from the KC-10's tail. Tiny blue lights illuminated the tip of the boom, swinging around in a small circle as the boom drifted and floated in the stream of rushing air.

Ammon tried to ignore the stirring boom and instead concentrated on the body of the aircraft as he moved aggressively into position. When the Bone was within eighty feet of the tanker, Ammon quickly drew his throttles back to idle. The bomber slid into position, twelve feet aft of the boom. As Ammon concentrated on maintaining this position, the boom operator extended the boom and slid it along the nose of the bomber. At first, the boomer missed the air refueling port, and he pulled the boom quickly away from the bomber to keep from smashing out one of the windows. Ammon sucked in his breath and then held it. His number two engine sputtered and also flamed out. Another half dozen caution lights flickered on. Morozov swore at him from the back cockpit. Ammon stayed in the contact position, waiting for the boomer to hook up to his Bone. Slowly, with exercised caution, the Boomer moved the boom back toward the tip on the B-1's nose. The boom slid across the thick metal as it searched for the receptacle block. Then, with a solid *clunk*, the receiver latched and accepted the nozzle.

Ammon glanced down at his fuel gauge. Twelve hundred pounds. He held his breath and bit on his tongue as he counted the systems he had lost when the second engine had flamed out. Two generators, two main hydraulic pumps, half a dozen avionics computers. The list went on and on.

But it didn't matter. The B-1 could fly with only two engines. It was dangerous, but not deadly. What he needed was fuel. He continually cross-checked the fuel gauge. Then he saw the numbers begin to increase. The bomber was taking on gas.

Four huge transfer pumps inside the tanker began to pump fuel out of their tanks and through the six-inch boom at a rate of over 10,000 pounds every minute. Ammon cross-checked the fuel gauge once again. It was passing through 3,000 pounds and increasing very quickly. He let out his breath with a sigh of relief, reached down and restarted his engines, then settled back in his seat and concentrated on staying in the proper position behind the huge tanker.

TORREJON AIR BASE, SPAIN

"Sir, I've located a carrier task force off the coast of Portugal, about three hundred miles west of Lisbon," the Torrejon controller said. "They may be within UHF radio range of the Wolf tanker. I'm getting a satellite link with them now." The controller was standing by the communications officer's desk. The CommOff looked up and rubbed his hands through his sandy brown hair, then glanced at his watch. 21:14. The refueling, if it was on schedule, was just about ready to begin.

"Do it," he commanded. "Tell the carrier communications center to blanket the sky with the message. The tanker should be monitoring guard frequency. Every aircraft has to do that. Tell them that would be a good place to start."

"Sir, it's already done."

REAPER'S SHADOW

Ammon looked at his fuel gauge. They had already taken on almost 130,000 pounds of fuel. It was good to be fat once again.

Suddenly, with another *clunk*, the refueling boom disconnected from his bomber with a mist of spraying jet fuel. The boom operator raised the boom and retracted its nozzle. Ammon heard his radio come alive.

"Heater four-one, that completes your off-load. You have received one-hundred-thirty thousand pounds of JP-8."

"Roger, Wolf," Richard Ammon replied as he pulled back on his throttles and began to descend away from the KC-10. The outline of the tanker began to fade and merge with the darkness as the Bone descended toward the ocean.

Ammon pushed the nose of the aircraft downward, establishing a 25 degree nose low attitude. They descended toward the ocean at over 20,000 feet per minute, cutting through the darkness toward the glistening ocean waves. He only had a few minutes to get down low. They would soon be close enough to the coast of Spain that, at any altitude above a few thousand feet, they would be detected by NATO's over-the-horizon radar.

Ammon didn't need to remind himself that the Americans knew he was coming. And they had fighters based all over Europe, as well as carriers in the Mediterranean Sea.

As he pushed the aircraft down toward the sea, Morozov spoke up from the rear cockpit.

"Looks like we got a little weather up ahead," he announced. "My radar is showing a huge squall line. I've got all sorts of radar returns. Looks like there are huge thunderstorms all across the Mediterranean Sea.

T H I R T Y - F O U R

U.S.S. AMERICA

THE AMERICA HEAVED IN THE FIFTEEN-FOOT SEAS, THE DARKENED FLIGHT
deck pitching into the night sky as the carrier crashed through the
waves. The carrier's superstructure was shrouded in a thick fog of mist
and saltwater spray. A freezing rain mixed with the crashing waves and
soaked the carrier's grated steel deck with a sheet of diluted salt water.
Strobes of lightning flashed through the sky while thunder crackled and
rolled overhead.

The Mediterranean weather had turned sour, a result of a low pressure system that had been slow in making its way across the plains of
central Europe. The system built up heat and energy as it crossed the
sun-baked land, then became unstable as it mixed with the moisture
laden troposphere that hung over the Mediterranean Sea. The result
was an enormous line of storms that now stretched from southern Italy
to the western coast of Turkey, rolling the entire Mediterranean with
high winds and bitter cold rain. Brutal lightning continually flashed
from the bowels of the mushroom-shaped clouds, arcing its way to
the sea.

On the best of nights, the flight deck of a carrier was a horribly
dangerous place to be. On nights like this, it was worse. All of nature's
elements—the wind and the sea, the rain and the thunder—combined

with man's howling catapults and screaming jet engines to form a Niagara of noise, lights, vibration, and confusion.

Three hundred men worked in the darkness to launch and recover the carrier's aircraft. Many of them were nearing exhaustion. Yet the night was young. It was only 22:15 local and the America was only halfway through it's second night launch. Aircraft were already waiting to be recovered. Hornets and Tomcats circled overhead, occasionally tapping into refuelers for gas as they waited for clearance to land. As soon as the second round of aircraft had been catapulted out over the water, the waiting aircraft would line up to make their approach to the carrier's deck.

An F-18 Hornet taxied up to the catapult and was quickly surrounded by sailors wearing different colored vests. One man communicated with the pilot through an elaborate dance of gestures and flashing hand signals, while two other sailors connected the fighter's nose wheel to the catapult bar. The pilot signaled his gross weight to the catapult controller, who set the catapult's steam engines at an appropriate setting that would blow the thirty-six-thousand-pound fighter across the deck. The pilot completed his final checks, ran his two engines up to full afterburner and pushed himself back in his seat. The catapult hissed, pulling her steel cables taut against the carrier deck. The cat director bent his knees and slowly lowered his hands to the grated deck. When his fingers touched the water-soaked metal, the catapult fired. Two seconds later, the fighter was airborne. It immediately turned away from the carrier as it climbed up through the rain.

By the time the pilot had passed through three thousand feet, he already had tuned up his radar and was sweeping the sky up ahead. He quickly took his appointed place in the armada of U.S. and NATO aircraft that were searching for the stolen bomber over the dark skies of the Med.

REAPER'S SHADOW

The B-1 continued through the night. She was more than halfway across the Med on her way to the Aegean Sea, the ancient vineyards of Sicily having passed just off to her left. She sped along two hundred feet above the dark ocean waves. Richard Ammon peered out through the darkness, squinting his eyes to protect his night vision from the flashing lightning that constantly filled the sky. The pointed nose of his bomber had picked up a faint and eerie green glow. The entire cockpit constantly crackled with sparkling flashes of faint blue light. Tiny fluorescent spider webs of electricity crawled up his windscreen, like a thousand outstretched fingers. Saint Elmo's Fire. It was beautiful and fascinating to watch, but very dangerous, for it indicated the presence of massive amounts of electricity. Of course, the possibility of a lightning strike was only one of the risks that a pilot took when he chose to fly directly through such powerful storms.

The turbulence alone was enough to rip the wings off of most aircraft. But the Bone bobbed along, slicing through the wind sheer and downdrafts with considerable ease. Two small winglets underneath her nose flickered in the wind, acting to stabilize the aircraft as it flew through the stormy night. The massive engines never even coughed, though with every passing minute they sucked in tons of rain-soaked air. Her radar continued to peer through weather, beaming through the turbulent wind and the rain to guide the aircraft over the white-capped waves.

This was perfect, Ammon thought. He couldn't have asked for anything better. The storm would almost assuredly hide the B-1 from any American fighter's radar. And even if they were to find him, it would take a very brave pilot to try and chase him through such a storm.

Ammon knew that he would be safe until he passed to the east of the storms. By then he would be over the Black Sea, and only a few minutes ride from the Ukrainian border. There the chase would end, for even if the Americans were able to find him, it would no longer matter, for the small fighters didn't have the range to pursue him past the Aegean Sea.

Richard Ammon scanned his instruments once again as the aircraft bounced along. Everything was functioning perfectly. The terrain-following system was flying the aircraft. There was really nothing for him to do.

He reached down and picked up his chart. He studied the black pencil line that depicted their desired flight path. It was a hook-shaped line that passed south of Sicily before turning northeast toward Greece and the Aegean Sea. Morozov had planned their intended flight path to avoid passing over any NATO airspace.

Ammon continued to study the map. He traced his finger along the line, following its crooked path until it passed just north of the island of Crete. There he let his finger linger. He glanced up into the darkness. The island nation was not far ahead.

Returning his eyes to the cockpit, Ammon stared at his weapons display and considered once again the horrible weapons that were stored inside the belly of his aircraft. For the thousandth time, he swallowed and shook his head in awe. He couldn't help himself. The magnitude of destructive power was enough to baffle the mind.

In his mind, he counted the weapons. Ten M-95 high-velocity bunker-killing missiles. The specialty weapon. Designed to kill military and civilian leadership as they cowered in their subterranean bunkers. Eight B-69 nuclear gravity bombs. General purpose destruction. Twenty-four megatons of fiery blast and smoking debris. Guaranteed to radiate for a hundred years, producing massive stretches of hot soil, glowing milk, mutant fish, and enough thyroid and bone cancers to fill every hospital bed within the whole of northern Russia.

Then there was the last weapon stuffed inside his bomb bay. The guided cruise missile. "The Sunbeam," Colonel Fullbright had called it. It was a weapon Ammon knew very little about. He didn't understand how it worked. He didn't know how it was guided. He didn't know its capabilities, lethality, payload, or speed.

All he knew was its range. About three hundred miles. Because that was how close he had to get to his target before he could spit the missile out of the belly of the Bone and send it on its low-altitude flight toward Moscow.

Which meant he had to fly at least eighty miles on the other side of the Russian border. Eighty miles north of their lines of defense.

Ammon drew in a weary breath, then turned his attention back to his chart. He followed the pencil line across the Black Sea to where it crossed the Ukrainian border. He followed it north, past the city of Kiev toward the Russian front.

There he expected to encounter the first of the Russian fighters. The whole of Russia's Southern Command—SU-27s and 29s, Mig 35s and 31s. They were all there, jammed along the Ukrainian border. Each of the fighters would carry a full combat load. About half of the aircraft would be dedicated to defensive-counter air, set up in a wide swath as a combat air patrol, watching and waiting for an attack such as this, prepared at a moment's notice to track any incoming Bandits and blow them out of the sky.

Ammon stared forward into the inky-black distance. They were out there. Waiting. He looked at his watch. It wouldn't be long. At the speed he was flying, he would soon be within range of the fighter's early-warning radar.

Just eighty miles. That's all he would need. Eighty miles beyond the Russian border. A quick run through the night. It would only take eight minutes. Eight minutes of luck was all he would need.

In a dash, he would cross the Russian border, hiding between the low hills, winding his way up the narrow valleys to stay hidden from the Russian radar. Then, once he was within range, it would only take sixty seconds to put the missile through its final countdown and send it out on its way. And then he was gone, escaping back toward the Ukrainian border by a slightly different route.

It would take the Sunbeam thirty-one minutes to reach its target in Moscow. By that time, Ammon would be more than seven hundred miles away.

THIRTY-FIVE

KHAR'KOV, UKRAINE

SGT SERGEI MOTYL SHIVERED AS HE LAY IN THE SNOW. THE AIR WAS brittle and cold. He sucked in the night air and tried to remain perfectly still. Through the winter haze he could see a tiny cluster of lights, shining in the distance. That would be the Ukrainian city of Khar'kov. Motyl had just crossed the border. He was now on the Ukrainian side.

He settled back, rested his head against his pack and stared up into the night sky. The small warheads that were crammed inside the canvas pack jutted against the back of his neck. It wasn't very comfortable, but Motyl didn't mind. He was hungry and tired and cold, but none of that mattered. In just a few hours, his mission would be over. In just a few hours, he would meet up with the man.

MOSCOW, RUSSIA

Vladimir Fedotov, the president of the newly formed Union of Soviet Republics, sat on a worn leather chair behind a huge, ornate oak-top desk. For a long moment he studied his visitor in contemptuous silence, then glancing at a small wooden chair, he indicated for him to sit down. General Smikofchen shook his head to decline, preferring to remain at attention while in the presence of his commander in chief. The president grunted as he reached into his breast pocket to produce a new package of cigarettes. While he fumbled to unwrap the tight plastic wrapper, the general took a quick look around.

Fedotov's office occupied one of the original structures that lay within the Kremlin walls. It sat at ground level and extended from the rear of the Armory, beneath the shadow of the Arsenal Tower. The structure was made from rough granite walls and ancient pine floors and was cold and damp and smelled of wet stone. Young Czarist officers had used this space to prepare themselves and their horses for battle. Even Catherine the Great had once used the room as a rendezvous spot with her lover.

Vladimir Fedotov could sense the ghosts of these ancient warriors as he sat within the thick granite walls. At times, he could almost feel their presence. And he spoke to their spirits, silently calling their names.

After lighting his cigarette, Fedotov considered the general that stood before him. He glared at the slender man with a look of disgust and contempt, then asked him to repeat himself once again.

General Smikofchen cleared his throat and spoke in a calm and even tone.

"Sir, we don't really know what the Ukrainians are up to. It seems to be some kind of scramble, but none of the fighters nor tactical bombers have yet made any attempt to cross the forward line of their own defensive positions. Though they make an occasional jab at our borders, by and large, they seem to be hanging back. It doesn't seem to make any sense. Their intentions are very unclear."

General Smikofchen paused for a moment before he continued, all the while staring at some invisible spot that hovered just above the president's head.

"But, sir, it is our guess that it is unrelated to the situation in the United States. We just don't see any connection at all."

Fedotov suddenly pushed back his chair. He hunched his shoulders and pulled in his neck as he settled against the leather backrest. Reaching out, he picked up a red-trimmed folder from his desk. It was a one-page summary of events that had occurred over the past eight hours. Fedotov flipped the cover page open and scanned the report once again.

While Fedotov read, General Smikofchen remained at attention, staring at the wall, watching the president with his peripheral vision.

He knew that Fedotov hated the bearer of bad news. And to bring him this report was not an assignment that General Smikofchen would have volunteered for. But as the Head of Counter-Reconnaissance Operations, he had the responsibility to tell the old man.

The general shifted his weight from one foot to the other as Fedotov scanned through the report.

RE: UNIDENT

TO: CYRUS/intolol/intrepid/inturn

AN: WH/Zu/2035/BASE

MESSAGE FOLLOWS

Beginning about 1419 Zulu, Russian WEST-HEM SINCCOMCOM began to note a marked increase in classified message traffic among the United States military. Initially the traffic was limited to organizations within the United States Air Force, but within an hour expanded to include Naval STRATCOM and CINCLAINT as well. By 1603 Zulu, a significant increase was also noted in satellite traffic. During the next hour, message volume was at such a level that U.S. communications systems were completely overloaded and a standby HF satellite was reactivated to handle the spike in coded-message traffic.

The communications included all sources and spectrums, was always encoded to at least a level-three security, and was accompanied by continuous counter-counter measures.

At 1615 Zulu, U.S. Strategic Command increased its state of alert. All of the Command's B-1 and B-52 bombers were placed on a two-minute response time. All Peacekeeper missile sites were ordered to DEFCON BRAVO.

At 2020 Zulu, our European Comm Center began to monitor radio transmissions between an American KC-10 air-refueling tanker and their command post in Torrejon, Spain, concerning an apparent security breach of some type within the United States military. Code name "Shattered Bone," the crisis has the attention of the highest levels within the United States government.

The sudden and marked increase in secure communications must certainly be related in some way to this unknown breach in security, but as of this time, we have yet to determine any further details.

Reconnaissance, observation, and intelligence operations continue.

END OF REPORT

President Fedotov tossed the paper back on his desk and looked at his watch. The heavy granite walls muffled every sound and the room was deadly quiet. General Smikofchen listened to Fedotov's measured breathing. Finally, the President sat forward in his chair.

"Okay, Smikofchen, explain to me, what's going on?"

For the slightest moment, General Smikofchen sucked on his cheek and didn't respond.

"Sir, it is too early to draw any conclusions," he finally answered. "Perhaps there is something there. Perhaps there is not. The simple and most likely explanation is this: the Americans have determined that our threat to use nuclear weapons is both real and imminent, and so, have ordered their forces to a higher state of alert to reflect the sudden escalation in hostilities. That would be standard procedure, sir."

Fedotov snorted. "And what about the sudden spike in secure communications?"

Smikofchen blinked his eyes several times and then slowly shook his head. "Sir, I wish we had some explanation. But the truth is, we really don't know. We feel that perhaps it is a result of the Americans warning their neighbors and consulting with their NATO allies over the impending crisis."

Again Fedotov snorted. "Stupid fool," he said in disgust. "It is far more than that. Can't you see? Can't you read?" He threw the report at the standing general and slammed his fist on the desk. "What about the intercepted conversations with the KC-10!? What about this thing, 'Shattered Bone?'"

Smikofchen opened his mouth and began to explain. "Sir, we feel—"

Fedotov quickly cut him off.

"No," he cried. "Don't feed me your crap. Don't lie to me, General Smikofchen. Don't pretend to me that you have any idea, when, in fact, you are clueless as to what is going on. The Americans aren't going crazy, beaming coded messages all over the world, just because they have seen what we do with our missiles. They have known of our intentions for days now. Their satellites see everything that we do. This isn't something which they just discovered and has suddenly sent them off in a panic.

"No . . . this is something very different. There is, within the United States, a developing situation which has nothing to do with our missiles. I can feel it. Something has happened over there which we do not understand. And uncertainty is never good news.

"Now, General Smikofchen, it is your job to find out what they are doing. It is your responsibility to find out what is going on. Now go. You have means. You have methods. You have options and hardware. So get out there and get the job done!"

KREMENCHUD-CHERCASSY, UKRAINE

The Ukrainian prime minister stole a quick glance toward his Director of State Security and his Minister of Defense. Andrei Liski and General Victor Lomov didn't take their eyes off of the tactical display screen.

Prime Minister Golubev watched General Lomov's eyes. They darted across the screen, never resting in their effort to take in and process all the information that was displayed on the screen. He watched as the general's mouth began to form a silent cheer.

"Yes, yes, yes," General Lomov began to silently chant. "Go, my sweethearts, go."

Prime Minister Golubev turned back to the tactical display screen. There he watched as hordes of Ukrainian fighters began to take to the air. They came from so many bases. Chernigov, Kiev, Varva, and Dneprodzerzhinsky. One by one, the fighters began to fill the airspace around the northwestern border of the Ukraine. They assembled into flights of four and squadrons of twelve and began to form a defensive line that led from Kiev toward the Russian border.

The fighters were stacked at intervals of three thousand feet in an effort to completely saturate the airspace they were sent to protect. By the time they were finally assembled, there would be almost eighty-five fighters in all.

It all was a part of the plan. And though, to the Russians, the line of fighters seemed to be nothing more than a poorly planned frontal attack, the Ukrainian pilots understood their real purpose.

Distract the Russian fighters. Keep the surface missile sites very busy tracking multiple targets. Keep the Russian forces so preoccupied with fake attacks from the west of Kiev that they would never even look to the east. Force them to muster their assets out west while Ammon slipped undetected across the lower belly of their borders, from a direction they would never expect.

So, the Ukrainian fighters would saturate the skies with fighters and missiles and fake attacks. Striking north, then turning back south, coming in high and coming in low, firing missiles when barely in range, they would harass the enemy forces with a muster of aircraft, machine guns, missiles, and men.

Turning his eyes to the bottom of the tactical display screen, Golubev looked to the northeastern part of his country, to the frozen and brown rolling hills that wrapped themselves around the eastern half of his nation. Although the Ukrainian radar couldn't pick up the low-flying bomber, he knew it was there. Based upon their pre-mission planning, at any given minute, he knew within fifty miles or so of where the bomber would be. He glanced at his watch, then looked back to the screen. The bomber would be just passing east of Khar'kov, a little over 200 miles away.

General Lomov turned to the prime minister. "Yevgeni, it is almost more than we could have hoped for." His eyes were bright with hope and anticipation. "Our battle with Russia is certainly over. It is now only a matter of minutes, my friend, before the Russians have a far greater concern than their dirty little war with our Ukraine."

REAPER'S SHADOW

Richard Ammon felt his stomach knot into a ball. He swallowed once again. His mouth was as dry as sand. He arched his back against the firmness of his ejection seat in hopes of relieving the fatigue and the soreness.

Ammon glanced to his right, through the canopy window. He could see the dim outline of Khar'kov as the city passed off in the distance, not more than forty miles away. Like a black hole in a starry night sky, the city's darkness stood out against the glittering layers of snow that reflected the dim light of the setting moon.

Turning his head, Ammon stared down at his CRT, the main computer screen that was mounted on the panel before him. The CRT depicted the terrain which spread out in front of the bomber, including the gentle hills, lakes, and occasional tower or strand of high-tension power lines. It also depicted a small dotted line that ran across the screen from left to right—the bomber's preprogrammed flight path.

The Bone sped along at almost seven hundred miles an hour and less than a hundred fifty feet above the ground. Because it was dark and he was flying so low, Ammon was not flying the aircraft, but instead, was allowing the onboard computers and radar systems to do their job of keeping the aircraft from hitting the ground. However, at this speed and altitude, if anything went wrong with the aircraft's terrain following system, it would only take a fraction of a second before the aircraft was nothing but a smoking hole in the snow. So Ammon monitored the flight very closely, splitting his attention between Reaper's Shadow's performance and looking ahead for enemy fighters.

"Any sign of activity?" Ammon asked tersely to the man who sat in back.

"Nothing yet," Morozov replied. The airborne sensor on his ALQ-161 defensive system was still up and down, working erratically at best, so Morozov didn't expect to see anything on his screen. But he knew the fighters were there. As well as the surface-to-air missiles.

"One-forty miles now to the border," Morozov announced. "Even with the scramble out west, the Russians will not leave their eastern flank completely unprotected. The fighters are out there. We could start seeing them at any time. So keep her low, my boy. Keep her down in the trees, and they'll never even know we are here."

Ammon didn't reply. Looking down, he studied his chart. He scanned his eyes along the Ukrainian border until he found what he was looking for, then took out a pencil and began to write down some numbers on the checklist that was strapped to his leg.

Ammon looked at his navigation computer and did some quick calculations. It wasn't far now. Fourteen minutes to the border. Another eight minutes after that. Twenty-two minutes in all.

THIRTY-SIX

REAPER'S SHADOW

"I'VE GOT TWO BANDITS!" MOROZOV CALLED. "ONE O'CLOCK. MEDIUM altitude. Tactical circle!"

"What are they?" Ammon called back. "How far out? Do they see us?"

"I . . . I don't know. I can only get our air-threat search system to work intermittently. It keeps dropping into test mode, and then shutting itself down. I can reset it, but it only stays on-line for a few minutes. But I saw them. Had a pretty good look. They are high, but I don't know their distance."

"No!" Ammon pleaded to himself. "No! No! Where did they come from? How could this be?"

Out of the whole eastern front, there couldn't have been more than a dozen Russian fighters that hadn't been pulled out to the west to guard against the massive Ukrainian aerial offensive. Maybe twelve Russian aircraft, flying six at a time, had been left to guard the whole eastern front, an area that stretched from Khar'kov to the Sea of Azov! More than five hundred miles of long, barren landscape and open, empty airspace.

And now two of them were up there, circling over his cowering head!

How could he have been so unlucky?

Ammon slammed his fist on the console and peered out into the black night. Sweeping his eyes across the horizon, he searched for any moving stars, indicating a light from the fighters. He searched for the faint glow of an afterburner engine, a wisp of a shadow, or any hint of the fighters that were there.

But he couldn't see a thing. He couldn't see the ground. He couldn't see the moon. He couldn't even see any stars, for a light overcast had just obscured the faint celestial light.

Glancing at his radar screen, Ammon rolled the aircraft into a slight left-hand turn to fall behind a small mountain that lined up to the north. Leveling the aircraft just below the mountain's crest, they crossed over the Russian border.

Sweeping low, jamming Reaper's Shadow through another tight cut in the rolling hills, they sped to the northwest. Below them and to their left was Russia's Fifth Brigade. The two thousand Russian soldiers of the Fifth Brigade were making their way along the highway, speeding to the west to act as reinforcements to the main battle front. To Ammon's right, sitting among an outcropping of huge boulders, were three surface-to-air (SAM) missile sites. Every twelve seconds—every time the SA-6 radar swung around in its circle to beam on the low-flying bomber—Ammon's headset chirped, warning him that the radar was looking, beaming in circles for targets in the sky. Ahead of the flyers, less than twelve miles, was a triple A, anti-aircraft site. Ammon looked at his chart to where the anti-aircraft gun would be, then gently turned his bomber to the right.

"Coming right, heading three-three-eight," he said into his mask. "Triple A site up ahead. This heading should keep us clear by at least seven miles."

Morozov quickly checked his threat screen. He had missed the presence of the upcoming triple A.

"Good catch. This heading looks good."

Ammon grunted, but did not reply.

DRISKMENKYOVOK HIGHWAY, NORTH OF KHAR'KOV

Sgt Keloslysky shot his eyes up to the sky with a start. What was that sound? It was horribly loud. Like a huge, sucking, high-pitched whine.

And incredibly fast. It grew from a whisper to a deafening pitch in only a few seconds. Suddenly, with a blast, the whine shifted in intensity and turned into a ear-splitting roar as a shadow flew directly over his head. He could actually feel the air compress around him, pushing on his eardrums as the aircraft shot by, seemingly inches above the snow-covered trees. Instinctively, he covered his ears. The roar faded off into the distance, even more quickly than it had come.

Sitting on the round turret of his T-80 tank, Keloslysky turned to his gunner, who was still staring up into the darkness.

"Did you see what kind of aircraft it was?" he asked tensely.

"Negative, sir. It came at us so fast! It nearly blew me out of my seat. But whatever it was, it was huge. And very low. I've never heard anything like that before."

Keloslysky listened as the roar of the aircraft echoed through the trees and bounced off the bare canyon walls.

"Think we need to report it, sir?" the gunner asked nervously.

Keloslysky shook his head. "Report what, Blosko? That we heard a big roar? That we saw a quick flash in the night? What good is that going to do? We're in the middle of a battle zone. There are probably a hundred aircraft overhead. Besides, it had to be one of our friendlies. And if it weren't, the air-defense guys know what they're doing.

"Now, let's get back under the hatch, and get on our way."

Keloslysky pushed the gunner's head back down into the steel turret, then waved to the driver to push through a small clump of trees.

DARK 709

Major Vasyl Peleznogorsk flew his fighter by pure instinct. He adjusted the throttles and airspeed, selected switches, maintained his altitude, and adjusted his radar, all without looking, doing it only by feel. Glancing to his left, he checked his wingman, who was still in a loose, night-tactical formation, one mile behind, 500 feet below him, and slightly off to his left. He monitored the tactical frequency on his radio, trying to get a feel for the situation as he listened to what little he could catch of the battle going on to his west.

He sat in an SU-27, the most advanced and maneuverable fighter in the world. When it came to finding, tracking, targeting, and shooting down other aircraft, the SU-27 was unmatched. It was better than the F-15. Better than the F-16. And far better than any NATO aircraft.

As he listened to his ground controllers, screaming directions to his squadron mates and vectoring them toward the incoming Ukrainian forces, he swore once again to himself.

How could he have been so unlucky?

All those marvelous targets. All those wonderful pieces of steel and wire. All the missiles and tracers and bullets. The hope and the glory. The thrill of a kill. The thrill of escape. The rush of quick heat in his head. It was life. It was death. It was all this and more.

He had been waiting for this moment for all of his life. Waiting and hoping and training.

The largest aerial engagement since World War II.

And he was missing it all.

He was stuck out here, hundreds of miles from the aerial action. Assigned to guard the eastern border. Assigned to drone in endless circles, searching the sky for attackers that he knew weren't even there.

So, just like Richard Ammon, who was 18,000 feet below him and twenty miles off to his right, Major Vasyl Peleznogorsk sat and cursed at his luck.

Only he did it for a much different reason.

REAPER'S SHADOW

Morozov was busily punching numbers into his offensive computer system. Their first target, a scattered deployment of mobile tactical missile launchers, hidden in a small valley and protected by a battery of SAMs and AAA, was still over two hundred miles to the north. But they were making good progress. It was all looking good. Passing the heavily defended border would be the most dangerous part. But so far, they were clean. No detection by enemy fighters. No detection by any of the ground-based radar or missile sites. Everything was going according to plan.

Morozov had already selected and programmed the weapon he would use to destroy the Russian nuclear missiles. A B-88, air-burst nuclear bomb.

Might as well start things out with a bang, he thought. Get things off to a real good start.

He finished punching the commands into his computer, double checked the coordinates, then sat back in his ejection seat and smiled.

D A R K   7 0 9

Major Vasyl Peleznogorsk slammed his fist once again. They were just wasting time. There wasn't anything here. And they needed him out to the west.

Glancing back, he checked his wingman's position.

"Dark seven-oh-nine, what do you see?" he asked tersely into his mask.

"Nothing here, Major."

"Yeah . . . I've got nothing but Bread," Peleznogorsk replied. Bread—code word for no action. No targets. Nothing to get excited about.

Peleznogorsk glanced at his radar and compared the terrain to his chart, then keyed his microphone switch once again.

"Dark seven-oh-nine, let's drop down to 4,000 feet. See if we can find any Bandits down low."

R E A P E R ' S   S H A D O W

Ammon looked at his time-to-target display. Thirty-five miles to the launch line. Just over three minutes to go. At two minutes, he would have to power up the Sunbeam's batteries and start to feed flight coordinates into its on-board computers. Up to that point, Morozov would have no idea. Prior to that, he still wouldn't know.

But at sixty seconds, when the Sunbeam went into its final countdown, a bright, red caution light would illuminate on Morozov's center CRT.

"SELECTED MISSILE IN FINAL COUNTDOWN," the message would read.

The instant the message displayed on Morozov's screen, Ammon would make a quick turn to the west. Pushing his throttles up, he would make his last dash to the launch line. Morozov would then see the missile in its final countdown. He would read the target destination. He would feel the turn to the west. And then he would know. It might take him a moment to put it together, but soon enough, he would finally understand.

W A S H I N G T O N ,   D . C .

President Allen took a quick sip of ice-water and swirled it around in his mouth before washing it down his dry throat. He looked at his watch for the thousandth time in the past twenty minutes.

"Any indication the Russians are wary?" he demanded once again.

"Negative, sir," the communications controller replied. "As of this moment, they have no indication. The Russian tactical communications are following a very familiar pattern. There has been no movement of any of their defensive air-patrols to the southeast. They still have their forces concentrated along the northwestern corridor."

Blake looked up, his face a tight wad of concentration, his forehead furrowed. "The missile will be airborne within two minutes, sir."

"Any word on the target?" the President asked for the fifth time in the past half-hour.

Blake shifted again in his seat. "No, sir. Not yet. But he's there. We will find him. I promise you that."

EYE 27-27 SATELLITE

Forty-five miles above the earth, centered above Moscow, the newest American satellite was working in high gear. Its enormous radar antenna had already been deployed and was being used to create a stunning visual scene, even through the darkness of night. Powerful infrared sensors, designed to detect the most minute differences in heat sources, scanned the target location with enough definition to tell which individuals were wearing coats and which ones were not, based on the heat that escaped from their bodies. Working in conjunction with a series of computer-enhanced telescoping cameras, the satellite beamed through its search area. And what it saw was no less than amazing. The detail was perfectly clear.

Inside its central computer, the satellite put the information together. The radar. The infrared. The laser sensors. The optical scene. It pulled it all together and overlapped the different images into one incredible display. Through the crystal-clear vacuum of space, it continued to search for Fedotov.

MOSCOW, RUSSIA

The president of Russia sat at his desk inside the old stable and stared at the tactical display board which was mounted on the far wall. The screen depicted the air-land battle as it occurred over the Ukraine. His swollen eyes ran across the depiction of the various aircraft that were preparing for battle. Twelve hundred kilometers away, the Ukrainian prime minister hunkered in a deep underground command post and stared at an identical screen.

As the president watched, he could not believe his own eyes. But there it was, right before him. Unable to be denied. The evidence could not be refuted.

For the past ten minutes, he had been watching the Ukrainians assemble what appeared to be every one of their remaining combat aircraft. The fighters had formed into five main groups and were sweeping toward the Russian border.

They were coming after his army with everything they had. They had scrambled every remaining fighter or tactical bomber, everything that could drop a weapon or shoot a gun, and sent them over the border. Didn't they know that they didn't have any hope?

Vladimir Fedotov suddenly felt very cranky. His fingers tingled and the blood roared in his ears. He fidgeted in an arrogant rage.

"Fools!" he cried to himself. Who did these guys think they were!? They would attempt to challenge his army! It was unbelievable! What did they hope to accomplish? He would smash them with a flick of his wrist. He would pound them into a red pulp of meaty mess. They wouldn't live to offend him again.

Vladimir Fedotov's breathing quickened as he turned to face General Nahaylo, his minister of defense.

"Tell me, what have you found?" he demanded. "What are they attempting to do?"

The minister of defense wiped at his nose. The winter was young, but already he was working his way through his third serious head cold. He quickly dabbed at his eyes, then shoved the dirty handkerchief into his pocket

"Sir, there is no reason to be alarmed. They don't have the forces to hurt us. Not even with such a massive attack. They are desperate, sir. That is all. They know we have readied our missiles, and now they do what little they can do. But it won't matter. Not in the long run. Within a few hours, the enemy fighters will not even have a home to defend."

HQ/NATIONAL RECONNAISSANCE ORGANIZATION, WASHINGTON, D.C.

There were only four men in the control room, leaving it dark and quiet, which was very unusual. Normally, the control center would have been crowded with satellite controllers, intelligence officers, Space

Command watch-supervisors, and other assorted technicians, busily going about their jobs as they hustled and jabbered with one another. But tonight, almost all of these men and women had been cleared from the room, leaving it lonely and quiet.

The satellite operations officer continued to punch commands into the computer to tighten up the picture. Beside him, the CIA and DIA directors watched in silent amazement.

An image of the Russian presidential fleet garage emerged on the enormous wall screen. Moving the satellite image just five or six feet at a time, the controller scanned the garage from above, using a combination of infrared and focused X-ray to cut through the thin metal roof and provide them with a picture of what was inside.

"As you can see, gentlemen, the presidential limousine is parked here, next to the door," the controller said, while using his computer mouse to draw a circle around a dull glob of light. "Based on this infrared return and an analysis of its intensity, we have determined that the engine block is quite cool. Between fourteen and seventeen degrees Celsius. Just better than ambient temperature inside the garage. The vehicle has not been used for some time. Therefore, the target must still be somewhere inside the Kremlin."

"Incredible," Weber Coy muttered, more to himself then the others.

"Yes, it really is," the operations officer replied. "In fact, 'incredible' might still be a bit of an understatement, for it would seem that, with the EYE, we now have a nearly unlimited opportunity to see pretty much whatever we want. All of it real-time. We watch as it happens. Instant gratification! What a beautiful thing."

"Okay, okay." the DIA director prodded. "We don't have much time. Let's go over to the square and take a look."

The operations officer nodded to the satellite watch controller, who punched another series of keys at his computer. The image on the screen faded away and was lost in a thick darkness.

Above the earth, the EYE moved its enormous phased-arrayed radar and infrared sensors just a few millimeters to the north. The optical cameras moved just a fraction of a degree while tiny sensors refocused the lenses.

Then a startling image appeared on the screen. This one wasn't infrared like the image before, but a relay from the satellite's video cameras. The lighting was dim and subdued, but bright enough that the men could clearly see the cluster of military vehicles parked outside the back entrance to Fedotov's quarters. They watched as a group of soldiers milled underneath a bright security light, talking and pointing to each other. They could see the rank on their shoulders. They could make out the mist of their breath as it condensed in the cold night air.

The lights inside the apartment were off.

"What do you think?" Coy asked the controller.

"I'm not really sure," the operations officer replied. "Let me see if we can get a good laser shot at the window." He nodded to the controller, who initiated the proper commands.

"What do you mean, laser shot?" the DIA director asked. "What good will the laser do us now?"

"Sir, the laser has many purposes other than to lock onto and designate targets. For example, what we are doing here is to focus the laser on the target's front window. If there is anyone inside who is talking, the laser will detect the vibration in the glass from their voices. This kind of technology is really nothing new. It's something we have been doing for over a decade now. It's just that this is the first time we can do it from one of our birds up in space."

Coy looked to the DIA Director and smiled. Such an incredible toy. He was proud.

"Just a minute, sir," the controller called out. "We are getting just a hint of vibration. Someone is talking from inside the president's quarters."

"Bingo!" Coy whispered to himself.

The operations officer turned to his satellite controller. "Let's go in and have a good look around," he said.

With a few keystrokes, the visual scene faded away and was replaced by an infrared image once again. The soldiers appeared ghost-like, their bodies nothing but blurry masses of white light. The heat from the vehicle engines burned brightly on the huge screen. The controller moved the picture to the inside of the quarters. Several white circles and half a dozen long, white lines filled the screen.

"These are hot water pipes and the hot water heaters," the controller explained while he circled each object on the screen. "This is the furnace. And this . . ." he paused for a moment, ". . . this looks to be a big-screen television. See how it glows. It is warm. It is on. This could be the source of our voices."

"Okay," Coy barked out. "It is really quite fascinating, but forget the tour. Just tell us if you think he's there."

The controller scanned through the rooms, then said, "Negative, sir. He's not there. Unless he's dead. There is no living source of heat. There is nothing alive in these rooms."

"All right, then let's keep on looking. And let's pick it up. We haven't much time. And who knows where the target might be?"

The controller punched at his computer. Forty-five miles above the surface of the earth, the satellite's sensors were moved once again. This time, they honed in on Fedotov's private office, a small cubicle of stone which jutted out from the back of the Kremlin.

Moments later, the operations officer shouted in excitement, "That's him! It has to be him! You can see him at his desk. He is watching some kind of screen. With his military officers all around him. It has to be Fedotov."

"Are you certain?" Weber Coy asked.

"Certain as we can be! It has to be him. Who else could it be?"

Coy rubbed the stubble on his chin, and then said, "Okay. Designate the target."

With the stroke of a key, the EYE was commanded to slip out of its search program and into its target-designator mode. Instantly, a four million watt, pencil-thin beam of invisible light lazed down from the satellite and locked onto the office, scattering a pool of reflective energy around the wooden shingles at the crest of the roof line. The Sunbeam would use the laser beam to home in on its target.

DARK 709

Major Peleznogorsk leveled off at 4,000 feet and pushed up his throttles to keep up his speed. The sky had cleared for a moment through a thin break in the clouds, and looking down, he could barely make out the dim outline of the barren hills and narrow valleys that ran northward from the Khoper River toward the city of Borisoglebsk. The low mountains sat in mute silence in the moonlit night.

REAPER'S SHADOW

Twelve miles to the south, Richard Ammon watched the time-to-target display on his screen. One minute and thirty-two seconds to go. The flight profile data was already loaded into the Sunbeam. Its internal batteries were up and running. The starter motor was standing by.

All that was left was the final countdown sequence. Sixty seconds to align the missile's internal gyroscopes and navigation computers.

Ammon looked out in front of his bomber. In the glimmer of the clearing night, he could just make out the Khoper River as it began to come into view.

It was time to go.

With a jerk of his hand, Ammon threw the aircraft into a sudden and tight left-hand turn. He felt himself sink into his seat from the force of the Gs. The Khoper slid underneath the nose of the bomber as Reaper's Shadow shuddered against the strain of the high-G turn.

Morozov called out in a panic. "What are you doing? Where are you going? Ammon, come back to heading three-five-two. Come on, Ammon, do it now!"

Ammon did not reply. Instead he rolled the aircraft out on a westerly heading, then reached down and began to punch the launch code into his navigation computer.

"Carl, where are you going?" Morozov demanded.

Still Ammon did not reply.

"Carl Vadym Kostenko . . . what are you programming into the computer?" Morozov shouted. Some numbers flashed up on his screen. "Ammon! I want you on a heading of three-five-two. That's three-five-two, Ammon! Turn it, Ammon! Turn it now!"

The aircraft continued to the west.

Morozov's voice filled Ammon's ears once again. "Ammon, think what you're doing to Jesse. What about her, you yellow-faced coward? Think of blood and pain and tears of sadness. You can't even imagine what my men will do!"

Ammon blinked his eyes and swallowed hard. His stomach rolled in hate and disgust.

With a start, he shook his head and finished entering the code into the system computer. He checked the numbers to ensure that he had not made a mistake. Then, reaching up, he paused over the "Enter" key on his computer's keyboard.

"Morozov, ol' buddy," he said very simply, "I think you should listen to me now. It's time for your little surprise."

Ammon jammed the computer's "Enter" button.

Immediately the coordinates of the missile launch line flashed up onto Morozov's navigation computer while a bright red light began to flash on his screen.

"SELECTED MISSILE IN FINAL COUNTDOWN"

The new time-to-target display showed Reaper's Shadow was only fifty-nine seconds from launching the missile.

Morozov wiped his hands over his face as he stared at his screen. For a long moment, he sat in quiet shock. What was this missile? Where did it come from?

And then it hit him. Whatever Ammon was doing, he wasn't working for him.

"Ammon, I swear I will kill you!" he shouted. "I swear, I swear, I will kill you! I'll rip out your heart and shove it down your throat! I'll—"

Richard Ammon reached down and disconnected his communication cord from the intercom box. There was no longer any reason to listen to Ivan Morozov. He pushed up all four of his throttles and once again was pushed back in his seat. The Bone began to accelerate, leaving a vapor trail of super-heated air in its wake.

All the while, the missile continued in its countdown. At ten seconds, Morozov felt the bomb bay doors swing open, dropping with a rush into the oncoming wind. At seven seconds, he heard a faint hiss and rumble as the missile starter-motors kicked in. At three seconds, he felt a quick rattle against the aircraft's frame, as two hydraulic pistons slammed against the missile, sending it downward with a sudden *thaat!*

The missile lurched as it dropped into the slipstream. Its internal ram engines ignited with a lightning-bright flash. And then it was gone.

THIRTY-SEVEN

DARK 709

"I'VE GOT MISSILE LAUNCH! I'VE GOT MISSILE LAUNCH!" THE RUSSIAN
pilot screamed into his mask.

"Where?" his wingman cried.

"Ten o'clock! Low! Keep with me! I'm going down to take a look."

Peleznogorsk rolled the SU-27 into a hard, descending left-hand
turn and armed up two of his missiles, at the same time keeping his
eyes on his own radar to watch the rough terrain that was rising to meet
him. He leveled off at 1,500 feet. The brilliant flash had sparkled not
more than four or five miles off in the distance. But now it was gone.
He rolled his radar's antenna to a look-down position so that he could
search the ground beneath and before him as he chased to the area that
had just flashed with light. Throughout the maneuver, he kept his eyes
constantly moving, darting, and peering through the sky.

"Papa! Papa!" he screamed into his mask. "We've got Bandits
launching Babies. I say again. We've got Bandits launching Babies!"

"Papa" was his ground controller. "Babies" was the code for an
unidentified enemy missile.

The controller was quick to respond. "Aircraft calling Babies, say
your call sign and location?"

"That's Dark seven-oh-nine. Dark seven-oh-nine. Confirmed Baby
at three-five kilometers north of Belgorod."

There was a long moment of silence.

"Dark, confirm, three-five kilometers north of Belgorod?"

Peleznorgorsk jammed his mike once again. "Affirm! Affirm! North of Belgorod." A sudden pause. And then, "Wait! Wait!" Peleznogorsk stared at his radar screen. He had seen it. A quick flash. Yes, there it was again. The aircraft was low. Incredibly low. It was in a turn. It's wings and back were rolled up in a tight bank, bouncing back enough of Peleznogorsk's radar energy to reveal the bomber's location.

"I've got the Bandit," the Russian cried. "He's low. Turning south."

The Bandit rolled level, and then disappeared from his screen.

"Papa, I can't get a good track. And negative on the ID."

Peleznogorsk pulled his radar display down to a five mile scope, the tightest beam he could have, in an attempt to focus the energy of his radar on the fleeing target. He threw both of his massive engines into full afterburner as the target pulled away. He strained his neck over the nose of his fighter, peering into the blackness of the night, looking for the enemy aircraft. The Bandit flickered once or twice, then disappeared from his screen as it dropped behind a low mound of hills. Peleznogorsk sucked in his breath and pushed up his throttles once again. Five seconds later, the target re-emerged on his screen.

"Papa!" Major Peleznogorsk called out. "I've got good trace, but I can't get a lock. Target is now three-one kilometers north of Belgorod and heading south."

"Have you got a good ID?" the controller cried. His voice was brittle and sharp. He was nearly in a panic. As the ground-radar controller, it was primarily his responsibility to find and track the incoming threats, and missing the Bandit meant that, at a minimum, he had just lost his job. He would spend the next two years of his enlistment cleaning floors. But it could be worse. And it would be far worse, if he allowed the bomber to get away.

The controller tightened up in his seat, his body rigid in fear and concentration, as the SU-27 pilot replied, "Negative ID, Papa. Negative ID on the Bandit."

"How many targets?" the controller shot back.

Peleznogorsk paused to consider. "Only one, as far as I know. I'm only picking up one on my radar. But who knows? Maybe there's more."

"Okay. Okay." the controller called back, relieved that at least it wasn't a major attack. "I've got Blade Flight coming down from the Despansky Cap. ETA . . . four point five minutes. They will be sweeping in from the west."

"Copy." Peleznogorsk replied.

"Now, what about the Baby?"

"Negative on the Baby. I can confirm the launch, but the missile simply disappeared." Peleznogorsk turned back over his shoulder to glance at his wingman.

"Two, do you see it?" he asked.

"Negative," his wingman replied.

"That's okay, Dark," the controller shot back. "Forget the Baby. We'll look for it later. How much damage can a single missile do? For now, let's go get the Bandit. ID him if you can. But don't wait for an ID to engage!"

Peleznogorsk glanced down at his radar. The image continued to flicker and bounce on his screen. It was still there, somewhere to the south. But it was starting to fade. It was pulling away. He only got a look at it about once every ten or fifteen seconds now. And it was far too vague a radar return to get a good lock for his missiles.

Five seconds after launch, the Sunbeam had accelerated to 740 miles per hour and dropped to only twenty feet above the frozen terrain. Its guidance systems kicked in and sent the missile on its preprogrammed flight path toward the city of Moscow. Using infrared sensors and radar, the missile mapped the ground up ahead, then compared the terrain with the data bank in its on-board computers to determine its exact location. It sped along the ground, not bouncing back, but instead absorbing the SU-27's radar signal, while lifting itself over scattered farm houses and rows of tall trees.

It screamed along at a breathtaking pace. Like a ghost, it sped toward the city. For all intents and purposes, it was invisible. There was absolutely no hope of shooting it down.

REAPER'S SHADOW

The cockpit was very quiet. Ammon hated the silence.

The Bone's defensive systems had fallen completely silent. Morozov must have shut them down. If there was anything out there, Ammon would never know it.

Ammon plugged back into his interplane communications cord.

"Morozov, we need the defensive systems up," he started to plead. "You've got to tell me what is going on. I've got to know where the fighters and SAM sites are, or we'll never get out of this thing alive."

Ivan Morozov didn't respond.

Ammon dished the Bone over a narrow lake and through a small cut in the hills. He pushed the aircraft as fast as he could as he made his way to the south. The aircraft vibrated quietly against the speed. He was pushing his ponies at a dead run, but without any information about possible threats, there wasn't much else he could do.

DARK 709

Jamming his fighter into tight, sudden turns, Peleznogorsk followed the aircraft as best as he could. Yanking left, he watched as the signal flickered on his radar screen. The Bandit had pulled away to almost twenty-eight kilometers now. His finger strained against the fire trigger on his stick, ready to fire the missiles. But the target-tone remained at an irritating shrill. It pierced his ears with its gyrating tone, but never settled into the familiar and constant low-toned growl which would indicate his missiles were locked onto the target.

The aircraft was flying so fast! Too fast. It couldn't have been a Ukrainian bomber. Nothing they had could keep up with this.

This wasn't making any sense!

Peleznogorsk then realized the fleeing aircraft had to be using some kind of terrain-avoidance radar to keep from smashing into the ground. And his target acquisition computer should be able to identify the type of radar it used. He quickly punched a few keys on his computer, commanding it to do an analysis of the fleeing aircraft's terrain-following radar signal.

Three seconds later, Peleznogorsk had his answer. And as he stared at the read-out on his screen, he couldn't believe his own eyes.

"Papa!" he screamed. "I've got a good identification. Target is an American bomber. I say again. Target is an American B-1 bomber. We are under a U.S. attack!"

MOSCOW, RUSSIA

Vladimir Fedotov breathed a sudden and angry groan, then turned around to face General Nahaylo. "Are you telling me it is an American aircraft? An American missile?"

The minister of defense wiped his nose. "Sir, there is absolutely no doubt. It is an American B-1 bomber. It launched some kind of cruise missile. And then turned away."

Fedotov raised an eyebrow. "Only one missile?"

"Yes," Nahaylo replied. This curious fact was not lost on either man.

Fedotov felt his heart beating faster. He took a series of short and shallow breaths. His hands, tightly clasped across his lap, began to tremble ever so slightly as he clenched his fingers together.

Cowardly American harlots! Killers! American pigs! How could they have resorted to this?

Staring up at General Nahaylo, he demanded, "Tell me, what is the range of this American missile?"

Nahaylo took a quick look at his notes. "We believe that the missile must be one of their ALCMs, sir. Max range, about 1,100 miles. Max speed, about 500 knots. Which would put the missile over Moscow in another . . . forty-five minutes. Assuming that Moscow is even the target."

WASHINGTON, D.C.

"Oh, sweet Mary!" President Allen cried. His face was a white sheet of pale flesh. His eyes were wide and dry with sudden fear. His hands trembled and shook at his side.

"Are you certain? How do you know?"

"Yes, sir. We are certain. The RC-135 orbiting over northern Turkey picked up the radio communications just seconds ago. A Russian SU-27 witnessed the missile launch. They just simply got lucky. And now, even as we speak, they are recalling their eastern fighters to join in the search for the Bandit."

"Sonofa. . . ." Allen's voice trailed off. He fell back in his seat and raised his eyes to the ceiling, as if seeking divine intervention.

"And . . . have they . . . confirmed the source of the missile?" Allen's voice was hesitant and hollow. He did not want to know the answer to this question.

Blake stared down at his feet and cleared his throat. "Yes, sir. They have. They have confirmed it is from a U.S. B-1 bomber. Don't ask me how. We haven't got a clue. But they know it was an American aircraft."

Allen closed his eyes and muttered to himself as his face took on an even lighter shade of pale.

"Have they passed along the information?" he finally asked.

"Yes, sir. By now, the entire Russian military and civilian battle-staff have been notified."

"And what about the bomber?"

"They are after it. That's all that we know."

Allen passed his hands over his eyes and cursed to himself. Blake stood before him like a whipped puppy. "Sir," he muttered. "There is the matter of the missile. We have to destroy it, sir. There is nothing more we can do. We must destroy it before it gets to its target. Every missile has a self-destruct mechanism. We can use the EYE to command the missile to self-destruct. And if we destroy it now, perhaps we can keep the match from the fuse.

"But if we don't stop the missile . . . if it reaches its target . . . well . . . who knows what could happen?"

"The situation has become very dangerous. Uncertain and unpredictable. Things could quickly spin out of control."

REAPER'S SHADOW

Richard Ammon had assumed that Morozov had turned so quiet because he was angry, which wasn't true. He was busy. Very busy. He worked as fast as he could, punching the new target coordinates and launch instructions into his computer.

So they never got within range of their targets. So what did he care? That didn't mean that the mission was over. All was not lost. He could still attain what they were after. It would just be in a different way. A more violent means. But the effect would be just the same.

With a final stroke of a key into his offensive computer, Morozov commanded five of his nuclear short-range attack missiles to their new coordinates and put them into their final countdown.

The target names appeared on his screen. Kursk. Voronezh. Orel. Kaluga. Novemoskovsk. All major cities. Industrial centers. Masses of Russian population.

In minutes, they would be reduced to a heap of molten cinder block and burning debris. The citizens would die by the thousands, vaporized into a black mist. Burned beyond recognition. Destruction to a nightmarish degree.

Morozov sat back.

He would have the last laugh. He would sizzle half of southern Russia, if that's what Ammon wanted. But the mission . . . his mission . . . his baby . . . it would not be a failure. Not while he was alive.

Morozov reached up and launched the first of the missiles.

The aircraft shuddered with a buzzing vibration. Ammon looked up with a start. His bomb bay doors were beginning to swing open. He glanced down at the weapons configuration panel. Five missiles were armed and ready to fire! The doors slammed open with a *thump!*

"No! No!" Ammon shouted as he watched.

But it was already too late. With a slap and a thump, the missiles were gone. He squinted his eyes from the flash of their engines. The five missiles' ramjet engines ignited with a lightning-bright flash, casting deep shadows across the dark sky. The missiles shuddered and wobbled in midair, then dipped toward the earth and sped away.

DARK 709

Peleznogorsk dropped his hands from his face as the light faded and then disappeared.

"I've got Babies! I've got Babies! Four . . . five . . . count 'em . . . five confirmed missile launches!" Major Peleznogorsk screamed into his mask. His fear was real and intense.

"Oh, geez," his wingman called out. "Did you see that, Lead. They looked like nuclear ALCMs. I could tell by the fat harpoon tips. I say again, the missiles might be armed with nuclear warheads."

"Papa! Do you read!" Peleznogorsk cried out. "We've got five suspected nuclear cruise missiles inbound."

The controller sat at his console in a horrified stupor.

"Oh, Mother, it's over," he cried to himself.

WASHINGTON, D.C.

The whoosh and rush of the helicopter blades filled the air. They beat at the tree limbs and lay the neatly trimmed grass flat against the soil as the three Presidential helicopters made their short approach to the White House lawn. The President and his party were already waiting. The helicopters had barely touched down before a small door just behind the cockpit swung open and a short step was extended out onto the grass.

Within just a few minutes, the three helicopters were airborne again. They flew in a loose trail formation, one behind the other, as they made their way across the Washington, D.C., terrain. Flying low, they turned westward toward the Virginia side of the city. As they crossed over the top of the Pentagon, an American Airline 727 was just climbing out from National Airport, which was only three quarters of a mile to the south.

President Allen watched the airliner as it climbed overhead. He watched as the aircraft pulled in her landing gear and accelerated northbound.

For just a moment, he could envision the aircraft's crowded cabin. He could picture the business men and tourists as they stared out of their small oval windows, watching the city slip by them, the monuments and buildings growing smaller as the aircraft climbed into the sky.

The President had to wonder. Was this the last time those passengers would look down upon this city? Were some of them leaving loved ones they would never see again?

"Lord, please don't let them be the lucky ones," he prayed as the 727 disappeared from his sight.

As the President looked down on the city, the word "cindered" kept rolling over in his mind. That was the word that the Federal Emergency Management Agency used to describe those who were left without warning and unprotected in the event of a nuclear detonation. "Cindered" was a term for the casualties. It was the government word for "the dead."

The helos whisked along, cutting through the cold air. The President watched the tree-lined Potomac slip underneath him, then leaned back and closed his eyes. The Presidential helicopters turned to the north. Following the Potomac River, they made their way toward the Virginia countryside.

MOSCOW, RUSSIA

"But, sir," Nahaylo was pleading.

"Don't 'but, sir' me!" Fedotov cried. "I'm not blind. I'm not stupid. Look at the screen, General Nahaylo. Look at the screen and tell me what you see!"

The general did not look away, but instead locked his eyes with Fedotov's. "I know what's up there, sir. I understand the critical nature of the situation."

"Oh, is that right?" Fedotov replied, waving his arms wildly toward the five dots on the screen. "Well, let me tell you something, General. Those are American cruise missiles. Now maybe they're nuclear. Maybe they're not. But do you really expect me to just sit here and wait, hoping they just go away!

"I have to assume the worst here, Nahaylo. I just can't wait until half of Moscow goes up in a ball of flames. We will be dead by then, General. You. Me. Everyone in this room. Then how do you propose we respond? Which is exactly what the Americans are hoping we do. Can't you see that. They expect us to wait around in a terrified stupor, hoping for the best, not choosing to escalate things, until it is too late, and we are vaporized into a cloud of black mist.

"So, no, I will not wait. I want our Satans in the air! Get me the launch box! Get me the codes! Now!"

General Nahaylo tried once again.

"Sir, I must remind you. The first missile, the stealth missile, has already been destroyed. Whether it flew off course and crashed, or simply malfunctioned, or just what, we do not know. It is possible the Americans destroyed it. But it doesn't matter now. It is gone. And though the other five missiles are proceeding to their targets, we still have a chance. It is possible that we might shoot them down. They are not as stealthy. They are not as fast. And, sir, most important, they might only be conventional weapons. We don't know that they have nuclear warheads. We must give it a little time. We must wait and see."

"No! No!" Fedotov shouted back. "I will not sit here and wait to be destroyed. I will not roll over like a dog on his back and expose my jugular vein. They. . . ," Fedotov pointed toward the red dots on the screen. "They are the ones who asked for this battle. They are the ones who started this fight. Without warning . . . without cause . . . without reason.

"So, don't sit there, my friend and tell me to be patient, when in reality, I am just waiting to die!"

Nahaylo stepped toward the president with pleading eyes. "Sir." The president knew what he meant. But he no longer cared.

President Fedotov turned from Nahaylo and nodded his head to the three-star general who stood at his side.

Within thirty seconds, he was handed a large, black, leather briefcase. It was eighteen inches long, with rounded corners, and a single brass lock.

The President picked up the briefcase. He was watched very closely by his military aides as he unlocked it and opened it up. He was surrounded by nine heavily armed and specially trained military guards. A look of puzzlement came over Fedotov's face as he opened the briefcase and stared at the unfamiliar keyboard. Anticipating he would need help, a command-and-control specialist emerged from the crowd of military advisors and came forward to talk the President through the launch codes and procedures.

It didn't take much time. Once the briefcase was open, it was only a matter of seconds before a single SS-18 ICBM missile was launched and sent climbing upward to its cruise altitude of 150 miles above the earth. Within five minutes, the missile was over the Greenland Sea on its way up over the pole.

Inside the missile, a digital computer was hard at work. Dual laser-gyros determined the missile's actual position and fed the information into the navigation computer. The navigation system then made tiny adjustments to keep the missile flying along its intended flight path.

As the missile leveled off in sub-orbit, the computer began to feed the target coordinates to the ten individual nuclear warheads. Two of the warheads were commanded to fall over the White House. Two were directed to Capitol Hill. Two were given the coordinates of the leafy, tree-filled courtyard that sat in the center of the Pentagon.

The Russians were strong believers in redundancy. They always sent at least two warheads to every priority target. Their philosophy was, if one missile was good, then two had to be better.

With six warheads targeted for D.C., there were still four warheads yet to be given an objective. The targeting computer continued to search its memory bank. After several seconds, it found what it was looking for. The coordinates of the secret Underground Presidential Command Center in central Virginia were then fed to the remaining four warheads.

When the four warheads descended back through the atmosphere, they would maneuver away from each other until they were two hundred meters apart. They would then spread into a box pattern. Their detonation sequence was set to "impact delay," which meant the warheads would not detonate until they had penetrated the soft earth that lay over the Presidential Command Center. By the time their mushroom clouds of glowing fire were sent climbing over the gentle Virginia countryside, the President of the United States would already be dead, recorded in history as one of the "cindered."

THIRTY-EIGHT

REAPER'S SHADOW

AMMON KNEW IMMEDIATELY WHAT HE HAD TO DO WHEN HE SAW THE missiles launch.

Jamming his engines into full afterburner, he pulled back hard on the stick. The Bone began to accelerate skyward, climbing through the air in a vertical angle. Ammon felt disoriented and dizzy as he stared up into the darkness. His head tumbled and his eyes lost their focus as nothing but sky filled his windscreen. He checked his altimeter. Eight-thousand feet. He rolled the aircraft inverted and pulled while hanging upside down in his harness, then rolled the aircraft once again. He was level at 10,000 feet. High enough. The signal to the missiles should get to them from this altitude.

Reaching forward, to the left of his seat, he flipped up a yellow safety cover, exposing the toggle switch that was hidden underneath. He pushed the switch down. A light tone began to sound in his headset as a message appeared on his CRT.

"SELF-DESTRUCT MECHANISM ACTIVATED. SELECT DESIRED MISSILE TO DESTROY."

Ammon began to furiously punch in the numbers. He would have to destroy the missiles one at a time. He finished punching in the coded indentifier of the first missile. He hit the "SEND" key. A two-second, coded, microburst radio signal was sent out from Reaper's Shadow's lower antenna, commanding the first nuclear missile to self-destruct. The last-ditch safety recall mechanism kicked into gear, blowing the missile into a thousand tiny pieces.

"MISSILE YB#$YB45 DESTROYED." appeared on Ammon's screen.

Morozov looked up and sucked in his breath.

"DO YOU WANT TO SELECT ANOTHER MISSILE?" the computer asked Richard Ammon.

"Y," Ammon tapped into the keyboard.

"SELECT DESIRED MISSILE."

Ammon typed as fast as he could. Morozov screamed and cursed from the back.

"YS86(^75AB." A tap on the SEND key. A three-second delay.

"MISSILE DESTROYED." flashed again on the screen.

Two missiles down. Three to go. Ammon continued to punch at the keys.

KERYCHOYA HILLS, NORTH OF KHAR'KOV

Sergei Motyl sat up with a jolt as the fighter sped by overhead. The roar from the aircraft had jerked him out of a fitful sleep. He looked to the sky and located the aircraft, its flaming tailpipes glowing a faint orange against the cold winter night. He watched as the fighter receded into the distance, toward the northwest. Within half a minute, it was followed by several more. All of them were flying very low, no higher than a thousand meters. Mig-31s, probably from Kazakiezainkpof, just on the other side of the border.

The fighters had disappeared. Motyl continued to stare to the west. The clearing in which he had been sleeping was small, but still it offered him a clear view at the now starry sky.

Suddenly, the air crackled and roared once again. Four more fighters flew overhead. These too were flying very low, but instead of continuing westbound, they climbed and began to circle overhead.

Motyl suddenly had an idea. This was it. The perfect opportunity to do a check on the product. Shooting down a fighter was something he would remember for the rest of his life. And Motyl didn't care who he killed. Russian, Ukrainian, it didn't really matter. He held them both in equal disdain.

Motyl rolled onto his knees and began to fumble in the darkness. His breath formed into tiny clouds of white vapor as he pulled one of the missile warheads from his pack.

R E A P E R ' S   S H A D O W

Ammon glanced at his navigation display. They had just passed over the Ukrainian border and were only a few minutes away from Khar'kov. He punched in the last of the numbered codes.

"MISSILE DESTROYED," appeared for the fifth time.

Ammon immediately pushed the nose of the aircraft toward the earth and hooked up his terrain-following system. The aircraft descended abruptly, dropping toward the ground at over 20,000 feet per minute. The darkness rushed up to meet him. He leveled off at 200 feet above the ground and began to pray.

He knew that by climbing so high to send the code to the missiles, he had certainly betrayed his position. Without the hills and terrain to hide behind, without the frozen ground to clutter up the Russian radar screens, without the benefit of low-level flight, he was no longer hidden. Every aircraft, every SAM site, every piece of aerial artillery, now knew exactly where he was.

And then he saw it. A sudden flash in the darkness. Straight ahead of him. Two Russian fighters. Their afterburners glowing orange against the night sky. He stared again. He could see the twin engines. SU-27s or Mig-31s. Like a pair of sharks, they moved through the night. He took a deep breath. One of them broke to the right. The other broke to the left. They knew something was there. Must have picked up a trace of his radar and were coming around to have a quick look.

Sergei Motyl heard the bomber before he ever saw it. He could hear and feel its massive engines as the aircraft approached from the north. Looking down from his hilltop, he caught an occasional glimpse of the aircraft's gray wings, the dark paint flashing against the white powder-topped trees. The aircraft was flying up the valley, approaching with incredible speed. Even as he watched, the bomber raised its pointed nose and began to climb up the mountain where Motyl stood hidden among the trees.

Ammon pushed himself down in his seat, shoved his engines into full burner and pushed the aircraft through the speed of sound. If he could outrun the fighters as they turned back to meet him, maybe. . . .

He felt something cold and hard poking into the flesh of his neck. Slowly he turned his head. The barrel of the gun jabbed even deeper. Ammon turned to look into Morozov's cold eyes. The dim lights from the instrument panel bathed his face in a pale green and blue. Morozov's thumb moved up to the hammer and pulled it back.

Motyl hoisted the SA-18 launcher onto his right shoulder. He had already loaded it with a missile. He flipped the battery on as the aircraft approached him. Peering through the optical sight, he followed the bomber as it flew over his head.

The sound from the four engines almost deafened him. It shook him and rattled his bones. He turned as the aircraft overflew him.

The receding aircraft filled the eyepieces. Motyl flipped the arm switch and pressed on the trigger.

The blast nearly knocked him to the ground as the SA-18 missile fired from the shoulder-mounted tube. The heat seeking missile immediately picked up on the aircraft. With 140,000 pounds of heat and thrust flying in its face, there was no way the missile would let the bomber get away.

Everything seemed to turn in slow motion. Ammon recoiled from the weapon. Morozov lifted his thumb from the hammer. Ammon closed his eyes.

A long moment of silence. Ammon waited to die.

Morozov called out over the roar of the cockpit.

"Carl, I wish that I had already killed you. That is my only regret."

Morozov moved his finger to the trigger of the gun.

The missile's flight lasted only two seconds. That's all the time it took to cover the 2,000 feet that separated Motyl and the receding bomber. The missile impacted and exploded on the aircraft's left side. As it detonated, it sent thirteen pounds of high explosives into the number one and two engines. The engines immediately blew into a thousand white-hot pieces of burning steel, then disintigrated into two hollow shells.

Baseball-size chunks of metal were sent flying through the Bone's tender wings and body. Some of these metal chunks were the shrapnel from the missile. Some were pieces of the GE-101 engines that had just blown themselves apart. Whatever the source, it didn't matter, the damage they did was the same. Hydraulic lines were immediately severed. Precious electrical cords were burned and cut. One partic- ularly large piece of steel made its way through the wing root, puncturing a huge fuel tank that ran along the entire length of the wing. As fuel spewed from the gaping hole, it immediately burst into flames. The heat burned through the number one primary hydraulic line, providing even more fuel for the blaze.

Sergei Motyl watched the aircraft explode into bright yellow flames. He stood for a moment, not knowing how to react. As he watched, the aircraft began to roll and descend down the back side of the small mountain. It soon was lost to his vision by a row of high trees. He waited and listened, expecting to hear a loud explosion as the aircraft impacted the ground.

THIRTY-NINE

REAPER'S SHADOW

MOROZOV WAS THROWN FROM HIS FEET AS THE AIRCRAFT RATTLED AND shuddered. The explosion blew him against the floor, his gun was thrown from his hand. For a moment he lay there in a daze. The aircraft bucked and rolled beneath him, bouncing him violently into the air. His face contorted in pain and rage. The entire cockpit was bathed in a faint red sheen as dozens of fire and warning lights began to blink on the instrument panel.

Morozov tried to stand. The aircraft lunged and cracked with whip-like force. He was knocked to the floor once again. Another explosion. Then a dull yellow light began to illuminate the cockpit; warm, like a flickering fire. It grew and began to blend with the harsh red lights that flashed on the instrument panel. Morozov felt the floor begin to tilt to his left as Reaper's Shadow began her death roll.

The cockpit blared with warning horns. The Bone continued to roll.

Ammon fought with the bomber. He shoved the stick all the way to the right. The rolling slowed, but then continued. The enormous bomber had already banked up to almost ninety degrees. Her nose began to drop toward the ground. Through the side of his canopy window, Ammon could see the dim shadows of the trees that sped by underneath him, less than one hundred feet below. They seemed to be reaching out, pulling him earthward, as the Bone rolled onto her side.

Ammon shoved his right rudder all the way to the floor, jamming his foot against the steel pedal. The aircraft's rolling motion stopped. Ammon glanced once again at the passing trees, unable to force them out of his peripheral view. He shoved again at the pedal. Then slowly, ever so slowly, a few degrees at a time, the aircraft began roll back to the right. It heaved and shook as it rolled to an upright position. Fiberglass panels began to vibrate loose from the cockpit ceiling. Ammon's main CRT screen shattered with a dull *paaang*, unable to withstand the violent vibration. The entire aircraft threatened to rattle apart.

Ammon glanced at his Master Caution Display, where there were no less than thirty warning lights flashing. He tried to note the more critical ones in an effort to determine how badly Reaper's Shadow was damaged. He began to count the systems that he had lost: two engines, three hydraulic systems, two of three generators, three flight computers, two main electrical buses. The list went on and on.

Ammon realized his time was almost over. There just wasn't much more he could do.

He glanced around the cockpit and saw Morozov in a heap on the floor. It was ironic. Morozov had chosen a very bad time to get out of his ejection seat.

DARK 709

Major Vasyl Peleznogorsk pulled his head to the right. He banked his SU-27 slightly up on its side as he scanned his eyes through the moonlit darkness.

There it was again, a flicker of fire. It flashed and then quickly disappeared. He stared down through the thick Plexiglas of his canopy at the spot where he had last seen the flame.

Then he saw it again. No more than six kilometers away, off at his two o'clock and very low. The aircraft couldn't have been any higher than thirty meters. He could see the fire as it burned, huge yellow and blue flames flowing back from the bomber, billowing horrible and bright in the night. He squinted at the burning aircraft. As his eyes focused in the darkness, he began to see the vague outline of the enemy bomber. It seemed to be in a slow roll as it sped along the ground.

"I've got good visual on the Bandit!" the fighter pilot screamed into his microphone. "Six kilometers, two o'clock, low!"

No less than fifty other aircraft, both Ukrainian and Russian fighters, heard the pilot's frantic call.

"Who's calling Bandit?" asked one of the Russian Mainstay airborne controllers. "Calling Bandit, say your ID!"

"Dark seven-zero-niner!" Peleznogorsk responded. "Two, have you got him? Low. Two o'clock. Five kilometers."

The slightest pause. "Two's visual!" Peleznogorsk's wingman replied.

"Control, we've got a positive visual identification. Heading one-four-zero, thirty-six west of Dergachi. Looks like he's on fire. I'm too close for missiles. I'm selecting guns. Seven-zero-nine flight is in for the kill!"

With that the SU-27 pilot banked his aircraft hard to the right. His wingman fell in beside him. The bomber's shadow wisped along the ground, illuminated by the fire that burned over the left wing. Major Peleznogorsk had the aircraft clearly in his target acquisition box, but it was still three miles away. He pushed his two throttles up to full afterburner and felt the Saturn/Lyulka turbofans push him back into his seat. He began to move in on the bomber. Once he got to within 1.5 miles, he would press the trigger on his cannon and blow the bomber away.

REAPER'S SHADOW

FIRE WARNING lights continued to blink insistently. Ammon reached up and jammed in his two fire suppression buttons. The fire lights remained on. He selected the reserve fire bottles. The fire lights didn't even blink, but continued to blaze in his face.

He was still on fire! He was sitting on almost fifty thousand pounds of fuel, and he was still on fire!

The fire was completely out of control. He was amazed that the white hot flames had not already burned through the protective firewalls that surrounded his fuel cells. By now, they surely were about to explode.

Morozov struggled to his feet. He thought for a minute about finding his gun. Then he shook his head. How could he be so stupid! Finding the gun was the last thing he needed to do.

He was nothing but a walking dead man if he didn't get back in his seat! That much was perfectly clear. He could see the flickering fire outside the left window. The aircraft bounced and rolled through the air. It could only be seconds away from exploding. There was nothing more he could do. Let Ammon die trying to be a hero. He was getting out of the jet!

Morozov began to struggle to the back of the cockpit. The aircraft shuddered under his feet, making it impossible to walk. Morozov dropped to his knees and began to crawl the four feet that separated him from his ejection seat. A thick piece of metal, part of an overhead hatch, fell down on top of his legs. He reached down and pushed the panel aside. Stretching his arms, he grasped a thick nylon hand-hold and used it to pull himself back toward his seat.

DARK 709

The SU-27 pilot was pulling inside of two miles. The bomber continued straight ahead. It made no effort to evade the fighter that was sneaking up on its tail. Apparently the B-1 crew didn't yet know that they was being pursued by one of the world's premier fighter pilots. The Russian pilot broke into a smile. It would be like shooting a bird in a cage.

REAPER'S SHADOW

The aircraft shuddered again. It was breaking apart, actually shaking itself into pieces. Ammon was thrown against the side of the cockpit. His head bounced around on his shoulders. He could barely see. He could barely think.

Reaper's Shadow bucked and rolled, then descended toward the earth. Ammon reached up for the ejection handles. The aircraft was less than forty feet above the ground and going down very quickly.

Ammon jerked up on the handles. The explosive bolts that secured the overhead hatches fired, blowing them free from the aircraft and leaving gaping holes where the hatches used to be. Ammon felt an incredible rush of air as the cabin depressurized around him. The cockpit filled with flying debris; pencils, paper, checklist, dust, carpet, maintenance logs. Anything that was not securely strapped to the frame of the aircraft was immediately sucked out of the hole. Even the checklist that Ammon had strapped around his leg was torn from its bindings and sucked away. A thick vapor of fog burst inside the cockpit from the moisture mixing with the super-cold air.

Ammon could actually feel the oxygen in his lungs expand in his chest.

His ejection seat fired its rocket, shooting him upward through the open hole and one hundred feet into the air. A small drogue chute opened to slow him down before popping the primary chute from its housing. With a violent jolt, the main chute deployed. Ammon began to slowly drift to the earth.

Morozov was just pulling himself to his feet when Ammon's ejection seat fired. The blast from the seat's rocket filled the cabin with heat and smoke and a dazzling white light.

Reaper's Shadow was traveling faster than 600 mph. The outside air flowed over the nose of the aircraft and across the smooth, polished skin with a force greater than the strongest tornado, creating an enormous vacuum of low pressure over the entire front of the aircraft. The pressure sucked at the inside of the cockpit with incredible force, pulling everything through the open hole. Instantly, four thousand pounds of over-pressure lifted Morozov off the floor and pulled him toward the open hatch, his arms and legs flailing around him. The pressure sucked him through the small opening, folding him over like a rag doll, breaking both of his shoulders and most of his ribs as he was yanked through the hatch-jettison hole.

Ivan Morozov was still alive as his body was blown up and over the tail of the bomber. He knew exactly what was going on. His mind was alert, for he hadn't the time yet to panic. But for the first time in his life, he felt honest fear. Honest, gut-wrenching fear. The horror was complete and mind-boggling as he realized that he was going to die.

Morozov felt the oxygen get sucked from his chest. He felt burning pain from his broken shoulders and ribs. He gasped, but couldn't breath. He arced over the tip of the B-1's twenty-foot tail. The burning aircraft shined in the night.

He felt the sudden rush of a bitter cold wind as he began to fall back to the earth. He had a clear sensation of falling. His body tumbled and rolled in the slipstream. He saw the trees coming at him at an incredible speed. He closed his eyes and started to scream.

DARK 709

For a few moments the SU-27 pilot lost sight of the bomber. He pulled his nimble fighter into a steep climb, pushing himself away from the ground so he could search the dark sky for any sign of the burning aircraft. He jerked his head around in the cockpit, looking left and looking right.

He leveled off at 9,000 feet and frantically searched all around him. The air was clear. Not a cloud in the sky. He circled once, eyes darting from side to side.

Then he saw it. A flash of light. A rolling ball of fire. Directly in front of him, a huge explosion rocked through the night sky, filling his cockpit with a bursting yellow light. He squinted his eyes to protect his night vision. But even through his half-closed eyelids, the pilot could clearly see the debris start to scatter through the air as the fireball rolled skyward and then disappeared.

The pilot watched for long moment, then pressed his microphone switch. "Control, this is Dark Flight. Scratch the enemy bomber. Seven-zero-nine has a confirmed kill. I say again, seven-zero-nine has a confirmed kill."

FORTY

OVER THE ARCTIC OCEAN

THE SS-18 BUILT UP SPEED AS IT BEGAN ITS DESCENT BACK TO EARTH. Enormous heat was generated as the missile began to pass through the hydrogen-rich upper atmosphere. The skin of the missile began to expand and glow against the heat and the pressure.

The missile was one hundred and ten miles above the surface of the earth and moving downward at a near vertical angle. It was within a few meters of its intended flight path. The ten individual warheads had all accepted their targets. Twenty-nine times every second, the missile's guidance and targeting computers did a complete self-check of their systems. Everything was in perfect order.

The SS-18 continued its descent, building up speed until it reached its terminal velocity of eight thousand feet per second.

In a matter of minutes, the SS-18's nose would peel back and spit out the ten warheads, each to home in on its target.

The missile was approaching the coast of Sweden before it was finally detected by the American early warning over-the-horizon radar at Reykjavík, Iceland. The radar center immediately began to analyze the size and speed of the sub-orbit missile in an attempt to determine what kind of weapon it was.

A huge mainframe computer began to track the missile's flight path. After tracking the missile for thirty seconds, the computer began to predict what the missile's targets would be. It soon determined the missile was heading for somewhere along the east coast, probably the mid-Atlantic, more specifically Washington, D.C. However, because the missile was an SS-18, with ten separate nuclear warheads, the tracking computer could only guess what each individual target would be.

Within seconds after identifying the target as an SS-18, the President of the Unites States was notified of the incoming missile. Seconds after that, the United States Strategic Command was ordered to Attack Option CONFINE.

The rules of engagement under CONFINE were simple. Under this plan, if any nuclear weapons were detonated on United States soil, a limited retaliatory strike was automatically authorized. There was no choice. It had to be. The military was instructed not to wait for authorization from the President. Instead, they were instructed to immediately launch a crippling retaliatory strike.

Attack Option CONFINE was a necessary holdover from the Cold War. It was an integral part of the doctrine of mutually assured destruction. CONFINE was a way of ensuring that the United States could respond to a nuclear attack, even if all of its civilian leadership was already dead.

What CONFINE lacked in flexibility, it made up for in its power to deter, for it promised any potential aggressor that he could not win at a nuclear war. Even if he were successful in eliminating all of the nation's senior leadership, he would not go unpunished. He would not be left unharmed to claim victory. Indeed, he would probably be counted among the dead.

MINUTEMAN III ICBM LAUNCH CONTROL CENTER F.E. WARREN AIR FORCE BASE, WYOMING

Lt Jason Pond turned to look at the senior launch-control officer. Capt Tracy Leaven's face was drained of all color. She appeared ghostlike under the milky lights of the launch center. Pond couldn't help but notice the trembling of her hands as she reached above her head to open the red box.

The alert message bells continued to ring through the chamber. They echoed off the cement walls and bounced from ceiling to floor. Red warning lights added their crimson glow to the dimly lit room. Printers clattered and rolled, drowning out the constant hum of the air purifiers and the equipment cooling systems.

Lt Pond turned back to his console. He stared at the key which he held in his hand. It pressed against his flesh, heavy and warm.

With great effort, he reached up to the red cabinet that hung over his missile launch console and inserted the key into his box. The key slipped smoothly into the lock. The door sprung open. Lt Pond reached in and pulled out a thick red binder. It was sealed in tight clear plastic and was clearly marked "TOP SECRET" on every side. Lt Pond used his fingernail to break the seal, then flipped open the binder to the tab marked "OPTION CONFINE."

"I've got a confirmed checklist," Capt Leaven called across the launch center floor.

"Roger that," Pond replied. "Standing by, ready to copy."

For almost thirty seconds no one spoke. Both officers sat motionless, strapped to their impact-resistent chairs by tight belts that ran around their waists.

Suddenly the alert message bells fell silent. Lt Pond and Capt Leaven sat up in their chairs. They each held thick grease pencils in their hands. They hunched over their binders like schoolchildren, anxious to copy every word.

Ten seconds after the bells stopped ringing, three huge ceiling-mounted speakers began to boom.

"*For bunker. For bunker. For bunker. Message follows.*" Lt Pond licked his dry lips as he stared at the plastic-covered pages of his binder.

"*Echo Lima Delta Two Charlie Two Charlie Seven Foxtrot Sierra Two Five Mike Mike Seven Niner Mike Hotel Whiskey Alpha Oscar Four Four.*

"*I say again. Echo Lima Delta Two Charlie Two Charlie Seven Foxtrot Sierra Two Five Mike Mike Seven Niner Mike Hotel Whiskey Alpha Oscar Four Four. Time now, twenty-three fifteen. Message complete.*"

Lt Pond stared at the thick, black grease pencil marks he had scribbled onto the plastic pages of his binder. He then began to compare them with the codes that had been previously typed in the code book. He went through the letters very carefully, reading them out loud as he went.

It was a perfect match.

"I've got a SPOTLIGHT!" Pond called out as he finished. He raised his head and looked across the room at his boss. She was still decoding her message. He waited for her to respond.

"Confirm item twelve," she yelled over to Lt Pond. Pond looked down at his binder to block number twelve. "Five," he called back.

Capt Leaven scribbled the number in her binder. She read through the coded message once again, reading every word, comparing every letter. Lt Pond glanced up at the clock. It had been almost three minutes since they had received the message. They didn't have very much time.

Finally Capt Leaven replied, "I confirm SPOTLIGHT." A long moment's hesitation. The room fell silent. The air stirred around them as the air conditioner kicked itself on. Capt Leaven didn't move.

Lt Pond waited. His right hand unconsciously dropped to the 9mm handgun that was strapped to his side.

Suddenly the captain straightened up in her chair. Her voice was firm as she gave her command.

"Break the sealed switches. Select blue on my command."

Lt Pond immediately broke open the red safety covers that protected a long row of switches that were set in the center of his console. He flipped each of the ten switches to "ARM," then reached up and inserted his key into a multicolored lock.

"Two is ready. Selecting blue," Pond announced in a raspy voice.

"Ready on my command," Leaven replied. "Ready, ready, now!" Both officers turned their key to the first position. Immediately, all ten of the Minuteman III missiles which they commanded were activated and put onto hold.

CAPS, TEXAS

Duane Marshall looked up from the fractured radiator that was now plaguing his tractor. It had frozen the night before, an early frost for central Texas, and the old tractor's radiator had frozen through.

Duane's farm was located just three miles from Dyess Air Force Base, home of the 7th Wing. His best piece of property, sixty acres of fertile red soil, was located directly underneath the departure end of the base's runway.

As Duane stood back from his wounded tractor, he heard the familiar sound once again. Three miles to the north, a B-1 was just taking off. It would be overhead in a matter of seconds. Duane brushed off the tips of his fingers and prepared to insert them into his ears.

The B-1 approached the empty field, accelerating from the northern horizon. Much as he hated the noise, Duane couldn't resist watching the aircraft as they flew overhead.

Even before Duane turned to look for the oncoming bomber, he knew the approaching sound was not the same. It sounded much lower and much more powerful.

He turned away from his tractor and looked to the north, squinting his eyes against the dry winter dust.

Then he saw them. Like geese raising from a corn field, they rose from the base. Taking off in six-second intervals, the bombers came, trailing one behind the other in a long, unbroken line.

The first bomber was nearly upon him. Duane stared in awe as it flew overhead. Even as he watched, three other B-1s chased after their leader and formed up on his wing. This formation was followed by six more. Screaming overhead they flew, sending thin contrails to blow in the wind. The bombers pierced the thick Texas air, pulling their dart-like noses skyward as they turned back to the north.

Duane Marshall watched until they had all disappeared. He had counted twenty-eight bombers in all. For twelve years Duane had been farming here in Caps, yet never had he seen so many aircraft take off all at once. And never so close together.

Duane wasn't much for reading the papers, but even he had some idea what might be going on. "Must be that darn Russian thing," Duane muttered to himself as he turned back to his tractor.

ONE HUNDRED TWENTY-FIVE MILES EAST OF JAN MAYEN ISLAND, NORWEGIAN SEA

The U.S.S. Georgia broke through the ceiling of ice very easily, her back hunched against the pressure of the four-foot flow. The submarine's thick steel hull crackled and popped as she emerged from the bitter cold waters of the Norwegian Sea. After breaking through the ice, the nuclear-powered submarine resubmerged to thirty fathoms. She had already pressurized her missile tubes with nitrogen to protect the missiles against the sea water when they were launched. Now all she had to do was wait.

Seventeen hundred miles to the southwest, a RC-135 command, control, and communication aircraft flew in a lazy orbit off the Newfoundland coast. Inside the aircraft, controllers sat at long rows of computers, radios, radars, and desks. They worked quietly as they concentrated on doing their job.

Under the belly of the aircraft was a round fiberglass pod. Trailed out behind the pod was a two-mile long strand of thick copper wire. Using an ultra-low frequency radio, the communication specialists that filled the interior of the RC-135 had been able to communicate with the U.S.S. Georgia as she sat under the ice.

Once Attack Option CONFINE had initiated, much of the responsibility for what followed was left up to the three-star general who commanded this aircraft. He would be the one who called all the shots.

Inside the aircraft was a small television monitor. The monitor was satellite data-linked to the radar site in Greenland and showed the flight of the incoming missile. Once Greenland began to lose its track on the missile, Headquarters Space Command, buried deep in the Cheyenne Mountains of Colorado, would accept responsibility for tracking. Space Command would track the warheads all the way to their targets.

Once the nuclear detonations were confirmed, the controllers aboard the RC-135 would broadcast a message, which would be relayed to units around the entire world. Within a very few minutes, all of the nuclear assets that were presently standing by would be commanded to launch their weapons.

As the RC-135 circled, it continued to receive messages and codes from various units, all of them associated in some way or another with Strategic Command. Most of the messages were meaningless garbage. Nothing but bogus message traffic whose only purpose was to assure that the command and communication systems were still in operation.

But as the controllers watched in terror as the missile on the radar screen descended through the air, they fully expected that to change. They anticipated that within the next ten minutes, damage reports would begin to flood in as the warheads detonated over their targets.

FORTY-ONE

MOSCOW, RUSSIA

"SIR, WHAT DO WE DO?" GENERAL NAHAYLO'S VOICE WAS DESPERATE. He stood beside President Fedotov's chair, his back toward the Tactical Display Screen, his eyes intense with emotion as he stared down at him. "We still have time," he continued. "We can destroy the missile. But we only have seconds. Once the missile opens up and the warheads have separated from their housing, it will be too late."

The general paused, waiting for the president to answer. Fedotov did not reply.

"Two minutes, sir!" the sergeant sitting at the missile control desk announced. He moved his right hand and flipped up a protective cover, exposing the small, red, self-destruct button that was housed underneath.

"Mr. President, I need your permission to destroy the missile," General Nahaylo insisted.

"Are you certain the bomber has been destroyed?" Fedotov asked once again.

"Yes! Yes! Yes! For the fifth time, sir, the bomber has been destroyed. It is gone! Our own fighters and the Mainstay have both confirmed the kill."

"And all of the missiles?"

"Yes! You know they are gone, sir. You saw them yourself as they disappeared from our screen. The Americans destroyed them. Everything's gone! Including the bomber! Now we just can't sit here. You simply must act! Only you can order the SS-18 destroyed!"

Fedotov continued to stare at the Tactical Screen. His face had become an unreadable mask, his eyes pale and dry. The seconds ticked by. General Nahaylo wiped a handkerchief over his stricken face and glanced at the young sergeant who sat with his hand poised on the button.

"Sir," the sergeant pleaded. "What do you want me to do?" He wasn't looking at Fedotov. He was staring at General Nahaylo. Sheer terror leapt from his eyes.

The command center was stone silent. Every head, every face, every eye, was turned toward Fedotov. No one spoke. No one breathed. No one moved.

Nahaylo grasped the back of President Fedotov's chair. "Sir! Thousands of people . . . maybe millions of people . . . are within seconds of losing their lives. No one will win. It is madness! You must do something. Now!"

Fedotov swung around in his chair and lifted a fist toward Nahaylo. "No! No, General Nahaylo! They started this fight. Not you. And not I. They are the ones who attacked us! But now I'm calling—"

"Sixty seconds, sir!" the sergeant cried out.

"—their bluff. They are cowards, and I will not back down. So, General Nahaylo, don't tell me what I must or mustn't do. Unless you are in charge here. Don't tell *me* what to—"

"Forty-five seconds, sir!"

Nahaylo grabbed Fedotov by the shoulders and pulled him around, staring him straight in the eyes. "President Fedotov, you *must* kill the missile!" he cried. "We must stop while we can! This isn't some kind of game here! This is life! This is death! This is war!" Fedotov pushed him away. Nahaylo held on. Fedotov pushed him back once again, then glanced at his guards in a panic.

One of Fedotov's body guards drew his weapon and held it at the ready position.

"Thirty seconds, sir!" the sergeant cried out. Sir! What do you want me to do?"

"Captain Blenko!" Fedotov called to his guard. "Arrest this man! Get this coward out of my sight!"

As the Captain began to move forward, he shot a quick look at Nahaylo. It was clear he didn't know what to do.

General Nahaylo glanced up at the approaching guard. He stared at his gun. He stared into his face. He glanced down at Fedotov, who was smiling.

Grabbing Fedotov by the ears and hair, he shook him like a rag doll, his eyes wild with frustration and fear.

"Vladimir! Vladimir! You must kill the missile!"

"You are a fool!" Fedotov choked.

"Fifteen seconds, sir!" the sergeant cried out. There were tears of fear in his eyes.

Nahaylo swung around to the controller. "Kill it! Kill it!"

"No!" Fedotov shouted. Nahaylo ignored him and lunged for the console. Fedotov grabbed at him. "Shoot him! Shoot him!" he cried.

At that instant, General Nahaylo's world came to a standstill. Every thought and emotion faded away as the cognitive process shut down. For half a second, his mind went completely blank. Then he saw them. His countrymen as they labored through life. What sin had they committed? How many would die? His wife and his children. Where were they? How could they survive? And finally he saw her, a tiny and blond-headed girl. She ran to him as she squealed out "Papa" and quickly climbed up on his lap. She was weightless and perfect and constantly smiling as she rested her head on his chest.

He only had one grandchild. But he wanted more.

"Ten seconds, sir!!" the sergeant cried out. "Nine . . . eight!"

General Nahaylo pulled out his pistol and shot Fedotov square in the chest, blowing him back in his chair.

"Kill the missile!" he cried again, while lurching for the self-destruct button.

The sergeant got to it first. He jammed it down with his finger so hard that he split the top of his nail. Half a second later, Nahaylo's hand slapped down on the back of the sergeant's pale wrist.

From a satellite high above the earth, a self-destruct command was sent to the SS-18 missile that was descending over the Virginia coast.

The missile immediately blew into a thousand tiny pieces. The warheads crumpled and burned and vaporized into powdery dust as searing-hot pieces of copper and steel began to fall to earth.

Inside the bunker, every man stood frozen in a horrified stupor. A heavy stillness hung in the air. The sergeant dropped his head on the console and buried it between shaking arms. General Nahaylo swallowed hard and lowered his head. The soft hum of computers seemed to fill the dead air. Crying, Nahaylo turned his back on Fedotov, tiny specks of blood dotting his face. He didn't try to wipe them away.

NORTHERN UKRAINE

Richard Ammon watched the fireball fade and disappear, a yellow explosion in the clear night sky. Only seconds before had he pulled up on his ejection seat handles. Just as his chute had deployed, he felt the jolt of overpressure as Reaper's Shadow had exploded in the air. Tiny pieces of burning debris and small chunks of metal shot outward, carried forward on a rolling wave of shock and heat. Pea-size fragments of wreckage pelted against his body and tore tiny holes in his nylon parachute.

He was safely out of the plane. But he was not uninjured. Both of his arms dangled uselessly to his side. A searing pain originated at his elbows and made its way up his shoulders, then down his spine. He had no feeling at all in either of his hands. As he dangled in his chute in the darkness, he tried in vain to raise either one of his arms. No good. They were both gone. Identical breaks, just above the elbow.

As he descended through the bitter darkness, he began to shiver uncontrollably. Shock was beginning to set in. His body heaved and shook as the muscles rubbed themselves together in a vain effort to generate some life-giving heat. The veins in his calves and thighs constricted to force the warm blood back up to the internal organs that lay protected in his chest.

He hit the ground with a solid thump, jarring his broken arms and sending piercing jolts of pain down his spine. He fell in a heap onto the shallow snowbank. His parachute descended around him. For a moment he lay there and shivered. He didn't move. He couldn't move. It simply was too painful. He willed himself to roll over and stand up. But the exhaustion was too great. He needed some time. Some time to rest. Then he would pull himself together.

He looked down at his arms, which hung at his sides. He tried once again to move his hands, staring at his fingers, willing them to bend, willing them even to twitch. But whether from the cold, or the fractures, or a painful combination of both, he couldn't move his hands. He knew that frostbite was now a serious possibility, and would lead to amputated fingers.

He lay on top of a shallow bank of snow and listened to the night. In his mind he said a little prayer. He felt so tired. So hopeless and alone.

Above his head, he could hear more fast-moving fighters. They appeared to be circling, at about 5,000 feet, maybe four miles to the west. He listened to the sound of their engines until they faded away in the wind. Then he listened to the breeze in the forest.

And wondered what he could do.

He had two broken arms. It was almost eight hundred miles to the Turkish border. He had little food. He had no warm clothes. He didn't have a map. The only items of any value were stuffed in the survival pack attached to his parachute. And with his broken arms, he had serious doubts that he could even get the survival pack open.

With enormous effort, he forced himself to roll over and propped himself into a sitting position. He felt dizzy and extremely lightheaded, but surprisingly, the pain in his arms was beginning to fade, although it was replaced by a tight and burning sensation. But even that seemed so far way, almost as if his arms were detached from his body.

Ammon puzzled on that for a moment. It seemed kind of odd. The lack of pain. Was that good? Was that okay? What did the lack of pain mean?

He continued to shiver uncontrollably. His muscles jerked. His teeth jammed together. He could feel his heart race in his chest. He knew that he had to get warm. He had to find some kind of shelter. He needed protection from the cold. And food. And a long drink of water. Yes, water was extremely important. A critical step in the treatment for shock.

Everything that he needed was inside his survival pack—the sleeping bag, plastic containers of water, fire kits, food bars, chocolate, and a warm set of clothes. Yet he was feeling so tired. So very tired. His eyelids were heavy as thick, velvet curtains. His legs were already asleep. All he wanted was to close his eyes and let the world drift away.

He shook his head and tried to think. He had to do something. Reaching deep inside himself, he forced himself to his feet, wobbling on unsteady legs. His arms flopped at his side. He fumbled in the night, searching through the darkness for his survival pack. He found it laying under a small evergreen tree, and fell down in the snow beside it.

For a long moment he stared at the pack. It was vacuum-sealed and extremely tight. It only had one tiny zipper. Ammon pushed at the pack with his right shoulder. A scream of pain shot down his arm and he fell back, suddenly faint, his head swimming. The pain seared to the marrow of his bones. He lay still, waiting for it to pass. Slowly it faded, receding to the back of his mind, where it seemed to throb with the beat of his heart. Ammon rolled gently to his knees. His arms flopped in the snow beside him. He turned the pack over, pushing it around with his chin until he found the tiny copper zipper. He tugged on it with his teeth. It didn't move. He jerked a little bit harder. It still didn't give.

And then he remembered. The zipper was soldered shut, a final protective measure to ensure the pack didn't open and spill its contents when the pilot ejected from his plane. It took twenty pounds of pressure to break the solder molds. Much more pressure than Ammon could exert with his teeth.

Ammon's heart sank. Leaving the survival pack, he stumbled to the base of an enormous white pine and fell down beside it. There, the forest floor was soft and dry. On the downhill side of the tree was an old fallen log. He burrowed himself into the bed of pine needles and pushed himself under the log. Using his teeth and feet, he wrestled the parachute together, bundling it and spreading it over his body. He buried his face in his jacket.

He wasn't so cold any more. He felt kind of fuzzy and warm, light-headed and free, as if his body were slowly sinking into a tub of warm water. It was where he wanted to be.

And he felt so tired. It was quiet and peaceful. The trees swayed over his head. The late-night stars were shining, sharing their innocent light. Maybe he would just close his eyes. Just for a moment. Rest. He needed to rest. Then he would get back to work. He would gather up his equipment and make some sort of plan. But for now he needed to rest.

It was so comfortable. This wasn't so bad. He could spend the night here. That's what he would do. Just lie here and rest until morning. His arms were feeling a little bit better. Maybe they were healing already. Wasn't that nice? The pine needles were so soft. He was feeling quite warm. He would close his eyes and sleep until morning.

Tiny vapors of white breath escaped from his mouth and disappeared into the black night. Ammon's eyes closed. His breathing became measured. He fell asleep. His head rolled to the side of his chest.

Inside his survival pack, an emergency locator beacon automatically beamed its emergency signal to the satellites that passed overhead.

LOS ANGELES, CALIFORNIA

Jesse awoke with a start. Her eyes bolted open, and she sat up quickly in her bed, her heart pounding, a tight catch in her throat. She wiped her eyes and swallowed hard.

She looked at the clock. Six-thirty. She looked to the window. It was just getting light. Slipping out of bed, she tiptoed to the bedroom door and cracked it open. The agent was spread out on the couch, still asleep. She went to the closet and dressed quietly, then slipped out of the apartment through the kitchen door.

The rain was slowly dissipating into a heavy mist. It was cold and wet, but Jesse didn't care, she was so anxious to get out of the house. She stepped out onto the wet grass and headed across the small lawn to the wooden walkway that led down to the pier.

Jesse walked along the beach slowly, her hands thrust into the pockets of her light jacket. She had on knee-length shorts and brown sandals, leaving her legs exposed to the cool morning air. Her hair was tied with a single white ribbon. A north wind blew at her face, blushing her checks and lifting her loosely wrapped hair past her shoulders.

The hard-packed sand gave a little under her light feet as she made her way from the beachhouse and walked north along the shore.

A pale sun tried pitifully to break through the thin overcast that covered the eastern hills, but it would be several hours before it would generate enough energy to warm the cold sand. By then, a dreary and wet fog would have formed over the bay.

It promised to be another miserable day in southern California. Just like the day before. Just like the day before that.

A flock of seagulls followed Jesse as she walked along the beach. They screeched in chorus at her, begging for food. They hopped along behind her, always maintaining a safe distance, occasionally spreading their wings as if to fly, then seemingly changing their minds. Too much effort to take to the air. Too much work. Better to stay on the ground and hobble along, hoping for a handout for breakfast.

Jesse ignored the gulls and their insistent noise and followed the beach for a mile. By then, the sun had risen completely, but still its warmth and heat remained hidden, robbed by the thin overcast and the cold ocean air.

Jesse turned and put the mountains to her back as she stared out over the waves. White caps turned the ocean frothy and washed hollow deadwood and black seaweed up onto the shore.

She turned and started to walk back to the beachhouse. The seagulls turned as well and continued to trail her as she made her way across the pale sand.

As she approached the apartment, she saw him. He was waiting for her on the back porch.

Jesse froze in her tracks. She saw the blue uniform. She saw the look on his face. Her heart stopped. Her breathing stopped. The wind stopped. The whole world stood still.

The officer reached out his hand. "Mrs. Ammon," he said with a struggle. "My name is Lieutenant Colonel Oliver Tray."

Jesse's hand shot to her mouth. She wanted to scream. She wanted to cry. She wanted to curl into a little ball and just disappear. She fixed her eyes on the officer and managed to mutter in a dignified tone, "He's dead, isn't he? Just tell me now."

Oliver Tray shook his head. "No, ma'am, he's not dead," he quietly said. "Now, will you please come inside? I have something to tell you, and we don't have much time."

FORTY-TWO

JOLLY 21

THE HH-60 PAVEHAWK RESCUE HELICOPTER DROPPED BACK FROM the air-refueling basket and descended toward the Sea of Azov. The HC-130 air refueling aircraft peeled off to the right and climbed up to 3,000 feet. Only a pale light defined the horizon. In six hours, it would be dawn. The mission had to be completed by then.

Thirty hours earlier, about the time that Richard Ammon was crossing over the northern Bahamas, the U.S.S. Ticonderoga had received her orders from the President of the United States. She immediately sent sail at top speed to the east, passing the southern coast of Greece before turning north into the Aegean Sea. As darkness fell, she sailed unannounced through the Dardanelles Straits and into the Sea of Marmara, pushing as close to the coast of Turkey as she dared. Two rescue helicopters were towed out of their hangar's, readied on deck, and put on a five-minute-launch-time alert. At six o'clock in the morning, they had received the call, but a decision was made to wait until nightfall. The mission was going deep, and they would need the cover of darkness. So the day was spent in intense mission planning. The satellite imagery was checked again and again. The coordinates and flight route were fed into the helicopter's internal navigation computers. The air refueling aircraft was quickly deployed to a remote airstrip in northern Greece. At twelve-eighteen local, the EYE satellite was moved 800 kilometers to the south in order to get a closer look. Peering down from space, it saw the signal. The orange and white parachute had been spread out in the clearing and folded into an X. He was still there. He was still alive.

By mid-afternoon, everything was in place. The pilots and pararescue specialists, or "PJs" as they were called, paced around their helicopters, snapping insults and jokes at each other, checking their gear, and watching the sun as it faded in the hazy sky. As the sun set over the blue-green waters of the Marmara Sea, one of the Pavehawks spun up her engines and took to the air.

Four hours later, the helicopter had finished air refueling and was speeding to the north, flying just five feet over the water. Approaching the Ukrainian coast, it pulled up to cross over a wall of white rock, barely clearing the crest of the pale granite cliffs, then dropped toward the trees on the other side. Its blades slapped the air as it pounded along. Two gunners stood at each of the side doorways, their 7.62 caliber mini-guns set on the maximum rate-of-fire of 4,000 shells per minute. Between the aft bulkheads, three PJs hunkered down in their seats and inventoried their rescue and medical equipment once again.

The helo was fighting a buffeting headwind from a bitter cold front that had moved down from the Arctic Ocean. The temperature was below freezing and dropping very quickly as they flew further north. The survivor was another 300 miles up ahead. He had been down for almost twenty-four hours. He wouldn't live another night on his own.

The night was pitch black. As dark as a cave. The pilots were using their night-vision goggles to see. The world appeared ghostly green as they peered through their goggles, but still they had no problem making out the trees, rivers, and valleys as they sped along. The helicopter remained very low, pulling up only to clear high-tension power lines and an occasional long row of trees. The pilots steered the helicopter through the valleys, staying clear of even the smallest towns. They made their way to the north, undetected by anyone except an occasional Ukrainian farmer who stopped and wondered at the noise in the night.

Ninety minutes later, the copilot heard the first tiny warble of the downed pilot's emergency locator beacon. The Pavehawk's internal computer also picked up on the beam and commanded a three degree change of heading to the right. It also updated the distance to the survivor. Only thirty-eight miles to go.

The satellite communications radio started to chatter, rattling out a deciphered code onto a three-inch-wide strip of white paper. It took the flight engineer a few seconds to notice the clattering SATCOM. It wasn't supposed to come on. Not here. Not now. They should have already been told what they needed to know. The flight engineer pulled the paper from the printer the second it stopped and read the report, then swore to himself.

"NRO detects unidentified Bandits in the area," he announced over the intercom system. "Multiple fast movers, riding shotgun for some choppers underneath."

One of the pilots grunted. "So we're not the only ones looking for this guy, huh?"

"No, sir. Not by a long shot."

A very long pause. The pilots knew there was more. "Okay, give it to us, Pup. What else have you got?"

The young flight engineer, no more than a teenager, read the SATCOM report to himself once again and then said, "Two Ukrainian brigades have been moved up from Khar'kov, with their associated triple A and support vehicles. They are fanned out in a search semicircle. They are estimated to be in the area now."

The pilot swore. One of the door gunners jammed his mini- gun off of safe and adjusted the focus on his goggles. The copilot stared at his navigation screen. Twenty-six miles to go.

"What side of the survivor are they approaching from?" the pilot hurriedly asked.

"Doesn't say, sir. But I bet we find out."

The pilot swore once again. "Two full brigades! Are you certain? Two full brigades?!"

"That's what it says, sir. Do you want me to ask for verification?"

The pilot paused for only a second. "No," he answered. "Screw it. Doesn't matter. So they want him. We want him worse. We'll be there in less than twelve minutes. Now everyone, you know what to do!"

Beneath them, the frozen ground scurried by. The door gunners trained their mini-guns to fire forward of the helo's position. One of them threw a huge green ball of bubble gum into his mouth. "Left gunner's ready!" he called out.

The pilot looked at the distance to the survivor's location. Twenty-one miles to go. He pulled back on the cyclic while adding a touch of power. The Pavehawk lifted gently over a 200 meter ridge of ancient glacial rock. Descending once again, the helicopter's four blades slapped at the air. The pilot followed the steering cross on his navigation computer and wondered for the thousandth time, Who is this guy we are after?

NORTHERN UKRAINE

When the sun had set, Ammon pulled his parachute in with his teeth and gathered it over his body, hoping to keep himself warm. But as the north wind picked up and the temperature dropped, he quickly realized it wouldn't do much good. He lay tucked up under the rotting log, shivering again from the cold. He had pulled his arms from the sleeves of his jacket and tucked them close to his body, not so much to keep them warm, but more to limit the pain that the useless limbs caused as they dangled at his side.

He was bitter cold. And very hungry. And far more thirsty than he ever had been in his life. He was lonely and tired and had given up hope. From his hole, he could just make out the north star. As he stared out into the darkness, his breath crystallized in the bitter cold, leaving tiny, white prisms of frozen breath. He couldn't feel his feet any more. When he closed his eyes, his lashes froze themselves shut. He swallowed a thick wad of spit and licked at the frozen moisture on the underside of the log.

The parachute signal had been his last hope. No, that was not correct. The signal had been his only hope. The only hope that he ever had. If they were looking, they would have seen the signal. If they were searching, they would have picked up on his locator beacon. If they had chosen to, they could have sent some type of rescue chopper.

But they didn't. He had waited all day. Holding on through the cold and the pain, hiding himself among the trees, he had waited. And now it was too late. It was too cold. He wouldn't last until morning.

A muffled sound drifted through the forest. Barking dogs. Through the trees. Far off in the distance. Then the sound of shouting voices. Ammon nearly stopped breathing. His heart dropped to the pit of his stomach, and he pushed himself even further under the log.

JOLLY 21

"Jeff, we've got a major highway up ahead," the copilot announced as he studied his moving-map-display. "I've got significant west-to-east traffic. Looks like a column of military vehicles. Turn left now, heading three-zero-zero. That should take us about a mile behind the last vehicle."

"Coming left," the pilot replied as he banked the helicopter aggressively up on her side. Inside his helmet, the tone of the locator beacon continued to build. The Pavehawk had a very good lock on the survivor's location, and he was just where they thought he would be. As the pilot rolled out, he, too, could begin to make out the dark ribbon of paved road that made its way to the east, along with a column of boxy vehicles with high backs and big tires. A dozen or so, mostly troop transports. No sign of any missile launchers or triple A.

The helicopter was just over a mile from the road, and barely skimming over the trees. They would pass behind the short convoy of trucks. The Ukrainians probably wouldn't even know they were there. With any luck. . . .

"Break right! Tracers in the sky! Get down pilot! Get her down now!" The right door gunner was screaming his head off. Both pilots jammed the stick forward to push the helicopter even lower toward the trees. Twisting his head to the right, the copilot saw a terrifying sight. Long arches of white and green tracers sprouted up from a small clearing in the trees to chase after the low-flying helicopter. Snaking lines of 23mm fire reached out with their long, bony fingers.

"Break left! Now! Now! Bring her around!" the gunner called again.

The pilot reacted by instinct. Pulling the chopper into a tight turn, he jerked up on the collective to add more power, which forced the helicopter around even more. Pulling back on the stick, the helicopter began to climb. Twisting through the sky, the pilot banked the chopper left and then right in an effort to break the attacking gunner's aiming solution. The copilot twisted in his seat, hoping to locate the incoming line of fire. At first, the tracers passed just over their heads. Then suddenly, they jerked to the front of their nose before trailing off below and behind them. The pilot let the helicopter drop. The top of the trees rushed up to meet them and began to brush their undercarriage. Broken pieces of wood and scattered pine needles thrashed through the air behind the fleeing chopper. The tracers died off.

The Pavehawk turned back to heading. Only eight miles to go.

NORTHERN UKRAINE

Ammon heard a shot fire out. Another fired twice in reply. The dogs snarled and barked at each other. He pushed himself deeper under the log and prayed that his parachute would not be seen. But he knew that it would. And he knew that even were he completely hidden, it wouldn't matter. They were coming. With the dogs, they would find him.

It was then that he heard the beat of the rotors. He sucked in his breath and didn't dare move, thinking the sound wasn't real. For a second or two, the sound faded away. Then, with a deep *whoop*, the HH-60 approached the side of the hill.

"I've got the landing zone straight ahead," the copilot announced. "There! On the south side. Near the crest. Just below the outcropping of pines."

"Yeah, I've got it," the pilot replied. "Are you sure that's the place? It's half the size I thought it would be!"

The copilot nodded his head. "Yeah, that's it. I'm certain."

In the back of the chopper, the rescue team began to store their equipment in preparation for the assault landing.

The pilot turned to the copilot. "Try the radio once again," he demanded. "Try both the primary and alternate channels. He's got to be there, and I want to hear his voice before we commit ourselves to going into such a small LZ!"

The copilot keyed his microphone switch, though he knew it wouldn't be any use. He had been through this before. The guy simply wasn't answering their radio calls. But still, he did as he was told.

"Unknown Hiker, Unknown Hiker, come up on two fifty-five point four." He paused for ten seconds, then keyed the switch once again. "Unknown Hiker, Unknown Hiker, if you hear this transmission, identify yourself by popping one of your flares."

The pilot slowed the helicopter and circled over the LZ, peering down with his goggles as he passed overhead. It was bare. No signal. No parachute. No fire or smoke from a flare. No sign of any life at all.

"Maybe his survival radio is busted," the right door gunner said. "Maybe he's incapacitated. You know, a broken arm or something. And with hostile troops all around him, you know he can't set off a flare."

For a moment no one spoke.

"Yeah, maybe you're right," the copilot finally offered. "But maybe he's already been captured. Maybe there is someone down there waiting for us. And maybe it isn't our friend."

The pilot set up for one more pass over the LZ. "We'll take one more look," he said. "Then we'll decide what to do."

The helicopter flew right over his head. Ammon could scarcely believe it. He rolled out from underneath the dead log, wincing with pain, and struggled to his feet, his eyes on the sky, following the sound of the chopper. The clear *whoop* of the blades reverberated through the night air. He stared into the sky as the sound receded into the distance.

"No! No!" he silently pleaded. "No, I'm here. You've got to come back!"

Then he heard them again. Shouts. And the dogs. They seemed to be gathering around him. The sounds echoed through the trees. He glanced up at the sky, not knowing what to do. He only had a few seconds. The helicopter would only make one more pass.

Dropping to his knees by the log, he bent over and buried his face in the dirt. Grabbing a thin strand of nylon parachute between his teeth, he staggered to his feet and dragged the parachute out from under the log. The sound of the chopper faded, then turned back toward his direction as it set up to make one more pass. He dropped to the forest floor once again. An animal bolted from the treeline to his right, rustling the leaves in his path. Ammon sucked in his breath as the rabbit scampered into the brush, its frightened eyes gleaming in the dark. Ammon bent over, his broken and swollen arms jolting with pain. He fought down the urge to cry out. Quickly, he grabbed more of the chute in his teeth, then pushed himself backward, sliding along the soft pine needles and powdery snow. Pulling the bright parachute from under the log, he stretched it into a thick orange and white streamer. Gasping for breath, he fell down on the ground. He listened to the sounds in the forest. And waited to see who got to him first.

"Jeff! He's there. He's laying on top of his chute!" The copilot was nearly screaming. The chopper passed over the LZ for the second time. "He's there. We've got to go in!"

Suddenly the aircraft shuddered and leapt to the side as the mini-guns started to blaze. "We're taking fire! We're taking fire!" The left gunner screamed. "I've got multiple targets, all along on this side!"

"Roger that!" the right gunner called. The six barrel Gatling gun spun on its mount, spewing white-hot bullets through the forest and trees, mowing down everything in its path. Within a matter of seconds, the two gunners had fired off nearly a thousand rounds of ammunition.

"Can we land?" the pilot asked in desperation.

"I don't know," the copilot shot back. "It's going to be tight. But let's get down there and see."

The pilot shot a quick look to his right. The copilot answered his question with a nod of his head.

The mini-guns continued to cut through the forest. The HH-60 shook and vibrated with every round. Two of the PJs pulled themselves to the door gunner positions and helped feed the chain of ammunition from the ammo bins to make sure the guns didn't jam. A white arc of light traced up to the chopper. The air frame buffeted violently as three shells passed through the thick aluminum of the tail boom housing. The pilot jerked the aircraft around and turned for the LZ while slowing down. They were committed. They were going in. The right gunner held his fire as he searched for a target. The chopper settled over the tall pines and came to a hover as it blew up dust and snow and small limbs from the trees. Slowly, it moved forward until it was over the small clearing on the side of the hill.

The left gunner called out over his mike, "You've got three feet on this side. Maybe four. But no more."

"Maybe two feet on this side," the right gunner called out. "You're going to take out some limbs, but I think we can do it. Now let's not screw around. This place is crawling with grunts. Let's get going. Let's bring her down now."

The pilot concentrated on holding his position, then shifted the huge helicopter two feet to the left. He pushed gently down on the power. The HH-60 immediately began to settle through the trees.

Ammon threw himself across the blowing parachute, then kicked it out of the way to keep it from being sucked up into the turning rotors. The sound of the two jet-turbine engines and spinning rotors beat at his ears. The downdraft nearly blew him over and he had to squint to keep the blowing snow out of his eyes. He tucked his face down next to his chest as he stumbled to the side of the clearing and fell behind the protective cover of the trees.

The soldier was no more than ten feet away. The Ukrainian jerked his machine gun up to his chest and let off a short burst of fire. A flash of light strobed the air, lighting the forest with an unnatural light. The tree limb next to Ammon's head exploded into a thousand pieces. Ammon turned and ran.

The copilot glanced down at the engine instruments and gave the pilot a quick thumbs up. The mini-guns had fallen silent for the moment. As they settled through the trees, the gunners lost their overhead view, and the enemy became more difficult to locate. A quick muzzle flash strobed through the trees. The right gunner let his mini-gun roll, saturating the area around the muzzle flash with a long burst of 7.62 caliber shells. The tree limbs gave way, scattering in every direction as he fired at the source of the light. The pilot took out even more power. The HH-60 dropped like a rock through the trees, cutting its way down through the broken limbs and blowing leaves.

Ammon ran awkwardly through the pines on the perimeter of the clearing as he watched the helicopter settle through the narrow hole in the trees. Debris and snow blew into his eyes. He felt the air break with a crackle as one of the door gunners opened fire, sending a burst of shells raining down through the forest to impact the frozen ground where the Ukrainian soldier had been. Ammon never looked back to see the result. The chopper was nearing the ground. He could see the look of the door gunner's face. He saw a PJ standing with one leg on the helicopter's landing gear, half in and half out of the cabin, a thick canvas belt strapped around his waist. He was waving at Ammon, beckoning him to come. Ammon left the cover of the forest and bolted toward the hovering chopper suspended three feet in the air. The forest lit up with a burst of machine gun fire. Ammon pushed his broken body forward, his arms still tucked in his jacket, his face covered with dirt and red mud. He slipped in the snow and almost fell down. Stumbling forward, he lunged into the PJ's waiting arms. The PJ wrapped his arms around Ammon's shoulders and pulled him into the air. Another set of hands reached down to grab him. The helicopter shifted just slightly. Ammon was lifted and jerked inside.

The pilots felt the Pavehawk sway. "Go! Go! Go!" the PJs screamed. The pilot pulled up on the power. The helicopter lurched upward through the trees, then quickly disappeared in the night.

EPILOGUE

AEGEAN SEA

THE TICONDEROGA ROLLED GENTLY WITH THE WAVES AS SHE SAILED south past the port of Izmir. The helicopter landing deck was clear of any aircraft, and a half dozen sailors ran laps on the deck as the ship cut its way through the seas. It was early morning. A heavy overcast, with rolling clouds and thin shafts of virga, reduced the visibility to less than a mile.

Below deck, on the third level, was the ship's infirmary. Richard Ammon was in room HB-12. The room was tiny, even by Navy standards, with flat, gray walls and steel pipes running the length of the ceiling. It smelled of ammonia and cleanser. A small vinyl recliner sat in the corner. The bed was wider than most. The sheets were navy blue. There wasn't a porthole, and the lights were turned down.

Ammon was asleep, and had been for the past twenty hours. His face was peaceful in the dim light. A thin sheet covered his body. His bare shoulders lay exposed to the cool air. His arms were wrapped in thick, white cloth and tucked down next to his sides. He was under heavy sedation, awaiting surgery which would come the next day.

A strand of soft hair brushed the side of Ammon's cheek and he turned his head to one side. Jesse leaned even closer and placed her hand on his shoulder. Her lips barely touched his skin as she whispered in his ear. Ammon stirred once again. Jesse whispered his name. Ammon slowly opened his eyes. A tiny smile spread across his face.

"Jesse. . . . Jesse. . . ." he started to say. His voice was heavy with sedation.

Jesse pulled her face back to look into his eyes while placing her fingers over his lips. "Shhhh . . . don't talk," she whispered. "Don't talk. Just rest. Go back to sleep if you want to. I will be here. I am here for you now."

Ammon lifted his head from the pillow. The room began to spin in a circle. His mind was groggy and weak. He blinked several times and then started to say, "But how did you . . . ?"

Jesse cut him off as she pressed her face next to his cheek. "Shhhh . . . not now. Just lay back and rest."

"But, Jesse. . . ."

Jesse pressed her finger just a bit more firmly against his lower lip. "I will tell you about it tomorrow. Or the next day. We'll have lots of time."

Ammon smiled and closed his eyes. A warm feeling spread over his body. She was right. They would have tomorrow. And the next day. And the day after that. Time was no longer a factor. He would never leave her again. She would be the first thing he saw in the morning. She would be the last thing he touched in the night.

He lay his head back on the pillow. Within seconds, he was sleeping again.

Jesse smiled and brushed a tear from her eye, then gently lay down next to him on the bed.